A BULLET FOR THE SHOOTER

HIT WORLD BOOK TWO

Larry Hoy & William Alan Webb

Hit World Press
Coinjock, NC

Chris Kennedy/Hit World Press
1097 Waterlily Rd.
Coinjock, NC 27923
http://chriskennedypublishing.com/

Publisher's Note: This is a work of fiction. Names, characters, places, and incidents are a product of the author's imagination. Locales and public names are sometimes used for atmospheric purposes. Any resemblance to actual people, living or dead, or to businesses, companies, events, institutions, or locales is completely coincidental.

Cover Design by Shezaad Sudar.

Ordering Information:
Quantity sales. Special discounts are available on quantity purchases by corporations, associations, and others. For details, contact the "Special Sales Department" at the address above.

A Bullet for the Shooter/Larry Hoy & William Alan Webb -- 1st ed.
ISBN: 978-1648551314

To all the brave men and women who fought the real war after 9-11.

William Alan Webb - Author Foreword

A Bullet for the Shooter began life as the novelette *Shoot First*, Larry Hoy's maiden entry in the then-nascent Hit World Universe. I found the character of Luther Sweetwater compelling from the very start and performed more of an editing role on that story than actual co-writer. Over the course of adapting "Shoot First" into this novel that changed, mainly because I had more experience in the longer format.

Larry's and my writing styles are quite different and yet oddly compatible. In my view, he is more from the Stephen King school of writing, using small details to build tension ending in something shocking and horrific, while I am heavily influenced by writers with a more spare style, like Roger Zelazny, where details and descriptions are limited in favor of narrative pacing. I would like to think that *A Bullet for the Shooter* is the best of both, but there is no question that the structure of this book is all Larry's, which is another way of saying that it *has* structure. After the frantic chaos of *The Trashman*, that may come as a relief to those who read that book.

The Hit World Universe is a challenge for me personally, because it can incorporate any and all of the bizarre ideas that constantly flow through my mind. That isn't necessarily the good thing it might seem, as those ideas sometimes transcend my capabilities to turn them into coherent prose. In writing *A Bullet for the Shooter*, therefore, the grounding of Larry's story structure relieved that pressure. This book is all the better for it.

William Alan Webb
Eads, TN
5 November 2020

* * * * *

Larry Hoy - Author Foreword

I met Bill Webb at a writers' support group in Memphis when he had just returned from a book signing at Fort Knox. I was kind of dumbfounded that someone could make a living in this business. Over the next year Bill was my mentor as I signed up for his writing classes and followed him around various conventions. Over time, I learned what made him successful: Bill has a disciplined work ethic, and he has never met a stranger.

Now, I'm not a complete beginner. I've published a fistful of short stories earning enough money that I could order a meal in any restaurant as long as it comes wrapped in paper and the main ingredient is grease. Then, one evening as I was crawling through Amazon, I saw that Bill had released a short story, *Kill Me When You Can*. I devoured it and thought, "Hell, I can do that!" So, I reached out to Bill and asked if he'd open up his universe to me.

We tag-teamed "Shoot First," and I made plans to build out the universe through short stories. But then Bill met Chris Kennedy and they told me to forget the shorts—it was time to turn this into a novel! That's where my idea for Luther Sweetwater came from.

Like Luther, I had plans. I sorta knew where I was going, but I was in deep over my head. In truth, Luther is my hero. He's not someone who can do everything, and he has to work for every step he takes. He has problems. Okay, he has a lot of problems. Just like things don't come easy for Sweetwater, writing this book didn't come easy for me. But oh, what a trip it was. Thank you for coming along.

Larry Hoy
Memphis, TN
7 November 2020

* * * * *

The Hit World Universe

September 11, 2001, was the blackest day in American history. A dozen hijacked airliners wiped out most of the American government and brought America to its knees. The population screamed for blood, but the government was in chaos. The senior surviving member in the line of succession was a junior Senator from Oregon who nobody had heard of outside his native state.

The Chinese, Iranians, and Russians all eyed the United States to see if the time had come for military action against American interests worldwide. The new president had only just been appointed and didn't have the political capital—or will—to risk World War Three. Indeed, he was on record as publicly blaming America for worsening relations with the Muslim world prior to the attacks. He called for restraint and refused to commit the U.S. military to go after those identified as responsible. "We brought this on ourselves," he said in a nationwide broadcast.

But Americans were having none of it, not even the constituency that had elected him. The wealthiest of the wealthy went to work behind the scenes, committing tens of billions of dollars to show America's enemies what happened when you dared attack us. The terrorists jeered and vowed more attacks, trying to provoke a response.

It worked.

The answer was the formation of a lavishly funded group of mercenaries hired by those wealthy private citizens. The mercenaries sped to the Middle East set on bloody revenge. The president threatened to arrest everyone concerned, but America's law enforcement agencies sided with the mercs, and he never pushed it beyond threats.

Impeachment loomed.

The money to finance the mercs was funneled through a dummy corporation called LifeEnders, Inc. They attracted the best black ops people America had, plus select others from friendly nations, with many either on detached duty from the U.S. armed forces, arranged by loyal officers who defied the chain of command, or they left the service altogether. The billionaires who supported them spared no expense to supply them with the best equipment available. They even lured some top-flight freelancers out of the shadows and into the fight. As always, money talked.

Within months, most of the men responsible for the 9/11 attacks were being executed on live American pay-per-view television, along with officials from the countries who supported them. Outraged protests from enemy states, and America's own president, fell on the deaf ears of the American public. The new chairman of the Joint Chiefs of Staff clarified that American military capabilities were at full strength and on high alert, but the president ordered them to stand down. Officially, the military obeyed. Privately, they defied their commander in chief, and let America's enemies know it. Rather than risk nuclear war and worldwide Armageddon, foreign countries backed down.

But Americans didn't want to limp along with a rump government that was wildly unpopular and had proved unequal to the emergency. As the federal bureaucracy struggled to restore itself and fill critical positions, the population demanded power be turned over to private corporations wherever possible. These new Corpses, a derogatory name for the corporations, replaced the bureaucracy with results.

With impeachment likely to succeed in deposing the president, and as a presidential recall petition passed 90 million signatures, America held a special election on September 11, 2003. Though challenged by the traditional parties, the Supreme Court deemed such a vote legal. Both parties nominated the usual candidates saying all the usual things, but the mood in America remained angry and combative, and through the summer a populist movement grew to draft Charlton Heston for president. The two political parties laughed off his efforts, but they misjudged the mood of the country. The actor won in a landslide write-in campaign, and with him, both houses of Congress swung toward revenge- and security-minded independent candidates. When the actor took office in January 2004, he had the strongest mandate of any president in American history.

LifeEnders, Inc. grew out of the mercenary group that struck back in the Middle East. The corporation found and eliminated threats to America, worldwide, with the speed and technique of a scalpel. When terrorist organizations were discovered within America, LifeEnders, Inc. found and eliminated *them*. Terrorists couldn't hide from their reach, and there was no appeal on their judgment.

As time went by, LEI, as LifeEnders, Inc. came to be known, also tried to end murder within America's borders; killers were met with swift Old Testament justice. But that didn't work. First, there were too many murders, and second, the regular police angrily opposed such intrusions into their areas of responsibility. So the government passed all the legislation and—more to the point—set all the corresponding fees and tax rates to finance private, legal assassinations under the quasi-governmental LEI. Non-contracted killings remained murder, with all the usual punishments, but contracted murder through LEI was the law of the land.

The street name for this new reality was Hit World.

Chapter One

Luther Sweetwater built his shooting nest on a table by the window, seven stories above the busiest street in downtown Dallas. It was far enough back that it couldn't be seen from the outside, even from the hotel across the street, but close enough that he could get a clean shot at anything on the road below. The rifle, a custom-built, LEI-supplied version of the Finnish SAKO TRG 42, chambered for a .338 Lapua Magnum round, stood ready on its stand.

His handler was a stern British woman named Ms. Witherbot, no first name offered. She'd told Sweetwater to hit the target while he was on his way to work, thereby doing him a favor, it being a Monday and all; Sweetwater was saving him from of a week of work. Probationary Shooter Sweetwater *yuck-yucked* appropriately, even though Witherbot's tone didn't sound like she was joking at all. Truth was, Sweetwater wasn't sure she could make a joke, but he needed some kind of mental defense mechanism. Maybe she knew that.

The dispassion of killing someone strictly for money was hard for Sweetwater, and while he'd asked repeatedly, they wouldn't tell him why he had to kill the guy. If there was a good reason, if the target was a pedophile or rapist, justification wouldn't have been an issue, but LifeEnders didn't explain things to trainees, they just issued assignments.

Sweetwater was in perfect position to take the shot when everything went to shit.

He laid his head across the stock of the SAKO and slipped his cheek into a fitted groove along the top. It was as if they had made the stock just for him, which they had. Test firing it at the range, he'd put ten rounds into a two-inch circle at 1,800 meters. The rifle was perfect, his aim was precise, and he was ready to hunt...but not necessarily to kill a human being for money.

He moved the scope up and down the lanes of traffic, using the magnification to inspect cars as they inched along Main Street. The sweet fragrance of top-shelf gun oil filled his nostrils. Not the cheap stuff used in the Marine Corps, but *the good stuff*, M-Pro 9. One refined drop and the action was smooth as glass.

The lens of the scope went black as a Cadillac came into view. Adjusting the sight to the rear bumper, Sweetwater found the telltale Texas plate that read BIG CASH. The target was in sight. He felt the veins at his temples pulse.

"Time to make your bones, Two-Bit," he whispered. Sweetwater hated the nickname that he'd been stuck with in the Corps, but like pilots and their call signs, you didn't get to pick what everybody else called you. Two-Bit is what his fellow snipers had called him, and Two-Bit he became. Now it was his call sign, or would be, if he ever got his badge and license to kill.

Sweetwater touched his left thumb to the tip of his middle finger. Sensors in the gloves triggered a call to his spotter, who he hadn't been introduced to.

"PS4213, request confirmation."

"Hold." That inhuman single word reply, fed through an electronic scrambler that disguised all voice characteristics, held the key to his future. A bead of sweat ran down his temple, and a rookie might have wiped it away, but years of intense sniper training kicked in and he ignored it. The Caddie sat locked in the bumper-to-bumper Dallas morning traffic, so he had time.

A click in the earphone alerted him that someone else had plugged into the call. Then the unmistakable voice of the British Bitch, Ms. Witherbot, said "wait" in a tone which held more rigid authority than Sweetwater believed a single word could hold. She apparently had added another line to the call, because it only took two rings before a strange man's voice answered.

"Cooper, here."

"Mr. Cooper," said a computer voice that came on the line, "we are pleased to announce that open enrollment into the Forest Green Health Care Program has been extended." There followed another click as Mr. Cooper hung up.

Witherbot's voice returned. "Please wait as we triangulate the location." Sweetwater knew she was talking to the spotter, not to him, or not *just* to him. For purposes of the evaluation, he was like a tool undergoing a performance test.

He tried not to lose concentration as he waited for the signal to shoot but couldn't help trying to guess if Witherbot's accent was really British, or maybe Australian. He had never been good at guessing accents.

"Fucking telemarketers," he growled, forgetting the radio link was open.

"Is that a serious remark?"

"Uh, yeah, sorry about that." He ground his teeth; first day on the job, and he was already showing his ass. "I'd hate for the last thing I'd heard on this Earth to be a telemarketer."

"What are you talking about, PS4213? That was us. We need the target to give us a voiceprint for confirmation, and a health care questionnaire works well as a ruse. It's a necessary precaution."

"Oh."

He shut up and watched as the Cadillac crept a few more feet through traffic. Most snipers were hyper-focused while waiting for the kill shot, but Sweetwater's mind didn't work that way. Then the brake lights on the car flashed and the driver's door opened.

"Spotter," he said. "The target is getting out. Am I good to shoot?"

"Hold, I do *not* clear you to execute the contract."

"How about you hurry those computers of yours? This is a perfect setup."

The driver got out and opened up the car's back door. A dark-haired man emerged, wearing a light beige suit. He only got one step away from the vehicle when a woman's hand appeared in the open door, holding out a black briefcase. The man turned back to the door and the crossed reticules of the scope met on the target's forehead, just above the bridge of the nose. Sweetwater recognized him from the briefing the day before.

"Spotter, I've got visual confirmation on Robert Cooper."

"Negative, Probationary Shooter," came the immediate reply, "hold your position. The trace has confirmed your target is in Toronto, Canada."

"The hell he is. I can see his face, he's right down there."

"I said 'hold' Shooter, you are negative for taking the shot."

The target took his briefcase and walked along the sidewalk. The rifle's reticules were now centered on the back of his head. It was an easy shot.

"Damn it, what's going on?"

"We have re-run the tracing program. Your target is tracking from Toronto."

"Well, your computers are wrong. I'm telling you that's the guy; he's right there."

Witherbot broke back in. "If you are so certain, PS4213, then you have the option to verify the target's identity using alternate methods."

"How the hell do I do that?" Sweetwater knew he didn't sound professional, but she was pissing him off. They had a perfect setup that was quickly going to shit. What was that old saying? All plans fall apart at first contact with the enemy? "I don't want to lose this shot. Spotter, give me the go, and we have money in the bank."

"You're talking to me now, PS4213," Witherbot said. "You can use your phone's fingerprint scanner and get the contract's thumbprint. That will verify his identity."

"How the fuck do I get his fingerprint?"

Her tone was scolding, like an English schoolmarm from an old movie. "If you want your place in the company, PS4213, then be resourceful and figure it out. Transmit the print as soon as you have it. I'll be waiting. And remember, you currently are not authorized to execute the contract, so any collateral damage is on you. Be careful. Oh, and one more thing. Do not curse when speaking to me, is that clear?"

He waited, but she clearly expected an answer.

"Yes, ma'am."

His earwig clicked as she disconnected the call.

Damn, damn, damn!

He looked around. The hotel room was a perfect sniper's nest with a picture window overlooking the road. He'd selected the ammo load to blast through the car's window if need be, while still maintaining lethal force. Plus, for Sweetwater's purposes, it had a comfy bed, an ice machine down the hall, and even cable TV.

Snatching up his Texas Rangers baseball cap and a bright blue windbreaker as an improvised disguise, Sweetwater headed out the door. Disgusted with how such a relatively easy assignment had gone off the rails, he flipped over the Do Not Disturb sign and moved it to the outer door handle.

"I hate fieldwork," he said and then sprinted down the hall to the staircase. He'd have to hurry.

Chapter Two

Downtown Dallas, TX

Sweetwater shouldered his way through crowds of pedestrians rushing to beat the clock and get to work on time. Whenever he stopped to crane his neck and search for the target, Mr. Cooper, people bumped him from behind and walked away cursing. He tried to speed up since it was less than two blocks to Cooper's office, and once inside there was no way Sweetwater would make it past the front counter security. And even if he somehow managed that, he couldn't imagine how he'd get Cooper's fingerprint. It's not like he could ask.

Pardon me, sir, may I please verify your identity so I can kill you?

Vicious curses followed him as he bulled through the crowds, no longer bothering with maneuvering politely around walkers. The sounds of downtown Dallas during rush hour filled his ears with a storm of blaring horns, screeching tires, and screaming drivers.

Somewhere ahead of him, an engine roared above the deafening din followed immediately by the unmistakable crash of breaking glass and the squeal of metal scraping metal. A car wreck, but Sweetwater ignored it, his business lay elsewhere, until a crowd of onlookers started gathering, completely blocking his way. Sweetwater shoved and pushed, but it was no good. He would never catch up with Cooper now.

Then he heard more screeching tires, followed by another crunching impact. A car horn blared like a wailing siren. Shards of steel and glass rained on the bystanders, who were scattering like a flock of grackles after a gunshot. Sweetwater sprinted down the rapidly clearing sidewalk to the intersection, not caring who he knocked down. Dread filled his stomach, and he didn't know why. He didn't believe in premonitions, and yet...

Once at the corner, the scene was clear-cut. A semi had turned left. A small Mercedes had turned right at the same time, and the sports car was now wedged up to its shattered windshield under the semi's trailer. The lady behind the wheel was in full-blown panic mode. The car windows muffled her screams as she wriggled against the airbag, but the horn worked just fine. The crash had jammed it in the On position.

The second accident involved a mid-size Chevy that was obviously following the sports car and failed to stop in time, rear-ending the Mercedes. It must have glanced off the back driver's side quarter-panel because now the little Chevy lay angled in the middle of the street. The three cars together formed a nice neat little triangle, completely blocking the intersection.

A middle-aged woman grabbed Sweetwater's shoulder, her voice a near shriek of panic. "It hit him. Can you help him?" She was pointing at the middle of the mess, and he followed her finger to the Chevy. The driver was unconscious, laid out across the steering wheel. Either the car didn't have an airbag, or it didn't deploy upon impact. White smoke plumed from the seams of the engine hood, obscuring vision, and adding to the overall chaos of the accident. The woman jerked on Sweetwater's jacket sleeve and pointed again to the middle of the accident. "Not the driver; the car hit a man who was in the crosswalk! It ran over him!"

Most of the crowd that had run away from the shower of debris was now holding up their phones, either taking pictures or videoing the carnage. None of them appeared to be calling 911. Sweetwater's Corps training kicked in and he ran to help.

From a dead run he slid across the trunk of the Mercedes and landed between the three cars. Steam and smoke boiled up from all three vehicles and he smelled hot oil and, ominously, gas. One of the radiators hissed from a puncture.

Sweetwater found Mr. Cooper splayed on the pavement like a roadkill armadillo. Blood covered the side of Cooper's head from a deep slice on his scalp. One leg was trapped under the Chevy, but he was still alive. His eyes were open as he gasped for air. Sweetwater dropped to one knee to check his pulse.

He pressed his fingers to the side of Cooper's neck and felt a pulse, but it was weak and was running as fast as a hummingbird's wing. Blood flowed in thick ribbons from his mouth and nose, and when he coughed crimson bubbles covered his chin. Sweetwater steadied Cooper's face and looked him in the eyes.

"Mr. Cooper, we've called for help," he said, hoping it was true. Surely somebody had. "Stay still and don't move, the paramedics are on their way." Then Sweetwater realized that he was actually trying to help the man, whereas minutes before Cooper was a target to kill in fulfillment of a contract. Now, lying on the hot asphalt in a spreading puddle of blood, the target had a name, had become an actual person.

A more experienced hitter would have ended the man's pain and collected on the contract, whether there were witnesses or not, and Sweetwater knew that's what he should do. God knew he needed the money, but he wasn't cleared to kill the man, damn it!

Suddenly, Cooper reached up and grabbed his arm with the powerful grip of a man who knew he might be dying. He pulled Sweetwater close and spoke in a croaking whisper, which was barely audible over all the noise.

"I have a daughter; you have to help me. I can't leave her like this," he said in between coughs, which left a fine spray of blood splattered on Sweetwater's cheek. The would-be Shooter reached out to peel Cooper's fingers from his coat sleeve but couldn't do it.

"Mr. Cooper," he repeated, "help is on the way." Reaching under the man to pull him to a sitting position, Sweetwater stopped when Cooper screamed in pain. He jerked back, afraid someone saw him. In the video-happy, "gotcha" post-9/11 world, everybody tried to be somebody by accusing anybody of anything. Fortunately, the smoke and imminent likelihood of a fuel tank explosion kept onlookers at bay.

"I've got money," he begged. "Help me. I'll make you rich." Tears ran down the sides of his face. He coughed again, and more blood spurted from his mouth. "I can't die like this...my phone...Can you help me find my phone? I need to call my wife." Sweetwater had to put his ear up to Cooper's lips to hear him.

"Sure." Sweetwater wasn't sure why he was helping the man, but he pawed through Cooper's coat pockets and retrieved the phone. He didn't know why his hands shook when he turned the phone on and held it where the dying man could see it.

"Call Shelly."

Luther felt a thick line of sweat running down between his shoulder blades as he sat crouched in the middle of the intersection. The phone rang four empty rings. Sirens screamed in the background, though they were still a few blocks away. If he acted right now, he could still complete the contract before they arrived. After six rings it clicked over to a recorded voice. Cooper gave a weak laugh. His head slowly drooped lower as he lay on the bloody asphalt. His skin grew pale.

"Hi, honey, I love you and Jenny with all my heart…" He panted and sucked in a wet breath. "I just wanted…" Then his hand fell away from the phone and his head slumped. Sweetwater reached out and lightly felt his chest. Two shallow breaths later, it stopped moving.

Sweetwater snatched up the phone, hung up, and slipped it into a jacket pocket. Still kneeling in the middle of the road, he apologized to dead Mr. Cooper that he couldn't save his life, the life of the man he was paid to kill. A heavy sense of guilt and sadness settled over him.

"Is he all right?" said a woman's voice from somewhere behind the Chevy. "I called 911."

It took all he had to pull his eyes away from the dead man. That's when he realized what death really looked like. Being a sniper had always felt like playing the world's most realistic video game. There was no screaming or crying. Line up the crosshairs, squeeze a trigger and presto. It was just a simple point and click. And, of course, he had never actually shot anybody.

He clambered back over the Mercedes. It was empty now. Someone had opened the passenger door, and the lady was standing on the curb, screaming obscenities at the empty tractor-trailer. Sweetwater craned his head around to see that the rig's passenger door was open and there was no driver anywhere, evidently adding fleeing the scene on top of whatever other charges were headed his way. What the hell, how much worse could it be?

The woman on the corner was back. She put her hand on his chest, and Sweetwater shrank back. He didn't like being touched by strangers unless they were hot, young, and female; she only scored one out of three.

"What happened?"

The excitement of the crowd was infectious. Some heard the question, saw blood on his hands and sleeves and gathered close to eavesdrop.

"He didn't make it."

Sweetwater retraced his earlier steps and shook his head. Mr. Cooper's pale death mask was burned into his memory. At the moment he died, Cooper's gory face had taken on a surprised look Sweetwater would never forget, as if seeing something beyond the world of men. Remembering it, he wanted to be anywhere except near the dead man. His pace increased until he was running from the scene of the crash until he found an alley where he leaned against one wall.

"Now I get it," he mumbled, panting, the confession falling unheard. "Everybody warned me. The closest I ever got to action was tagging paper targets." Turning into the alley he slowed to a shamble, feeling hungover, and moved away from the bloody street. "God help me, I didn't know…"

Chapter Three

Downtown Dallas, TX

It was about five miles to LifeEnders Inc. Worldwide Corporate Headquarters. Sweetwater walked the whole way. Once he ducked into the alley it didn't take him long to get away from the crowd. The twin wrecks attracted people like buzzards to a dead deer, all of them climbing over each other to get video of someone else's tragedy. At the next trash can, he stripped off his hat and jacket and used one of the coat's sleeves to wipe the blood off his hands. Then he used the rest of the walk to calm down and think.

More than once, he wiped his hands across his shirt. There was no blood left, but he could still feel where Cooper's fingers had dug into his arm. Some inner sense told him that the memories of the last half hour would never fade, and not just what he'd seen, either. The trauma left the odors surrounding the dying man imprinted on his brain like a carving in stone. The unique stench of hot asphalt, blood, fear, smoke, oil, excreta...all of it combined to form the unique reek of Cooper's death, an unforgettable stench. But for Sweetwater, by far, the worst of it was the dying man begging for help, words that would forever haunt him.

He was the first person Sweetwater had ever watched die. He'd been at the capital on 9/11; he had seen more than his fair share of bodies, but Mr. Cooper died right in front of him, which made it personal. *Then I stole his phone like a fucking needlehead,* he thought. The only difference was that he planned to swap it for a lot more than just a bag of smack.

25

His fingers slipped into his pants' pocket for at least the tenth time, and traced the smooth plastic case, the last thing Cooper had ever touched on Earth. Then he realized that he was caressing the phone of a dead man and jerked his hand out. He wiped his fingers on his shirt again.

Somewhere out of sight, an ambulance sped away as the sirens blared out a warning. Sweetwater suddenly wondered if Mr. Cooper was in the back. Maybe he'd been wrong, and he wasn't dead; maybe they'd revived him and he was on his way to the hospital where he would eventually ask for his phone and remember the stranger who'd crouched over him and knew his name.

Objectively, Sweetwater knew there was no chance of that. Cooper's shattered body and mangled leg trapped under the Chevy, the blood covering his face and the fading strength in his fingers, the fading pulse that finally stopped. He was as pale as a corpse when he finally died because he *was* a corpse. Nobody could have saved him, yet Sweetwater still felt guilty, like he had failed.

Because, he realized, he *had* failed. He'd had a chance to fulfill the contract and didn't take it. Killing a man who was almost dead would have solved everything. Cooper had been nearly dead anyway, right? But Sweetwater would have passed his probation, gotten his license, and been on his way to getting paid. Kill targets, get paid, right? He'd read something like that in his favorite science fiction series.

Or if he had just trusted his gut and taken that damn shot, he would have been golden. The British Bitch might not have liked it, might even have washed him out, but by now he probably would have been stretched out in his hotel room, sipping a cold rum and Coke with a porn movie on the tube, and a fat fee in his bank account.

Instead, he was trudging across downtown Dallas, determined not to tell Witherbot about his self-doubts. Whatever he felt privately wasn't relevant, not if he wanted a license. Because a Shooter couldn't empathize with his or her contracts. Once they signed for a job it was a legal and binding document, and they sure as hell couldn't let it affect their performance. A signed contract meant the target had to die. It was just that simple.

In another part of Dallas, Adrian Erebus hit the controls to the air conditioner with his palm. It had finally died with a wheeze and cough. Instantly the vents started blasting him in the face with the dry burning heat of Texas. A red light appeared on the dashboard, warning the engine was overheating. He checked the temperature gauge and saw the needle was pegged to the far right.

"Sorry, Herbert." He looked into the rear-view mirror and caught sight of his eight-year-old son engrossed in a book. The boy's T-shirt was already showing sweat rings under the arm pits. "It might get a little hot. I'll see if we can catch a breeze."

Erebus rolled down the driver's window, and then the passenger's side. "This is the best I can do, buddy. You going to be all right?"

The boy in the reflection held up his thumb without looking up from his book.

"All right, this shouldn't be too long. Once I get a chance to talk with your mom, we'll all head home together."

Heat rose from the mall parking lot in waves, like mirages in the desert. Erebus adjusted the focus on the binoculars, and he spotted her car as she came close. Her pink Porsche tended to stand out in a crowd. Her car slowed before turning into the underground parking garage. He caught sight of her face for a brief second as her car disappeared. Her red hair was pulled back, and she was wearing a large pair of sunglasses.

In that brief second, he knew she was unhappy and ready to come back to him.

"I knew it."

He angled the binoculars up, scanning the side of the building. He could already picture their reunion. He'd sweep her into his arms, and she'd kiss him. Then he'd dance her around the room, as the music played their song in the background. Then when the song ended, they'd each take Herbert by the hand and walk back to their car.

He returned the binoculars to the glove box. She was still sharing the penthouse with some rich guy, and it couldn't be seen from this side of the building. Erebus turned the ignition key, but the engine just clicked. And even more frustrating, there were more warning lights on the dashboard.

"Hey buddy, you up for a little walk?" He looked into the rearview. Herbert closed his book and sat up. "Good boy, let's go." He quickly rolled up the windows and locked the doors. He paused only a second to consider, but finally retrieved the binoculars before shutting the car door. "All right, let's go see if we can find out what your mom's up to."

Chapter Four

LifeEnders Incorporated, Worldwide Corporate Headquarters, Dallas, TX

L uther stood outside the building's front doors and went through the mental exercises he'd learned at Scout Sniper School to slow his pulse. Security likely had him on multiple cameras, while facial recognition scans had undoubtedly already identified him. He just stood there as seconds ticked away, but he wasn't ready to go in and have his voice crack from nerves. It was child's play to hit a target a thousand yards away. Dealing with corporate managers—that was hard.

Four sets of beveled glass doors opened into the LifeEnders, Inc. Worldwide Corporate Headquarters building. The lobby was an elegant mix of form, function, and ostentatious wealth. On the wall behind the long security desk, fifty feet inside the doors, hung the LEI logo. Sweetwater took a deep breath and then slowly exhaled. Inhale for four seconds, hold four seconds, exhale for eight seconds, repeat. He had practiced the breathing mantra of snipers for so long it was almost second nature.

Time to get this over with.

He marched to the security desk and smiled with a confidence he didn't feel, knowing he'd likely been monitored the entire time he stood outside the door. The receptionists didn't bother to hide their suspicion as he approached, squinting with barely suppressed contempt. Heat flushed Sweetwater's cheeks as he read the judgment on their faces, as if they knew he'd screwed everything up.

"Luther Sweetwater, PS4213," one receptionist said before he could speak. "How may I help you today?"

Her clipped tone and officious manner made her seem middle-aged, her dark hair pulled back in a bun and wearing a simple black suit coat over a white blouse. Her face was at his level, five-foot-six, with a posture that suggested she would probably have been more comfortable in a uniform.

"Do you know all your people by sight?" he asked, in a lame attempt to start a conversation.

"The ones in the city, yes." Her face gave nothing away, as if she were reading a weather report. "The ones I don't recognize the computer does. Now, please, how might I help you? We are very busy at the moment."

Sweetwater let his eyes roam from side to side around the empty lobby. Busy?

"I was working a contract today and, well—"

"Yes, Ms. Witherbot is expecting you. Room 4-C, please. Down the hall on your left." She cut him off and turned back to stare at her computer terminal.

"Why didn't you just say that to begin with?" His voice was louder than necessary, but a quick glance confirmed the reception area was still nearly empty. "Thanks," he said, managing not to let his resentment inflect the words. He wandered through a maze of hallways in search of the elusive 4-C without finding it. On what he could have sworn was the third time walking past the same spot, it suddenly appeared on his left.

The doors were made from a thick layer of frosted glass. He pushed through them a little too hard, trying to make a tough guy impression. The doors slammed against the office wall. The stern face of Ms. Witherbot scowled at him from behind a paper-covered desk.

"PS4213, I'll thank you not to slam doors in this building," she said, her accent becoming stronger as she enunciated each word, as if speaking to a toddler.

"I'm sorry," he said, not really all that sorry.

"I understand matters got beyond your control?"

"You know that's not what happened!" he shot back. "I had things under control, but you two screwed it up."

"Really? Please explain, Probationary Shooter 4213, how your inability to execute your contract was due to my error."

"I, uh, well, yours and the spotter. Probably more the spotter's fault."

"I was the spotter."

"Uh...you were?"

"I perform multiple duties, but, please, you were about to explain how today's loss was not your fault."

"You told me not to shoot. You told me Cooper was in Canada."

"How do you not already know the answer to your implied objections? Did you not just complete the training course on rules and regulations? Per federal law, a probationary Shooter must have his targets verified. This is for your safety and ours because until you receive your credentials LEI accepts responsibility for your work. We must verify your competence, and we have Federal inspectors who routinely examine the execution of every contract. This isn't a nuisance animal species we are dealing with here at LEI, like armadillos or coyotes, these are human beings with constitutional rights. We have to be right every time. So, with probationary shooters we use an abundance of caution to verify targets.

"One method you witnessed was voice pattern recognition, and as we confirm the voice pattern, we triangulate the phone signal. That is exactly what I did for you, which is how we learned Mr. Cooper was—is—in Canada."

Sweetwater's temper flared, as it did when he felt he was unfairly challenged, and he slapped the table without thinking first.

"Are you calling me incompetent?"

"I wasn't, but upon reflection perhaps I should have been. You are an untested element who was unable to fulfill a contract due to circumstances beyond his control, but self-control is something within your power. Please see that you exercise it in the future!"

"Sorry…and…?"

"And here you are. I assume you want me to give you another opportunity?" She leaned back in her chair and rested her elbows on the arms, steepling her fingers.

"Yes, I do."

"During your aptitude interview, you told our agent you understood the delicate nature of our work, yet you argued with me when I told you to stand down and initiated a foot pursuit that may or may not have contributed to the death of a non-target. Collateral damage may be acceptable when executing a valid contract, but not merely to ascertain a target's identity. You were insubordinate and sloppy, and you opened the company to a punitive lawsuit. In our business, we simply can't accept anything less than perfection."

"I completed the contract," he said, consciously keeping his teeth clenched.

"You did what?" Now she sat forward with her thin eyebrows climbing up her forehead. "I authorized you to collect additional identification. You were not cleared to execute the contract. If you're saying you killed that man, then you could be in serious trouble, PS4213. That would be murder."

"Only if he wasn't Cooper." Sweetwater considered tossing the dead man's phone on her desk, but remembering her admonition of a moment before, he reached over and carefully put it on the gleaming wooden desktop. As he did so, he couldn't help glancing up at the lady who held his fate at LEI in her hands. She had a heart-shaped face behind stylish glasses, and despite the severe bun, he realized she was really very pretty. Maybe even damned pretty.

"What is this?" She waved her hand at the phone. For the first time, he noticed dried blood spots along its face. "Are those bodily fluids?"

"Sorry, I didn't see that. I think it's just blood."

"Just blood…and how is HIV transmitted, Mr. Sweetwater? Isn't it by blood or other bodily fluids?"

"I guess it is."

"And you took this from the dead man, I presume?"

"That's his phone—Cooper's, I mean. I figured you could open it up and find out why he showed as being in Canada."

She paused for a moment, holding his eyes like an owl that has spotted prey. She turned and pressed a few buttons on her computer. "Jason, could you come up here for a moment?" Her eyes did not leave his.

"Sure thing. What's up?"

"I have a cellular phone I need you to look at."

"Be right there."

"You could just lift his fingerprints," Sweetwater offered.

She clicked a button on her keyboard as she continued lecturing. "If this turns out to be what you say it is, then perhaps we can identify the technology the target used to hide his location. Perhaps he knew someone wanted him dead and this was to throw them off the trail, or perhaps he was having an affair and wanted to throw his wife off the trail. If there is something that will do that, it could be a valuable tool for us to have. Of course, that is, *if* this turns out to belong to the target. Do you know the consequences if we find out this did not belong to your contract?"

"If it's not Cooper, I'm screwed."

"Yes, you would be a murderer. We would be legally obligated to report you to the Dallas Police."

A young man appeared in the office doorway. Thick dark hair covered his cheeks, but his chin was shaved bare. "Hello?"

"Jason, could you examine this phone, please?" She still didn't touch it, merely gestured toward it. "This man believes it has software that can spoof the users' location to our system."

"Yeah, sure, but if it does, I'm not surprised. Some of the really hard-core black hats can spoof almost anything. I'm betting it has some new VPN program on it. Movie pirates use them to hide where they work. It'll only take me a minute to know for sure." He picked up the phone, careful to only touch the sides. "I'll call you as soon as I know."

The British Bitch had obviously not expected that but kept up her stony façade without a twitch. Only a slight narrowing of the eyes gave her away.

"Very well, thank you, Jason." She paused long enough to let Mr. Muttonchops clear out of the room. "Where were we? Oh, yes," she continued, her accent becoming even more clipped as she continued what Sweetwater realized was a scolding. He also noticed her tone wasn't quite as accusatory as before. "I asked you to retrieve a secondary form of confirmation of identity, and yet you still executed the contract, without authorization?"

"Well...all right, I didn't exactly kill him," he finally admitted.

"You did, or you didn't, which is it?"

"He got hit by a car."

"I knew that much, but you said...so you did not complete the contract?"

"Not technically, but I know how this works. If he was fleeing, you guys still get paid all the same."

"That is irrelevant. And even if you're correct about his identity, there is no reason to credit you with the contract. If he spotted you, then you might have a case to be paid. Perhaps we should send a bonus check to whoever was driving the car."

"I was getting the ID like you told me, but I lost him in the crowd and the next thing I knew he got hit by the car. I pulled his phone so you could close the contract."

"Yes, but that is not what we pay for."

"You wouldn't let me do what you pay for, remember?"

"Again, irrelevant."

"Not to me!"

She opened her mouth to reprimand him but was interrupted by a chirp from her computer. She closed her mouth, her lips pressed into a thin line, and hit a key. Jason's voice came from the speaker.

"I got the phone open, and I was right; the guy has a VPN on his phone. It's pretty simple. I should be able to adjust our interface. We won't get fooled by this program again. And, for the record, I confirm this was Robert Cooper's phone."

"Thank you." She clicked the button on the keyboard to end the call. "Well, Mr. Sweetwater, it appears that you have earned your second chance."

"So now it's 'Mr. Sweetwater'?"

"Would you prefer I use your number?"

Sweetwater realized that it was a serious question. She was trying to be accommodating. He noticed, for the first time, the slight upturn of her nose, and how at just the right angle it gave her a pixyish look. She was also younger than he'd thought, maybe 45 or so.

"No, that's okay. So, I've earned a second chance for what? Didn't I fulfill the contract?"

"Don't be absurd! Stealing a dying man's phone does not fulfill a contract, even if we get paid for it. A Shooter does not earn his or her credentials through an accidental death. If you would like another chance to properly execute a contract, I will allow you that."

Well, aren't you a sweetheart? But the truth was he really didn't have much choice, so he gave her his best smile and hoped it didn't look as fake as it felt.

"Fine, thank you. What do you have?"

She faced her computer and typed and clicked for several seconds. "Yes," she said to herself. "This will do nicely." A printer on the corner of her desk hummed to life. She snatched up a single sheet of paper the instant it finished printing and slipped it into a manila envelope. She handed it over like it was an X-ray which indicated whether or not he had terminal cancer. "Here is your new contract: Grace Allen Tarbeau. Let's hope this one goes better than the last; it is most lucrative. Your fee will be most handsome, even at the reduced rate of a Probationary Shooter. Now, if you don't mind, I have several other duties to perform."

"Sure."

After leaving the office, Sweetwater rolled the envelope into a tube and stuffed it into his back pocket. It was LEI policy that subcontractors always review offers in private and that all such offers be delivered as hard copies. Before he headed back to his hotel room to read, however, he stopped at a liquor store with thick black bars on the windows and graffiti outside. Money was tight, so he got the biggest bottle of the cheapest stuff he could afford. After putting it on the checkout counter, he laughed and pointed at the bottle.

"My favorite brand," he said, "Old Hangover."

Chapter Five

S weetwater had been on a high school field trip to DC on September 11, 2001, when the world changed forever. The tour bus was a mile from the Capitol when the first plane hit it. Most of the kids screamed, and the bus driver tried to turn around, but the traffic was too heavy. Instead, they abandoned the bus and ran, scattering when the second plane struck the dome. Another plane flew into the White House. Everybody else ran away from the flames, but he ran toward them.

Even years later, Sweetwater still didn't know why he did what he did next; teenagers do weird stuff. He guessed that he somehow felt it was his duty as an American to help clean up after the attack. Once his teachers finally located him, covered in smoke and rock dust, they locked him in his hotel room with three roommates, but Luther Sweetwater was not a kid to meekly follow orders he didn't agree with. It got him in plenty of trouble in high school. He pried the window open and climbed down the brick wall two stories to the ground.

Even years later, he could remember the stink of burning jet fuel as he climbed over debris looking for survivors. One memory in particular haunted his dreams. He'd scrambled over a big chunk of marble when his foot slipped, and he slid onto a pile of glass. Luther fell across the body of a man with a "Vietnam Vet" tattooed on his upper arm. Luther delicately rolled the body over to check if he

39

might still be alive. The man's face was cut from the glass-covered painting he had fallen across. A look of pain was pressed onto the man's face from when he passed.

Luther looked at the painting, stained with the dead man's blood. It was the portrait of President Lyndon Johnson. Luther didn't recognize the portrait at first, but years later he researched presidential paintings and found the restored image.

The days that followed were filled with endless hours of recovering mangled bodies from the rubble. He and his fellow workers lined them up in rows across the street from the Capitol. Hundreds of bodies were laid to rest side by side with nothing more than a sheet to protect them.

More volunteers came in to help, only to leave just as quickly. Digging out broken and burnt bodies took more mental and physical strength than most people possessed. Days in the rubble stretched into weeks. They ate whatever they were given, by whoever gave it to them, and slept anywhere they could. Unknown to Sweetwater, his parents had driven to Washington from rural West Tennessee, since all flights were still grounded, to look for him. Somehow, he hadn't even thought to call them during the chaos. Nothing mattered except the digging, and sometime during all that chaos the desire for revenge turned into an obsession. He had trouble resting. When he stopped for sleep, ghosts turned his exhausted sleep into nightmares.

The high school senior had to do something or go insane, so the next day he found a Marine Corps recruiting station and enlisted. When his parents found out, they tried to squash it, but he was three weeks past his 18th birthday. It was barely a week later, and he was in basic training and, after that, Scout Sniper School. Like the right hand of God, Sweetwater vowed he would smite the terrorists who had struck at the heart of the nation.

The spring of terror turned into a baking summer in boot camp. While training on the shooting range, he was told he qualified for sniper training. He spent the days crawling through the North Carolina dirt with a .50-cal on his back. Evenings were spent waiting for his orders. It was accepted knowledge that the United States would be going after whoever instigated the 9/11 attack. However, the new commander in chief seemed too timid to commit the necessary troops or do much of anything.

Daily news reports stressed the frustration of the nation and the desire for retribution. While the military was sent to reinforce the borders, the skeleton government recalled most of the overseas military and their families.

After an exceptionally hot day of training, Sweetwater's Marine division was gathered together in the base theater where they were patched into a live news feed. A dozen men were dressed in black, and all of them held automatic rifles. In front of them a lone Arab man knelt with his hands tied behind his back.

One of the men in black stepped forward and pulled down a scarf that was across his face. "My name is Turrell Smith. The people behind me are my brothers and sisters in the LifeEnders. We are *not*," Smith paused for emphasis, "I repeat, we are *not* representatives of the United States Government. We are the hammer of revenge against those who dare to attack our nation."

Smith looked side to side, meeting the eyes of each man standing beside him. "We could no longer stand idly by and watch our government cower before cowards hiding in caves on the far side of the world. Those who think they can destroy the United States will discover their mistake as they choke on their own blood, as will the traitors within our borders. Hatred for America will no longer be accepted." The man put his foot on the back of the kneeling man and pushed him to the ground. The man fell flat to his stomach, unable to catch himself.

"This piece of filth is named Osama bin Laden. He is the man who orchestrated the attack on our country. This man sent a handful of terrorists to hijack a dozen planes and kill thousands of innocent Americans in cold blood. Since our government did not act, we did. We are Americans, and we will not allow our republic to die without a fight. We are LifeEnders…we are the hammer of revenge." Smith pointed directly into the camera. "All you Marxists and terrorists and those who would raise your hand against the red, white, and blue should pay attention."

Smith knelt beside the bound man identified as Osama bin Laden. With a jerk he grabbed a handful of hair, lifted bin Laden's face from the dirt and angled it to the camera. "If you still dare attack us, then remember this." Smith dragged the bound terrorist closer to the camera. Sweat and dirt mixed into mud on the man's lean, bearded face. Smith continued. "If you attack our country, we will find you, and you will find out why we are called LifeEnders."

The sound of leather against steel came from off camera, then the barrel of a gun appeared beside the head of the bound man. Bin Laden whimpered and tried to move his head away.

"Rahmatan min fadlka!" Mercy please!

"We'll give you the same mercy you showed those people in the Twin Towers."

The gunshot echoed through the movie theater speakers. The opposite side of bin Laden's head blew out like a tornado hitting a mobile home. The force of the bullet knocked him over.

The theater on base exploded in cheers, drowning out the live feed. All the Marines were on their feet, shaking the seats in front of them, stomping their feet, and pushing each other on the back with such force that only other Marines could remain standing.

The entire country became one, giant block party. Luther celebrated the LifeEnders' victory through the night and well into the next morning. The next day, those who were eligible put in their separation paperwork. They had seen the new American heroes, those who didn't ask permission to avenge the country—they just did it—and a huge percentage of eligible service members wanted to join the mercenary group.

S weetwater pulled the drapes closed and took care to overlap them so no light could leak into the darkened hotel room, which also had the effect of muffling traffic noise. Then he filled the sink with ice and dropped a few cubes in a plastic cup. Usually, this was when he did a light workout before dinner. Being small of frame and stature, he packed on as much lean muscle as his body could take and still maintain his agility. But tonight was different. Now, he needed to drink.

The new contract lay on the bed. Seeing it twisted his gut in knots, while dread filled him over what he might find there. Before watching Cooper die, the idea of being a licensed Shooter had meant big paydays, fast cars, and faster women; a lifestyle he'd always dreamed of but never thought could happen. Now he understood what death really meant, that he would be taking away everything a person had, or ever would have, whether they deserved it or not.

Instinct told him the new contract would be a bad deal, and that concerned him most of all. Assassins couldn't have qualms about killing people; it was the entire job description, and yet here he was.

Cracking open the cheap whiskey, he threw the plastic cap across the room, as if acknowledging he wouldn't be resealing the bottle. He half-filled a glass of yellow-brown liquid, hoping it would help him sleep through the night. Every time he closed his eyes, Sweetwater saw Robert Cooper bleeding out while half-pinned under the busted-up Chevy, like some afterimage you get from staring at the sun too long.

Flopping onto the bed, he rolled onto his back and opened his eyes, but Cooper's image didn't go away. Instead, the dead man stood beside the bed, bent over so his pale face could study Sweetwater with a quizzical expression.

"So, is that glass half full or half empty?" the hallucination, or the ghost, asked.

Blinking, Sweetwater rolled onto his side, drained the glass without coming up for air, and refilled the cup until whiskey spilled onto the table.

"Fuck you, Cooper, go away," he said. "You're not real. You're at the coroners right now, getting your fluids drained down a steel sink. Your problems are over now. Leave me alone." He choked down half the glass in one long pull. The full glass hadn't bothered him, but the second one felt like he'd swallowed acid as the whiskey ate its way down to his stomach. He put the glass down, sat up in bed, and then doubled over as he coughed from the cheap booze, rasping "smooth" between gags. When he could breathe again, he threw the rest of the booze back and fought to keep it down.

Cooper stood up and laughed. "I think we both know that's not going to happen." Then he vanished.

Sweetwater covered his eyes with his forearm. This wasn't going the way he'd imagined.

Night fell as the day's events replayed over and over in his mind. When he uncovered his eyes, the darkness startled him. Weren't ghosts more likely to show up in the dark?

Instead of turning on the lights, Sweetwater got up and pulled back the curtains, allowing the window to frame the glow of downtown Dallas at night. He sat on the bed, forearms on his thighs. He felt beads of moisture run down the outside of the plastic cup and drip onto his pants, leaving a wet spot that eventually brought him out of his reverie. He shook his head to clear it, and the brownish liquid called out to him. Sweetwater tipped the cup back again, and again, and again. Each slug went down a little easier and went from burning his throat like Drain-O to being smooth as the finest Irish whiskey.

His head a bit wobbly, he opened the manila envelope to study the contract, but first he sipped the last of the watery whiskey, crunched the last ice cube, and stumbled to the sink to get more. He was stalling.

He knew he'd had more than enough but tipped the bottle into the plastic cup anyway. Once the cup was full of booze and ice, he was out of excuses to stall. Like yanking a bandage off a cut, he ripped out the single sheet of paper.

The target's picture was in the upper right corner, an image of a young woman in her early thirties: Grace Allen Tarbeau. Her mouth was twisted in an off-center smile as she posed for the camera. Taken in a rural setting, she had some silly polka-dot top hat on her head. Under the hat brim, curly red hair poured out. A few freckles sprinkled her nose. Everything framed her emerald green eyes. She was gorgeous.

Yet Sweetwater saw something else there, too, although he couldn't put his finger on what it was. Sadness touched her eyes in a way he'd never seen before, and her smile seemed more determined than happy. A feeling told him this woman had seen bad times.

Leaping from the bed, he dropped the paper and ran for the toilet. He made it to the bathroom, but not all the way to the crapper, and threw up the whiskey along with chunks of the meatball sub he'd eaten for dinner. Heaving, he looked up to see Cooper's ghost sitting on the edge of the bathtub, leaning his elbow against the sink, holding his face in his palm. His skin had a light gray tone.

"You really going to off the girl? I got twenty bucks says you don't."

"Why do you sound like a 1930's movie gangster?"

He leaned back and shrugged. "Why are you asking me?" Using his left index finger, he touched his temple and then pointed at Sweetwater. "I'm a figment of your imagination."

"Are you?"

"Oh, you believe in ghosts! Is that what you think I am?"

"I don't know. Hell, I don't care, just go away!"

"Make me."

That brought another round of retching, followed by dry heaves. Once Luther's stomach finally calmed a little, he crawled on all fours to where he'd left the bottle, took a swig to rinse out the taste of vomit, and spit it into the sink.

"The answer's not in that bottle, Two-Bit," Cooper said. "It's between your ears."

"How did you know my nickname?"

"C'mon Luther, you're a smart guy, so quit playing dumbass."

"Fuck you. You're dead."

"And you didn't do it, which means there's still time to save yourself."

"Shouldn't you have started rotting by now?"

"Did you go blind, too? I have." Cooper shook his head, and little bits of skin flew off. Then he rose and started to walk through the bathroom wall. He paused and glared at Luther. "Think first, think again." It was a twist on the unofficial motto of those with a license to kill, "Shoot first, shoot again."

With a wave, Cooper disappeared into the wall. Sweetwater pushed himself very carefully to his feet, and then, somehow, made it back to the bed, using his hands to move along the wall. Staring at the ceiling as the room swam around him, he lay there for hours waiting to pass out.

He awoke to a wet pillow and dried tears crusting his eyes.

Chapter Six

Downtown Dallas, TX

The angle of the early morning sun blazed like a high-powered laser through the hotel room window, and it was aimed right at Sweetwater's eyes. Covering his head with a pillow didn't help. The sun was out there, and his eyes were not happy about it.

A cough brought enough spit into his mouth to allow him to taste cotton and sour vomit. Months had passed since he last had such a bad hangover, with pain lancing his brain at even the slightest movement. He could only move one body part at a time, and then only slowly. The process took nearly three minutes, starting with his left leg first, over the side of the bed, then the right leg. Sit up sideways and, finally, a stop to gasp for breath. The carpet felt wet under his feet and reeked of something stale and foul, but he was afraid to know why. The only thing he knew for sure was that LEI would be charged extra for damage to the room. Locking both legs against the edge of the bed, he scooted his butt until he nearly fell off and, with a deep breath, pushed to his feet.

Sweetwater had expected pain, but not like what came next. It was as if somebody had stabbed his head with an ice pick. The muscles of his shoulders spasmed and he almost gave up and went back to bed. He passed the window and a caught a sunbeam. The sunlight laser was back. He winced from the pain of the light searing through his closed eyelids and hitting the burned-out embers that used to be his eyes. The laser kept driving and blasted out the back of his skull, cauterizing everything along the way.

With his eyes closed tight, he waved his arm around like a blind man. He just happened to catch the back of a chair and waited for the world to stop its roll, or at least for the corkscrew to slow down. He leaned over the back of the chair, grabbed the armrests, and used it like a walker to shuffle to the bathroom. The merciful God above had protected most of the ice in the sink, and with the stopper closed, the part that had melted was still pretty cold. After opening the tap and filling it to the brim, Sweetwater plunged his head in as deeply as it could go, spilling water over the counter and onto the floor.

The cold water muted some of the pain and all but extinguished the burning fire in his eyeballs. A second plunge lasted longer, until he couldn't hold his breath a second more. After diminishing the pain, Sweetwater found he could walk, sort of, and choked down everything left in the whiskey bottle, maybe two fingers, letting the alcohol burn out the leftover taste from the night before.

He returned to the sink and dipped his head again. The whiskey didn't stay in his stomach long enough to be absorbed. Since his employer was paying for his meals, Sweetwater ordered pancakes, orange juice, a carafe of coffee, a bottle of ibuprofen, and a pitcher of ice water from room service. Bacon came with the order, but he didn't think that was a good idea until the pancakes settled his stomach, then he wolfed down all three slices. Thirty minutes after breakfast, he felt human enough to re-enter the world.

After showering and brushing his teeth, it was after two when he finally called the LEI offices and asked for Ms. Witherbot.

A single ring and the clipped British accent spoke and gave him a different kind of headache. "Good afternoon, PS4213. What can I do for you this fine day?" Sarcasm dripped from the receiver.

"You knew it was me?" It was a stupid thing to say, but his brain function hadn't passed 50 percent yet, maybe less.

"Caller ID is a wonderful invention; I'm surprised that you haven't noticed it in the last twenty or so years."

"I just want to confirm the contract you gave me yesterday."

"Is there a problem?"

"It's just not what I was expecting."

"Oh? How so?"

"She's a girl."

"A female, yes. Were you expecting Hitler? Thirty-five percent of our contracts target females. Your introductory packet specifically indicated that we are gender-neutral on accepting and authorizing contracts. To do otherwise violates federal discrimination laws. So, as long as it complies with ancillary government regulations specific to our industry, we accept it. If you cannot accept those conditions, then this is the wrong line of work for you."

"She can't be thirty years old."

"Actually, she is thirty-two. Did you even read the contract?"

"I skimmed it…and yeah, I remember now. Thirty-two."

"You barely got past the picture," said a third voice. "You saw her tits and forgot everything else."

It was Cooper, sitting on the other bed smoking a cigarette. He had taken on a weird blue pallor.

Sweetwater tried to ignore him.

"If there is a problem," the British Bitch went on, "I'll withdraw your application. No muss, no fuss about it. I will assign this target to the next Probationary Shooter. You go back to your old life and never contact us again."

Cooper laughed. "Old life, ha! You didn't have one." Smoke trickled from his nostrils.

"There's no problem, ma'am. I just wanted to confirm."

"I confirm the target, Grace Allen Tarbeau. Also, just in case you have not completed reading the contract, the requested time limit on this contract is tonight. The request comes with a bonus clause the company would very much like to collect. You must be on site, but we'll have a cover identity ready for you."

"Tonight?" *Fuck!* She said nothing more, waiting him out. "I didn't seen that." More silence. "I'll be ready. Thank you." There was a *click* and the line went dead. He heard a faint echo…was *his phone tapped?* What a stupid question; of course it was.

Sweetwater's hand trembled as he reached for the contract. "It's just the whiskey shakes," he told Cooper as he started to read.

The dead man's laugh echoed as if from the crypt. "Sure it is, and cigarettes are gonna kill me." He rolled backward as he laughed at his own joke, and then sank out of sight into the bed.

Chapter Seven

Downtown Dallas, TX

The sun was still a couple hours from setting when Sweetwater took an elevator to the top of the Renaissance Tower, one of the tallest skyscrapers in Dallas, feeling remarkably decent, testimony to the amazing results that an overdose of pain meds can have on a hangover. A brass plate in the building lobby said the building was 720 feet tall. That made for a long elevator ride. The numbers on the floor display continued to climb.

His stomach gurgled as the drugs melted into his system. The pancakes were long since digested, and he was craving something sweet, like a big slice of cake or a brownie, but it was too late for that now. It was time to get on with the job. The elevator doors opened with a *ding,* and he was in a small room. The glass wall opposite the elevator revealed more of the Dallas skyline than he'd ever seen before.

As soon as he stepped out, a balding man in a white suit coat grabbed his arm. The head waiter, or maybe the organizer, Sweetwater couldn't decide which, because he looked like an undertaker rather than a guy who made sure the flowers were just so or everybody got enough food and drink. According to the British Bitch, this cadaverous guy would provide his cover story.

"You're late," the man said, looking down his nose. His long white tuxedo coat looked like a movie prop, emphasized by the matching white tie. All that white made him look like a funeral director in Heaven.

"They told me to expect you here at six; it is now twenty after."

"Yeah, sorry about that, I couldn't find a place to park." The guy's attitude reminded Sweetwater of a fast-food manager he'd worked for, the kind who always harassed you over meaningless bullshit just because he could. He gave him a nickname, the way he did everybody he met…the Skeleton.

"Excuses are worthless. Remember, if you are early, then you're on time. If you're on time, you're late. If you're late, well, that is just unacceptable."

"I'll try to remember that in the future."

The man was at least six feet tall, but he couldn't have weighed over a hundred and twenty-five pounds, a walking skeleton with sunken eyes and a long, bony nose. Sweetwater was half a foot shorter but forty pounds heavier, and all of it muscle.

"Walk this way," said the Skeleton. Without waiting to see if Sweetwater followed, he turned and strode away.

The roof of the building was an open-air patio. Beside the little elevator room were a few shelters. Greenery grew in concrete receptacles scattered about the roof, with wrought-iron tables and chairs organized here and there. A small crowd of over-dressed people, like those you see at campaign fund-raising events, mingled and pretended to be enjoying each other's company. Even somebody as unsophisticated as Sweetwater could smell the phoniness.

The shelters were there for food prep. There were platters of hors d' oeuvres and champagne flutes by the hundreds standing on tables and trays. The Skeleton led him past everything to a rack of suits, black slacks, white jackets, and black ties. He plucked one from the front of the frame.

"Here, try this one." He gestured towards the changing tents by waving the back of his left hand. "Be quick about it. The party starts in half an hour."

"Who are these people?" Sweetwater said, gesturing toward the ones already there.

The Skeleton gave them a half-second glance. "Who they are isn't important. They are the clients, and that's all that matters. Now hurry up and get dressed."

In the tent, he stripped out of his street clothes and into the Halloween costume. The pants were a little long. Fortunately for Sweetwater, he was wearing his cowboy boots, which didn't exactly match the waiter getup but added another inch of height. Before he put on the jacket, he opened the travel bag he'd brought with him.

Inside were the special tools he'd requested from LEI, including a shoulder holster with a Sig Sauer P320 equipped with a suppressor and loaded with subsonic, hollow-point rounds. After checking to make sure one rested in the chamber, he positioned the holster to hold the pistol barrel down along his ribcage. Opposite of the pistol, he clipped on his old USMC Ka-Bar, for good luck. Finally, he shrugged into the white dinner jacket. Like his pants, it was just a little too large, which worked to hide the pistol and harness perfectly.

Sweetwater had to hand it to the British Bitch, serving as a waiter was the perfect cover—silent, ignored, invisible. It was too bad the Skeleton wasn't really an undertaker because he'd soon have some new business.

Erebus sat at the bus terminal outside the Renaissance Tower. According to the newspaper he'd found, the rooftop party would be starting anytime now. From a shopping bag as his feet, he withdrew his binoculars and scanned the outside of the building.

"You know buddy, the shopping bag was a great idea." He craned his neck to try to catch sight of the rooftop plaza. "Herbert, keep an eye open for your mom. Let me know if you see her."

"Hey, buddy, what are you doing out here?" called a voice from his right.

Erebus quickly returned his binoculars to the shopping bag and looked up to see a large man in a dark gray suit, and wearing dark sunglasses despite being in the shadows cast by the buildings to the west, with a suspicious wire running into his right ear.

"We're not doing anything; just waiting for the bus."

"We?" The man tilted his head.

"My son and I."

"Uh-huh. There is only one bus route that picks up at this stop, and it has passed twice."

A chill ran down Erebus' back. "Oh, I didn't realize that." Silence stretched out between them. "We were waiting for the number three bus." He hoped there was a number three bus. The other man kept staring at them. "I guess we need to go find another stop. Do you know where the number three picks up?"

The man didn't respond. Erebus realized that the man hadn't moved since he first arrived, so he picked up his shopping bag and started walking away. "Come on, Herbert, let's go see if we can find your mom."

After turning the corner, he turned to follow the side of the building. "Maybe we can find somewhere else to wait. I have a lucky feeling today is the day we bring your mom home."

Across the street was an open parking garage. "There's a spot we can wait. Come on." He knew she was counting on them, and he was not going to let her down. When he spotted Grace, he would whisk her away from the nightmare she was trapped in. No matter how late, he'd speed over there and sweep her into his arms. Then they'd all race back to Tennessee where they could spend eternity loving each other. Life would be different for them all, especially Herbert. The boy needed his mother.

It was an hour before the Skeleton finally gave Sweetwater a platter and told him to walk the floor. Since it was Texas, he strolled around the patio offering people a meatball made from Wagyu Beef and veal. If nothing else, he discovered what he'd always assumed, that the rich knew how to live. He finally couldn't hold back his hunger any longer, so he'd ducked behind a tent with three meatballs left on his tray and downed them, one after another. Damn! They were the best thing he'd ever tasted.

The view was tremendous. The sun was dipping below the horizon, and the sky was ablaze with red and orange and one long streak of pink. Blue and green lights flashed through the water of a long infinity pool that ran along the east side of the tower, contrasting against the colors of the western sky. Hidden speakers played background music, nothing so loud as to prevent people from mingling, but just loud enough to quiet the obnoxious Mr. Cooper from chattering in Sweetwater's brain. Thankfully, the ghost was nowhere to be found. Sweetwater had never been a waiter at a party like this before. For that matter, he'd never seen a party like this before, outside of movies and watching overpaid celebrities glamming it up on TV.

But now it was time for business. If he wanted to be a professional, he needed to act like one. The reassuring weight of the pistol against his ribs confirmed that this would be a walk in the park, like shooting fish in a barrel, or whatever cliché best fit the situation.

When Grace Allen Tarbeau stepped out of the elevator lobby and onto the deck, Sweetwater didn't want to kill her, he wanted to run away with her.

She was dressed in a long dark-velvet gown, and he thought it was a great choice. A slit ran up the skirt, nearly to her waist. With every step she took, her perfect, shapely leg peeked in and out of sight. His eyes worked up that long leg to find a waist that called him to wrap his arms around her and pull her tight against his chest. Thin, silver straps fell over her bare shoulders, holding the dress against her in an alternating not-quite-tight-enough and not-quite-loose-enough way. Bouncing red curls framed her face as she stepped onto the patio, but to him, the most fantastic thing about her was her eyes. Anybody who saw those eyes could never again deny the existence of God. They sparkled like a flashlight shining through emeralds. It seemed impossible that she'd only recently been a poor girl from rural West Tennessee.

She walked past Sweetwater without noticing him. He caught just a hint of a fragrance that inspired images of a Tennessee spring, and the way she carried herself tempered his lust. The wholesome allure from the photo was no longer there. Money was said to change people, but it had warped Grace Allen. To her, Sweetwater was just part of the decor, someone to be ignored. Which made things much easier for him.

Sweetwater waited until nobody was looking his way and ducked into one of the changing tents. Serving staff scuttled along in a choreographed dance he'd been part of but didn't really understand. He pulled out his phone. "PS4213 requesting confirmation." He kept his voice low.

"That's her," the now-familiar British voice said. "You are confirmed, PS4213. You may execute the contract."

"You sure you don't need to give her the telemarketer call?"

"Sarcasm is not appreciated, PS4213. Did you see her carrying a phone?"

"No, but—wait, you can see her?"

"You have no need for that information at this moment. You asked for a second chance, and this is it. You lied to us about executing the contract on Mr. Cooper, which is totally unacceptable, but then you recanted and brought us good intel about spoofing software of which we were unaware. That is the only reason you have been given this second chance, and there will not be a third. However, I believe you can do this, PS4213. I think you have it within you to be a first-rate Shooter, so go execute the contract."

"Right," he said, packing as much bravado into the one word as he could. Except the truth was that his mouth had gone dry again. Most people would have seen though Grace's bullshit, but Sweetwater didn't want to see through it. Sweetwater passed through the kitchen and picked up a silver platter of champagne flutes, the sweet smell of alcohol making his stomach churn.

But when he exited the tent, an epiphany hit Sweetwater like the venom of a cottonmouth racing through his body. Without consciously realizing it, something had changed, like a switch in his brain had been flipped.

He wanted that license.

Chapter Eight

Downtown Dallas, TX

Sweetwater returned to the party and worked the crowd. The white coat made him invisible. All around the rooftop people mingled and chatted about inane trivialities, unaware that a predator walked among them. They were sheep, and he was a wolf. No, not a wolf, he was a lion. He was the king of beasts, and the rest of them were just gazelles standing around waiting to be devoured.

On full alert now, he kept his body relaxed and fluid, yet ready to leap in any direction as he'd been taught. Sweetwater slipped into the herd using them as camouflage to stalk his prey. Not too close and not too fast. The hunt required patience.

He stopped five feet away from Tarbeau, making sure that he could see her in his peripheral vison. Prey always recognized a predator's eyes, so he didn't let her see his. He didn't want her to get spooked, the last thing a Probationary Shooter needed was some rich guy as collateral damage. Especially not Dennis Roy Tarbeau, eldest son and grandson of the scions of Tarbeau Oil. Killing him would raise a shit storm, whether he was legal collateral damage or not.

The tall, broad man walking two paces behind Grace Allen was her husband, and he looked unhappy. She walked toward the edge of the building and held a hand out behind her, without bothering to look at her husband, who followed in her wake. He dug a pack of cigarettes out of an inside pocket, lit one, and put it between her

61

fingers. Only then did Grace grace him with a smile, and for a fleeting instant Sweetwater knew why he'd married her. The brilliance of her white teeth against the high cheek bones and dark red hair made for beauty most men would die for.

Or kill for, as in Sweetwater's case. He didn't know who wanted her dead or why, and he didn't care anymore. At least, he mostly didn't care. In the back of his mind were stories about some franchise owner who'd fallen in love with his target and claimed he'd killed her, only to have her double-cross him and show up at headquarters. That earned him a hefty price on his head, and the girl walked away rich after suing LEI. It was meant to be a warning against feeling empathy toward your targets, and, now, being so close to Tarbeau, he understood the warning.

Paralleling her path, he judged that it wasn't time to close on them yet, but he moved to cut off any avenue of retreat. His prey wasn't going to get away, not this time.

They stopped at the edge of the building and turned to face the crowd. Flashes lit up the night as photographers fought each other to capture the perfect shot. Grace Allen, the lovely gazelle, stood framed against the sky just as the stars began to appear.

The time had come. Sweetwater shifted the tray of champagne to his left hand and reached into his jacket to pull out the Sig. But in his excitement, he had lost situational awareness, and, as he should have expected and planned for, sometimes shit happens. Someone grabbed two of the champagne flutes from behind him, which unbalanced the tray and caused it to slip forward. Compounding his mistake, Sweetwater let go of the pistol instead of shoving it back into the holster as he reached up to catch the tray. But it was too late. The half dozen remaining glasses fell from the tray and shattered on the floor. Champagne spattered anyone nearby. Every eye glared at him, as if he had ruined their lives and not merely spilled some carbonated wine.

"You stupid ass!"

A large man grabbed Sweetwater's lapels and shoved him backward. He stumbled, hit the low wall around the roof's edge with his knees, and bent forward to stare at a 56-story drop into nighttime nothingness. The silver platter sailed out of his grasp, spinning end over end out of sight. And then he felt something else move his jacket, something heavy. *The pistol!* It slipped free and followed the silver tray toward Elm Street far below, bouncing once against the side of the building before tumbling away. Hands grabbed the back of his coat and jerked him back to solid footing.

The monster of a man spun Sweetwater around and towered over him. "Listen, asshole, I'm sorry I pushed you so hard."

"It's fine," Luther mumbled, craning his neck both left and right to see around the big man. Grace Allen Tarbeau was gone. "I'm fine." He stumbled past the man, and Sweetwater was grabbed by the shoulder and spun around.

"Then perhaps your worthless ass could go grab a towel for my wife. You dumped that cheap champagne all over her." Sweetwater thought the guy might have once played in the NFL. Holding a fist full of jacket, he pulled the waiter-assassin close and pretended he was brushing off dirt, but his whispered tone was anything but friendly. "And do it now."

Sweetwater wanted to crush the man, and unlike his younger days, the Marines had taught him exactly how to take down someone much larger than himself. A hard knee to the balls, an upper cut with the heel of your hand, a kick to the kneecap or inside of the ankle...there were lots of ways. But that wasn't why Sweetwater was there.

Focus, Luther, focus.

"Honey, please." The woman beside him finally spoke. Her thin white gown was near transparent where the drinks had hit her, and with the dress clinging to her skin everyone could see that she wasn't wearing anything underneath.

Then it happened. The man brushed a hand over Sweetwater's holster. With a sudden jerk, he pulled the jacket away to expose the now-empty shoulder holster and Ka-Bar.

"What's that?" someone asked.

"He's got a gun!" someone else yelled, despite the holster being empty.

The sophisticated party broke down into chaos, like a Three Stooges movie without the pie throwing. People screamed and ran in every direction at once. Sweetwater tried to pull away from the man's grip, but NFL-guy wouldn't let go. People backed away as if he might shoot them, even though his hands were empty. If he still had it, Sweetwater would have given NFL-guy a hole in his forehead and gone after his target.

Many of the party goers ran toward the elevator, even though the little lobby was already jammed. Too short to see over the crowd, for an instant the panicked crowd parted just enough for him to see his target and her escort disappear behind a row of potted bushes.

Sweetwater looked up at NFL-guy. "Let me go."

A low grin crept across his mouth. "What if I don't, little man?"

Sweetwater kicked out to the inside of his right knee. The guy's leg buckled and bent in a direction it wasn't designed to do. Screaming, the big man let go and fell to his hands and left knee, since the right sure as hell couldn't bear any weight.

Sweetwater couldn't resist bending low and whispering in the man's ear. "Just remember, I asked nice. This is on you."

He started to walk away. NFL-guy wasn't his target, after all.

"You stupid fuck, I'm going to sue you for everything you have." Then he spit on Sweetwater's prized boots.

Target or no target, nobody disrespected Luther Sweetwater like that. He was a fuckin-A Marine scout sniper, and he'd be damned if anybody ever treated him that way ever again. He'd die first.

Pinching NFL-guy's ear, he pulled it sideways toward his lips. "You want to sue me, after nearly killing me? Listen, asshole, if I ever see you again, if you ever bother me or try to sue me, I'll break your other leg and throw you in the Trinity River, you got that?"

The man nodded. The wife had scrammed. Sweetwater pivoted with his hips to put all of his weight behind the low hook. With a soft crunch, NFL-guy's head snapped to the side, and his body went limp as he fell face down. Just to add insult to injury, Sweetwater stepped on the downed man's back and walked over him.

His phone chirped but he didn't answer. It was probably the British Bitch asking what the hell he was doing.

In the few seconds that had passed, the center of the roof had emptied. Sweetwater headed for the row of potted plants while pulling his Ka-Bar free of its sheath. There was nowhere for her to run now; he was the lion, and she was the cornered gazelle. And if hubby got in the way, he'd get cut up, too.

Sweetwater saw her trembling as he stepped behind the bushes. She was even more breathtaking up close. Gone was the extreme arrogance of the poor country girl trying to act like she came from

Old Money. Instead, he saw reflected in those remarkable eyes the terror that all prey must feel at the moment of death. She froze, even as Dennis Roy pulled desperately on her arm, trying to pull her away to safety.

"It's time," Sweetwater said, unsure if he was talking to Grace Allen or himself.

Tears flowed down her cheeks as she mouthed the word "no" over and over, but without sound. Hubby stepped forward a pace, but Sweetwater pointed the tip of the knife at him.

"You're not part of this, but if you get in the way, you'll get hurt."

Dennis Roy Tarbeau stepped back.

"Why are you doing this?" he asked, in a tone he probably thought was conciliatory, but came out dismissive and demanding. Sweetwater doubted he even realized how the words sounded.

Grace Allen found her voice, although it came out as a squeak.

"Please don't do this."

Her escort, her husband, nodded in acceptance, which disgusted Sweetwater. If she had been Luther's wife, he'd have spent every last ounce of his strength defending her, but not this guy, he seemed almost complacent about it.

Fucking coward.

For an instant Luther considered killing the husband, too. He could say it was collateral damage, but he rejected the idea. Knowing the British Bitch, she probably had cameras recording the whole thing.

Sweetwater moved his left hand over her eyes, and her knees buckled. The tip of his knife caught her just below her rib cage. The tip parted the dress like warm butter and cut into her flesh, but only a quarter of an inch, enough to draw blood but not cause real damage.

The sudden pain caused her to jerk back to her full height. Eyes wide with terror, she held her breath awaiting the thrust. He tensed, ready to strike her below the sternum and then pull upward in a fatal gash.

Instead, he dropped the Ka-Bar. He staggered two steps back, his mind once again flipped. He was going to kill somebody for money! What the hell was wrong with him?

"Oh, for heaven's sake." The other man wrapped his arms around his wife's waist, and in one motion hurled her over the wall. Her screams echoed down the concrete canyons of downtown Dallas.

Gaping, Sweetwater looked at the man who, until a moment ago, appeared to be a loving husband unable to protect his wife. "What did you do?"

"What I paid you to do!" Then he put a hand to Sweetwater's chest. "Listen to me, you little fuckup. Officially, I did nothing. You threw my dear bride to her death."

"What?"

"You are the assassin, right?" It was more of a statement than a question. "Am I correct? You're with the corporation?"

"Yes." The word was flat in his ears.

"I feel cheated having to both pay you and do your work for you. If I could, I'd file a complaint with LEI, but lucky for you I can't. Somebody might find out that I hired you, and how would that look?"

"It's legal."

Tarbeau's face turned to stone. He held up a small electronic device that Sweetwater recognized as a personal scrambler, used to interfere with cellular and video transmissions at short range.

"Be glad no one knows the truth, you worthless fraud. Our business here is done. May I suggest that you make your own way out?"

"What?"

"Are you dense? You did your job, now go get paid while I mourn my late bride."

Sweetwater watched Tarbeau shuffle off, weeping into his handkerchief, wondering what had just happened. Then he went looking for the emergency stairs.

"Hey, you." Tarbeau had paused in his sobbing.

Sweetwater turned back to the man.

"Don't forget your knife."

Chapter Nine

Downtown Dallas, TX

Erebus stood just inside the parking garage, scanning the rooftop of the Renaissance Building with his binoculars. That side of the building had far less traffic than the other, which made the chances of them being spotted much lower, but he could only watch the back of the building where it was mainly deliveries. Occasionally, the binoculars would give him a glimpse of someone peeking over the side, but it was never his red-headed angel. He considered crashing the party and rescuing her, but who would watch Herbert while he was gone? It's not like he could drag along an 8-year-old and fight off Grace Allen's kidnappers, too. He glanced to where Herbert was sitting, his back against the wall, his nose in a book as usual.

"What are you reading now, buddy?"

The boy held up his book. Erebus recognized the cover: *Lord of the Flies*. He remembered it as required reading when he was in high school. "Wow, where did you get that one? That book might be too scary for you." Erebus couldn't' remember much about the book except for the nightmares. Herbert shrugged and opened it back to his page. "All right, but if you have nightmares, let me know okay?"

The boy nodded.

He heard an odd sound, like something hit one of the tower awnings, followed by a dull *clunk*, like a metal pipe hitting the asphalt. Adrian snapped to attention, scanning up and down Elm Avenue, looking for the source of the strange noise. It took him a moment in the half-illumination of the streetlight, and then he spotted a small glinting thing lying next to a delivery truck parked along the curb.

Was this a message from Grace Allen? Had she sent him a message? "Stay here, Herbert. I'll be right back." He slipped his binoculars into his bag and ran out into the street.

It was a pistol. Adrian stared it, wondering how it got there. Why did someone have a gun on the roof? Did Grace Allen throw it to him?

He picked it up, pinching the barrel between his finger and thumb like a dead rat. He spun it around. The part in the handle had popped out and he could see bullets jammed inside. Erebus thought for a moment; was it called the magazine or the clip?

Another sound caused him to jump, much louder this time and definitely metallic. A thin tray had hit with a *clang* and rolled across the ground until it came to a rest leaning against the curb. Erebus scanned into the darkness for any more gifts from his wife, but the sky was clear.

He looked down at the gun like it was a roadkill skunk. He didn't like guns, and Grace Allen knew that. They had agreed they wouldn't have any guns in the house because of their child. Neither of them could fathom the thought of Herbert finding a gun and hurting himself.

Adrian was about to drop the nasty thing but stopped; if this really was something from Grace Allen, if she really wanted him to have it, well...

He dropped the gun into his shopping bag. Then he scooped up the clip, or magazine, and the pieces from the handle, and stuffed those into the bag, too. He started back to his hiding place before he remembered the silver tray. If the gun was a gift from his wife, then this was too, and she must have meant it as a gift. So, he retrieved it from the curb and slipped it in with the rest of the stuff.

He was halfway back to the parking garage when he heard a scream from above. He turned just in time to see a woman tumbling through the air. Spotlights ringed the tower every ten floors, shining upward, and in the glare from one of them he saw red hair trailing the woman like a flag. When she reached the tenth floor he caught sight of her terrified face as she spun.

He took two steps to run and catch her, but only had time to scream Grace Allen's name before she struck the pavement.

I t was fully dark outside when Erebus realized he was back in his car, speeding away from the dozen police cars surrounding Grace Allen's shattered body. The speedometer on his old maroon Taurus read 95 miles per hour. Tears covered his face like sweat, and he couldn't stop hyperventilating. Had he really just seen his angel die?

He glanced into the rear-view mirror. The back seat was empty. Fresh panic overwhelmed him as he stabbed his thumb on the button to turn on the overhead light. Herbert had curled against one side door and fallen asleep. Erebus took a long look at the boy and turned out the overhead light.

He glanced at the speedometer again and this time he saw the needle was pegged at the car's maximum speed so he eased his foot off the gas until the needle eased back down to 35.

Thoughts ran through his head, each one blurring into the next. How had his wife died? Was she really dead? What was he going to tell Herbert? Where were they going? What was next? Where were the treasures his wife sent him? Did someone push her? Did anyone else get hurt? Was that horrible Tarbeau man behind this? Is that why she sent him the gun? Would he be able to find whoever killed her? Did the gun even work? What was he going to tell Herbert? What would happen to him without his mother?

While Adrian muddled through his thoughts, a car came up behind him and turned on its bright headlights. They were on a simple two-lane road which didn't allow much of an opportunity for the other car to pass. He glanced in his side mirror and was blinded. Erebus took his foot off the gas pedal as he tried to blink the glare out of his eyes. His head rocked forward as his back fender was bumped.

"What the hell?" he yelled. He locked both hands on the steering wheel to hold the car steady, but he was still having trouble seeing because of the other car's lights shining in his eyes. "Dammit, turn down your lights!" Erebus tried to rub one eye with the palm of his hand.

Suddenly, the glaring light was gone. The car engine roared as it came alongside him, moving forward. Erebus stopped rubbing his eyes and stared through the window, trying to get a look at the driver, but dark-tinted windows prevented that. Then the small car drew even with his left fender and signaled before moving back to the lane.

"No way, asshole," he said.

Erebus accelerated to stay even with the other car's back fender. The other car started drifting over into the lane and Erebus turned left to bring his left front fender into the other car's back right fender, like he'd seen police do on TV. The car's back end swung left as Erebus slammed on his brakes. The driver overcorrected, and an instant later the vehicle spun out in front of his slowing Taurus, bouncing over the shoulder. Its front tire caught in a roadside gulley and it flipped side over side into the field along the road.

Erebus stopped, got out, and looked both ways; nobody coming. The other car lay upside down, the roof crushed. Moving toward the hissing wreck, he looked through the back window, checking for signs of life, but the window tint defeated him again.

"Serves you right," he said in a scolding tone, "you shouldn't blind folks with those brights of yours, especially a guy with his kid in the car."

Erebus glanced toward his son in the back seat of his own, and fortunately it appeared Herbert had slept through the whole thing.

He left the other car behind in the ditch as he drove off without looking back, smiling now. Fifteen minutes later, he pulled over at a convenience store and got some road snacks and a bottle of sweet tea. While filling up, he noticed the fender of his car was dinged up and figured someone must have hit his car when it was parked at the garage back in Texas. He admonished himself for not thoroughly checking the car before he left. People were such animals.

It didn't matter though, by morning they'd be back in Memphis. Then he'd start looking for whoever hurt Grace Allen. No matter how long it took, somebody was going to pay.

Memphis, TN

A week later, Sweetwater was home in Tennessee when some ham-fisted jerk pounded on his trailer door so loud that a flock of grackles took off in a cloud of black.

The noise interrupted a bad dream, which was nothing new. He didn't have pleasant dreams anymore, just nightmares, although the perpetual hangover and headaches that went with them might have had been at least partly his fault. He reached for a jar of his uncle's shine, only to find it was empty.

Whoever the someone was, they wouldn't stop hammering at the door.

"I'm here," he yelled, and instantly regretted it.

It was like Dallas all over again. The room swam as he lurched to the door, arms out in case he fell. The floor kept shifting underfoot and wasn't to be trusted when he wasn't still drunk. The trailer was very old and rotten in places.

"Hold on, damn you!" It wasn't a yell, more of a series of loud grunts. Hand over hand, he moved along the couch to the wall, then a side shuffle to the door. It took three tries for him to finally separate the chain latch. With a final grunt he flung the door open to the sound of empty cans and bottles being scattered along the floor.

"Waddayawant?" It all came out as a single slurred word.

"Luther Sweetwater?" A short, portly man stood outside wearing a red polo shirt with a strange logo on it. Sweetwater squinted, trying to read it, but couldn't.

"Do you see anyone else here?"

"Sign here, please." He held out a clipboard with a sheet of paper on it. Sweetwater yanked it out of his hand and leaned back against the door frame to try and read it. The print was even smaller than the logo on the shirt, so he brought the paper right up to his nose to find a signature line.

"Right here, please." A chubby finger pointed to a line at the bottom of the sheet.

"I see it." After scrawling something like his signature, he pushed the clipboard back without looking at the man.

"Thank you, sir." The delivery man ripped the top sheet away from the copies below it and passed the paper to Luther, along with a small, padded envelope. The logo on the envelope was large enough to read: LEI.

"Have a nice day," the delivery man said with a knowing smile.

Sweetwater slammed the door and refastened the chain.

He grabbed a corner of the envelope and ripped it in half. The first thing he saw was a check with the LEI logo in the corner, and a lot of zeroes beside the numbers 2 and 5, as something metallic fell to the floor and rolled a few feet away.

On the ground, face up, was a badge. "Certified LifeEnder, No. 00777."

Chapter Ten

Erebus stared down the barrel of the pistol. The men from the gun range said it was a Sig Sauer P320. One of them asked him how the barrel got scratched, and he made up some nonsense about dropping it, which he could tell they didn't believe. They also told him the magazine—it wasn't a clip he found out, it was a magazine—hadn't been damaged when he "dropped" it, and he bought another one because they'd been so nice and even paid for a lesson on how to fire the gun. Strangely enough they used practice bullets, which Adrian hadn't known existed. They told him the ones in the original magazine were expensive and way too good to practice with.

One other thing he had learned was just how loud it was. Now, shivering in the damp night, he was looking to see if there was a bullet ready to fire, since he'd only shot the pistol that one time. His ears rang for hours after that, but one thing he hadn't expected was for his fear of firearms to vanish the instant he'd squeezed the trigger. There was power in the gun, and he liked the way it felt. Adrian had never had power before.

The Sig still scared him some, but if that was the gun that Grace Allen had sent him to avenge her death, then he had to quit worrying about being afraid. Like a tough guy he'd seen on TV said, it was time to "man up." A willingness to use the gun wasn't the same as actually knowing how it worked, though, despite the men at the gun store going over the basics, and now he wondered if there were still bullets in the weapon, as if they might have somehow escaped and run off.

So, standing in the shadowed alley, he tried to maneuver the barrel so the streetlights might pick up glints off the nose of a bullet. But the barrel was too long to see anything, and he slid the pistol back into his jacket pocket and patted the fabric. Guns scared the hell out of him, kept repeating his brain, even though he wasn't sure it was true anymore.

Blowing on his hands, Erebus rocked back and forth and cursed the cold. Because of the high humidity, winters in Memphis seeped into your bones so you didn't really feel warm again until spring, and tonight was like that.

"Come on, you lowlife, how much can you eat?" he whispered, watching the couple shove gooey slices of Hawaiian pizza into their mouths. The pizzeria's grand front window was fogged up, but not enough that he couldn't see. It pissed him off to watch them talk and laugh between bites. The girl smiled as she flashed her eyes at the man sharing her table, and his shit-eating grin enraged Erebus. *Just you wait asshole, pretty soon you're going to know what it feels like to lose the one you love,* he thought. He didn't like cursing, even in his private thoughts, but sometimes no other words fit the situation.

Erebus didn't think of himself as a killer, though, not really, and sure as hell not like *him.* As for the woman, she had to know who she was out with. She had to know the crimes he'd committed. She was sharing her pizza with a man who destroyed lives and snuffed out happiness for mere money, and it was payback time.

Erebus couldn't stop rubbing his hands together. Gloves would have helped, but he didn't underestimate his target. The man he was going after was a Hitman, and gloves might cause him to fumble the pistol at the critical moment and shoot the wrong person. He slammed his fist into the palm of his other hand; he vowed that wouldn't happen. It couldn't happen. That would ruin everything.

The girl stood up and walked toward the back of the restaurant, probably heading for the restroom. The Hitman waved over their server to pay the bill.

"Finally," Erebus whispered. He turned and walked a few steps down the alley, flexing the cold muscles in his legs, and then returned to his spot to watch the couple leave.

They came out of the pizzeria and turned left, walking south along Main Street.

Erebus slipped around the corner, out of sight, swung his arms to get the blood flowing and sucked down air to work up his courage, even though it seared his lungs with cold. He took out the pistol and pulled back the slide, tilting it to look into the cylinder again. The bullets were still there.

Feeling like he was in a movie, Erebus slipped the gun back into his pocket and followed the couple at a safe distance. He felt his body warming up as he walked.

"Tonight, lover boy. Tonight you're gonna know what it feels like."

Julia draped Bonney's arm around her waist as they walked along Main Street, snuggling into the crook of his left arm. Whenever she'd strolled with a man in the past, he had always held her with his right arm, but this time Bonney politely shifted her to the other side, away from the street.

"Are you cold or just feeling snuggly?" he asked.

The young woman looked up to meet his eyes. "Maybe a little of both? Are you complaining?"

Bonney took his arm back, peeled out of his suit jacket, and draped it over her shoulders.

"How's that?" He slid his arm around her back again, drew her close, and rubbed the outside of her arm. "Better?"

She pulled the jacket collar across her nose and breathed in the scent of his cologne. Last Valentine's Day, she'd gotten him a bottle of Eternity for Men, her favorite, and he'd worn it ever since. "Yes, thank you." She took his hand and pulled his arm almost up to her shoulders…almost. "That just about does it."

They continued walking arm in arm down Main Street, two lovers enjoying each other's company on a cold night near the Mississippi River. They intentionally strolled away from lighted streets that lined the trolley line through the dining area of downtown. Most tourists to Memphis ignored Main Street; they seemed to prefer the bright neon and the noise of Beale Street. Tonight, Bonney led them through the quiet romance of Court Square Park, in the dark, romantic, secluded, and potentially dangerous middle section of the street.

A horse-drawn carriage passed going the other way with a couple huddled under a thick, fluffy blanket, snapping pictures at the classic buildings lining both sides of the street, which necessitated the use of bright flashes. That destroyed the mood he'd been trying to create, but annoyed as he was, Bonney nodded at the people in the carriage as the horse *clop-clopped* the carriage out of sight.

When they arrived at the fountain in the center of the park, he looked down at the girl in his arms. He shrugged his shoulder. "I'm gonna need my arm back."

She stuck out her lip bottom lip in a pout as he withdrew his arm from her grasp.

"One second," he said. He reached into his pocket and held out a handful of change, selected two pennies and offered her one. "Make a wish."

Julia pursed her lips and cocked her head. Ignoring the copper coin she instead picked out two quarters. "Cheapskate," she said, but it was playful. "You first."

Bonney bowed his head for a moment as if praying, and then flipped the coin into the fountain. Dim light reflected off the quarter's silvery surface until it struck with a *plop* and created a circle of ripples.

Julia bowed her head, took a deep breath and held it. With her eyes closed tight, she kissed the slug and threw it toward the fountain. She didn't open her eyes until she heard the splash of water.

"What did you wish for?"

She gave him a playful nudge in the ribs with her elbow. "You're not supposed to ask that...so, what did you wish for?"

"I thought you weren't supposed to ask that."

"No, I said *you* weren't supposed to ask. I didn't say anything about me."

Bonney laughed and hugged her close for a moment, then spun her to face him. "Honey, I need your help to make my wish come true."

"Here? Aren't there cameras?"

This time he laughed even harder.

"Not that. Or not that right now. Later, yes."

She looked up to his face. His little crooked smile seemed to shine in the moonlight.

Billy reached into the collar of his shirt and brought up the edge of a gold chain. It took him a moment to open the clasp behind his neck. When he had the ends apart, he pulled a necklace from under his shirt. Hanging from the chain was a key.

Julia reached up and pulled the key close for a better look. It was a simple door key.

"I don't get it." She squinted at the key as if she was working on a puzzle.

"That is the key to my apartment. I think it's time you move in with me." Bonney wrapped the chain around her neck and fastened the clasp behind her neck. Then he leaned down and kissed her on the side of her neck right where the chain rested. "Tell me you'll move in with me."

"I'd love to," she said in a whisper. "I love you so much, Billy, but…" her voice caught as she twisted the key in her fingertips. Her expression became pleading. "…I can't. I don't want to be your live-in mistress. I want you forever or not at all." She pulled the chain back over her head. "I know that sounds ridiculous in today's world, but it's how I was raised. Sex I can rationalize…well, not really, but I have. But moving in together is different."

He put a hand out to stop her, pulling her arm down until it rested between her breasts. It wasn't a sexual gesture, and his smile became gentle. "I figured that went without saying. At least, I hoped it did." Lowering himself to one knee, Bonney withdrew a small black box from his pants pocket and held it out between them. "That's why I brought this." Inside was a gold ring with a brilliant cut ruby whose facets glowed in the dim lighting. "Julia, I don't want you to move in with me for a while, I want you forever. Marry me?"

She reached out and slid her fingers along the ring just to convince herself it was real and not some dream. "Oh my God…" She reached out to touch his hand. "I love you so much," she said, then pulled him forward and kissed him.

When they finally broke for a moment, both lovers were short of breath. "Do you like the ring?" he asked. "It's not a—"

"It's perfect." She cut him off with another kiss. Then he felt her stop responding, and she leaned backward a little.

"Hello?"

Annoyed at being interrupted, Bonney turned his head to see a middle-aged man in dark slacks and a University of Memphis Tigers jacket standing under a streetlight. Caught off-guard, he reflexively half-spun toward the man and moved his right arm away from Julia's back. Instinct flashed warnings to his brain.

"I'm sorry to intrude," the man said. "Uh, sorry, I couldn't help overhearing…congratulations?" The man held out a piece of paper. "I'm really sorry to disturb y'all, but there's nobody else out here to ask." He stepped closer to the couple, still holding out the paper.

"What is it?"

Bonney stepped between the stranger and his new fiancée, his hand slipping to the grip of the pistol on his belt.

"I'm really sorry. I just need directions. I certainly didn't want to disturb you."

"Where are you trying to get to?"

"I'm supposed to meet my buddy at the Peabody Hotel lobby bar. He said anybody could tell me how to get there, but so far nobody could." The man took another step. "I've got the address, but I got turned around somewhere." He held the paper in his left hand, while his right disappeared out of sight. Bonney noticed, and he knew what was coming, but with cameras everywhere, he still had to let it play out, or he'd be the aggressor. It happened precisely as he knew it would, and he knew how to keep Julia safe during what came next.

First, he took the paper and pretended to skim it, while keeping his focus on the man.

"This is just a Subway receipt."

He saw the man pull a Sig Sauer P320 from his right jacket pocket, but like an amateur not a Shooter, and far too slow against a trained killer like Billy. Before the mystery man could point his gun, Bonney's Kimber Model 1911 .45 caliber was aimed at his forehead. It was a big gun to carry concealed, but experience had taught him to appreciate stopping power.

"Keep the gun pointed down, mister, and you can walk away from this."

"I got the five-dollar footlong," the man said, with more bitterness than those words should contain. It took Bonney a second to follow the non-sequitur. "You know what that sandwich and you both have in common? You are both selling a lie!"

The man changed as he spoke. Where he had first appeared hunched and timid, blending into the background, now he seemed to grow inches in height as his back straightened. He rolled his shoulders and rocked his head to the side with an audible *crack*. Although flabby and pale, Bonney now recognized the insanity latent behind those bulging eyes. Crazy people were damned dangerous.

"I've got no idea what you think is going on, mister, but I'm just out spending the evening with my girl here. If you were after my wallet, I'm guessing you've figured out that you can't have it, so ease up on that pistol before somebody gets hurt."

Julia's shaky voice came from behind him. "Billy, what's going on?"

"Don't move, honey, I've got this. The man needs some fast cash and picked the wrong people to target, that's all." Even as spoke, the gun never wavered from the man's head. As for his words, Billy knew better. The man had found *exactly* the target he was after.

"William Bonney," the mystery man said through clenched teeth. Unlike Bonney, his hand shook so bad that if he fired, the bullet was as likely to hit a passing trolley as either of them. "I know who you are, and I know what you do."

"Listen, buddy, I have no idea what you're talking about, but I'm sure we can talk this out."

The man laughed again, but with a bitter edge. "So, you just happened to have a gun ready?"

"This is downtown Memphis after dark, so yeah, I had a gun ready."

"You can't fool me; you kill people for money. Your code name is Billy the Kid. You are an assassin for LifeEnders. You have executed six contracts for the company. You are a Memphis…"

Bonney's heart froze over when he heard the name LifeEnders. Julia didn't know, and he didn't want her to know, but he also didn't want to kill the man. That would attract too much of the wrong kind of attention, and if he did Julia couldn't avoid finding out his profession. Instead of blowing out the back of the man's skull, he shifted to his right foot and without warning launched himself across the eight-foot distance separating them.

He wrapped his hands around the gunman's arm, but adrenaline gave the guy added strength, and he jerked his arm free. The pistol went off and the deafening report echoed through the park, scattering the few other parkgoers off into the darkness. The man with the gun brought his hands up and pressed them against his ears, more evidence that he didn't know guns. Bonney could see him screaming, but his own ears were ringing, and he couldn't make out the sounds. His world froze.

The gunman backed away, out of Bonney's reach, and brought the gun back up even as Bonney did the same with the Kimber, but his arm wavered. He focused on the barrel, trying to bring it back in line with the man's forehead, but he was unsteady. He overcompensated and the barrel swung wide. Bonney's brain seemed sluggish as he struggled to aim...then his arm started to drop from the pistol's weight, until his arm hung limp, the pistol pointing at the ground.

Bonney saw horror twisting the gunman's face. Had the man really shot him? How could that happen? The other man paced in circles, waving the gun in his hand, and the truth flashed through Bonney's mind: he was dying.

"You did that. It's not my fault!"

Billy felt his body sway as a wave of nausea drove him to his knees. He reached for his forehead, but blood dripped from his hand, and instead he stared at it, wanting to vomit.

I'm not dying, he told himself, *I'm engaged now, I can't die. It's just some blood, and I can handle blood.*

Then the gunman's screaming finally penetrated through the fog as his brain started to shut down.

"You did that! Not me, you! You, you, you! You did that." The man backed away two more steps, fear choking his voice. "You did that. You grabbed my hand, and the gun went off. It's your fault." The man in the Memphis Tigers jacket turned and ran.

Bonney couldn't seem to catch his breath. He swayed on his knees, and his head seemed to weigh twenty pounds as he tried to follow the path of the man who'd just shot him. Like a flash of lightning, Julia's face made him turn and nearly fall over as he scanned the suddenly empty park.

He found her.

She lay crumpled on the ground, and even in the darkness he could see the bloody hole in her chest. The still functioning part of his brain guessed that the bullet that hit him must have been a through and through. He struggled to crawl to his fiancée, each breath a burning torture, as blood poured from his chest to the cobblestoned sidewalk that crisscrossed the park. Julia had fallen on her side, facing him. He could see no rise or fall in the shirt that was plastered to her chest by her blood. Once he was close enough, he could see no life in the eyes that reflected the streetlights surrounding the park.

Still gripping his unfired pistol, he fell on his side as the strength left his body.

Why hadn't he fired? Why hadn't he honored the threat?

Conscious thought faded. He felt no pain, only a pervasive sense of guilt.

I could have saved her…but I failed.

Then he couldn't remember why he was laying on the ground, or why Julia looked so strange. Thoughts became formless, and then images flashed by like a movie running at 50 times normal speed. He felt the air leave his lungs, and his last thought was panic because he desperately wanted to draw another breath but couldn't. The lights of the park grew progressively dimmer, and a few seconds later everything turned dark.

E rebus pushed his overweight body into a pounding run toward an alley west of the park. He had to move before the cops got there, except Erebus wasn't the sort of man who moved more than necessary in his everyday life.

He had screwed this one up, but good. Erebus knew he could never tell Herbert about what he had done tonight. Revenge for his mother's death or not, he couldn't risk seeing the disappointment in his son's eyes. Herbert would never understand his father murdering someone regardless of the circumstance, or even if it was an accident. True, he'd gone there to kill Bonney for killing Grace, but hadn't he changed his mind and resolved just to scare the man? Yes, yes, he had, and then Bonney grabbed his hand.

"It's not my fault." Erebus repeated the refrain with every step.

He'd been sloppy, though, that was his fault. He'd gotten too close to a licensed killer for God's sake! What was he thinking? And the girl...no, he wouldn't feel sorry for the girl, she got what she deserved. If you date a killer who lives by the sword, then you'd better be ready to die by the sword. That was in the Bible.

Wheezing from the effort of jogging to the alley, Erebus climbed a fire escape to the adjacent building's roof. It was only a three-story building, but he barely made it to the top before collapsing on the roof, where the chill breeze dried the sweat streaming down his face, and gasps of foggy breath trailed away into the night.

Once he was able to catch his breath, he managed to crawl to the ledge and peek over the side. From his vantage point, he could see the entire park and all of the surrounding streets. The park's canopy of tree limbs would have blocked his sight lines during summer, but winter stripped the branches of their leaves, giving him a clear view.

Within four minutes, the cops showed up and swarmed the scene, setting up Klieg lights while dozens of flashlights crisscrossed the area. A dozen patrol cars disgorged double that number of officers, who set up a perimeter using crime scene tape and then spread out to look for clues. Erebus knew it was only a matter of time before they found him.

A tall detective in plain clothes—because what else could he be—pulled out Bonney's wallet, called to a slender woman and showed it to her. Within 20 seconds, it was over. The female detective spoke into a hand-held radio, and all of the uniformed cops packed up and left. The detectives waited for the coroner and her crew to arrive, but, after a brief conversation, they loaded the bodies into a meat wagon and left, followed within minutes by the detectives.

Court Square Park was once again a dark, quiet place on a cold winter's night. The only signs of recent violence were dark smudges on the footpath and a single police cruiser parked at the curb. It reminded Erebus of a scene from some movie, where a dozen men invaded a guy's house, but he killed them all and then a cleanup crew wiped up all the blood, wrapped the dead bodies in plastic, and hauled them off.

Teeth chattering, Erebus wanted to go home and crawl under his warm blankets and tell Herbert all about what he'd done. His son might or might not understand the circumstances, and Erebus dreaded telling him, so when he saw an excuse to stay, he stayed. They both needed to know why the cop in the car was sticking around, but whatever the reason was, he hoped they found out soon. It was damned cold up there.

Chapter Eleven

Downtown Memphis, TN

The brown waters of the Mississippi River swept passed on his left as Luther Sweetwater drove north along Riverside Drive. He'd really been looking forward to today's lunch meeting with some high school buddies at the old Pyramid, now converted to a sporting goods store-slash-hotel-slash-restaurant. He felt great. The morning was lovely, bright, and crisp, but not too cold even that close to the river. What more could a man ask for out of life?

That's when his phone started playing "Killing in the Name," a song by Rage Against the Machine that was his ring tone for LifeEnders. He'd once laughed at the irony, but now he dreaded hearing the first four power chords start their haunting melody. He reached over and touched the button to accept the call, making a mental note to change the ringtone.

"This is Luther—" he started, but the voice of Ms. Witherbot cut him short.

"Yes, Mr. Sweetwater, I have a job for you." The heavy British accent felt like a hammer pounding nails into his ears with every word.

"Yeah, I'm not available at the moment. I have a lot going on. You need to find another Shooter."

"You have passed on every job I've sent your way. I'm starting to think you may not appreciate the opportunity you have with the company. Would you like us to cancel your credentials?"

"It's not that, I…" He let the sentence hang, unsure just what he wanted to say because she was right.

"Unfortunately, neither of us has a choice this time. You are the man we have on site, so the job is yours whether you want it or not. I refer you to Article 4, Section A17 of your contract."

"Wait, this is a Company Priority?" Company Priorities paid double; that got his attention.

"Yes, and before you make some weak excuse, it's a simple retrieval. We'll not be requiring you to execute a contract."

"Oh." Now that was more like it. Double pay and he didn't have to kill anybody? Sign him up! But Sweetwater didn't want to give in that easily. Even though the company had credited him with his first kill, he hadn't really done it. He'd only taken credit to get paid and still wasn't sure he wanted his LEI badge and License to Kill. "So, what do you need?" The sound of defeat filled his voice, just to let her think he wasn't happy.

"One of our assets was murdered last night, and in your city as it happens. We need you to retrieve his credentials, nothing more. As you know, collectors and forgers would pay a lot to get their hands on an authentic LifeEnders badge and License, so we simply can't allow them to get into the general population. Retrieving those credentials is our utmost concern. I'm sure you can appreciate the situation we are in. Do you have any questions?"

"There's another Shooter in Memphis?"

"There was. Were you not listening?"

"Shouldn't I know details like that?"

"Why?"

"Are there any more?"

"Again, Mister Sweetwater, what difference would it make?"

She had a point. So Sweetwater sighed, trying to sound reluctant while secretly planning how to spend the money. "No, I understand. Where do I need to go?"

"Turn right at your next light."

He leaned forward to get a better look through the windshield, searching the sky for a helicopter or something else hovering above. "Are you tracking me? How do you know where I am?"

"Of course, we are tracking you. You are a licensed Shooter, so we follow you wherever you go. Now concentrate. Turn right onto Beale Street."

"I don't think I like that."

"Oh, stop being childish, Mr. Sweetwater, and follow directions."

A tracker under the car; it had to be, he thought. He'd get rid of it the first chance he got, but, for the moment, Sweetwater followed the voice on his phone like it was a British GPS. She directed him to a side road that took him to Court Square Park, where a single police-man was leaning against the wrought-iron fence surrounding the large, two-tiered fountain. Sweetwater pulled to the edge of the street and killed the engine.

"The man you need to talk with is Sergeant Green. He has the credentials."

"How many Shooters do you have in Memphis?" Luther asked.

"That's on a need-to-know basis. Focus, Mister Sweetwater, and notify me once you have taken possession of the items."

"**P**lease tell me this is going to be fun."

Sweetwater jumped sideways into the closed driver-side door and twisted to face the grotesque figure sitting in the truck's passenger seat. The dark gray skin of what might once have been a woman was stretched tight over angles of skin torn in places to show the white bones beneath. Damage to her face left it flat, like she'd died under the blows of a baseball bat. Tangled red hair fell past shrunken shoulders, while an expensive cocktail dress hung loose on her frame. Eyes still filled her sockets, but no light filled them.

He tried to speak but nothing came out.

"Being dead is so fucking boring."

"Go away; you can't be real," he said, fumbling for the door latch, like a trapped animal clawing at a cage.

"I was real," she said. "Until you and my husband decided to kill me."

"Huh?"

"C'mon, Luther, I know you're not stupid, Eamon told me all about you."

"Eamon?"

"Me!" said Mister Cooper, who materialized in the seat between them. His face and body had deteriorated badly since the last time Sweetwater had seen him. "That was my first name, Eamon Cooper. I filled Grace Allen in on your bio and back story. I didn't think you'd mind."

"You look like a meat loaf."

Cooper shook his finger. "Be original, Luther, you stole that line from a movie."

"Son of a bitch!"

Sweetwater worked the door handle until it opened.

He slid from the truck and paused for a moment to let his heartrate subside. Grace Allen Tarbeau waved from inside the truck, then she and Cooper disappeared. Sweetwater walked to the uniformed officer, not nearly as upset as he wanted the British Bitch to think he was with his assignment, but damned freaked out by the hallucinations. Still, with any luck, he could still make lunch with his friends. He could really use some sane company right about then.

"Sergeant Green?"

"You Sweetwater?"

"Yeah."

The policeman threw him a wallet and turned to go. It fell short and landed on the walking path. Inside was a familiar LifeEnders badge. Opposite the badge was a man's LifeEnders ID and a deceptively plain, government-issued card with another photo, his License to Kill. Sweetwater bent to pick it up and, still crouching, read the name, William Bonney, like the legendary Billy the Kid. During his time in sniper school he'd heard the name. He looked up just in time to see the officer climb into his cruiser. He called out and ran toward the cop.

"Hey, wait up."

The window of the cruiser lowered with a hum and stopped, leaving only a three-inch gap. "What now?" the man asked in a voice that said he was already late ending his shift.

Sweetwater looked back toward the park. "Is that it? You already finished the investigation?"

"What investigation? You see those red stains on the sidewalk. That's where they died. Live by the sword, die by the fucking sword. Frankly, the only reason I'd give a shit who killed that lowlife is to shake their hand."

"Was he alone?"

"You mean whoever did us all a favor and shot your asshole butt-buddy? How should I know?"

Sweetwater felt the anger flush his neck but kept his voice calm. Not wanting to kill people wasn't the same as thinking about doing it.

"I meant, was the victim by himself?"

"There was a girl, she took a bullet, too. Now get the fuck away from my car." The hum returned as the window slid back up. The cop extended his middle finger and drove away.

Sweetwater walked back to the fountain. Just as the officer said, there were two dark red blotches on the sidewalk.

The stain nearer the fountain was more or less circular and about three feet across. Somebody had bled out completely there, without moving, probably dead before they fell. Along one side was a smeared blood trail that might have been left from small wheels, as if someone had pushed a shopping cart into the sticky puddle and then reversed it back out. But why would there have been a shopping cart? He wasn't used to inspecting crimes scenes, so the question rolled around for half a second until his brain snapped out the answer: a medical gurney, of course. They'd contaminated the scene without giving a shit.

The other blood pattern was long and narrow, more of a smear than a pool, and not nearly as bright as the other stain. Someone had crawled as they were bleeding out. Visualizing the scene, he found the spot where the first victim was standing when they were shot.

Sweetwater put himself in line with the center of the two blood stains and slowly walked away from them. His eyes scanned the ground and spotted a gleam. He bent down on one knee and brushed aside the grass to expose a brass shell casing.

"Son of a bitch," he whispered. "They really don't give a fuck who killed them. They didn't even fucking try."

He knew cops hated Shooters, but seeing how little they cared about Bonney's murder made him realize they *really* hated Shooters, as in "not caring if somebody killed them" hatred. And what about the girl, whoever she'd been? Couldn't they at least do an investigation for her sake?

Sweetwater stood up and patted his pockets to identify the different lumps: keys, pistol, pocketknife, wallet, creds…wait a minute, that wasn't where he kept his credentials, those were Bonney's. It felt weird having two Licenses to Kill on his person when he wasn't sure he even wanted one.

Disregarding that, he took out the knife, flipped open the blade, and dropped it point down so the point sank into the earth just to the left of the bullet casing. He jogged back to his truck, grabbed a wadded up McDonald's bag off the front passenger's floorboard, carefully opened it, and dumped the crumpled cheeseburger wrappers in one of the park's garbage cans. He snatched up an unused napkin and hustled back to his knife.

Careful to use the napkin, he picked up the brass, making sure to only touch the ends. Then he gently tucked the napkin around it so as not to smudge any fingerprints, and laid it into the McDonald's bag. Finally, he got back in his truck and called Witherbot.

"Two-Bit, do you confirm that you have the credentials?" The British accent came out loud and strong and condescending…But there was something else there too, something he couldn't quite finger. Sweetwater thought that if she wasn't such an absolute bitch all of the time, she might even be hot.

"If you track them as well as you say you do, then you already know I have them."

"Yes. Now please take them to the airport. Your contact will meet you outside the terminal. You are to pick her up and follow her instructions."

"What are you talking about? What contact? You said this was a simple pickup job."

"We have decided to send in a resource to investigate the incident. We have to prevent this from happening in the future."

Something wasn't right; he could feel it. She knew more than she was letting on. He wasn't sure why he cared but decided to keep her talking and see what happened.

"The cops here aren't going to do an investigation. They didn't even process the scene. I really don't think they did more than haul away the bodies."

"Bodies? As in plural?"

"Yeah, you must already know the Shooter's name was William Bonney—"

"Of course, we do."

"But there was a second victim."

"How can you be so certain?"

"Two blood patterns, that's how, separated by about five feet. Plus, the cop waiting for me said he was with a girl. One of them bled out where they fell, the other dragged themselves toward the first one before the reaper got them. I'm guessing Bonney was the crawler."

"Why do you say that?"

He shrugged, even though she couldn't see him. "Just a guess."

"Do you have an ID for the second victim? What did the police say?"

"He essentially told me to fuck off."

"Damn. Could the second body have been the killer?"

"How should I know? But I found a bullet casing."

"Where?"

"A few feet from the blood stains. It was just lying in the grass. I didn't think to check for a second one, but I'll go back and check when we hang up."

"Do that, please." Luther heard clicking on a keyboard for a minute or so, and then some low whispering before she finally came back. "All right, Mr. Sweetwater, we need you at the airport in an hour. Until then, we ask that you investigate the scene some more before it rains, or someone else disturbs it. As you have discovered, due to the nature of our business, our relationships with the local police are sometimes strained. Be sure to secure the credentials and report to the airport in an hour. Do you understand?"

"Sure. So, does this kind of thing happen a lot?"

"Thank you, Two-Bit. We'll be in touch."

"Before you go—"

"Yes?"

"Is it in your job description that you have to be such a bitch?"

The line went silent, but it didn't drop. Sweetwater thought he heard an intake of breath, then a *click*, and finally a dial tone. Somehow, someway, he knew he was probably going to pay for that.

Sweetwater figured that walking the murder scene again would at least kill some time until he had to leave for the airport, and laughed at the pun.

Bent over and careful where he placed his steps, he examined the nearby grass, checked the garbage cans, and even eyeballed the fountain. Other than a couple of panhandlers and some guy on a bench eating an early lunch, nothing presented itself. As he worked the site, nobody hassled him, nor did he see any police, detectives, or crime scene investigators. Nobody cared what he was doing, or even paid much attention. When he ran out of time, one thing was clear, LifeEnders wasn't getting any help solving the murders.

Back in his truck, his phone played the guitar riff that signaled a call from LifeEnders as he turned on the engine. He pressed the button to accept the call without looking.

"Lemme guess, you couldn't live without hearing my voice?"

"Are you attempting humor, Two-Bit?"

"You know I don't like that name, right?"

"And I do not appreciate being called a bitch."

"I should have known better than to answer. Look, I'm just leaving, because I've been examining the scene. I'll be at the airport in about twenty minutes."

"Acknowledged, Two-Bit—"

"I really don't like that name."

She ignored him. "However, the flight has been delayed. You will most likely beat it there."

"Say it ain't so. I'm heartbroken."

"Ours is not a humorous business, Mr. Sweetwater."

"No shit? You mean we're not killing people because it's fun?"

"Perhaps you're not cut out for this line of work after all."

"Or perhaps I'm just tired of taking shit from my handler for reasons I can't understand. If you don't like me, just say so."

He figured that would really bring out the woman's nastiness, but strangely it seemed to have the opposite effect.

"Thank you for your dedication to our cause."

"We have a cause? I thought we did this for the money."

"Yes, that's true enough, and everyone must earn a living, but, yes, ours is a cause. Perhaps one day there will be time to discuss it with you."

He listened for sarcasm but didn't hear any. She actually meant it.

"Now you've got my interest. I'll buy the first round."

"Please don't be late. Your contact will be on the flight from Dallas arriving at Concourse B."

"I'll be there," he said, her civility throwing him off stride.

He dropped the truck into gear and wove his way toward the highway. Just like every other day in Memphis, it was packed.

Chapter Twelve

Downtown Memphis, TN

Sunlight shining through his eyelids woke Erebus, and a glance at his watch told him it was past 11 am. Stiff, hungry, thirsty, and cold as hell, it took him a few seconds to orient himself and remember why he was on a rooftop overlooking Memphis' Court Square Park. The warmth of the morning sun had made him drowsy and, after the long night's vigil watching the cop in the cruiser, he'd fallen asleep. Now he jumped up to see if he was still there. He was.

And, for once, his timing was perfect, because a man in a nondescript brown pickup truck parked in front of the cop car. A short, stocky guy in his twenties met the police officer by the fountain. After a brief exchange, the policeman tossed something to the newcomer and took off, but the guy followed the cop, and they raised their voices enough that Erebus heard a snippet of what they said: "the only reason I'd give a shit who killed that lowlife is to shake their hand." The MPD car took off faster than seemed safe to Erebus.

The new man walked back to the park, inspecting not just where the shooting occurred, but the entire park and even the fountain. Once it looked like he picked something up from the ground, but Erebus couldn't tell what it was. Then it struck him…the bullet casing, or whatever they called it. When the man at the gun store showed him how to shoot the pistol, Erebus distinctly remembered the empty bullet flying out of the gun and landing among thousands of others on the floor of the firing range. That must have happened again, and now the guy down there had it.

Could it somehow be used to find him? Forgetting his fatigue and hunger, Erebus climbed down the fire escape, earning an odd look from a homeless woman pushing a baby carriage full of aluminum cans through the alley, and then lumbered to his car down the block.

Two parking tickets were stuck under his windshield wiper, fining him for an expired meter, but after you've killed somebody, two 20-dollar fines didn't mean much. Now he just had to make sure not to lose the guy in the pickup. His work was just getting started, and he couldn't risk being stopped, not now. Herbert wouldn't like it if they got caught before finishing what they'd started. He wouldn't like that at all.

"Fuck!"

A repeated *dub-dub-dub* came from under the truck, and it lurched to the right when the front passenger-side tire blew out. Sweetwater grabbed the steering wheel with both hands, knuckles whitening as the truck vibrated and tried to roll. He clenched his teeth to keep them from hitting each other. Stuck in the middle lane, with oblivious idiots passing on both sides, he hit his turn signal and took his foot off the gas. A blue SUV on his tail honked, and the driver flipped him the finger.

"Come on, fuck wads!"

Angry faces cursed him as he tried to get over, but nobody let him in. One guy actually laughed and paced him, acting as a blocker to keep him from getting over.

"Are you serious, motherfucker?"

The guy rolled down his window and yelled something. The blue SUV roared past on his left, honking. Cars in his lane swerved to pass him on both sides, but they couldn't get around on the right, either. He was boxed in.

The tire had begun to shred now, and soon enough he'd be riding the rim. If he stopped in the middle lane, it was only a matter of time before somebody either slammed him in the rear or ran over him as he darted to safety off the roadway. There was only one way out that he could see, even though he hated the idea. Risking it, he let go with one hand and dug out his car gun from the center console, an LCR Ruger .38 Special. Small enough to fit in the limited space available, the Houge grips cut down on recoil. It was a simple and reliable gun, and when he lowered the passenger-side window and pointed it at the jackass who was blocking him on the right, the man floored it and took off.

"Think twice next time, fuckhead," he yelled at the guy's back bumper.

But still more cars switched to the right lane, and as the tire wore away, he began to lose control. Another car came up behind him, and when it couldn't change lanes to get around, the driver pounded on his horn. Sweetwater felt like popping off a few rounds out the back window just to shut him up.

Finally, he saw a break in traffic and chanced jerking his truck to the right. That forced drivers to swerve into the breakdown lane to get around him, but at this point he didn't care if they rolled over.

Horns kept blasting as he crept down an off-ramp. He was finally able to pull into a graveled area leading into a merge lane and brought his truck to a merciful stop.

It took him half an hour to change the tire. As he worked, he was forced to keep one eye on the traffic as it flew past, since most drivers considered the shoulder an additional lane. He rolled the old tire along the edge of the pavement, trying to figure out what happened. The tires weren't that old. They should have had a couple years before they needed replacing, and a blow out? He didn't even know tires could still do that.

They were badly damaged, and it was hard to be certain…but was that a hole on the sidewall? With all of the dust and noise he couldn't get a very good look, but it sure looked like a round hole. Could a rock have done that? It didn't seem possible. Or maybe…maybe it was a bullet hole? Before he could do any further review, a police cruiser pulled up behind him, lights flashing. He tossed the tire into the bed of his truck.

The officer rolled down the passenger-side window a crack and motioned Luther to come on over.

"Looks like I missed all the fun," the officer said over the roar of the traffic. "Need help?"

Sweetwater drew a sweaty arm across his face, which did no good since his shirt was drenched from the effort of changing the tire.

"Naw, I'm good, but thanks. Maybe next time."

"Well, go ahead, and I'll help you get back on to the road. When you're ready, we'll pull out together."

"Right, thanks again. I appreciate the help."

"Sure thing, and be careful out there, it's a dangerous world."

The cop grinned, and all Sweetwater could think to do was stand there and blink. Was there some underlying message in the cop's words, or was he just being paranoid? There was no time to worry about it, because, a few seconds later, the cruiser slipped past his truck and the cop waved. Then, true to his word, the cruiser turned into the first lane of traffic, and just as Moses parted the seas, the traffic did the same. Sweetwater pulled out behind the cop and continued west. But the back of his neck felt like somebody had shot with him a tazer.

What the hell was going on?

Maybe the tire blew out, and maybe it didn't. And maybe the asshole on his right had been nothing more than that, an asshole, and maybe the cop just happened to show up after he'd been working for half an hour. Nothing but maybe, maybe, maybe…or maybe none of that had happened by accident.

It only took another seven minutes to get to the airport, and Sweetwater pulled into the cell phone lot. A large screen displayed the list of arrivals and departures, showing the flight from Dallas had landed ten minutes earlier.

Sweetwater killed the engine and settled down to wait, but seconds later his phone rang from an unknown number.

"This is Luther Sweetwater."

"Mr. Sweetwater, my name is Teri Warden. I believe you are my contact."

The voice on the phone sounded like that of a young girl. What started out as a great day hanging with friends had turned decidedly weird.

"I'm just outside the airport, where should I pick you up?"

"I'm at the B Terminal exit. Flash your lights when you arrive so I know it's you."

"On my way."

As he approached the terminal, he scanned the people to try and match the voice to a face. Most were in groups, and the singles seemed to all be middle-aged businesspeople. He pulled his truck up to the curb and flashed his lights twice. He was about to do it a third time when the passenger door opened and what appeared to be a teenage girl tossed a small suitcase on the floorboard and climbed up into the seat.

"All right, let's go."

"You're my contact?"

"Either that or I'm setting you up to take the fall as a sex trafficker."

"That's not funny."

The girl's smile would have fit perfectly on a world-weary hooker. "Sure it is."

"I didn't see you when I pulled up."

"Sorry, habit of the job. When you're my size you work from the shadows. Down to business. Do you have the other Shooter's creds?"

"Sure, right here."

She had to be older than she looked. Hell, at first glance, she barely looked old enough to fly without an adult. Then, at second glance, he changed that opinion. The truth was that parts of her body looked very grownup. A cop motioned him to pull out of the terminal, so he did. Fumbling in his pocket, he handed over Bonney's wallet and ID case.

She pulled the badge and license out of the wallet. Then she connected a short cable to a covered port on the back of the badge, while she attached the other end of the cable to her phone. Luther glanced over while he drove, to try and catch what magic the girl was doing.

"So, what's that?"

"I'm pulling the audio and data files from the recorder."

"What audio files? Has that badge been recording what I say?"

"Relax hot shot, we only use it in dire circumstances, but, yeah, your badge records about six hours of sound. The mikes are sensitive enough to pull in normal conversation from about five yards out, and that includes the fact that it's usually closed up in a pocket. It also has a GPS tracker along with some other data points. It's all keyword activated, using a proprietary algorithm we developed, so it starts recording whenever it detects potentially hostile words or tones. Welcome to *1984*."

"It's the 21st Century."

She glanced to see if he was kidding, then shook her head and went back to fiddling with the badge.

"I heard you were like that," she said.

"Like what?"

"Like that."

"Like that *what?*" he said, not understanding her word game.

Warden grinned.

"Witherbot was right, this is gonna be fun."

Chapter Thirteen

Southwest Memphis, TN

Traffic was still heavy as they left the airport and got back onto I-240, heading east to avoid any traffic jams through downtown. Sweetwater tried to keep the conversation going but the girl—or woman, or whatever she was, the female named Teri Warden—all she did was focus on her phone. He kept taking quick glances at her, but the glare off the screen kept him from seeing anything.

Without warning, something slammed into the truck, forcing it right toward the guardrail. Red stars raced across his vision as his head bounced off the driver's side window. It was only by instinct that he turned to the left, counteracting his skid so they hit the rail parallel instead of head on.

"Hang on!"

A glimpse of his passenger in his peripheral vision showed that she'd already pulled out a pistol. That settled that; she was not a kid.

Sparks flew as he bumped against the guardrail at 75 miles an hour. Another hit rocked the truck, throwing both of them hard against their seat belts. Sweetwater fought to keep the wheel straight as black smoke reeking of burning oil boiled from the engine into the cab. He tried to wipe away the tears with the back of his hand as a kaleidoscopic corona of flashing colors gave him tunnel vision. The part of his mind trained as a Marine sniper warned him that if the airbags deployed they were screwed. Then the wheel started to turn in his hands.

Glass fragments from the driver's side window sprayed his neck and cheek as a bullet zipped past his jaw and shattered the passenger window. Bits of trash and garbage flew out the newly made hole.

"Shit!"

But whoever had them targeted hadn't reckoned with the mysterious woman. While he fought to keep the dying car from rolling, Warden fired past him, out what was left of his window and into a red sedan. Enough speed had bled off by now to give him back some control over the truck until, with a lurch, the front end dove into a ditch while the rear end went up and over.

The seatbelt dug into his shoulder and chest, and the airbags exploded as the truck flipped over. The roof smashed into the ground, and all the windows shattered, blowing safety glass in every direction. Something hard hit him in the back of the head, and his arms went limp. He was vaguely aware of dangling upside down before he blacked out.

"Hey, you!" said a disembodied voice, followed by a tap on the shoulder that sent him swaying back and forth in his seat belt. "We've gotta get you out of there."

A pounding inside his skull felt like somebody hammering nails into the bone. He concentrated and opened his left eye a slit, but the right one seemed stuck. Regardless, it made his disorientation worse. He looked up to see the ground through the web of the shattered front windshield, and muddy grooves gouged into soft soil leading back toward, what he assumed was, the interstate. Puddled on the ceiling was a pool of black blood, growing larger, drip by drip.

He tried to move his arms and twist free, but his body responded as if tangled in a net. Pulling himself upright using the steering wheel didn't work either, and left him panting from the exertion.

"Hey, you, can you hear me? Cops and EMTs are tied up some-place else; it'll be a while before they get here."

Sweetwater! That was his name. For a second he couldn't think of it and panicked, but remembering it centered him again. Was that somebody yelling through the window? Probably. He tried to answer, but his mouth felt as though somebody had stuffed it full of cotton, so it came out like "murr." He ran his tongue over his lips and finally managed to say, "Help me down," in a thick slur.

"Sure, yeah, I can do that."

Sweetwater saw a hand reaching toward him…holding a knife? The face of the man holding it wouldn't come into focus, and sud-denly it was gone. For a second or two he saw nothing, until new faces appeared at the window, men and women.

"Hang on dude, the ambulance is on the way!"

"And the po-po."

"Mrrr…" he said.

Beside him, the girl-woman from LEI sat cross-legged on the ceiling of his truck holding a bloody rag to her nose.

"You look great," she said. "The whole swollen eye thing really fits you."

She fished something from out of her jeans pocket and laid it in his right palm, curling the fingers around the handle of a pocketknife. "Cut yourself down before this thing blows up. There's gas everywhere."

"Mrr…"

The helpful people outside his window told him to stay put, that he might have a neck injury or internal bleeding, but Sweetwater's brain was starting to clear, as was his sense of smell. Like his passenger said, he could smell gasoline now and also caught a whiff of cigarette smoke.

Some dumbass was smoking outside the car!

Adrenaline flooded his body, and he jammed the blade under the belt and pulled. The belt slipped away, and he fell upside down out of the seat. He tucked his head as he fell, but when he hit the roof of the cab, he bounced his head again. Stars popped and spun in his vision.

Sweetwater feared nothing more than fire, so death in a flaming truck kept the adrenaline flowing. The pain vanished as he scrambled to climb out, and arms reached in to help him. His passenger's voice screamed at someone to put out their fucking cigarette.

Sweetwater felt someone grab at his shoulders and start pulling. He dug his heels and pushed as best he could. He felt bits of glass poking into his back as he slipped through the driver-side window. More hands grabbed his arms and joined in the pull. The smell of gas permeated the air as he turned his head and felt dampness on the grass.

"Go! Go! Go!" someone screamed. Then there was a *whoosh!* followed by a wave of heat. The hands holding Sweetwater let go and left him flat on the grass. Rolling onto his hands and knees, he put his head down and scrambled away from the burning grass. Heat grew on his legs and someone threw a blanket over him and rolled him through the grass. Finally, the hands returned to his shoulders and started dragging him again.

Once away from the fire, his saviors helped him to a sitting position, where he could only stare as flames engulfed his truck. Thankfully, it didn't explode, and the oily black smoke boiling into the sky meant that it wouldn't, a solid sign that the remaining fuel had seeped from the tank before the fire started.

"I only had a quarter tank left," Sweetwater said to no one in particular. While he was surrounded by people, none seemed to be listening. "It costs fifty bucks to fill that bad boy."

"Money isn't everything."

Still stunned from the wreck, the appearance of the badly decayed form of Eamon Cooper didn't even startle Sweetwater. Whatever Cooper was, ghost or delusion, he sat cross-legged in the grass beside the bloodied Shooter.

"You again," Sweetwater said. "So, this is an ongoing thing?"

"Apparently so, but I guarantee it's not my idea."

"Or mine," said a female voice from his other side, one he now recognized.

"You know I didn't kill you, right?" he said to her.

"Excuses, excuses. You were there to do it."

"But I couldn't do it. I want you to know that."

"Who gives a shit? Dead is dead, but I'm not the one who matters now."

"Huh?"

Grace Allen Tarbeau turned away, a tendon in her shoulder popping through a jagged spot torn in the dried-out flesh.

"I tried to talk her into warning you about what's going on," Cooper said when Grace Allen didn't say anything more. "But she refused, and it's her call."

Sweetwater nodded and blinked, as if this all made perfect sense.

"Okay."

"I dislike you for accepting a contract to kill me, Luther," Grace Allen said, "but I do appreciate you changing your mind. So, I'll tell you one thing: it's Herbert you've really got to worry about. Not Adrian, Herbert. You would do well to remember that."

"Who is Herbert?"

"I don't appreciate you that much."

"But…what about you, Cooper, you could tell me."

"Sorry, cowboy, I don't like you that much, either. You took a contract to kill me, too, even if you didn't go through with it. That stings a bit."

And they both vanished. Morbid onlookers now lined the bank of the ditch to watch Sweetwater's life go up in smoke, yet none of them reacted to Cooper and Grace Allen dematerializing like Samantha in *Bewitched*.

Huh.

So, either they were actually ghosts that only he could see, or smashing his head into the window had caused a concussion. Flames caught Sweetwater's attention again. Tilting his head, he grabbed a handful of grass and threw it at the burning vehicle. He'd loved that truck; it was brand new. Well, almost new, it was only eight years old, and that was the newest he had ever owned.

T he police were the first to arrive.

By the time they got there, Sweetwater had snapped back into the present and forgotten Eamon Cooper and Mrs. Tarbeau. The cops secured the site of the accident and tried to get the traffic moving again. After they verified Sweetwater's and Warden's identities, they pretty much ignored them. One cop made sure to give Sweetwater a ticket for failure to control his vehicle, reckless driving, and littering, but refrained from arresting him.

At least the EMTs checked them for concussions and the like. They treated Sweetwater for some minor first-degree burns on his legs by cutting away the bottom of his jeans and rubbing some anti-biotic cream on the red areas. Ten more seconds and the fire would have burned him badly, but the quick action of the bystanders prevented it from being much worse. They both refused trips to the hospital, and Warden assured them that she could handle the situation. Why they talked to her and not him, Sweetwater didn't know and didn't ask.

When the fire department finally arrived, there wasn't much left to do except hose down the burned-out hulk and any remaining hotspots. The cop who issued Sweetwater his tickets came back and passed him a small card.

"Call this number tomorrow, and they'll tell you how you can go about getting your truck back."

The cop dropped the paper short of Sweetwater's fingers, and it fluttered away in the breeze, but he snatched it out of midair with lightning fingers. There were reasons he'd made it through Scout Sniper School, with reflexes and hand-eye coordination topping the list. The nasty smile disappeared from the cop's face, and he stalked away.

"Memphis PD really loves you, don't they?" Warden said.

Sweetwater's face had been cleaned and bandaged, but his right eye was swollen nearly shut. He opened his mouth to ask her name, then remembered that she'd already told him, and that it was Teri something…Warden, Teri Warden. With his mouth hanging halfway open, he asked her age instead.

"That's not a very polite thing to ask a lady."

"Are you a lady?" he said, although a split lower lip turned it into a mumble.

She shrugged. "I like to think not."

"So? Your age?"

"How old do you think I am?"

"You're either twelve, or sixty-seven."

Warden liked that, and let him see her perfectly straight, china-white teeth in a playful smile.

"Something like that."

A line of blood had dried under her left nostril, and she licked at it with the tip of her tongue. Sweetwater stared as she dragged out the moment, both of them sitting in the grass as cars roared by on the interstate above and emergency personnel packed up. Finally, as the fog cleared, things began to come back to him.

"We're hunting a killer," he declared, as if it was a great discovery.

She barked a single laugh. "And aren't we doing a helluva good job of it. I don't suppose you got a look at the dickhead who did this?"

"No, the first I knew was when my head hit the window. Everything else was a blur."

"This makes two attacks on LifeEnders assets in one day, or a day and a night."

"Three," he said. "I think somebody shot out my tire on the way to pick you up."

Warden instantly came alert. Gone was any lingering young girl persona, replaced by someone who was used to being obeyed. "Why didn't you tell me that sooner? Shit, my brain's a little rattled. We need to find a place to hole up."

"Ya think?" With returning sense came returning sarcasm.

"Hey, this is your burg, not mine. You've gotta have a safe house, right?"

"My apartment."

"Oh great, yeah, nobody would ever look for us there."

"Well, I do have a place outside town. I only got the apartment because I had the money from my first…job."

"How far out?"

"A ways."

"That'll have to work. Let me get us a ride."

"You know people in Memphis?"

"I know people everywhere."

Chapter Fourteen

When construction began on LEI's underground, nuclear-blast-proof Command and Control Center Project, CCCP—a tongue-in-cheek swipe by the ultra-capitalists of LEI at the Cyrillic abbreviation for the unlamented Union of Soviet Socialist Republics—it was universally dubbed the Kremlin. The contractor joked that he was digging so deep they might bring in a gusher. Once finished, the reality of what he had built far out-stripped even the most awe-inspiring oil well.

The Kremlin was a 300-foot square room with rows of round pillars supporting a roof ten feet high. Hundreds of people, and a few highly secret, experimental cyborgs and androids, manned hundreds of workstations, clacking away at hundreds of keyboards while staring at hundreds of monitors that lit their faces with an eerie blue glow. In many ways, it resembled every secret bunker ever depicted in movies, books, or video games, with two exceptions, the massive ultra-high definition video panels that took up all of one football-field-length wall, while the other three walls each showed live feeds from the beach near Galveston, Waimea Falls on Oahu, and a treetop view of the Guatemalan rain forest.

The other difference was the circular glass tube which extended from floor to ceiling in the room's center. Thirty feet across, it contained three desks and chairs, and banks of electronics to serve the three women who worked inside. Nor did their demeanor leave any doubt about who ran the whole operation: Cynthia Witherbot, Assistant Director of Domestic Operations, whose desk sat in the exact center of the entire Kremlin.

Among the multiple video displays arrayed around her desk, Witherbot concentrated on one that had been sent from a junior programmer under the mistaken belief it was anonymous, but she didn't care about that. What concerned her was the security video which purported to show one of the senior programmers doing something nefarious.

Mickey Hallum had been with LEI from the very start, but as Witherbot knew all too well, longtime employees sometimes grew resentful at not earning what they felt was fair when a corporation succeeded like LEI had, and that led them to use their position of trust to make up for what they felt they were owed. She hadn't caught Hallum yet, but that didn't mean anything; he was just that good.

"Madam Assistant Director," a voice said in her earbud, "I have a call from Teri Warden on your private line."

"Put her through, Lakesha." Warden's voice came through immediately, with a lot of background noise that sounded like traffic. "Teri, I'm here. What's going on?"

"Someone ran us off the road, Assistant Director. I'm okay and Sweetwater's got a nasty bump, but I don't think he's hurt bad. We need a car."

"Was this done intentionally?"

"Oh yeah. I'd bet it was whoever killed Bonney. I got off a shot but didn't hit him."

"Collateral damage?"

"No, none."

"Very well, then, we obviously have a Hunter on our hands. I'm issuing a special contract under 'Name Unknown,' please let me know if you identify him so we can change that. Do whatever it takes to kill this person. Hunters cannot be allowed to get away with their crimes."

A light blinked on her computer to indicate she had a call from Mister Keel.

"Yes, ma'am."

"Teri," Witherbot said, pausing to control her voice. "You do not have permission to be killed or seriously injured performing this mission, is that clear? Sweetwater is the Shooter, not you. Let him take all the risks; it's what he's trained for. I'll thank you not to force me to arrange final services for you."

"You just don't want me haunting you, Mom."

Witherbot's mouth turned into a firm, and highly displeased, line.

"I've told you—"

"I have another call. 'Bye."

Seventeen minutes later—and five minutes after the carcass of his truck was hauled off—a yellow Prius pulled off the interstate to where they'd been told to wait. A man got out and climbed into a nondescript, tan, four-door Ford that had also pulled onto the shoulder.

Sweetwater had one foot in the car when he stopped and turned to look back at the burned grassy area where his truck had come to rest.

"Hold on, I'll be right back."

"Where are you going?"

He explained about the McDonald's sack and the brass casing, and Warden joined him to look for it. Chances of it surviving the fire intact seemed slim, and now they didn't even have the wreckage to look through, but miracles did happen. Maybe it fell out or something.

Limping back to the site took all of the energy he had left. The short afternoon had begun to wane, so Warden went ahead and started rummaging around the area. Dropping to his hands and knees, he sifted through bits and pieces of what had once been his most prized possession and didn't realize she'd wandered back until she returned minutes later holding a white bag over her head.

"Let's get out of here."

Once back in the Prius, Sweetwater didn't want to drive but she gave him no choice. "I don't know how," she said, with a mischievous smile that made her look thirteen.

Hell, he thought. *Maybe she is.* Then he looked at the adult part of her. *No way. Twenty at least.*

"I'm staying off the interstate this time," he said.

She nudged the McDonald's bag. "You really eat that stuff?"

"I don't just eat it; I *like* eating it."

"Gross."

"Yum."

"I've been thinking about your place outside town, and that won't work either. We need to get a hotel room."

The whiteness of his teeth when he smiled contrasted against the grime and bruises on his face.

"Works for me."

It took her a second to understand the innuendo.

"I'd rather eat fast food."

"I can be fast," he said, instantly regretting it, but she answered before he could add anything.

"Most men can. I'm not sure that's a reason to brag, though."

An hour later they were in a hotel room. Warden settled in like she had done this a thousand times before. Sweetwater got his own room, which he only agreed to when she paid for it using a LifeEnders credit card.

She set up her laptop on the room's desk and connected it to the TV using a cable she'd brought. Then she used another port on the computer to connect her cell phone.

Lying face up on one of the double beds, arm over his eyes, Sweetwater wanted nothing more than to fall asleep. His face hurt, his neck hurt, and his legs hurt. Hell, it was easier to list the parts of his body that didn't hurt than the ones that did. The mattress was firm, and the pillowcase smelled clean when he took in a deep breath and slowly exhaled. He felt the stress slipping off him, like water off a duck's back.

"So, what's the plan?" he asked without uncovering his eyes.

"Staying alive, to begin with."

"I'll co-sign that. Then what?"

"Why is it my job to figure that out?" Warden said.

"Because even though you look like a freshman in high school, I've got a feeling you've done this before."

"Was that a compliment or an insult?"

Moving his arm, he peeked at her for a second. She had stopped messing with the computer stuff to turn his way.

"Let's go with compliment."

"Stop gushing and keep it professional."

"But you—"

"Sshhh! I've got this ready, so let's hear what the badge recorded."

Sweetwater propped himself up on one elbow, as if watching the screen would somehow provide extra information. Warden pulled up a program and loaded the audio file she'd pulled from the badge. With a few clicks of her mouse she queued up the final five minutes of the recording.

"Here we go."

As the audio played, the program added a separate line for each new voice. A deep baritone male voice came from the speakers as a red wavy line jumped on the display.

"Wow, he asked her to move into his place," Sweetwater said.

"What?"

"Aren't you listening? This is some romantic stuff right here."

The program recognized a new speaker and the red line turned to blue. Warden thumbed a key to turn up the sound.

"Good for her, she turned him down."

The blue line switched back to red, identifying Bonney as the speaker again.

"Wait a minute!" She paused and held a finger up as if daring him to speak as she listened.

Sweetwater raised both hands as if surrendering to a gunman. They heard Bonney propose to his girlfriend—he called her "Julia." Luther turned to stare at the wall.

"What a jerk," Warden said as she slapped the space bar to pause the playback.

"Are we listening to the same thing? He just proposed. Isn't that generally a good thing?"

"He only proposed after she said she wasn't going to move in with him. Do you think he would have done it if she'd agreed to move in? Hell no, he wouldn't. He's just working some kind of angle. I know this kind of guy, not personally, but his type, and he'll keep pressing until she gives in. There will never be a wedding date. I'll bet you a hundred dollars he didn't even give her a diamond."

"You do remember they're dead, right?"

"So?"

"Tell you what, let's go to the coroner's and ask what kind of ring she had on."

"Yeah, we can do that, assuming the cops didn't lift it."

"C'mon, don't think like that. Just because they don't like us doesn't make 'em thieves."

"Damn, you really are as naïve as Witherbot said you were."

"She said that?"

Warden only glared at him, and since he didn't know why, Sweetwater wished he'd kept his mouth shut. Obviously, there was more to her relationship with Witherbot than he knew about, or than he wanted to know about. Knowing other people's business could be dangerous in Hit World, even for a Shooter.

"Let's hope your faith is rewarded. We're hunting a dirtbag killer, and I don't like it when somebody tries to kill me."

Sweetwater wondered if Teri realized the irony of her words. She pressed the touchpad on the computer, and the playback continued. The program switched between a red line when Bonney spoke and the blue one when the girlfriend did. When a new voice entered the audio, its line was green.

"Hello? I'm sorry to intrude…uh, congratulations?"

"That must our guy," she said, as the man's voice came from the speakers. She paused the playback.

"What's threatening about that? It sounds pretty innocent to me."

"The algorithm doesn't pay much attention to words when deciding whether to activate or not, it measures voice stress, tone, volume, and a lot of other factors that we wouldn't pay much attention to. This is definitely our guy."

"If you say so."

She restarted the recording.

Sweetwater jumped at the gunshot, which showed up as a thick white line on the monitor. The recording stopped shortly after.

"That's it. The badge stops thirty seconds after it detects the owner's heart stopped."

"That kind of tech cost somebody a wad in R&D."

Warden shrugged but said nothing.

"Well, that gives us something to go on, anyway," he said.

"All right, pretty boy, tell me what it gives us?"

"The killer knew our guy. He called him by name. I don't think he knew the girlfriend because he never spoke to her. Neither of the victims knew the killer. But I'm not telling you anything you didn't already know."

"How do you figure?"

"Because that's obvious stuff, and if you couldn't see it, you wouldn't be here. If I've learned anything about LEI, it's that they don't leave much to chance, especially that barrel of fun Ms. Witherbot."

"I admire her, but there's been at least one time she was wrong."

"Yeah, about what?"

"You. You come across as a good old boy, but you're not quite as useless as she made you out to be."

"Gee, thanks. Now who's slinging compliments?"

"I can run Bonney's old cases; see if anybody made threats."

"That's a place to start."

"Not much of a start. If we're looking for friends, relatives, or lovers of complete contracts that list could number in the thousands."

"LEI's databases are heavily protected, right?"

"Of course."

"So, for our killer to know Bonney's identity means they either interacted personally or he accessed the database. That would either make him a world-class hacker or able to afford one."

Warden pressed her lips together for an instant, but it was enough.

"What aren't you telling me?" Sweetwater said. He sat up on the bed, and any playfulness was gone from his voice. "Out with it."

"There's nothing else, dude; you're imagining things."

He stood up, balling his fists. She reached into her purse, but he grabbed her wrist and pulled her hand out. It clutched a .32 revolver, the same one she'd used that afternoon, which he easily twisted out of her grasp. Despite her tiny size, once he saw the gun Sweetwater had assumed she was also some sort of martial arts expert and expected a fight. He didn't get one.

"Are you serious? Are you really here to kill me?" He didn't bother hiding his anger.

"Don't be ridiculous."

"You'd only…what, shoot me in the foot? You know, just to teach me a lesson?"

"There are things you don't know and don't want to know."

"Is that supposed to make me feel better?"

"Look, trust me when I—"

"Trust?" Sweetwater felt his face flush, and it was all he could do not to hit her. "You were about to pull a gun on me!"

"Ssshhh! We're in a hotel room. These walls are thin. Listen, I just wanted to get your attention; I wasn't going to shoot you. Whatever you think you need to know, trust me when I tell you that you don't! You don't *need* to, and you sure as hell don't *want* to!"

"Now you keep it down. These walls are thin, remember?"

"Damn but you really are an asshole. I think you nailed it a minute ago."

He squinted, which only involved his left eye because of the swollen right. The truth was, Sweetwater didn't have a clue what was going on, and as he watched her face, he couldn't help marveling how perfectly her full lips matched the heart-shaped face.

"How so?" he said, coming back to reality. "What did I nail?"

A fantasy of her answering "nail me" flashed through his brain, but only lasted until she spoke.

"Go back and listen to the killer's voice. He's not a hacker, or another hitman, or anything of the sort. He's a normal guy. If he was a pro do you think he'd have left Bonney alive to crawl to his girlfriend? No, he'd have put two more in the back of his head to make sure he was dead."

"So, what's next?"

"I can run his audio file through the databases, but it's going to take time and the odds aren't good."

"What about the McDonald's bag?"

"Yeah, that's right. If we can lift a print, that might be all we need. Good job, Two-Bit, we might make a detective out of you yet."

"I hate that name."

Chapter Fifteen

Southeast Memphis, TN

Warden leaned over to dive into her backpack, but Sweetwater stopped her.

"Any more guns in there?"

"Yeah, four Uzis and a Carl Gustaf."

He frowned, wondering how she knew about the M3 Multi-role Anti-armor Anti-personnel Weapon System, better known as the Carl Gustaf recoilless rifle. Maybe Warden just knew the name and was being a smartass, but somehow Sweetwater doubted that. LEI never did anything by accident, and from what he knew of the company, it was risk averse in the extreme, so if the petite—petite what, girl? Woman? Which was she? Woman, he decided, because no matter what she looked like, LEI would never trust someone underage with so much responsibility. So, if the petite Teri Warden was an expert with a Swedish-made military recoilless rifle, he wouldn't be shocked.

Muttering, she opened panels and zippers and rummaged through her clothing. Sweetwater kept her pistol in his hand but pointed at the ground. Trust had to start somewhere.

"Damn, where is it?" She opened another panel, giving access to even more hidden pockets. "Ah!" She pulled out some clear plastic panels and cords, along with a round metal appliance. She cleared a space and laid everything on the desk. "I've always wanted to try this."

She assembled the thin sheets of plastic into a six-inch cube, leaving one side open. Once she finished it, she put it beside a small hot plate-type device.

"Now to play mad scientist."

From the pile of parts, she selected a small tray and tipped in a bit of powder from a glass ampule. She added a little tap water and swirled it around until the powder dissolved, laid the bullet casing inside using a pen, and gently placed the tray inside the cube. "This needs to cook for a while."

"How long's a while?"

"Long enough to eat something. Isn't Memphis supposed to have some good barbecue?"

"Best in the world."

"I've heard that before. Any good places around here?"

"On every corner."

"Do you have to kill your own pig?"

"Huh?"

She pointed at the pistol.

"Oh."

She held out her hand.

Hesitating, he finally laid it in her palm, and she slipped it into a holster under her pant leg.

"Lead on."

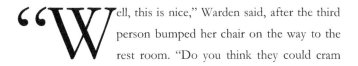

"Well, this is nice," Warden said, after the third person bumped her chair on the way to the rest room. "Do you think they could cram any more tables in here? We're not packed in tight enough yet."

"It's part of the flavor. It's cozy."

"It's stupid."

"You'll understand once the food gets here."

"If somebody grabs my ass there will be trouble."

"I'll remember that," he said, looking down then glancing up.

One side of her mouth curled upward in half a smile. "See that you do."

The waitress, a heavy-set black lady who'd worked there for decades, kept flicking her gaze at the swelling around his right eye. At his suggestion, they both ordered combo plates with banana pudding and sweet tea. The waitress nodded and returned to the kitchen, twisting her bulk through the tightly packed tables like a ballerina.

"I haven't had banana pudding since I was a little girl."

"You've never had banana pudding; you only think you have."

"Don't make a promise you can't keep."

"You'll see." They paused as the waitress returned with their drinks. "How long you been with LEI?"

"Mmm." She licked her lips. "Damn, that's good. You can't get sweet tea just anywhere. I'm technically not with LifeEnders. I'm with the SP."

"The Secret Police? I thought they were just a bunch of hackers living in their mother's basements."

"Well, my mother lives with me, and I have a basement office. Of course, I own the house."

"Is that true?"

She smiled. "Maybe."

"Does she know about your work?"

"She does. She works for LEI."

"No shit? She's not a Shooter, is she?"

Warden smiled behind a glass of iced tea. "Not lately."

"So, does the SP have classes where they teach their operatives to fire at moving vehicles while in a car rolling end over end, or were you just improvising?"

Her brown eyes crinkled ever so slightly, the only indication he might have overstepped his bounds.

"What about you? Isn't it said that all Shooters are inbred alcoholic rednecks that live in rusty old trailers?"

"Changing the subject, huh? Okay, I'll play along. All that's true, but I've been dry for a month now. The rest is mostly right on the nose."

"Good. Now that we've got the awkward small talk out of the way, do you have any new ideas about who's trying to kill us? I do have to say you did a good job finding that brass. Not to downplay your skill, but even a crack-head cop should have found it."

He shook his head. "If they gave a shit they would have, but we're on our own. I'm surprised they didn't just leave the bodies where they found 'em."

"That's becoming more and more common, Luther. The boys in blue resent us, and I guess I can understand why."

"You said 'us.'"

"You know what I mean."

"I think I do, yeah. 'Us' has a pretty definite meaning."

Warden ignored him for at least the fourth time that day, and talked right over him, but Sweetwater knew she was hiding something.

"It was still a good find."

"They don't like us even a little bit," he said, still on the earlier point, "as you witnessed today. Even though the homicide rate has dropped to almost nothing."

"It's down, yeah, but think about all those police jobs they don't need anymore, all of those union police jobs lost by union police members who no longer pay union police dues."

"Why is everything always about money?" he asked, leaning back as the waitress put their food on the table. But as she reached across the table, his eyes widened. Why *was* everything always about money? The thought nagged at him and wouldn't let go.

Warden missed his change of expression, though, and was already digging into the mound of barbecue on her plate.

What was he missing?

"So, you'd work for free?" she asked around a mouthful of baked beans. "I'll tell Witherbot if you want. Damn, this is really good."

"Point taken." Using his incisors, Sweetwater stripped the meat off a rib bone in one pull, although he didn't really taste it.

"What's the matter?" she said, licking her fingers before wiping them on a napkin. "Food not good, 'cause mine's great."

"Food's fine. Just trying to work something out in my mind."

"About our killer?"

"I don't know. It's like I can almost touch it."

"I hate when that happens. Think about something else, and it'll come to you. Tell me how you joined LEI; it's not for just anybody."

"I'm betting you've read my file."

She nodded, picking up her first rib. "I have, but they don't tell the whole story. This doesn't have any sauce on it."

"I ordered dry ribs, they're better than wet. There's nothing really to add. I signed on to kick al Qaeda's ass, the Marines trained me to be a sniper, then our pussy of a president wouldn't let us engage the enemy. I watched the Enders do the job I'd trained to do and vowed to join 'em. Except by the time I could the mission had changed."

"Did any of your fellow Marines resent the Enders?

"Of course they did. Me, too, for a while. Mercenaries getting paid big bucks to do the jobs we'd all dedicated our lives to doing? As Marines, we did what we were told, but that doesn't mean we liked it. A lot of it was jealousy."

"And now you know why the cops hate you. All of those murders for hire, angry spouses, business murders, all of the premediated killings they used to get paid to solve, are now legal as long as you're hired to do it. Courts don't like you, either, and for the same reason. LEI is bad for the whole criminal justice business. Plus, they're still getting jack for a salary while you're getting paid big money to kill people, which they're supposedly paid to prevent. To them you're just a bunch of criminals with a license to kill."

"We are licensed under the law."

"C'mon, Luther, don't play naïve again. Even if I'm not a Shooter, we're on the same team, so let's at least be honest between us. We're mercenaries."

"That's just politics."

"Of course it's politics. Everything is politics."

"You know a lot about a lot for a teenage girl."

Warden smiled as if there was a joke to which only she knew the punchline. She slurped up the last of the tea and put her glass to the side for a refill.

"That's cute. My job ages you faster than anything else I know. I spend all day, every day, digging out all the dirty little secrets everyone tries to hide. I find the really bad guys that our field operatives, like you, can't find. Once I track them down, we send that data to LEI, and they turn it over to you. Sometimes I have to wade through shit and depravity you can't imagine."

"In case you didn't know it before," he said, picking up a spoon as the waitress put a bowl of banana pudding on the table, complete with vanilla wafer and homemade whipped cream on top, "humanity sucks."

Chapter Sixteen

"Y ou're not gonna admit I was right, are you?" Sweetwater asked, standing on the restaurant's steps while trying to remember where he'd parked.

"I said it was good."

"It wasn't good; it was fantastic."

"We have different definitions of that word."

"I wouldn't put that half sandwich that's in your purse too near me then."

"You're still hungry? After all that?"

"Maybe."

After what had started as a fun day with some friends and wound up with him being almost run off the road, then flipped, and torched, Sweetwater was surprised how sanguine he felt with his stomach full of smoked pork. Then he tensed and straightened, eyes roaming the darkened parking lot.

"Is that pistol in your purse?"

"I won't shoot you over the sandwich, if that's what you're worried about."

Instead of responding, Sweetwater stared where he thought he'd seen a shadow near their car. Only a single streetlight lit the gravel lot, and they'd had to park the Prius at the far end. He'd started to develop a sense of awareness for possible danger, like he could feel it, and after two attempts on his life in one day, a third seemed more than plausible. If it was nothing more than paranoia, he could live with that.

"Let me have it," he said, holding out his hand. She picked up on his tone and followed his gaze. "Stand behind me."

She hesitated only a second then did what he said.

"What did you see?"

"I don't know. Maybe nothing, but for a second I thought there was a shadow over by our car."

"It's pretty dark out there."

"Stay here," he said.

"I'm coming with—"

"No, you're not. If there's somebody out there hunting us, I don't want to have to worry about you, too. Unless there's something you're not telling me, get back inside."

Now she hesitated longer, and Sweetwater got the impression there *was* something she wasn't telling him, but then she ducked through the restaurant's front door. Calling the police would only get him laughed at or cussed out so, holding the gun at high ready, he moved into the lot.

He quickly got away from the lights around the restaurant porch and crouched to present a smaller target. A couple walking toward the front door spotted him and veered away. At the first chance, he ducked behind a car and began working his way toward the Prius.

A scuffling of gravel alerted him to someone running away. Still not willing to present a target, he didn't pursue until he heard a car door slam, followed by an engine starting. Then he sprang forward, but he only caught a glimpse of a car as it sped off. When it passed under a distant streetlight, he thought it had four doors and was red.

Warden pulled on a latex glove and retrieved the bullet from the hot box. Holding it under a desk lamp, she turned it over, and they both saw a dark smudge on the side.

"Is that it?" Sweetwater said.

"That's it. Let's run it through the system and see if we can get a name."

"We have a system? I figured we'd take it to the cops."

"Right, because that's worked so well up to now. You think you're the first Shooter they've treated like flaming dog shit?"

"So what kind of system do we have?"

"Same as theirs; we're tied into CODIS and all the federal databases, but with restrictions the police don't have. Which is why we're gonna use theirs."

"You're gonna hack it?"

"Thank God I didn't have to draw you a picture."

"What the fuck is your problem? At dinner you acted like a human being, and I was beginning to like you. Now? Not so much."

"Holy crap, dude, grow a pair. At dinner we were off the clock. Now I'm working."

She took a picture of the print with her phone and sent it to her computer. Then she brought up a program with warnings about it being the property of LifeEnders, Inc., and promising dire consequences for any unauthorized use. Given that LEI was in the business of killing people, he assumed hackers might think twice about trying to break in. Warden pulled a small device out of her backpack, plugged it into a port on the computer, pressed it against her right eye and waited. There was a *beep* and the computer flashed positive

identification and unlocked the program. After uploading the fingerprint, she pushed back in the swivel chair.

"Now we wait." But seconds later there was a *ping*, and an alert
flashed on her screen. Suspicion crept into her voice. "That was too
fast."

A new window opened on the screen. It was Luther Sweetwater's
booking photos. Of course, all LEI assets were required to be logged
in the FBI databases.

"Big yuck and very funny," he said. "Now run it for real."

Warden clicked a popup-window.

A headache had been growing all afternoon and finally became
bad enough to distract him, so Sweetwater fell onto one of the double beds and bounced, his headed landing on a lopsided pillow. The
cool fabric felt good against his injured face.

"That *is* the real print, dumbass. I can't believe you didn't wear
gloves. Don't you watch cop shows? Everybody knows you're supposed to wear gloves if you're handling evidence at a crime scene. I
just wasted hours to develop your fingerprints." Warden turned back
to the computer and started clicking.

"Listen, I don't know how it got there, but I didn't leave my fingerprint on that casing, I only touched the ends. I never touched the
side." He sat up on an elbow, his expression serious but not glaring.
"You're really not fucking with me, are you?"

"Not even on your birthday."

"Do you have a fingerprint kit in your bag?"

"Why?"

"Humor me."

"Sure, I've got one."

"Run my prints."

"I don't work for you, you know? If you want me to do something try asking like you don't own me."

"Please."

She spun in her chair and met his eyes. "You really didn't touch the brass?"

"Positive. I used the napkin in the bag to pick it up. If you'd said it had ketchup on it, that would have been possible, but I only touched the ends."

She stood up and started crawling through her bag of endless pockets again. "Come here, we'll double check just to be sure."

Sweetwater rolled off the bed and let her press his fingers, one at a time, on an ink pad and then along the edge of a sheet of paper. Satisfied with the clarity of the prints, she opened the camera on her phone.

"This is the print from the bullet casing." She enlarged the image using her fingers, which blurred the lines on the photograph, but not enough that it wasn't useable. Then she moved the image along the prints until she found the match.

"It's your right thumb. No doubt about it. Here, look for yourself."

Sweetwater shifted his gaze back and forth five times, until he was satisfied there was no mistake; the prints matched.

"How can that be? I swear to God that I have never seen that brass before I found it at the park." He searched her face, as if somehow he'd find the answer there. "How did he get my print?"

"Coffee," Warden said and turned back to her computer.

"He got my prints from coffee?"

"No, dummy, the coffee is for me." She cracked her knuckles and rotated her head from side to side until it popped. "This is what

I do, it's why I get the big bucks. I sift through all the white noise to catch the bad guy, and you bring me whatever I need to do that. Right now, I need coffee."

"You get progressively less cute by the minute. There's a machine at the end of the hall, I'll be right back."

"Stop!" She turned to Sweetwater. "None of that machine shit; I need real coffee. Go find a Starbucks or something. Mocha with soy milk, biggest one they've got." She waved with the back of her hand, dismissing him.

"I thought you wanted coffee." He left with a laugh.

"Don't mess with my java, Marine. Not all of us have lost all sense of taste. Now go; I have work to do."

Chapter Seventeen

Midtown Memphis, TN

Erebus' hands shook as he tried to push the key into the door. He fumbled it, dropped it, bent to pick it up, and snapped his head from side to side as he knelt in front of the door.

Did they know? They had to by now, didn't they?

But no blue lights lit up the street. There weren't even any suspicious cars. Sure, he'd taken his license plate off, but how many 10-year-old maroon Ford Tauruses could there be in Memphis? Not that many.

With no cops in sight, he retrieved the key and steadied his hand before jamming it hard into the lock. He got the door unlocked and went inside, easing the door closed behind him. After locking all four deadbolts, he listened for a moment for signs of an intruder. Satisfied that he was alone, Erebus walked into his bedroom and stuffed the gun into the bottom of his sock drawer. He closed the drawer and took a deep breath, thinking about the last twenty-four hours. He'd gone toe to toe with a real-life killer and lived to tell the tale.

Giggling, he realized he and Pat Garrett had something in common: they'd both killed Billy the Kid. Then he almost got the other guy, too, and would have if not for the Good Samaritan who'd dragged him free of his death trap of a truck. Looking into the dresser mirror he inspected the folds of his jawline, thinking he wasn't such a bad-looking guy.

147

He spotted Herbert stretched out on the bed. The boy had his nose in another book.

"Hey, buddy." His son never looked up. "I'm sorry I was gone so long. I wanted to be back a long time ago, but I had a big job to do." Herbert turned a page, but still didn't look up. A strand of dark hair fell forward but the boy left it hanging. "I hope you didn't stay up too late reading." Herbert held up his thumb. "Well, that's good, how about I make us some hot-dogs? Sound good?" Herbert lifted his thumb again. "All right, I'll call you when they're ready."

He hurried down the hall, past the extra bedroom to the kitchen. He moved mechanically to prepare the food as his mind replayed everything. Now that it was over, Erebus felt kind of proud. He'd never been an action kind of guy, yet here he was, avenging the woman he loved in a way he never thought himself capable of doing.

They ate their dinner in silence. Even then Herbert didn't look up from a heavy hardcover book bound in brown cloth. Erebus bent his head to see the book's title, nodding in approval. *Endothermic Reactions and Their Role in Demonology* by Silar van Troost. It was gratifying to see him reading something worthwhile, instead of junk like history or social studies.

The boy finished his dinner quickly and retreated back to his own room, never looking up from the book.

Erebus pulled a cold Busch from the refrigerator and sucked down a third of the can, not bothering to wipe foam off his upper lip. With his son off reading, he pulled a short stack of photos from the top of the fridge and sat down at the kitchen table.

The top picture was a glossy 5x7-inch photo of a black man in a white polo shirt. Written in blue marker across the top was "Asshole," and under that "William Bonney." Using the marker, he scrawled the word "Dead" in front of "Asshole." Despite the man being dead, Erebus curled his lips before setting the picture on the table and shuffling through the others.

"There you are," he said, selecting the photo of the man he'd been chasing all day. He read the name out loud, slowly sounding out each syllable, "Luther Sweetwater." He was a young guy with dark hair, cut short but tousled on top, over a square face. There was a seriousness in his eyes that pissed Erebus off, like the man thought he was better than everybody else.

He flipped the photo over. The back was filled with a short bullet type resume. Just the usual: age, height, weight, and such. The only detail of note was that Sweetwater had trained as a USMC sniper and was recruited out of Memphis. His LEI call sign was listed as Two-Bit. In the box indicating contracts executed, there was a number one followed by an asterisk, but with no indication of what the asterisk meant.

Erebus licked his teeth and sucked down the foam at the bottom of the beer can. Scratching his nose, he ignored the oil it left on his fingers after having gone nearly two days without a shower. For several long minutes he sat, the harsh light of the cheap overhead lamp hanging from the ceiling, memorizing every detail of Luther Sweetwater's photo.

"You're just a rookie asshole, but that don't matter, an asshole is an asshole no matter how long you've been doing it. And you ain't gonna be doing it much longer, Mister Luther Sweetwater from Semple, Tennessee. It's like the Lord says, if you live by the sword, you die by the sword. That might not mean anything to you, but, in this house, the word of God is the law by which we live."

He laid the picture back on the table and smoothed it flat.

"I almost got you today, and you don't even know who I am, do you? No, you ain't got a clue." He paused, as if waiting for the image to respond. "But that's how you guys play it, right? That's how you like it done? You shoot somebody in the back and then run off with your thirty pieces of silver. Well, don't you worry none about who I am, you'll know soon enough. Your day is coming, Luther Sweetwater. Enjoy life while you can."

Erebus got up and fetched a second beer before heading to his little den, where he fell into a ratty old recliner sitting across the room from an old-style television. A crack in the naugahyde pinched his butt, but he was used to that. He picked up the TV remote and tugged on a lever handle to recline the chair.

Maybe the ten o'clock news would have video of the burning pickup truck, or some cute blonde would be breathlessly standing at the site where William Bonney and his whore girlfriend bled out. Erebus would like to watch either story or, better yet, both. But it wasn't to be. Against the usual drive-bys and government corruption, the shooting death of some guy and his girlfriend in a dark downtown park barely raised an eyebrow, and a fiery wreck on the interstate was so common that passing motorists barely slowed down anymore. If he was going to attract attention to his crusade, Erebus knew he'd have to ramp things up.

Sweetwater opened the door to the coffee shop and the rich aroma of roasted beans rushed out to embrace him like a lover's hug. From behind the counter came the hiss of steam, followed by the grumble of milk bubbling into froth. He stopped to savor the moment, like when he ground coffee beans near the entrance at Costco and people commented about how good the caffeine permeating the air smelled. A glass display case of picked-over tarts, cakes, pies, and donuts nevertheless had two slices of carrot cake left, and while they looked a little dried out, and dinner still sat heavy on his stomach, it was going to be a long night. He decided to get those, too.

It took him over half an hour to move from ordering a couple of five-dollar coffees that had a longer pedigree than most thoroughbreds, to actually leaving the shop. After making small talk with a cute older woman in line ahead of him, his mind turned to figuring out who their attacker could be and, more importantly, their motivation. However, when he finally left, careful not to spill even a drop of the precious brown fluid, he was no closer to an answer than when he arrived.

None of it made any sense.

The cardboard bands around the coffee cups only protected his hands for so long before the heat started to hurt. Quickening his pace toward the lobby elevators, Sweetwater punched the button for the 3rd floor with his elbow as he tried to hold the cups without using his palms.

"She senses we're here, you know," said a male voice from behind him to the right.

Startled, Sweetwater bobbled both cups, but their tops held and none of the coffee splashed out. A moldy odor suddenly permeated the elevator's vinyl-paneled cage.

"Goddamn it, Cooper, stop doing that!"

"He's not doing anything," answered Grace Allen Tarbeau from his left. "It's you who keeps summoning us, not the other way around, and I'm getting kind of sick of it."

"I thought you were dead."

"I am, as you should know all too well."

"I didn't kill you."

"Maybe not, but you gave my lowlife husband cover and then collected the check. The rest is just semantics."

"If you're dead, then why does it bother you to keep haunting me? I mean, is there really a lot to do? It smells to me like all you're doing is rotting."

"Now that was rude, Luther," Cooper said. "It's not like Grace Allen asked to die."

Sweetwater could see his fuzzy reflection in the steel elevator doors, but nobody else. Whatever Cooper and Tarbeau were, they didn't have reflections.

"I'm sorry?"

"You aren't now," she said. "Now you're just being a jerk. But you will be."

"I don't know what that means," Sweetwater said.

Cooper answered, "We're not at liberty to explain."

"Explain what?"

"If I can't explain, then I can't explain why I can't explain."

The elevator dinged upon reaching the 3rd floor. "Please, just go away."

"We will," Cooper said. "But remember, if you need us then you have to reach out to us, not the other way around."

Stepping out into the hallway, Sweetwater glanced back into the elevator to respond, except it was empty.

"I haven't been drinking enough lately," he said in a low voice.

Thirteen steps down the hall, he used his foot to bump Warden's hotel room door in place of a knock. The door creaked open until he saw her in a shooter's stance, the gun pointed at his chest.

"Just take my coffee lady, you don't have to shoot me over it."

"That's not a bad idea. What took you so long?" she said, taking her cup. She paused with it halfway to her lips. "Who were you talking to?"

"What?"

"There's a presence around you—presences, plural."

"I don't know what you're talking about."

"Huh. Okay, forget it. Anyway, I think I've figured out part of this."

Sweetwater put his cup down and blew on his hands to cool them.

"Stop being a baby and sit down," she said, shaking her head. She pulled up a page and moved to the foot of the bed so they could both see the flat screen TV. There was a picture of a short, balding, overweight man wearing a tweed sport coat and black-rimmed glasses.

"So who is this?" he asked.

"That is Adrian Erebus. He's a high school math teacher here in Memphis."

"Yeah, I'd believe that. So why am I looking at this guy?"

"I've got this really tricked-up voice recognition program a black hat buddy of mine wrote, so I ran a search," she said, her voice hanging a second too long, leaving him to wonder what she was leaving out. "I got lucky. He uploaded some classes to his school's website, and the program found it. Turns out, Homeland Security has a very good database that tracks voices and all the program had to do was access it."

"Homeland tracks high school websites?"

"Homeland tracks everything."

"And they share it with LEI?"

"Sort of, they share it with Special—" She stopped and then started again. "They share it with various agencies on an as-needed basis, as well as a few other governments. They built it for China, but the FBI and CIA were quick to jump on board to track terrorists. Then Homeland swallowed it."

"That kind of shit gives me a headache. So, you're sure this is the guy who killed Bonney? It's hard to believe that such a pudgy, middle-aged cliché could take out a trained assassin."

"There's a 99.72 percent certainty. Besides, if you think about, that's exactly who could do it. Bonney would have alerted to an obvious danger, but somebody like this Erebus wouldn't appear much of a threat. That could have slowed down his reaction time."

"Can the computer tell you how he got my fingerprints? Or even better, why the hell he's doing this?" Sweetwater stared at the man's face, searching his memories.

"Not from the jump, but then I did my thing."

She left-clicked the mouse and a new picture appeared on the screen, that of a young red-haired girl in a baseball cap, with a ponytail hanging out the back and freckles ringing her nose.

"Her name is—"

"Grace Allen Tarbeau," he said, his voice dropping to a stage whisper.

"Yeah, how did—"

Warden stuck out her left hand, wobbling, her eyes gone wide. Jerking her head in both directions, she grabbed Sweetwater's arm for support with such force that he felt her nails digging into his skin.

"She's here," Warden said. "She's here with us right now."

"Who's here with us?"

"The dead woman, Grace Allen Tarbeau, her spirit is in this room."

Despite his own experiences, Sweetwater gave her a look that universally translated as, "Oh come on, you don't really believe that, do you?" Meanwhile, he scanned the room just to make sure.

"I think you're tired."

"Fuck off, Luther. I'm not tired and I'm not extra, but I am psychic. She's here, listening."

"The dead woman."

"Exactly, her newlywed husband put a contract on her and now she's here in this room. Ain't love grand?"

"I know about Grace Allen. I completed that contract. It's the 'in this room' part I'm having trouble with." Sweetwater looked into Warden's eyes. "She was my first. So, what does this have to do with Erebus?"

"He's my ex-husband," said a voice very close to his left ear. Sweetwater jumped off the bed and whirled, leaving Warden to scowl in confusion. Behind her, Grace Allen Tarbeau was sitting across the bed, with Eamon Cooper standing near the window smoking a cigarette. Tarbeau's skin had turned a dull black, crossed by large fissures where bloating was ripping the body open, and it hung in strips from her cheeks. Most of her hair had fallen out, but a few red strands remained. As for Cooper, his face was mostly a skull now.

"What?" Warden said. "What's the matter?"

"Nothing. I thought I saw a spider."

"She knows we're here, Luther," Cooper said. "Tell her, she'll believe you."

"She's here," Warden said. "In this room, right now. There's a dude, too."

"I'm a 'dude?'" Cooper said. "I don't feel much like a dude."

Sweetwater closed his eyes and shook his head. "You don't look much like a dude either, more like you're auditioning for a *Ghost Rider* remake," he said, talking to Cooper but forgetting he should be replying to Warden.

"What are you talking about?" Warden said. "I didn't say I was a dude. And *Ghost Rider* sucked, why would anybody remake it?"

"Sorry, I—"

"Wait a minute…no crap, Luther, you can see them, can't you?" Warden said. "You're talking to them!"

"Oops," Tarbeau said. "You done got caught."

Sweetwater flicked his eyes at the rotted corpse on the bed, and then back to Warden. He wasn't a man who sighed very often, but he did then.

"They aren't real, Teri. My therapist says they're hallucinations based on my feelings of guilt."

"Fuck that shit, they're every bit as real as we are. You're a Sensitive."

"I'm a Shooter!" he said, with more force than necessary. He hadn't meant for it to come out that strong; it just did.

"A Sensitive Shooter." Cooper laughed, sucking the cigarette down to the filter in fleshless lips. "That's like being an honest politician."

"I'm not a Sensitive," Sweetwater said. Keeping up with a four-way conversation where Warden could only hear his part brought his headache pounding back with a vengeance. Suddenly he felt very tired. "You're the most cynical corpse I've ever met."

"Keep me in the loop, Luther," Warden said. Something had changed in the way she looked at him. The slightly amused expression she had worn all day now showed some respect. "Stop throwing shade, I can't hear them, but I know you can."

"God, she's one of those," Tarbeau said. "Shade, what the fuck kind of talk is that?"

Sweetwater pointed at Tarbeau and scowled. "Leave her alone."

"Or what? You gonna kill me again?"

"You said your appearances are up to me, right? That I can control them?"

"Not exactly…"

Sweetwater heard the lie in her hedging answer. "Yes, you did, that's exactly what you said. So, here's the deal, either you leave Teri alone and don't hassle her, or stay in your grave and don't come back."

Cooper howled in amusement, a fresh cigarette burning between the bones of his fingers.

"That goes for you too, Cooper."

"You tried to help me, Luther. I've got nothing against you. As for her…" He gestured at Tarbeau with his chin. "I haven't known her very long, but I get where her husband was coming from."

"Fuck you, Eamon," Tarbeau said.

Sweetwater clenched his fists and leaned forward, pitching his voice loud without yelling. Red stars swam in his vision. "Go away, both of you!"

"I know when I'm not wanted," the dead woman said.

"I'm not sure you do," answered Cooper.

They both faded away.

Warden's mouth hung open. Usually that would have filled Sweetwater's brain with X-rated thoughts, but this time the headache pounded down the muscles of his neck into his shoulder blades. A cramp along his right scapula sent him leaning forward to stretch it out.

"They're gone, aren't they?" Warden said.

"Yeah," he said, sitting on the other bed to face Warden. "They're gone back to wherever dead people go…for now."

The coffee had cooled enough to drink without blowing on it, and for a couple of minutes they did just that, without speaking. Whatever awe she felt wore off quickly, however. Warden peeked into the bag, found the carrot cake, and offered Sweetwater the first slice, which he declined. She ate the whole thing in big bites, pouring crumbs from the foam container into her mouth like the crushed chips at the bottom of a potato chip bag. Then she licked bits of creamed cheese icing off the inside top.

"Ready to talk about it?" she said, eyeing Sweetwater's carrot cake.

"Since you obviously believe that I was really talking with two corpses, how come this doesn't bother you more? Cooper's been hanging around for months, and it still freaks me out."

"First, they aren't corpses. A corpse is the body of a dead person or animal."

"They look like corpses. They're even more rotten every time I see them. Cooper isn't much more than a skeleton, and Tarbeau looks like a meat loaf."

"You stole that from a movie."

He sucked on the inside of his cheek. *Had everybody seen that film?*

"If they aren't corpses, then, what are they?"

"Entities. Or, since you know who they are, ghosts."

"I don't believe in ghosts."

"It's probably time to start."

"You never said why this doesn't bother you."

"Sure I did, you just weren't listening. I'm a Psychic, Luther; I always have been. I can't see entities or ghosts, but I can sense their presence, and sometimes I can communicate with them. You're a level beyond me; you're a Sensitive, but I'm guessing this is your first experience talking with those on the other side, right?"

"I'm not even sure there that I believe in the other side."

"So, who've you been talking to?"

"I don't know! My head hurts."

"Damn you're delicate. Do all Marines need testosterone shots, or just you?"

That brought his head up.

"When I first saw you, I felt guilty because I thought you were hot but underaged, and it felt creepy. Less than twelve hours later, and you're not so hot anymore, and I don't give two shits how old you are."

"There ya go," she said, way ahead of him in knowing what was going on between them. "There's the hothead I've heard about."

"What does that mean?"

"Never mind. Let's get back to work. You say Grace Allen Tarbeau doesn't look so great anymore, and I believe you, but she sure as shit did in this picture. I'd hit on her, and I don't go that way. There's something wholesome about her, but look at those eyes—she knew just how hot she was."

"Then how'd she wind up with a loser like Erebus?"

"I know, right? She is *so* far out of his league. And get this, they had a kid, a son, but he died when he was eight, under suspicious circumstances. It happened right here in Memphis and MPD investigated. They didn't find enough evidence to charge anybody, but the cops had Erebus marked as the prime suspect. They thought he did it in some kind of rage.

"Grace Allen took off after that and headed for Texas. Then, two years ago, she married Howard Niester Tarbeau, who I think you've had the pleasure of meeting."

"The piece of shit who threw her off the Renaissance Tower."

Warden nodded. "She probably lied to Howard about her previous marriage. His family comes from old oil money, and he wouldn't like that. So he took out a contract on her. Adrian must have figured out who completed the contract."

"Then why did he go after Bonney first, and not me?" Sweetwater asked. "Hell, why shoot Bonney at all? It's not like we resembled each other."

She tapped on her teeth, eyes flicking back and forth, then stopping and meeting his gaze.

"Fuck me," she said. Before he could make a smartass remark about having to see her ID first, Warden jumped up, punched her access code into her phone and made a call. "Wait here," she said, then went into the bathroom.

Sweetwater kept trying to make sense of it, but fatigue had really set in by now. Too many adrenaline rushes in one day, too bad of a headache, and feeling anxious—alternating with being pissed off— had all combined to leave him feeling hollow. He tried to make out the mumbling through the hotel room walls but could only hear sounds, not words. Five minutes later, she was back.

"This isn't good, Luther, this isn't good at all. The law requires a licensed training agent to oversee every qualifying kill—"

"I've read the law. So what?"

"Then you must have missed the part about TAs being present when the contract is executed."

"Uh…"

"That's what I thought. It was tacked onto the original bill authorizing LifeEnders to mollify some of its opponents and get it passed. Apparently, nobody has ever actually used a TA the way the law says to—it's all phonied up to make it look good and the TA gets a small fee for letting their name go on the paperwork. Guess who your TA was."

"Billy the Kid?"

"Correct on the first guess; Mister William Bonney himself."

Chapter Eighteen

Sweetwater needed to think. He knew he wasn't the smartest guy who ever lived, but when he got out of his own way, he could be damned clever...if only he wasn't so damned tired. Leaning forward, elbows on his knees, and with closed eyes, he buried his face in his hands.

Think, Luther, think!

"So, this Erebus guy was once married to my qualifying kill, Grace Allen, and somehow he got hold of the paper trail about who pitched her off of that roof. Or who he thinks pitched her off."

Warden nodded and gulped some coffee. "That's what we know for certain, yeah. Now let's think about what we don't know."

"How did he find out?"

"That's the number one question, but we're not gonna learn that here and now. What else?"

Bright sparkles filled Sweetwater's vision, and it helped him think. He didn't know why, it just did.

"I think it's safe to say it was Erebus who tried to kill me on my way to the airport to pick you up, which means I could have been his primary target."

"Kinda obvious about him trying to kill you, but I don't agree on the primary target part."

"Did I tell you that I got a glimpse at the guy?" he said.

"And you low-keyed that?"

"I honestly just remembered."

"Fuck, dude, how did you get your creds? Okay, describe him, think back to what you saw, and only what you saw. Don't think about Erebus."

"It was half a second, before I got you—"

"See it as a photo in your memory. Focus on it and tell me what you see."

"His upper body was obscured…he was—I saw his face, but it looked weird, twisted…angry. He's fat, flabby cheeks, and a weak double chin. Piggy little nose—"

"Any ink, scars, deformities?"

Sweetwater finally lifted his head and nodded.

"Yeah…he had something wrong with the right…no, no, the left side of his face. It's like—like part of it was missing."

"Where on his face?"

"Cheek." He touched the point of his own cheekbone, near the temple. "Right about there."

"Good, that's pretty distinctive. What else?"

He shook his head. "That's all I've got."

"All right, if you think of anything else, say so."

"How did you learn all this?"

"I'm a girl."

"Seriously, I'm asking for real. How old are you really?"

Warden cocked her head. "Fifteen."

"I'm leaving."

"You are extra-extra Luther. You're kinda cute, but, dude, go take a manhood pill. I'm twenty-four. Wanna see my ID?"

He held up a palm. "I'm good, thanks."

"If we're done with the drama, let's go back to you being his target. I can only think of two ways he could have singled you out. First, he saw you pick up the bullet and tracked you that way."

Scowling, she fell silent and stared at the wall. Sweetwater admired her ability to shift focus so quickly and tried to wait her out, but when she gave no indication of continuing, he couldn't stand the suspense anymore.

"Yeah, and, what's the second way?"

"LEI has a mole."

"How do I respond to that?" Sweetwater said.

"Frankly, I have no idea. This is off the charts. I was expecting to find out almost anything, except that somebody slipped through LEI's security protocols. But that would also explain your fingerprint. If they hacked the database, they could also tamper with my access and substitute yours for somebody else's. I've gotta call the BB."

"The what?"

"Not a 'what,' a 'who.' The BB, the British Bitch…Cynthia Witherbot."

That brought him up straight. Had Sweetwater called her that in front of Warden? He didn't remember doing so. And her first name was Cynthia? Did he know that already? He also couldn't think of how to ask if he'd been indiscreet, but then she saved him the trouble.

"That's what everybody at LEI calls her. Honestly, I think she likes it."

She held up a finger to stop him from replying, pulled out her phone, and called the British Bitch to let her know they'd been compromised.

Again.

The Kremlin, LEI Worldwide Corporate Headquarters, Dallas, Texas

The assistant director of operations ended the call and eyed the Kremlin without turning her head. She'd been about to go home, having worked nearly 22 hours straight at that point, but news of a mole confirmed her worst fears. It had to be dealt with at once, without delay, and the first step was to issue a contract for the guilty party. She couldn't fill in the name yet, but Cynthia Witherbot had a strong suspicion that when she could, the name would be Mickey Hallum.

The rifle blasted away, set to full automatic. A man in camo jumped out from behind a pile of crates, aiming directly at him, but Erebus was faster. He swung the big ring sight onto the bad guy's center of mass and fired, and watched his tracers vaporize the guy into scattered pixels. Then he pushed pause.

The time on Erebus' phone read 2:43 am. Sleep had been hard to come by ever since he'd seen Grace Allen die, but sitting on the roof all the previous night, then following the guy in the truck, seeing him live through the crash, and missing another chance to kill him at the restaurant—it was all too much for his system. Exhaustion dulled his mind, yet he was restless, like that time he'd taken steroids because of poison ivy and didn't sleep for a week. He played the game by reflex. It wasn't fun like it used to be, and Erebus thought he knew why; once you experienced the high of blowing away real people, in real life, their electronic surrogates in a video game no longer provided the same excitement.

After thinking about it all day and night, Erebus had discovered that he liked killing people. Unlike math, which had a relentless logic that had always appealed to his orderly mind, eliminating bad people had a visceral thrill unlike anything he'd ever known. Not only was he making the world a better place, but shooting Bonney and his whore had been fun.

Now he had a new target: the guy in the truck, Luther Sweetwater. And, surprise, surprise, he was also part of Grace Allen's death. This Sweetwater guy had been some sort of apprentice Shooter, and even though Bonney was listed as the actual killer, Sweetwater had somehow been part of it.

Things just had a way of working out. He and Herbert wanted to kill every licensed killer, first in Memphis, and then everywhere. Sweetwater would have been on the list anyway, but now God had dropped him into their laps, and they could both get their revenge. Erebus for the woman he loved, and Herbert for his mother. It was all so perfect, and now Sweetwater was about to discover the truth of the old saying. Karma really was a bitch.

"Luther, wakey-wakey."

Warden stood beside the bed, calling down to him. Sweetwater reached up and rubbed his face, to find his pillow damp with drool.

"What time is it?" Sweetwater rolled onto his back and stretched. He was reaching for the wall when Warden's hand came down with a hard slap right in the middle of his belly. He bolted into a sitting position with a cough.

"What the fuck?"

"Let's go! We've got actionable intel in the form of Erebus' address. Get ready, it's time for you to go to work."

"Actionable intel?" he asked, while rubbing his eyes. "Did you get that off TV?"

"I'm a reader, not a watcher. Hurry up."

"Did you sleep?"

"I'll do that ten minutes after you put a bullet into Adrian Erebus' head. For which you'll now be paid, by the way. You have a contract for him. Now, let's go."

Sweetwater stood.

"Did you get through to the British Bitch?"

"Oh yeah, and she wasn't happy. But finding the mole will take time. They can't let him or her know they've been discovered, otherwise they might cover their tracks, and LEI needs to seal this off before they can do even more damage. Who knows what else they've disclosed? But she doubts the fingerprint results were compromised."

"That's impossible."

"Not according to her, it's not. She said there's one possibility you may have overlooked. Did you receive a pistol when you went after Grace Allen Tarbeau?"

Sweetwater blinked twice before answering. "The Sig."

"Chambered in 9mm. The same that put down Bonney and his girlfriend."

"Fuck. He was there. Erebus was in Dallas when Grace Allen died. It's the only explanation that makes any sense."

"Looks that way, yeah. You could summon Tarbeau and ask."

"Like hell I can."

"But you can."

"I'm not convinced they're even real, and if they are, I sure as hell don't know how to summon them. And on top of all that, I don't want to! My mom is a religious woman, and she didn't bring me up to commune with the dead. That's a mortal sin, so forget that. Besides, we don't need any more proof that Erebus got the gun in Dallas. Nothing else makes sense."

"Guns aren't my thing, but would it still work after being dropped from such a tall building?"

"I don't know, but he could've gotten it fixed. Is there any coffee left?"

"There's a machine at the end of the hall."

"I hate machine coffee."

"You offered it to me earlier."

"I know."

She laughed at that. "You're not quite the dumbass you want people to believe."

"I don't want anybody to think that!" Especially not really cute girls my own age."

"Get us some coffee, big boy. I can take it if you can."

"But it's *so* bad."

"Embrace the suck, Marine."

Chapter Nineteen

Midtown Memphis, TN

The Prius glided to a stop in an old residential neighborhood where bars were bolted over windows on every house and piles of refuse lined the curb. A couple bags of garbage had been ripped open as if by animal claws—probably raccoons, Sweetwater thought—and their contents littered the street and clogged the gutter drains. There was a run of oily water in the gutters.

Sweetwater opened the door and felt the cold air suck away his breath. Damn, he hated winter. They were parked across the street, so he joined Warden, putting the car between them and the house.

"Think he's watching us?" she said.

Something had clicked inside of him the instant he opened the car door. He was in the field again, on the hunt, in the environment he'd twice been trained for, once by the Marines and again by LEI. The hesitant awkwardness he felt around people vanished as his mind went into predator mode.

"We have to assume he is." Sweetwater looked at the revolver like he was in a restaurant, and the food didn't match the photo on the menu. "Why didn't I bring some hardware when I came to Memphis? I always carry a weapon, always, except today."

She shrugged. "Be glad the TSA allows LEI people to bring firearms on commercial aircraft, or we wouldn't even have that."

"I should have bought something heavier on the way over."

"At two am?"

His narrowed glance betrayed the killer within that the Marines had recognized, the drive that got him accepted into Scout Sniper School. It wasn't killing people that bothered him about LEI, it was killing people his personal moral code didn't think deserved it. With Adrian Erebus, however, that wasn't going to be a problem.

"Shooters know people," he said. "Day or night, it doesn't matter. I should have brought a better gun."

"Fine, you fucked up," she said, unimpressed by his intensity. "But it's too late now. If he has seen us and we pull out to go buy some heavy artillery, he'll be in the wind, and we'll never find him."

"Let's get this over with."

The house was simple brick. Sweetwater guessed it was about as long as his trailer and with a comparably simple layout. The door was in the middle of the wall and a barred window was set on either side, while a wooden garage door with no windows hid whatever was parked inside.

The sidewalk buckled upward from the roots of an enormous oak tree, with overgrown paving stones leading from the street to a small front porch. Sweetwater headed straight for it; the cold forgotten in the heat of the moment. His right hand gripped the revolver inside his front overcoat pocket. Displaying it openly might give the owner, in case Erebus did not still live there, a defensible reason to shoot him. He was so fixated on watching the windows for signs of a gun pointing his way, that Sweetwater missed when Warden veered off to the left.

"Over here, cowboy," she stage-whispered. "The front door is for Jehovah's Witnesses and bill collectors. What we need is around the back."

Great, he thought, *in through the back door.* Now Erebus could kill them and the cops wouldn't blink an eye. Not that they would have anyway.

The back of the house was just as simple, one door accessed by two concrete steps, framed on either side by barred windows. Warden took the steps carefully, as one corner had fallen away, and cracks made them appear unstable. She twisted the doorknob. Turning to Sweetwater with a quick head shake, she pulled a small black leather case from the breast pocket of her jacket.

Opening it, she pulled out two thin strips of metal, stuck one in her mouth, and held it between her lips. She dropped to one knee, bringing her eye even with the door handle.

"Yes," she mumbled around the lock pick in her mouth.

He kept his own voice low and the pistol ready. "I didn't say anything."

Warden took the pick from her mouth and alternated working it with one she already had inserted. Her gaze never left the lock.

"You were going to ask me if I knew how to do this."

"I was?"

"You were, and I answered yes. You never know what skills you'll need on this job—wait...damn, I almost had it." She stuck her tongue between her teeth and tilted her head to one side. A few seconds later, she pinched both picks in one hand and twisted the knob. The door opened an inch. Standing, she slipped the lockpicks back into their case and into her jacket, and then stepped aside.

"After you, Marine."

"And here I thought I was just arm candy."

"That's me; you're the gofer."

Sweetwater pulled out the pistol and entered the house, gun at high ready, finger on the trigger instead of the guard. He'd been drilled and drilled that you only did that when a shooting could be imminent, which it probably was. The screen door had squealed when he eased it open, exactly like the one on the back of his mom's house where he grew up. More than once as a teenager he'd tried to sneak inside after curfew, and because of that damned door she'd caught him every time. Now it happened again, except, instead of facing his mother's wrath, he might have to face a killer.

Once inside, he put his back against the inner wall and shut the door. That shut off the only illumination, since heavy curtains blocked the room's windows. It also left Warden outside, where she should be safe.

He was in the kitchen and, based on what he'd assumed about Erebus, it threw him. The counters were cleared off, the sink was empty, and the only thing out of place were some papers sitting on the kitchen table. Slowly, he moved to clear the house as he'd been taught.

A small den off the kitchen was barren except for a recliner, flat screen TV, and a gaming system with multiple controllers. There were no snack bags, soda cans, ashtrays, or any of the typical detritus of a video gamer. Sweetwater found that weird, but he couldn't stop to worry about it, and kept moving through the house. As he passed the front door, he noticed that it had a chain and more than one deadbolt. He smiled at the stupidity of blockading the front door but not the back.

A short hallway led to a small bathroom, which was empty save for a toothbrush and tube of paste sitting in a glass, and a bar of soap resting on the sill of the tub. He went back to the hallway and crept toward the last room, ready to shoot, drop, or roll. The door was closed. He stood to one side and reached for the handle. He forced himself to take three deep, silent breaths before he slowly turned the knob and gave it a soft push.

Sweetwater stayed behind the wall, bracing the pistol with both hands. He stepped back, listened, and dove into the open doorway, barrel first. Nothing happened.

Dim moonlight filtered past closed curtains and hinted at forms in the darkness. Feeling exposed, Sweetwater took two steps forward. Like the rest of the house, the bedroom was spartan. A mattress and box spring lay against the far wall, with the sheets and blankets drawn tight and a single pillow perfectly centered eight inches from the far end. Not a crease marred the surface of the pillowcase. It wasn't pass-inspection-Marine-boot-camp good, but it was close.

Against the wall sat a simple dresser with nothing on top. The last potential ambush place was the closet. Sweetwater slipped around the bed and placed himself with back flat against the wall, and then reached out with his left hand. Instead of opening it cautiously, this time he twisted and threw the door open. It bounced off the wall with a bang. He caught it with his foot and spun inward to face the closet, but it was too small to hide a person.

Shirts and slacks were in a line on hangers evenly spaced across the closet. The darkness made it impossible to tell for sure if they were sorted by color, as he believed, and that matched the theme throughout the house, only the essentials and everything in its place. He'd known neat freaks in his life, sure, but that neat? Sweetwater turned and walked back to the kitchen, less wary than he had been, but not by much.

"It's clear," he called out.

Stepping into the kitchen, his gun came up as a reflex, the sights lined up on the forehead of a fat man hunched behind Teri Warden in the center of the kitchen. Warden stood with her hands out to her sides.

A single LED bulb lit the space, hanging over the table by a strand of braided macramé which was attached to a cheap copper dome lamp. It was set to one side so it lit Warden's left side and enough of the man's face for Sweetwater to see details of the damage to his left cheek. He could see just enough of the scarred-over hole to realize why the edges of the wound appeared so jagged; they were teeth marks. Somebody had bitten out a chunk of the man's flesh. It was the same man he'd seen on the interstate and in the photos Warden had pulled up of Adrian Erebus.

Erebus was easily twice her weight and six inches taller, which meant that she didn't make for a very good shield. Sweetwater could tell that the deformed man had the back of her jacket bunched up in his right fist and was using it to hold her tight against him. He was holding an automatic pistol in his left hand which was pressed against the side of Warden's jaw. The sight on the revolver never wavered from Erebus' left eye. But despite being a helluva good shot, Sweetwater's sniper training kept him from simply shooting the man. Where being a quarter inch off with bullet placement might cost Warden her life, he wasn't willing to risk it using an unfamiliar weapon whose sight might or might not be calibrated correctly, loaded with unknown ammunition, whose trajectory properties he didn't know, and in tricky lighting. Not unless he absolutely had to.

Despite the weather outside, a trickle of sweat caused him to blink his right eye. The tableau held for what seemed like hours but was really less than ten seconds. Neither man moved. Warden's icy demeanor had cracked a little, and she once again appeared to be a scared little girl, gulping little breaths and trying not to hyperventilate. Sweetwater heard her whimpers, and their eyes met, but even as she sobbed and sniffled, she also winked.

Fuck me, she's good.

Erebus finally broke the silence.

"Luther Sweetwater," he said. Something in the man's voice sent a shudder through Sweetwater's shoulders, like the guy was overacting in a bad horror movie. "I know who you are."

"Goodie for you. I've always dreamed about being popular with the local psychopaths."

Even Warden showed surprise at that comment, and he saw something new in her eyes. Respect, maybe? She drew a deep breath, and he realized her breasts were larger than he'd noticed before and wondered if she'd done that for his benefit.

Situational awareness, Luther, maintain your situational awareness. But damn!

Trying to distract the madman, Sweetwater adopted a heavy Bronx accent, forgetting that Rocky took place in Philadelphia.

"Yo, Adrian, why don'tcha do us all a favuh here and lowa youse gun." Then he paused, finally recognizing the Sig, and realized how his fingerprint got on the brass casing; it *was* his gun, the one he'd lost on top of the Renaissance Tower, except the last time he'd seen it, it was plunging toward the street. Erebus caught the revelation as it crossed Sweetwater's face, and grinned.

"Yes, Mister Professional Hitman, Mister Destoyer of Innocent Lives, this is your gun. You killed Billy the Kid and his slut girlfriend with it, and now you're going to kill this bitch, but fortunately for me I'll shoot you before you can complete your work."

"That can't be the same gun Adrian; there's no way any weapon could survive that kind of fall and still work, not even a Sig Sauer."

"You assassins are all so stupid…but I guess you'd have to be to kill people for money, wouldn't you?"

"Then explain it so even an idiot like me can understand."

"Awnings, moron, it hit an awning, bounced, hit it again, and *then* hit the street. All the energy was gone. It's a simple equation."

Fuck! That makes sense. Nor was the guy what Sweetwater had expected. He was grotesque, yeah, but not a raving lunatic. Erebus' file said he was a math teacher, and that's exactly what he sounded like.

Until he didn't. Erebus frowned until his eyebrows neared touching, and something changed in his eyes. Sweetwater had never seen it happen before, but knew madness when he saw it

"You are one of those assassinsss." He drew out the last S, but what worried Sweetwater was that it sounded so natural coming from him, like when a hissing snake sounds so much like what you think it should sound like that you don't believe it. "You destroyed the most beautiful flower on Earth, and for what? Money! That's right; I know what you did, and I know why you did it. You killed Grace Allen to hurt me! We were back together, and you wanted her for yourself!"

And then Erebus changed back, just like that, so his expression showed no signs of the madness that had inflamed it mere seconds ago. Sweetwater squinted at the abrupt change. Now, aside from the hole in his face, he again looked like a teacher whose unruly students had no doubt made fun of him during class. Regardless, Sweetwater now had no doubts that he was insane.

"She brought hope and light into the world and you murdered her," Erebus continued, in a matter-of-fact tone. "So, just as that other man watched his beloved die, you might have to watch the brains of your bitch girlfriend leak out of her head before I kill you."

"She's not my—"

"Shut up with your lies!" Now he started blinking, and Sweetwater knew that was a bad sign. Erebus only glanced at her and kept talking. "Unless you obey me to the letter, then, maybe you will both live a little while longer. Now, I'm going to back out of here and leave with my gun pointed at you. If you want a shootout, then maybe you'll kill me and be able to call nine-one-one and save your girlfriend here, but then maybe I'll kill you, or maybe we'll kill each other. If either of those happens, she'll bleed out because she gets the first bullet. It's your choice."

Sweetwater fired, but not to kill. That was too dangerous, there was too great a chance he'd hit Warden, so he aimed for the man's ear to give her a chance to slip out of his grasp. She bobbed her head forward, hoping it was far enough out of the way that Erebus' shot would miss.

Except Erebus didn't shoot Warden, instead he used her as a shield and whipped the gun down and fired at Sweetwater. Warden whirled and jammed the heel of her hand up into Erebus' nose, smashing it in a spray of blood. He staggered backward and fired two rounds wildly on his way out the door. Both missed.

Sweetwater rocked back like he'd been hit under the sternum with a ball peen hammer. His mouth agape as air rushed out of his lungs from the impact, he saw Erebus backing out the door with blood covering his face. He tried to aim the revolver, but his arm didn't work right. Touching his chest with his other hand, he blinked when it came away covered in blood. He glanced up at Warden and saw shock and horror on her face. Then everything drew into a little pinprick of light, and he felt himself falling.

"Now you know what it feels like," whispered Grace Allen Tarbeau. Down on hands and knees beside him, she brought her decayed face within inches of his. "Death ain't all it's cracked up to be, big boy."

"Shit!" Warden said.

She didn't scream, but her brain automatically shifted into survival mode, with her first priority making certain Erebus didn't come back to finish them both off. Pulling the revolver out of Sweetwater's hand, she turned to the door, ready to fire, and carefully made sure he wasn't right outside before bolting it closed. He might still shoot through the window, but it was a tough angle. Sweetwater didn't look good, so she forgot Erebus and knelt beside the wounded Shooter. Folding back his coat, she found the center of the spreading circle of blood on his shirt, grabbed a towel that was draped across the front of the sink, and pressed it to the wound. With her free hand, she managed to use her cell phone to call for help.

"Nine-one-one, what's your emergency?"

"I..." she started. She paused when she saw the front of her phone was streaked with blood. Blood seemed to be everywhere. The kitchen towel was quickly turning red.

"Hello, nine-one-one, what's your emergency?"

"My friend has been shot."

"What is the address, ma'am?"

Warden closed her eyes and focused on answering the woman's question. After giving it, she thanked the dispatcher, who started walking her through the basic steps of controlling the bleeding. Warden already knew them and told her so, but the woman kept talking, which distracted her. It took seven minutes for the EMTs to come running through the back door, which she got up and unlocked, by which time his breathing had become labored.

"Is he gonna die?" she said, knowing how it made her sound but unable to stop heself before the words came out.

"Please step back," answered a stocky black woman. "We're gonna take good care of him."

"Hey, looks who's here!" Eamon Cooper said, hoisting a whiskey glass with four fingers of some amber-golden liquid in a toast. "I figured we'd see you sooner rather than later, Luther. Thinking about joining us permanently?"

Luther Sweetwater sat up—or thought he sat up, it was hard to tell—in an empty white space with no walls, floors, or ceiling.

Cooper stood nearby sucking on a cigarette while sipping the alcohol.

"Not if I can help it," Sweetwater said. "Where is 'here?'"

"I don't know; where dead people go, I suppose. What about you, Grace Allen; do you know where we are?"

She stood several paces away to his right, gulping down a banana split from one of those glass dishes made just to serve the ice cream concoction.

"No idea," she mumbled, with half a banana sticking out the side of her half-decayed mouth. Once she'd sucked it down with a loud slurp, she continued. "Goodness, excuse me boys, that wasn't very ladylike. I always assumed this was Heaven."

"If so," Cooper said, "it's not at all what my Baptist preacher father said it would be like. No trumpets or angels or any of that stuff. To be honest, if this is eternal bliss, it's damned disappointing. Except for the booze and cigarettes whenever you want them; that's not so bad."

"So, I'm dead?" Sweetwater asked. Nothing felt solid beneath him, as if he was simply floating in midair, yet he didn't feel any sensation of floating.

"You ask a lot of questions, Luther. Let me get you a drink," Cooper said.

"I warned you about Adrian," Grace Allen said. "He's a wicked, wicked man, but he's not stupid. You underestimated him."

"You could have told me that."

"And you could have stayed home and nursed your hangover instead of going to the R-Tower to shoot me! Besides, I *did* warn you."

"You told me to watch out for somebody named Herbert."

"Are you always so fucking dense? I told you that Herbert was worse than Adrian. I never said Adrian wasn't deranged."

Cooper laughed. His glass was full again. "She's got you there, Two-Bit."

"Don't call me that!"

"That's your Shooter's handle, isn't it? Two-Bit Luther?"

"I don't like that name!"

"And we don't like being dead," said Grace Allen. "Yet here we are. You don't like being called Two-Bit, yet that's your name."

"Two-Bit, Two-Bit, Two-Bit ..." they chanted.

Sweetwater clapped hands over his ears, then everything went black.

"We've got him back!" yelled the other EMT, a skinny guy with a name patch that said Tommy Nokio. "He's mumbling something about not calling him that. Who is this guy?"

Warden told them Sweetwater's name but not his profession or what he was doing there. The three of them huddled around the wounded man, trying to stop the bleeding long enough to safely transport him to the nearest ER. Warden stood right behind them, hunched over with her hands on her knees, watching.

"Luther, can you hear me?" asked the black woman. "I'm EMT Tanyika Dolkins, we're gonna take good care of you. Can you hear me?"

To everyone's surprise, Sweetwater opened his eyes, scanned the faces looking down on him, and settled his gaze on Warden.

"Heaven's not all it's cracked up to be," he said, then passed out.

Chapter Twenty

Sweetwater knew right away that the man on the operating table was him, even as the nurses and doctors scrambled in response to the flatline monotone coming from the heart monitor. His perspective was from 20 or 30 feet directly above the OR, but, instead of confusing him, it clarified things; he was dead, and his soul had left his body.

Well, shit.

At least nothing hurt.

"Kind of disorienting, huh?"

Eamon Cooper. Of course he would be here.

"Not really. I'm dead, right?"

"For the moment, yeah, but they're still trying to revive you, so who knows? You might make it yet."

Sweetwater finally turned toward Cooper and was surprised to see that he looked like he did when alive, not all rotted like a corpse that had burst from internal gasses.

"You're looking pretty good these days," he said.

"Thanks, I've been working out." A lit cigarette appeared between his fingers.

"No booze?"

Cooper shrugged. "No matter how much I drink I never get a buzz, so it seems kind of pointless."

Sweetwater pointed at the smoke. "But those?"

"I'm addicted."

A delusion addicted to nicotine…Sure, why not?

The answer to his unspoken comment came from behind. "We're not delusions, Luther, and we're not hallucinations. We're ghosts."

He whirled to see Grace Allen Tarbeau.

"Is that supposed to make me feel better?"

She shrugged. "Thought you might like to know, that's all."

"What I'd like to know is why I'm dead. What's this all about? Why did Erebus kill Bonney and try to—fuck, I guess he killed me, too, didn't he? Okay, so why did he kill me, Bonney, and Bonney's girlfriend?"

"To clarify," Cooper said. "You're dead, but you might not stay that way."

"If they're gonna save me they'd better hurry."

"Time runs different here, wherever 'here' is. We could talk all day and only ten seconds might pass out there, or down there, or wherever 'there' is."

"This is goddamned confusing."

Cooper held up a hand. "You might want to hold off on the whole taking God's name in vain thing. We haven't met Him yet, or any angels or all that stuff, but you never know."

"You want to know why Adrian went after you and Bonney?" Grace Allen asked. "Okay, I'll tell you. Listen up, it's a long story, and I've thought a lot about how to tell it."

"We fell apart, sweaty, panting, smelling of sex, and with the evidence of our lust strewn all over the room in messy heaps. Not just our clothes, or the blankets and pillows, even the mattress hung halfway off the bed frame, with us still on it.

"His name was Bryan; it doesn't matter where I met him. The part about him I liked most wasn't the foreplay or the sex, although God knows he knew what he was doing there. It was after we'd make love, the way his eyes traced the curves of my naked body. It's like he didn't want just the physical side of me, he wanted all of me, to really bond with me…Well, it's hard to explain to men. But nobody had ever wanted me before. Growing up all the boys just wanted inside my pants; they didn't much care about anything else.

"Everything about that night is burned into my memory. A single exposed bulb on the ceiling lit the room, making the sweat glisten. His eyes lingered on my breasts as they rose and fell as I breathed. I could feel his love, like you can feel the heat of a campfire from ten feet away. I felt a bead of sweat slip down my belly into my crotch and watched him watching it. I never had a more intimate moment with anybody.

"I rolled up on one elbow and did the same thing back at him, letting my eyes drift along his body until I got to his groin. Without looking away, I licked my lips."

"Okay!" Sweetwater said, holding up his hand. "TMI!"

"Do you wanna hear the story?"

"Yeah, but you can leave out all the porn stuff."

"And you can fuck off, Two-Bit. And, yeah, I know you hate that name, but tough titty said the kitty. I'll tell it my way or not at all."

"Shit…go on."

"You sure?"

"I might as well know why I'm dead."

She cleared her throat, which seemed odd to Sweetwater.

"Where was I? Oh yeah, I remember...'My God, don't you ever get enough?' Bryan said, laughing and rolling flat on his back. I reached out and touched the head of his—"

Sweetwater closed his eyes and cringed.

"—manhood. 'With Adrian, yes,' I said, 'once a year is plenty, but not with you. With you, once an hour is more like it.'

"'Once an hour? I won't survive that for more than week,' Bryan said.

"'Maybe, but what a way to go,' I replied.

"He blocked my hand with a pillow, and I put on my best pouty face. That used to get whatever I wanted from the boys in middle school, but Bryan just laughed. 'I'm going to need a minute. That was quite a workout.'

"'I'm thinking about teaching classes,' I said.

"He wagged his finger at my nose and said, 'Don't you dare.'

"I remember every detail of what happened next, every smell, every sensation, even the sounds his stomach made when I laid my head on it. It's like being dead has actually sharpened my memory. I can see it all like a video in my mind. Weird, huh? My brain cells have all turned to mush by now, but I feel smarter than I ever did while alive.

"Anyway, we screwed like rabbits for the next few hours. Adrian was away at a teacher's conference in Little Rock, and we had all the time in the world. Or so I thought. After the third time, Bryan closed his eyes and finally gave in to his exhaustion and passed into unconsciousness, and I finally let him. I'd well and truly worn him out, poor guy."

She laughed a little to herself.

"A couple of minutes later I did the same. Everything was quiet and perfect."

"I always knew Adrian had a temper, but I had never seen him like what happened next. The door frame splintered, and the door swung free to bounce off the corner of the bed. Bryan and I both sat up, and I heard him cry out when he saw a man standing in the doorway."

"The charming Mister Adrian, I'm guessing," said Cooper. He sucked the latest cigarette down to the butt, exhaled, and wrinkled his nose in dissatisfaction. Another one materialized.

"It was Adrian, all worked up into a state like I never saw before. I married him because I'd had some rough boyfriends over the years, truckers who promised to leave their old ladies and never did, drug dealers who beat me up, even one guy who tried to pimp me out. Adrian wasn't much to look at, but he had a steady job teaching in the Fayette County School System, benefits, a house he'd inherited from his mother. He wasn't fat back then, either; that happened after…Well, I'll tell that in its own time."

Sweetwater interrupted her. "I hope you don't think I'm hitting on you, but you're a damned fine looking woman. Couldn't you find somebody better?"

"Go ahead and hit on me, what do I care now? But c'mon, Luther, think with your other head, we're from the same county. Hell, we might have been neighbors. Everybody I knew grew up in a house with wheels, every guy I met just wanted to get into my pants. All except Adrian; I met him when I roller skated to his car at the drive-in near the town square in Semple. He wasn't like anybody I'd ever gone out with, but he seemed nice. So, when he asked me out, I went. Things went from there.

"He treated me like I was a princess and took great care of me. I can't complain about any of that. But I'd be yin' if I said I ever loved him, and sex with him was never better than something I had to tolerate. Then after our only child was born—that would be Herbert—the sight of Adrian started making me sick. Just looking at him made me want to throw up; I don't know why. Maybe it's because of what our son became as he got older…

"Anyway, when Adrian caught me with Bryan, he came through the door like some kind of wild animal, waving a hammer and screaming. I'd never seen him like that before, at least, not with me. He'd gone off on other people, sometimes to the point where I thought he'd wind up in jail, but he never so much as raised his voice to me…until them.

"He buried the claws of the hammer into the bedroom wall and pulled out a big chunk of plasterboard and called me all the names you'd expect him to: fucking bitch, whore, slut, all of those, and I'll never forget the spit flying out of his mouth as he yelled. I knew he'd gone crazy, and I mean *insane* crazy.

"I knelt and tried to get between him and Bryan, but he shoved me away, and I fell off the other side of the bed and hit my head on the bed frame. I think I passed out for a few seconds. Bryan was bigger and stronger than Adrian, but when I came to Bryan was on the floor with my husband kneeling on him. Bryan called out something like 'wait, please don't,' and tried to grab Adrian's arms, but I guess it was one of those situations you hear about where adrenaline gives somebody super strength.

"With this twisted, horrible grin, Adrian lifted the hammer high overhead and tried to hit Bryan with it, except they wound up wrestling instead. Bryan managed to catch his arm on the way down, with Adrian still screaming all kinds of stuff about Bryan never fucking another man's wife again, and how could I do this to him and our son, and all kinds of stuff.

"I tried to make him stop, but I was still naked, and when he saw me it made him so mad that it gave him extra strength. He jerked his arm free of Bryan's grip and threw his arm backward before bringing the hammer down on Bryan's head. And that's when I heard this horrible, wet crunch.

"I crawled around the end of the bed on my hands and knees because I had this sick feeling I knew what had happened, and I was right. Adrian was frozen, staring back to where Herbert lay on the floor, the claws of that goddamned hammer jammed into his forehead. His face was turned my way and his eyes were open. I knew right away that my boy was dead.

"Adrian forgot all about Bryan and fell to his knees beside our son. He idolized that boy; Herbert was his world. He cried and hugged our dead eight-year-old son and kept telling him to wake up, it was all gonna be okay, that kind of stuff. Bryan took off, but I couldn't move, I just sat there on my haunches for a while...I don't know how long it was, just a while...and then suddenly I snapped out of it.

"I leapt up and tackled Adrian the way I'd learned playing football with my brother. He was still holding Herbert, but I knew he was dead. I clawed at his face and neck, I tried to get the hammer away so I could use it to kill him, I really don't remember most of it. But Adrian didn't really fight back, except to keep me from getting the hammer, he just kept looking at Herbert's awful, bloody face where—dear God, I'm dead and it still sickens me. Where grayish stuff had started oozing from his forehead."

"Oh fuck," Cooper said, all traces of sarcasm gone now. "I have a four-year-old girl—had a four-year-old girl, Nottie we called her, and I guess they still do. Losing her would have killed me; I could never have functioned again. I'm so sorry, Grace."

"Me, too," Sweetwater said. "I don't have kids, but I'm really sorry you had to go through that."

Grace Allen shrugged. "Thanks, but it sort of hollowed me out. After a while, I quit mourning my son because I don't think I could anymore. I'd just run out of emotions; I'd run out of grief. That sounds terrible but it's true. Herbert was dead because I couldn't control my own lust, and I turned an otherwise decent man into a murderer."

"I don't think we're qualified to judge you," Sweetwater said. "Least ways, I'm not."

"What happened to Adrian after that?" Cooper said.

From somewhere else a new voice interrupted the conversation, a female voice, with some sort of beeping in the background.

"Pulse is weak but it's there," she said, and then was gone.

Cooper and Grace Allen both turned surprised glances on Sweetwater.

"Who was that?" he said.

Cooper conjured up a cigarette. "I think you might return to the land of the living soon."

"I'll hurry it up then," Grace Allen said. "Herbert's death was my fault. Adrian wasn't a prize catch, but despite a nasty streak, he'd never hurt anybody before, and he tried hard to be a good husband. It was me who wasn't satisfied and betrayed him."

"Nobody has right to hit somebody else with a hammer," Sweetwater said. "Except in self-defense. This isn't your fault."

"That's rich coming from you," Cooper said with uncharacteristic bitterness. Usually, he wore a smirk and had a tone to match.

Grace Allen shook her head. "No, he shouldn't have done that, but I think seeing me naked with another man made him snap, and if that didn't, I know that killing Herbert did. He threw me off and knelt there, holding our boy close to his chest, with Herbert's brains leaking down his chest. It was horrible.

"His face was red and wet when he looked over at me, and then something changed. His eyebrows went up and he pointed at me. 'You did it!' he screamed at me. A big drop of Herbert's blood dripped from the end of his finger. 'What did you do, Grace? Why did you kill our boy?'"

Grace Allen turned away from the two men, wiped her nose with a tissue that appeared in her left hand, coughed, and continued.

"I got to my feet because I'd seen that same kind of look enough times to know what was coming. Adrian's face had twisted with rage, and as I met his eyes, I knew he would kill me if I stayed. He seemed to be looking through me, not at me. A knot of ice formed in my stomach, and I couldn't move. I once hit a deer on a dark night on Highway 195, just outside of Grand Junction. It just stood there, frozen in my headlights, and I felt the same way. Then Adrian started climbing to his feet.

"Something snapped me out of my trance, and I ran. I abandoned my son and my husband, and I ran to save my own worthless life. I remember shivering and feeling cold, but I wasn't sure if it was from sweat or terror. I'm still not. I ran down the staircase and snatched the spare keys from the back door.

"Adrian came after me, yelling and pounding down the stairs, but I got to the door in plenty of time to get away and started working on the locks. I should have gotten away clean, except my fingers shook, and I'd started to panic. I fumbled with the chain lock and twisted the doorknob. It took a few seconds to register that it was still locked, and then Adrian grabbed my shoulder. After that…everything happened in a few seconds; it takes longer to tell it than to live through it.

"'You're not getting away that easy!' he screamed at me. I tried to reason with him, but he was way too far gone for that. His fingers dug deep into my skin, and he had the hammer ready to hit me. I didn't doubt for one second that he'd kill me where I stood. The look in his eyes was…awful.

"I looked around for anything I could use to defend myself. The block of knives by the sink was too far to reach, but I saw the coffee pot off to my right and reacted, there wasn't time to do anything else. I swung it hard as I could into the left side of his head. Blood and glass flew everywhere, some of it wound up in my hair, and Adrian made this horrible noise, like something you'd hear in a horror movie…but Adrian didn't let go.

"Any hesitation in his eyes was gone, he raised the hammer and there was nothing more I could do so…so I lunged forward and bit him. I was aiming for his nose, but he turned at the last second and I got a mouthful of his cheek. I bit down as hard as I could. My mouth filled with blood, and he shoved me away.

"Adrian staggered backward, screaming and swinging the hammer blindly, and damned near hit me in the jaw. I'm pretty sure he fell down. I ducked just in time, 'cause if he'd connected, I would have been dead long before you threw me off that building, Two-Bit—"

"I didn't do that!"

"Hush and lemme finish before you get jerked back."

"He might stay dead," Cooper said.

"And he might not," Grace Allen said. "I had seconds to save myself, and I knew it. I still had the keys in my left hand and this time I got the door open. I didn't care if I was naked and covered with blood, or that my heart was beating so hard I thought I might die from it. I ran for the driveway. I had a 1987 Olds Firenza with most of the paint gone that didn't always start on the first few tries, but that night it started up as Adrian came running out the back door. If it hadn't started, he would have killed me, simple as that. But it did and I stomped on the accelerator, fishtailing as I hit the street. And that was it; I never saw him again."

"How could that be it?" Sweetwater said. "What about your son, wasn't Adrian arrested for murder?"

Grace Allen hung her head. "I never called the police. Herbert was—there was something very wrong with Herbert."

"So, what did you do? I mean, you were nude, right?" Sweetwater said.

"Yeah, so I couldn't stop and ask for help. You know what would have happened in that area of Semple. So, I drove to my mom's house in Moscow. We're the same size. She was passed out drunk, but her scumbag boyfriend was there. He'd flirted with me from day one, and the second he saw me, bloody and with gouges in my shoulder, instead of helping me or calling the police, he bent me over a chair and raped me. Right then and there. Didn't ask anything, didn't even care that mom was snoring on the couch. He just pushed down on the back of my neck to hold me in place and fucked me until he was done."

"Oh shit," Cooper said, genuinely stunned. "Damn…what did you do?"

She shrugged. "By that point I was an emotional wreck; I'd watched my husband assault my lover, my son was killed, I was assaulted and raped. The only thing I wanted was to get away, so I grabbed some clothes from my mom's closet and told him to either kill me or give me a hundred bucks to keep quiet. He didn't have that much, but he did give me seventy-three dollars. That was enough to get me to Texas."

"What happened once you got there?" Sweetwater said.

"Don't ask. But then I met the ultra-rich Dennis Roy Tarbeau, and the second I saw him I was determined to become Mrs. Tarbeau. He made me sign a pre-nup, but if the marriage broke up after a year, I got three million dollars. So at the end of a year, I turned into the Ice Queen."

"You didn't love him, I take it," Cooper said.

"Oh, but I did. I couldn't imagine being more in love…until our wedding night. Dennis liked whips, which might have been all right, except it wasn't the fantasy he liked, it was the welts they raised…on me. His favorite game was Slave and Master."

"That's disgusting!" Sweetwater said.

"Don't be such a child," Cooper said, sounding annoyed with Sweetwater for the first time. "What goes on behind closed doors in a marriage is nobody else's business."

"Yeah, but—" he started, but then began to sink into whatever the whiteness was he'd been lying on. "Hey, what's going on?"

Cooper saluted with his cigarette. "Congratulations, look like you're gonna make it. See you soon, Luther."

"The boyfriend's name, what was it?" Sweetwater yelled. "Quick!"

"John Cleve Stuart!"

Then he was gone.

Chapter Twenty-One

Midtown Memphis, TN

Erebus heard the broken pieces of driveway bouncing off the underside of his car the same way it had the night his wife had to leave. He would never forget that *thunk-thunk* sound, not if he lived to be ninety. And he would never forgive the man who kidnapped Grace Allen and stole her car, the man whose name he'd only later learned was Bryan. Now that he was on the vengeance trail, if he could find Bryan, he'd shoot him just like he'd done to Sweetwater. And after that, he'd go after the guy down in Texas who kept her as a slave, that Tarbeau guy. He'd get them all.

Speeding away from his house reminded him of that whole awful night ten years earlier. He remembered all the blood and how it stung his eyes, leaving him squinting at the broken coffee pot and the open back door. Somehow, even then, he knew he'd never see Grace Allen again.

After the coffee pot hit him in the face, which he was pretty sure was done by Bryan while Grace Allen hugged him in the kitchen, he was stunned and it took him several minutes to slowly roll to his hands and knees, and then to his feet. When he wiped the blood from his eyes, they were both gone. He staggered outside and heard Bryan driving off in Grace Allen's car.

The pain in his face forced him back inside. At the kitchen sink he wet a towel in cold water and pressed it to his face. When he

199

pulled it away, the towel was soaked with blood. He rinsed it, took a few ice cubes out of the freezer, wrapped them in the towel, and pressed it against his left cheek. He walked back to the staircase, using his right hand on the walls to steady himself. All of those memories were quite clear, but after that, things got fuzzy, which he assumed was due to the head wound. A concussion most likely, although he never had it diagnosed.

Erebus wound up at the foot of the staircase, unable to mount the first stair because there were two first steps. He remembered that part clearly, the double vision and how hard it was to stand up. He leaned on the banister until it wobbled and nearly collapsed, and he felt strength draining away at the mere thought of going upstairs.

Only the vaguest memories remained of walking out the backdoor, like he was seeing everything through deep water, and none of it made sense. Later, he realized Bryan must have returned to finish him off and kill Herbert, and, somehow, he'd seen things through Bryan's eyes.

On the back stoop he—Bryan—found the gas can Erebus used for the lawnmower and had forgotten to put away. He carried it back into the house and started shaking it, sprinkling the fuel through each room, but hurrying so it didn't evaporate. A few minutes later he found himself again standing at the foot of the staircase. At first Erebus wondered where he was, since the view was what Bryan saw, but Erebus must have been upstairs with Herbert, which would explain how he saved his son.

As though he were watching a movie, he watched as Bryan poured the last of the gasoline on the staircase, dropped the empty can, ran back to the kitchen, rifled through the drawers until he found some towels, and piled them on the kitchen counter. Over the vent-a-hood he found a box of kitchen matches and lit the towels. Once they were burning, he grabbed one and threw it into the front room. Orange-yellow flames ran across the floor, climbed the front curtains, the chairs and couch, and licked up the walls.

Bryan grabbed the remaining towels and threw them at the foot of the staircase. Heat blasted him in the face as a rolling fireball enveloped the stairs as it roared upward to the second floor. Erebus stared through Bryan's eyes, transfixed by the flames all around him.

Sweat poured down his face, and when he wiped it from his eyes, his left hand came away red. That was the moment when his own memories cleared a little, when he no longer saw things through Bryan's eyes, and since the fire was raging upstairs, he must have already carried Herbert to the back yard, to safety. He *must* have.

The night was dark as he blinked in the firelight of his fully involved house. Somehow a wad of wet paper towels had wound up in his left hand and the heat from the flames drove him toward the back fence. Distant sirens grew louder by the second, but all Adrian could do was turn his head and watch as the roof caved in on everything he had ever owned or loved.

Except Herbert.

He still wore his pajamas, but stood next to his father reading a paperback, although how he could see the print in such deep shadow Adrian didn't know. It was enough that he had saved his son and the boy was safe.

His wife had left him the keys to the Ford Taurus with the rear bumper held on with tie-downs. Guiding Herbert into the backseat, Adrian didn't wait for the police, EMTs, or fire department. He started the car and, when he reached the end of the driveway, turned left, heading away from town and the hospitals there. Destination unknown.

The Command and Control Center for LEI Worldwide in Dallas bustled with activity at all times of day or night. The glass in Cynthia Witherbot's office at the center of the Kremlin had turned opaque as Servilius Tandro approached, passing two banks of workstations. What happened in her office was nobody's business except hers and whoever was with her, in this case the unfortunate Head of Communications Security. The mere electrification of the glass told the center all they needed to know about the tenor of the meeting, however; Tandro was in for one of the British Bitch's infamous tirades.

Arms folded and her familiar scowl set firmly on her face, only Witherbot's eyes moved as Lakesha buzzed Tandro into the office. He stepped to the front of her desk. A curt nod told him to sit.

"You know why you're here."

"Yes, ma'am. The leak."

"Well?"

Tandro drew a deep but silent breath. "We're getting close to finding him."

"You said that last week."

"He's very good at hiding his tracks."

"You said that last week, too. You keep saying 'he.' Have you at least determined that much?"

"Uh, no, ma'am, that's just a figure of speech."

"So, you've made no progress."

This time Tandro raised his finger. "Actually, ma'am, we have. Whoever the mole is, he or she is very, very good at this sort of thing, but they did make one mistake. They bounced an access request seven times before relaying it through a server in Nigeria, after which—"

"Spare me the details, Servilius, that is your job, not mine. Just tell me the status of the investigation."

"Speaking from his or her point of view, this could have been a fatal error, but tracking it down will take a lot of time."

Fatal indeed, she thought.

"How much time? Need I remind you that lives are at stake?"

Tandro pointed to the wall. "Ma'am, someone out there is betraying everyone who works here. I know it has happened once before, but this is the first time since I've been here, and, since it's my job to prevent this sort of thing, I take it very, very personally."

"All right then, Servilius, I believe you. But mark me well, no matter how much I like you personally, I need to see results, and soon. Is that clear?"

"It is, ma'am. Very clear."

Once Tandro had gone back to his own office, Witherbot left the glass energized and drummed her fingers on an open file folder on her desk. Whoever the mole was, he or she had to vanish quietly. Things like this were much better handled without muss or fuss. One day the guilty party was at work like any other day, the next they were simply gone. Nobody would know for certain what happened to them, although in a corporation that earned its money by killing people, it wouldn't be hard to guess. Still, it was that slight bit of uncertainty that kept everyone in line. Maybe they'd gotten a quick and painless double-tap to the head, but maybe torture was involved. LEI didn't exactly have a reputation for leniency toward its enemies, as its history of tracking down bin Laden showed. And if the corporation that grew from that beginning would never do such a thing now, it was useful for people to believe they would. It went a long way toward preventing the next mole.

But a quick shot to the back of the head? That was another story.

Witherbot picked up the encrypted line and dialed a number only she and Director Keel knew.

"To what do I owe the pleasure?" said a perfect baritone voice with the slightest hint of a Welsh accent. Witherbot couldn't help smiling. The previous time the accent was Swedish.

"Very soon I will need you and your brother's special talents, Ribaldo. Stand by for my call."

"What about Steed?"

She rolled her eyes, even though nobody could see her do it. "Dear God, no."

Witherbot outlined the situation.

"Might I speak freely?" Ribaldo said.

"That depends on what you have to say."

He chuckled. "You don't need Jürgen and me, Assistant Director, and I believe you know that. You need Steed."

Chapter Twenty-Two

The short pipe bomb weighed less than two pounds. In the pocket of Adrian's raincoat, it pulled down on the garment but not so much that it was obvious. He flipped up the collar to keep the rain out, which, when combined with the old school fedora, did an excellent job of making him invisible from any overhead cameras or any passersby. Not that anybody else was roaming the streets on a night like tonight. Grace Allen would have called the storm a frog strangler.

He splashed down the sidewalk as the cold December rain came down in sheets. He could see his target parked along the edge of the road, a 1969 black Corvette Stingray. The car belonged to Mark Shields—one of those LifeEnders assassins, code name Mad Mok.

The car was in the valet parking lot outside one of those steak restaurants where you pay one price, very high, and eat all the meat you want, the kind that Adrian had never been inside because he couldn't justify spending that much for dinner. Food was just food, after all; it all wound up in the same place. But it upset him that such a lowlife trigger man was inside eating a fine steak dinner that was paid for with blood money.

Adrian turned off the sidewalk to cross the street, but as he stepped off the curb he slipped and fell, just in case anybody was watching. Cameras would no doubt record him, but it was so dark and the rain so heavy, not even facial recognition would be able to ID him. Or so he told himself.

He fell into the street right behind the back bumper of the '69 'Vette. He pulled the bomb from his pocket, reached under the rear of the car, and pressed it against the gas tank. Except it didn't stick. He moved the pipe bomb around, pushing it against various parts of the car, until he finally heard a soft *thud* as the magnets grabbed onto something.

He got to his feet and brushed off his jacket, which, given the deluge, seemed pointless. Nobody seemed to notice Adrian's fall, or much care what he was doing. A valet might have been watching from a stand in front of the restaurant, but he couldn't be sure even of that. He turned his head side to side to make sure nobody was paying attention, reset his hat, and resumed walking. The cold rain soaked his shoes and ran down the back of his neck, but he barely felt it. He crossed the street, walked around a building, and back to his waiting car, where he had a good view of the Stingray.

Herbert sat where he'd left him in the back seat. The boy resembled a big, green marshmallow wrapped in a forest green winter coat. Like every other moment of his life, Herbert never looked up from his reading. This time it was *At the Mountains of Madness* by H.P. Lovecraft. Adrian never wondered how Herbert was able to read in the near total darkness.

"I've heard of Lovecraft, but I've never read him," he said. "Is he as good as they say?"

Herbert held up a thumb. His son had grown quieter since Grace Allen was killed, as if the boy knew what had happened to his mother. Not that Adrian had mentioned the accident to Herbert, but somehow the boy seemed to know. A boy needs his mother, he figured. It must have been a special connection between mother and son. That's how the boy knew. That had to be it. And now the boy was grieving for his mother.

He grabbed a pack of peanut butter crackers from the passenger seat and popped one into his mouth. Reaching over the seat, he put them in reach of his son.

"Hungry?"

Herbert just kept reading. The boy hadn't eaten much lately and it was beginning to worry Adrian. It wasn't healthy for anybody to mourn that long, especially a growing boy.

He thumbed the controls of his smart phone and brought up a music channel. He kept talking to Herbert without really expecting an answer.

"It was a good idea you had. About the bomb, I mean. I can't tell you how much safer this is than trying to shoot someone. You're a very smart young man, son, and I'm so glad we're doing this together."

Herbert nodded and waved without looking up.

Mark Shields glanced at the maître d' as he surveyed the dining room.

"Jonathan, this was a fantastic meal, and the steak was excellent. Please pass along my compliments to the staff." Raising his glass of bourbon in a silent toast, he swirled the liquid around the glass and then held it to his nose. The smell of caramel, smoke, and just a hint of cherry enhanced the pleasure of the liquor before he drained the last swallow. "The bourbon was also perfect."

"I am very gratified by your kind words, Mr. Shields. It is our pleasure, as always."

"So, what did Adam serve me?" Shields said. He always let the bartender, Adam, select the bourbon for his meal. The senior bartender knew more about alcoholic drinks than anyone in the city, and was Memphis' only Certified Bourbon Steward. "I really liked this one. The sweet oak flavor, just the right amount of heat." He gave the now-empty glass a final sniff. "Damn that's good."

Jonathan smiled, pleased that his friend approved of the whiskey. "Would you care for another?"

Shields held up a hand. "Thank you, but I'm driving."

"Very wise of you, sir. Adam asked me to pass along that tonight's selection was a limited release from Buffalo Trace called Pappy Van Winkle 25. It is, shall we say, available only to those with the most discriminating palate? May I inform him that you approve of his choice?"

"You may tell him he's a damned genius. I hope it's not too gauche to ask for a doggie bag."

"Of course not, sir. Our four-legged friends deserve the best, too. I hope you have an exceptional evening. If you'll excuse me." The maître d' turned to go.

Mark sniffed the empty glass. "Jonathan?"

The man turned to face him.

"Maybe a double to go?"

The other man gave a small nod and waved to his waitress before disappearing into the back room.

Ten minutes later, the young woman brought him his check in a leather wallet. She also carried his coat. She sat the wallet on the table, then reached under the coat and pulled out a simple brown bag. She placed it on the table with a slight clink of glass.

Mark signed the check, unsurprised at the bill's four figure total, and pulled on his coat. When he picked up the bag, he felt the shape of two long bottles and smiled as he remembered the flavor of the bourbon.

Worth every damned cent.

"Thank you, Rachel. It has been an extreme pleasure, as usual." He passed the wallet back to the young lady and headed for the door.

Shields rarely let anything bother him, but now he felt both more content and more energized than usual. Life was good! He stood in the doorway for a moment, breathing in the aroma of rain, which had a way of disinfecting the stink of the city and leaving it smelling fresh and…not clean exactly, but natural, like all the steel and concrete and asphalt weren't manmade monstrosities but rather the handiwork of Nature.

He tucked the brown bag inside his coat and trotted to the car. The wet Corvette sparkled as raindrops reflected under the streetlight. He unlocked it and slipped inside, where the smell of the rain was replaced by that of oiled leather. Mark placed his package in the passenger seat and slipped his key into the ignition.

The engine came to life with the low-throated grumble of a predator, and Shields felt the vibration under his feet and buttocks like he was riding a tiger. This was the ride for a Shooter, and despite the custom modifications that could turn it into a rocket whenever he wanted, there was no need to show off. That wasn't the point. He knew what it could do, he knew the power under the hood, and that was enough. So, he conserved the engine as he cruised down Poplar Avenue until he saw the on-ramp to Interstate 240.

Adrian was worried the sleek Corvette could leave his little Ford in the dust whenever its owner wanted and get out of range too fast for him to set off the bomb. He considered blowing it up at the curb but decided to stick with his original plan. The Ford's engine coughed a few times, but the engine caught, so he dropped it into gear and chased after the black car.

"Here we go, Herbert. Keep your head down, son."

Adrian moved his little car from lane to lane as he slowly gained on the killer. Three—no five—car lengths, he told himself. That should be close enough. Ahead, he saw a streetlight turn from green to yellow then red. The Corvette was stopped. Adrian stopped behind it, keeping a three-car-length distance even though there were no other cars between them. It was perfect. This way no innocent bystanders would get hurt.

Then another car pulled up behind him and blasted its horn. He froze for a second, unsure of what to do. Quickly, he turned on his emergency lights and waved for the car to go around him. He'd just have to keep tailing the 'Vette and wait for another chance. The car behind him finally changed lanes to pass him on the right. It was a Mercedes SUV. Adrian glanced over and saw a middle finger sticking out the driver's partially lowered window. The car was past him before he could respond.

"Thanks, asshole, that makes things easier…"

If he wanted to get them both he'd have to time it perfectly. He'd done the math a dozen times in his head, and he was pretty sure that three car lengths was far enough, but with Herbert in the car he couldn't take any chances. He reached for the garage door opener attached to the sunshade visor and waited.

When the light turned green, both the 'Vette and the Mercedes started forward, more or less parallel to each other. Adrian paused, his mind calculating distances…and pushed the button.

The blast shook the Ford even as he hit the gas pushing the car into a hard U-turn. A wave of heat pushed it sideways until he regained control. A yellow-orange fireball rolled into the night sky and the hulk of the Corvette drifted to the curb. The Mercedes kept going despite the flames on its hood and roof.

Adrian pulled to the curb a couple blocks away and opened the door.

"Stay here, son, and keep your head down. Don't let anyone see you. I'll be right back."

He ran toward the burning car.

What traffic there was had come to a stop behind the Corvette in the westbound lanes, but not those going east. Apparently, boiling black smoke and the chance of being caught in a secondary explosion wasn't dangerous enough to stop some people. So, Adrian had to dodge cars to cross the street and get close to the burning mess. A few courageous people braved the rain to try and help, but most stayed in their cars. As he passed them, he could see more than a few of the faces were lit by their phones. Odds were good the cops would be on site soon.

The back half of the car was gone, the fiberglass body melting at the break. Bits of smoking wreckage lay in a rough 75-foot-wide circle around the wreck. Adrian moved closer, until the heat from the burning car seared his skin, even thirty feet away. He skirted around the side of the car and, with his hands blocking most of the glare from the fire, peeked between his fingers. The initial flames had subsided as the gasoline burned off, and through the smoke, dark, and rain he could make out a few details in the firelight. Something charred and vaguely manlike sat upright in the driver's seat. The head of the body was leaning forward as if it were sleeping with its chin on its chest.

"Get used to the feel, you murderous turd. You get to feel that for the rest of eternity."

Adrian grinned as he said it out loud. He'd not only discovered that he enjoyed killing bad people, he liked cursing, too. There was a freedom to it all that he'd never felt in his life. It didn't occur to him to keep his voice down, besides, the roar of the fire drowned out everything else.

Satisfied his test run had gone perfectly, he traced his steps back to his car. The few people who had tried to help hadn't approached anywhere near as close as Adrian, and as he walked back to his car, they called encouragement and told him how brave he was to try to help the poor man. He waved back, reveling in a moment of adulation.

"How bad is it?" someone asked.

"As bad as it looks. That guy never had a chance."

Back at the Ford, Adrian watched the fire burn until he heard the sound of sirens. "I think it's time we get gone, Herbert. What do you think, bud?" He didn't bother to check his son's response. The boy would give him a thumbs up. He always did. Herbert, clever boy that he was, was still only eight years old. He loved his father and trusted his father to do what was best, and Adrian took that responsibility very seriously.

Driving east on Poplar, Adrian turned on the car radio and pounded the steering wheel to Queen's "Another One Bites the Dust." If that wasn't irony, he didn't know the meaning of the word.

The bomb had been more of an experiment than anything else; Herbert's idea of how to carry out the rest of their mission. The boy pointed out the dangers inherent in going toe to toe with professional killers, people whose very job title was "Shooter." Herbert's bomb suggestion evened the odds. It just took a little research on the internet to find plans for a simple pipe bomb, and an even simpler activator. He bought a lot of fireworks for their gunpowder but hadn't needed much of what he'd bought since the car's gas tank provided the majority of the explosive force. The bomb acted more as a trigger than anything else.

Now he just had to figure out the best way to use it in a hospital. Assuming Sweetwater lived, of course.

Chapter Twenty-Three

Elvis Presley Trauma Center, Memphis, TN

Voices, faint and muffled...followed by nothing. Not blackness, not dreams, not even the ghosts of Cooper and Grace Allen, just...nothing.

Until...something? A faint line of light, maybe? Beeping, the scuffing of shoes on linoleum, words...and Sweetwater realized he couldn't move. He was aware of his body again, but he couldn't move it. His brain felt like it was stuffed in cotton. Thinking was hard, exhausting.

He slept.

Another sound; a soft beep. Different from the earlier one. *Beep. Beep. Beep.*

He slept again. Time had no meaning, no way to separate and organize the visceral memories that were all he could recall later.

After the beeping, his next memory was that the air smelled different. Still not fully conscious, Sweetwater tried to take a deep breath, but it hurt his chest too much. Short shallow breaths didn't produce pain. But the air smelled different, or didn't it smell at all? Now there was no odor, just air passing through his nostrils on the way to his lungs. His nose itched, now it was clogged. The beeping came...back, *beep, beep.* Sweetwater made a concerted effort to open his eyes, but they were so heavy, and he was so tired.

He slept.

Someone held his hand and there were voices around him. Sweetwater listened, trying to make sense of what he heard, but his brain was like a rusty generator coming back to life, slow and sputtering. Was that crying? Someone squeezed his hand. Did they say his name? He tried to squeeze back, but his hand wouldn't obey. He tried to…and then he slept.

Sweetwater scrunched his eyelids as sunlight burned through his eyelids. Was he still in that hotel room in Dallas? He wanted to sleep. He was so tired, but the light wouldn't let him. The dry mouth and headache felt like the whiskey hangover. He fought down a moment of déjà vu and groaned.

"It's about time you came back to life," said a harsh woman's voice with a British accent. "I can finally go home now. Keep me informed."

Am I in hell?

A second female voice had a different tone.

"Stop it, Mother! Sweetwater? Luther, are you in there?"

Sweetwater tried to bring his hand up to cover his eyes, but he didn't have the strength to lift it more than a few inches from the bed. He turned his face away from the sunbeam with another groan and tried again to open his eyes.

This time his eyelids parted. His vision swam, but he was able to blink the blurriness away. He took it all in with a few glances: hospital bed with him in it, wires, monitors, tubes, and IV lines. In the far corner was a small desk with a laptop and a rather uncomfortable looking office chair. Then the sunlight became too much, and he closed his eyes again.

"Luther," the nice voice said. "Thank God you're back."

"Light," he rasped. He coughed, which brought with it a spasm of intense pain. He hissed through his teeth as the pain leveled off then slowly subsided. Someone gave his hand a gentle squeeze. "Where?"

"You're in the hospital, Luther. You were shot."

"Which?"

"They call it the Med, but its real name is the Elvis Presley Trauma Center."

Name, name…He knew her name. He knew that he knew it but couldn't place it. She was the computer hacker…Teri something. Her name was Teri. He tried to open his eyes again, but they seemed to be glued shut.

"Teri," he tried, although it sounded more like "tay-ree." "Teri Warden."

"Good job, Two-Bit!"

"Hate that name."

"I know. Sorry. I'm here, Luther." She squeezed his hand, "I'm going to get the doctor. I'll be right back."

"Mmmrrr…"

He gave a shallow nod. Everything hurt; his chest, his head, even his feet were cramping. He focused on shallow breaths as he waited for Warden to return.

"Mr. Sweetwater, how nice to finally meet you." It was a woman's voice, strong and confident, but not a voice he recognized. "I'm glad you have returned from the dead."

He opened his left eye enough to allow in a sliver of light. A tall black woman in scrubs and a doctor's coat stood beside the bed inspecting him.

"Not as glad as me." It was barely a whisper, but the doctor smiled.

There was a rustling and the sunbeam that was tormenting him seemed to fade.

"That help?" Warden said.

"Mmrrr…"

A hand reached out and took his wrist, two fingers slipping to the inside. "I'm Doctor Tamika Wilson. You give us quite a scare, Mister Sweetwater, but your vitals are fine now. How are you feeling?"

"Hurt like hell." This time his voice was stronger and clearer, as his body seemed to be waking a piece at a time. "Feels like I've been shooted."

Wilson squinted at him until she realized he'd used the wrong word on purpose. After giving him a brief examination and making notes on the clipboard, she hung it up and waggled her fingers goodbye. The Mona Lisa smile fit her face better than a broad grin.

"Try to not get shooted again, if you can help it," she said and left.

Opening both eyes in the reduced light, Sweetwater could squint enough to see Teri Warden's young face. She was prettier than he remembered.

"Did I hear the British Bitch?"

"Don't tell her I told you, but she's been here for a couple of days. Making sure anybody and everybody knew they'd better save your silly ass."

"I have a silly ass?"

"Her words, not mine."

"How would you describe it?"

"Somebody's feeling better, but your drip is shit."

Sweetwater glanced at the IVs feeding into his arm. "Huh?"

"Don't go 404 on me now, Two-Bit."

"English?"

Warden closed her eyes and shook her head, but her tight smile was indulgent. "Jeez, dude, it's like talking to my dad. I said you look terrible. 404 means don't be a moron. As to your ass, it looks like it's on your face. You need a bath and a shave and maybe a haircut."

"How close did I come?" he said, turning his head away from her.

"To dying, you mean?"

He nodded.

"You flatlined on the operating table and again in post-op, but it wasn't the bullet that got you, it was the blood loss. The bullet struck the sixth right rib at an oblique angle and deflected out your side. It broke the rib and the force drove it inward, where it nicked the lateral thoracic artery. That's what nearly killed you. If it hadn't punctured the artery, they'd have wrapped you in gauze and sent you on your way."

"The story of my life. Can I have some water?"

"Sip it. If you gulp you could choke."

Warden held the blue hospital cup close enough for the straw to brush his lips. He caught the end and sucked in cold water, gulping anyway.

"I thought I told you not to gulp," Warden said, giving him a look that obviously meant "are you trying to kill yourself again?"

He grinned and laid his head back, barking a laugh at his own joke before he even spoke.

"Don't expect me to ever tell you that."

"Oh Christ, that's gross."

Sweetwater laughed harder, grimacing as pain shot through his chest. He coughed, which hurt even worse, but he kept giggling anyway.

It was like the time in high school when he fought an offensive tackle nicknamed Rolls, for the rolls of fat around his neck, when he tried to snake his date to the junior prom, right there on the dance floor. The guy outweighed him by 130 pounds and, as expected, Sweetwater got his ass beat, but not before kicking Rolls hard in the nuts. Although bleeding from a busted nose, Sweetwater stayed at the prom, got slapped on the back by most of the other students and got laid afterward. Rolls collapsed and crawled away, crying most of the way. Regardless of how bad it hurt, Sweetwater and his friends laughed until they cried then, too, like it was the funniest thing that ever happened. Of course, it didn't hurt that they were drunk out of their minds.

"I'm sorry," he said once he stopped laughing, which happened when the pain got his full attention. "Oh fuck, that hurts."

"Serves you right, but since I'm so awesome I'll get the nurse to bring you something for the pain."

"There are those pretty gray eyes, I heard so much about," said another voice, almost cutting Warden off as she spoke. A thin African American woman in a nurse's uniform came in and raised her eyebrows at Warden. "I brought you something for the pain, Mister Sweetwater. Are you allergic to anything?"

"Work."

"Aren't we all? But what about drugs?"

"Not that I remember."

"He's not," Warden said.

"Are you his wife, sister, or girlfriend?"

"No, but I work with him and we have access to his medical history."

"HIPAA allows that?"

"In our line of work, yes, it does."

"Do you work for the government?"

Warden pursed her lips, as if trying to think of how to phrase her answer. "Hypothetically speaking, if we did have government jobs that were so sensitive that HIPAA laws didn't apply to us and I shared that with a nosy nurse who didn't have a security clearance, what do you think would happen to her?"

The nurse's face went completely blank, but there was no mistaking the animosity in her eyes.

"Take these," she said to Sweetwater, placing two oblong white pills into his hand, followed by the water cup and straw. He wasted no time doing as she told him.

"I'm sorry about my friend," he whispered. "She's not a very nice person."

"No, she's not."

The nurse left without another word. Sweetwater couldn't help giggling again.

"They stitched your artery back together," Warden said. "But if you keep this up and rip out the sutures, don't count on me calling anybody."

222 | HOY & WEBB

"They bring dinner around six, but that's three hours from now. If I get you something to eat, do you think you'll keep it down?"

"No promises, but a Big Mac would be great."

"I was thinking more along the lines of a protein shake. They have them downstairs in the gift shop."

"Not my first choice."

"We have chalk and brown chalk flavors."

"That sounds yummy," Sweetwater said. He closed his eyes and lay his head on the pillow. The pain meds had started to kick in. "And who can resist brown chalk?"

"Good choice. And if all that protein makes you puke, I won't have to clean it up."

Sweetwater heard soft footfalls as she left the room, then he slept.

He jerked awake at the scrape of a chair, which caused him to cry out in pain. Coughing brought more pain, which led to him sucking in air in shallow breaths, which led to him hyperventilating. He clenched his teeth and grabbed the rails of the hospital bed.

"Fun times, huh?" Warden said.

She held out a rectangular carton of chocolate protein drink with a straw in the top. He took a sip and leaned back.

"The doctor came back while you were gone," he said, "and said what I needed more than anything now was sex. Lots and lots of sex."

Warden considered that for a moment. "I think I agree."

"You do?" he said, surprised.

"Yeah, and I can't think of any reason not to do it while you're here."

"You can't?"

"Nope."

Was he really hearing her right? In truth, sex was the last thing he wanted, but Sweetwater would never admit that to Warden. He'd noticed how the cheeks on her otherwise heart-shaped face had tiny little bulges along the bottom, which he found adorable. So if she wanted to screw him in his hospital bed, patched artery or not, sign him up!

"Lock the door before that nasty piece of work nurse comes back."

"I don't lock hospital doors, Two-Bit. Besides, it'll take me hours to get to your place and back anyway. I'll need your key, and you need to tell me where you keep your blowup dolls and if there's a special one you want me to bring."

A light knock at the door got their attention. A balding, heavy-set man holding a tray of dishes covered in plastic wrap stood in the doorway beside a cart filled with shelves.

"Dinner?" he said nervously his eyebrows raised. "I can come back."

The monitor showed spikes for Sweetwater's blood pressure and pulse rate. Warden laughed until tears ran down her cheeks.

"E asy, cowboy," said Teri Warden's calm voice from the right side of his bed. The cup with the straw returned to his lips. "Drink some."

"You're not my mom," he said in a scratchy whisper.

"Thank God for small favors. But ssshhh…you overdid it last time."

"How long was I out this time?"

"Just a couple of hours."

"Why do I feel like shit?"

"That's a side effect of getting shot."

The lighting in the room was dim and darkness showed around the closed blinds. Despite that, Sweetwater squinted to study her face. She really was cute…not that he'd tell her that. He grabbed the end of the straw in his lips and sipped the water between coughing spasms. It took him just under a half a minute to quiet the coughing fit.

"There's more you're not telling me, isn't there?"

"Huh." Rising from the orange-seated chair, Warden walked over to peek through the blinds into the darkness outside. "She really did underestimate you."

"Witherbot?"

"Yeah. All right then, here's the rest of it. When the bullet hit your rib, it didn't just puncture your artery, splinters hit your lung and it collapsed. Apparently, that really complicated what the ER surgeons had to do to save you. Somehow, they found out about you being a Shooter, and when you died they wanted to let you stay dead right there on the table…"

"What happened? Did you do something?"

"Not me, no. Shit, Luther, look at me, what could I do even if I wanted to? It was Witherbot. She was here less than two hours after you were shot, and the surgical staff got the impression that their lives depended on them saving yours."

"Holy fuck, she did that for me?"

"You're a Shooter now, Luther; she'd do that for any of us…I mean, you."

"Because of her I'm still here?"

"More or less, yeah. I know she's not the most cuddly boss you could ever have, but once you're in, you're in. She takes care of her own. And let's face it, this isn't a cuddly sort of business."

"How long have I been here?"

Before she could answer, a nurse came in, followed by the doctor. Apparently satisfied with the readings on his chart, she handed the clipboard to the nurse. Her stony-but obviously unhappy expression hadn't changed from her first visit. She pulled out a pen light, stepped close to Sweetwater, aimed the light into his eyes one at a time, and straightened. The whole process took no more than five seconds, which told Sweetwater all he needed to know about the quality of care he could expect.

"You have been with us for five days. You came in with a single gunshot wound to the right side of your chest. You underwent a complex surgery and died twice but were revived both times." She dropped the pen light into her pocket and stuck two fingers in Sweetwater's right hand. "Squeeze my fingers."

Sweetwater made fists around the doctor's fingers. The grip was there but the strength was gone.

"That's fine." As if reading a perp his rights off a laminated card, the doctor informed him of his condition. "The bullet struck your sixth rib and exited, most of the damage was caused by bone splinters in your lung. By the time you came in you'd also lost a lot of blood."

The doctor pulled down the bed sheet and raised his gown to inspect a couple of tubes that disappeared through a cut in his belly. The clear tubes were full of yellow pus and blood.

"That's appetizing," Warden said.

Sweetwater snapped his eyes closed. "Oh god, Doc, warn a fellow, would you?" He turned his head to the side, but even with his eyes closed and head turned he could still see the image of the tubes in his brain.

"I was told you were a tough guy." Her tone could have flash frozen boiling oil.

"I'm just not a fan of asshole doctors."

Warden half jumped out of her chair. "Luther!"

The doctor ignored her. "Next time I'll let you stay dead, Mr. Sweetwater, and I'm willing to bet there will be a next time." She didn't storm out, however, as Sweetwater expected she might. "You are now in recovery. All that's left is letting your body recover from the trauma. How fast your strength returns depends on how well you follow the rehabilitation protocols, but you should be fully recovered within three months. Do you have any questions for me?"

"How long will I be in here?"

"That is mostly up to your body. Probably another five days to a week."

"A week?"

"Yes, and even then you'll have to take it easy. Stay in bed. If you try to do too much too soon, you'll just be putting undue stress on your body."

"Right. Look, I'm sorry we got off on the wrong foot."

The doctor hung up the clipboard. "If you need anything just ask one of the nurses." She turned on one heel and left.

"I think she wants you to ask her out," Warden said.

"She *is* my type."

Warden raised her left eyebrow in a question.

"Rich."

"And you know this how?"

"She's a doctor."

Warden leaned back, rubbed her eyes, and made a point of shaking her head so he could see it. "God, I hate it when the British Bitch is right."

He began to drowse again from the latest dose of meds the nurse had given him during the doctor's visit. "Are you sayin' I'm stupid?" The words were barely out before he began to snore softly.

"Not stupid, Luther," she said, "just naïve."

Chapter Twenty-Four

Elvis Presley Trauma Center, Memphis, TN

The Med, as the Elvis Presley Trauma Center had been known in Memphis for decades, was the only Level One trauma center for more than 150 miles in any direction. As such, and despite the new draconian laws regarding murder, gangs kept the trauma bays filled with gunshot victims to go along with the usual drownings, people cut from mangled cars, and drug overdoses. Rush hour came between midnight and four am.

The wail of an ambulance roused Sweetwater from a drugged sleep at 2:26. He'd half-rolled onto his right side, and through half-open lids read the digital clock beside his bed. Teri Warden snored lightly on the bench-style couch against the outside wall under the blinds, with the only light coming from a recessed fixture over the nurse's station near his room. Lying in that position hurt Sweetwater's chest so, after closing his eyes again, he rolled onto his back to go back to sleep.

But in the same way that some people could sense danger, he could sense the presence of...something else. Through the fog of sleep, he cracked open his left eye.

"Ah!" he cried, trying to scoot backward on the mattress. Two empty eye sockets set in a face of flaking black skin leaned within inches of Sweetwater's nose. Straight, white teeth grinned past the char-broiled remains of lips that had vaporized in fire.

Warden kicked off her covers and was at his bedside within seconds.

"What?" she cried, her hair tangled. "What's the matter?"

"That!" he said, pointing at the ruined face, which hadn't moved.

"Huh?"

"Can't you see him?"

"Luther, wake up, you're dreaming."

"No, I'm wide awake! He's right here, all burnt up like somebody poured gas over Gumby and tossed him a lit match."

Involuntarily, Warden took a step back and straightened. Glancing around the room, she had the same wide-eyed expression as paranormal investigators on all those TV shows.

"They're here, aren't they? That Cooper guy and the woman, Grace Allen Tarbeau."

The roasted face filled Sweetwater's vision. To see past it he had to move sideways a few inches. Four other figures stood nearby. He recognized two in the back as Cooper and Grace Allen despite their advanced states of decomposition: Cooper by his ever-present cigarette and Grace Allen by the sparse strands of red hair draping down her forehead. Over the shoulder of the burned-up figure was a big black guy with his arms folded, standing beside a slim brunette. Despite their dark color, both had a greenish hue with patches of dark red. Neither looked happy to see him.

"Fuckin' A, they're here! They're here in the back, but now there's five of them, and Barbeque Boy won't get out of my face!"

Warden turned as footsteps grew loud in the hallway, undoubtedly the nurse coming to find out what the yelling was all about.

"Luther, ssshhh, they're gonna think you're tripping."

But Sweetwater wasn't listening, he was fixated on a flap of crispy skin hanging off the dead man's chin. When the corpse spoke, his teeth appeared to be champing like a horse.

"My name is Shields, dickhead," he said. "Mark Shields, and it's your fault I'm dead right now."

The night nurse was tiny, but came through the door ready to kick ass.

"What's going on in here, Mister Sweetwater?"

"Bad dream," Warden said, stroking his hair like she was his girlfriend. "It's okay, this happens sometimes."

Sweetwater's mouth hung open as Shields came close enough for him to smell the charred flesh, and he didn't say anything as the nurse checked his vitals.

"Fuckin' rookie," Shields said. "Fuckin' incompetent, mother fuckin' new guy fucks up and I get killed. One minute I was livin' the dream, filled up with the finest beef steak and two bottles of forty-thousand-dollar whiskey sitting on the seat next to me to drink whenever I felt like it. And the next thing you know I look like the stuff you scrape out of a dirty oven. I had a '69 Corvette, shit for brains. Better than any wet dream you've ever had. A gorgeous, sleek, black 1969 Chevrolet Corvette that's now a heap of melted fiberglass, and it's your fucking fault! I was single, good lookin', and gettin' laid with a different girl every night. I had three million in the bank—three fucking million dollars! And now I'm not just dead, I've gotta listen to some swinging dick Marine asswipe call me Barbeque Boy, and I don't fucking like it!"

"I don't even know who you are," Sweetwater said. It was impossible to read facial expressions in a man with no eyes, nose, lips, and with skin the consistency of an unwrapped Egyptian mummy.

The nurse glanced at Sweetwater and then at Warden. "I'm Dottie Laforce, Mister Sweetwater, I've been your nurse the past two nights. Don't you recognize me?"

"The nightmare rattled him," Warden said. "He just needs to go back to sleep. He'll be fine in the morning."

Sweetwater's eyes looked past Shields to the black man.

"You must be Bonney," he said.

"No, not Bonnie, Dottie," the nurse said. "Dottie Laforce. Are you all right Mister Sweetwater?"

He finally heard the nurse's voice and focused on her. Having said his piece, Shields backed off a little.

"I'm fine…uhh, Dottie, right? Sorry, I get weird dreams sometimes and it takes a while to shake them. I'll be fine."

"You can't go gettin' excited or moving around a lot. You've gotta lie as still as you can. I know it's uncomfortable, but you've got to."

"You know what's uncomfortable?" said the woman with Bonney. "Being dead, that's what. It's cold and dank and all you've got to do is watch your body rot off your bones."

"I'd kick your ass if I could," Bonney said, and Sweetwater had no doubt he meant it.

He ignored both of them as best he could. "Thanks for checking on me, Bonnie—I mean Dottie. Sorry. I'll be fine."

It took another minute to convince her, but eventually Laforce left, came back with two sleeping pills and two pain pills, and waited for him to take them. Only then did she leave for good.

"Having fun yet, Luther?" Cooper called from the back of the room. The orange ash of his cigarette flared as he inhaled. Sweetwater briefly wondered how he could smoke without functioning lungs before Bonney got his attention again.

"Those pills are gonna knock you out boy, but don't think you're getting off that easy, 'cause we aren't going anywhere. We'll be here when you wake up."

"For how long?" Sweetwater said, regretting how weak it sounded the instant the words left his mouth.

This time Grace Allen answered. Her lower jaw had come unhinged as the muscles holding it in place decayed, so now it just flopped around as she spoke.

"Until this is over," she said.

A drian Erebus huddled in the tiny motel room's bathroom. The television was blasting in the other room, some action movie with lots of machine guns and explosions, the kind of thing Herbert loved to watch.

From his back pocket, he pulled out a rumpled photo with the name Mark Shields written across the bottom in red Sharpie, along with the asshole's code name, Mad Mok. He picked up an old Zippo, flicked the little wheel, and ran the flame along the bottom edge of the photo. The film on front bubbled as the paper backing burned. With a stylized snap of his wrist, the lighter clicked shut, bringing images of Humphrey Bogart to his mind. If any man knew how to handle a lighter, it was Bogie. Fire climbed along the photo's edges and curls of smoke tickled the bathroom smoke detector. Nothing happened. Dead batteries, he assumed.

The flames licked his finger like tiny yellow tongues. Erebus watched them burn his flesh. Pain shot into his hand, which fascinated the part of his brain that craved stimulus. But there was too much yet to accomplish to allow real damage to the finger, so he dropped the blackened photo into the toilet and the flames went out with a hiss. Then he flushed. The ashes broke apart in the swirl and disappeared through the hole in the bottom.

Just like Mark Shields, burned, gone, and forgotten.

He opened the bathroom door, waving his hands to scatter the smell of burning paper. Added to the room's overall dirty odor came the reek of mold when he opened the mini fridge and grabbed a can of Busch for him and a Coke for Herbert. His son lay stretched out on the bed watching TV on a set so old it had a picture tube. When he put the can of soda on the floor, unopened, Herbert leaned around him to keep watching the movie.

Erebus used to open the cans for his son, but lately Herbert wasn't finishing them, he'd just leave the cans sitting around, going flat. When Erebus accidentally knocked over an old, mostly full can of soda, it made a nasty mess that attracted ants. Now he just left them sealed, his son would open it when he was ready. If the boy didn't drink it, he'd just put it back in the fridge later.

Erebus sat down on his bed and looked at the television, not really watching it. "You remember the guy that broke into our house last week?" A memory of the house on fire intruded on his thoughts and became part of the narrative. "He's the one who burned it down and tried to kill us, remember? A friend of mine said he was still alive." Erebus sat quiet for a bit, wondering just how much he should tell Herbert. "I'm worried he might come after us again. Really, son, I'm worried he might come after *you* again. He wants to kill you because you're my son. He hates us because…because of your mom. He thinks if we're dead, she'll run off with him." Herbert didn't react, his eyes stayed glued to the TV. "Everything I do is to protect you, you know that, right? I really got lucky last time, son. If he catches us again…he'll be more careful next time. I think he'll kill me—kill us!" The last part came out just a bit louder than a whisper.

Erebus wiped away tears to hide them from his son. He didn't want Herbert to see just how afraid he was of Luther Sweetwater in that moment. Sometimes he wasn't. Sometimes something came over him, and he could stand up to a charging elephant. But now he was scared.

Herbert frowned, scowled at his father, and sat up. Erebus could feel his son's disgust. It was like a black mesh curtain thrown over his head. Herbert held up his hands, balled them into fists, and put his hands together, the knuckles touching. Then he pulled them apart and uncurled his fingers.

"Boom."

Erebus blinked, his mouth open as if stupefied. Herbert rarely spoke to him.

"Another bomb?" The concept blew his mind, sort of. He thought back to the burning fireball of the Corvette. The mere thought of something like that going off in a hospital horrified him. He had never killed an innocent before, and a bomb that big going off in a hospital might kill a bunch of people. Why would Herbert tell him to do that? Unless…of course, the boy saw what Erebus didn't. People that helped hitmen kill innocent people couldn't also be innocent; they were every bit as guilty as the killer, and guilty people should die.

"All right son, I'm convinced. Let's say that we build another bomb. How do we get it to him? He's in the hospital. How do we get it in there without getting caught?"

During his career as a teacher, Erebus preached his own theory about synchronicity and, as if verifying its validity, at that moment, a commercial came on television advertising an upcoming beauty pageant. Two women stood side by side while an announcer read a name. The camera zoomed in for a close up on one of them. Somebody placed a tiara on her head and another person put a bouquet of red roses in her arms.

"Of course," Erebus said. "We won't even have to go in the hospital. Wait until I tell that blowhard Tyler Easton about this. Let's see him make fun of my theory *then*." He glanced over at his son and realized the boy hadn't opened his soda. "I'm going to need your help again son, since it looks like we're back in the bomb-making business."

Sweetwater scrunched up his face. "Sorry that you saved my life?"

Warden paced a few seconds before answering, and Sweetwater noticed she had the slightest roll to her right hip.

"No, I'm sorry I dragged you into that place. I should have called the cops or something. We never should have barged inside."

"That's kinda my job, you know."

"No, it's not. You're a trigger man. Your job is to complete contracts, not go toe to toe with slobbering psychopaths." She looked up, and he saw how closely her cheekbones resembled the British

Bitch, cheekbones now streaked with tears. "Stop being so under-standing, damn it, I almost got you killed. This was all my fault, so get mad at me. Go on, yell, cuss, throw a shoe."

Sweetwater felt one side of his cheek raise in a half-smile. "The shoe might have to wait a few weeks. But, you know, I thought I *was* a trigger man." He paused, wondering just how much to confess. "Look, I'm not very good at this job. Working with you to trace down that crazy fuck was the most fun I've had." He paused again. "Well, right up until he shot me; that part sucked." He laughed, which sent pain ripping across his chest and armpits. Gritting his teeth, he grabbed the bed rails and fought through the urge to cough. After five seconds the spasms eased, and Sweetwater relaxed back into his bed.

"Fuck," he said through shallow breaths, "I can't handle any more coughing." Warden came back to his bedside. Something about her brought out the tough guy in him. At least, as tough as he could be lying in a hospital bed with tubes in his arms.

"So, partner, can you track down this piece of shit and get us an-other shot at the title?"

"He might kill you next time, Luther."

"Not possible. Nobody gets to shoot me twice."

Chapter Twenty-Five

Elvis Presley Trauma Center, Memphis, TN

"I was hoping you'd want back in the action," Warden said. "It's hard to know how people will react to a near-death experience." She fetched her tablet from the desk in the corner and pulled up a data sheet. "I'm not sure what you remember, but this is what we know. First, his name is Adrian Erebus."

Sweetwater remembered some of the discussion from before he was shot, but Warden was on a roll so he stretched out in the bed and listened. He had been awake for an hour and was already feeling as if he had run a 10K.

"Erebus married Grace Allen Erebus at Third Assembly Missionary Baptist Church near Semple, in Fayette County, Tennessee."

"They had one son, Herbert Wilson Erebus. Nothing noteworthy happened until approximately ten years ago, when it all went to shit. In one night Herbert died inside the family home. The Tennessee Bureau of Investigation was called in because the house burned to the ground and the fire chief declared it arson. Only the TBI had the resources to investigate it properly. After a reconstructive autopsy, the cause was listed as a blow to the head with a hammer or hammer-like instrument.

"Adrian Erebus drove himself to a clinic in Oakland, who immediately called an ambulance. Apparently, he was cut to ribbons and almost died from massive blood loss. As for Grace Allen, she disap-

239

peared not to be heard again for ten years. The rest of that story you already know."

"Her new husband put a contract on her."

"Yes, but hold that thought. First let me tell you about the old husband, Adrian. When Adrian left the hospital, he was the primary suspect for the murder and house fire, although there really wasn't much evidence tying him to it. The sheriff and district attorney thought they'd found their man, and they pushed hard for a confession, but Erebus was catatonic and never said a word to his interrogators. He was declared a menace to himself and others and, with no relatives stepping forward, he became a ward of the state. They locked him in a sanatorium, until five years ago when he just walked out."

"How do you walk out of a sanatorium?"

"Evidently it's pretty easy. The police report said Erebus was ninety-five percent catatonic. He'd move if directed to do so, but never on his own. If no one led him, he'd just stand there. He couldn't feed or clean himself. The story was that they stood him in the garden every day for some fresh air, even in the rain, because if they didn't, he'd start whimpering. That went on for years until one day, when they went to bring him back inside, he was gone."

"That's not very helpful."

"When I found his address and we raided his home I didn't know any of this. I should have. It should have all been accessible, but it wasn't—"

"How come?"

"I don't know. It was just blind luck that Erebus was there at all. A one in a million shot."

"It didn't feel all that lucky to me."

Teri looked up from her tablet, confused. "Oh, I'm sorry. I didn't mean for it to sound like that. But bad luck is still luck."

"Never mind; keep rolling."

"Well, that's all I have on Adrian."

"Then tell me about Grace." Luther covered his eyes with his forearm. "Why did her husband sign a contract on her?"

"LEI doesn't ask, and they *never* write it down. As a guess, I'd say the bastard was trying to protect his fortune, and it's a good bet that he didn't know Grace was previously married or had children."

"But the kid was dead for almost a decade by then."

"Mister Moneybags had a *lot* of moneybags. I'm pretty sure he was one of the original investors that financed LEI's creation, back when they were hunting al Qaeda."

"So old money doesn't like being lied to?" Sweetwater asked. "Who'd have thought it? But if that's true about him financing the hunt for bin Laden, why would the company send a probationary Shooter instead of a seasoned vet?"

"I think you're looking at it wrong. What if nobody else was available on such short notice, but Tarbeau insisted on Grace Allen being killed that night?"

"Huh, that could be it."

"Remember, this is all speculation, but, yeah, that's what I think. LEI pressed you into service because a powerful backer wanted his wife dead, and you were it for choices. The why is harder to say. Of course, you could just ask Grace Allen the next time you see her..." Warden raised her eyebrows and waited for his answer.

The room door swung open and the nurse came in, holding a paper folder in one hand and a pair of plastic bottles in the other.

"Mister Sweetwater, have I got a treat for you." She pulled a rolling table to the side of his bed and placed the plastic bottles on the steel top. "As promised, I brought you some protein milk."

"I thought that was a threat, not a promise," he said.

"Don't be like that. Each bottle has the same nutritional value as a full meal. I brought you one of each flavor." She twisted the top off the brown bottle and inserted the straw from his water cup. "Give it a try."

"Do I have to?"

Dottie smiled, but it was the faux sweet, knowing smile of a 7th grade home room teacher, or a night nurse at a trauma center who'd heard it all.

"We could do it intravenously," she said. "Drinking it's a lot of easier."

"You can put that stuff into his veins?" Warden said.

"Not safely, no."

Sweetwater motioned for her to raise it to his lips, and he took a short pull on the straw. The flavor reminded him of room temperature milk mixed with saw dust and dryer lint. He choked down a mouthful. "That's terrible. Why would you give that to a person?"

"I'm supposed to tell you how good it is for you, but between you and me, I think they use this stuff to get people out of here as soon as possible. Voluntary checkout against doctor's advice, see, most of our patients don't have insurance."

"We do," Warden said. "We have excellent insurance."

"Oh. I wonder if accounting is aware of that?"

"Water," Sweetwater gasped.

The nurse handed him the cup of water and the carton of protein milk to Warden. "Can you take care of this for me? Give him as much as he can keep down." Then she touched Sweetwater on the leg. "I'll stop by before my shift is over, but I have other patients for now."

Seconds after stepping into the hall, she stuck her head back into the room.

"Pardon me, Mister Sweetwater, are you allergic to flowers?"

"No," he said. "Why?"

"Delivery for you."

She stepped aside as a delivery man carried in a large basket of flowers.

"Who likes you that much?" Warden said.

"Nobody I know." He motioned for the delivery man to put them on a table next to the bedside chair. "Excuse me, who sent those?"

"Beats me, sir," the man said. Stocky and middle-aged, the man wore heavy horn-rimmed glasses and a surgical mask. "I just deliver where they tell me."

"What's with the mask?" Warden said, obviously suspicious.

The man answered on his way out. "They told me he was contagious."

"Who told you that? He was shot."

But the man had gone.

"What the hell?"

Sweetwater tried to think, but the needle on his energy tank was pushing E. He choked as the chalky flavor of the protein drink still coated his tongue and motioned for more water.

"More drink first," Warden said. He sipped and made a face.

"Yummy for the tummy."

"I get why the nurse is trying to poison me—she's a sociopath—but what have I done to you?"

"Finish the bottle, you big baby."

"You have no idea how bad that stuff is."

"You'll sleep better on a full belly, and I can do my work while you sleep."

Warden searched the flower arrangement for a card, or any sign of who sent them, but came up empty. Not only did it not make sense, it was downright suspicious. Or maybe she was just being paranoid. Whatever the case, after a thorough inspection turned up nothing, she sat in the corner chair and dialed a secret number.

"Problem?" said Cynthia Witherbot, in place of hello.

"I don't know. Last night I pulled the file on our suspect Adrian Erebus, and there wasn't much there. Hacker's intuition told me it felt scrubbed, so today I tried some of the federal databases directly, without going through the LEI interface."

"And you discovered information not contained in our file." Witherbot said it as a statement, not a question.

"Yes."

"The implication being that this Erebus person…what? Bribed one of our techs?"

"I don't know; I'm just telling you what I found. Those are dots I can't connect."

The pause that followed made Warden wonder if the call had ended, until Witherbot finally said, "Is there a place on the dark web where someone goes to sell access?"

"Sure."

"Start your search there."

"There are a *lot* of sites like that!"

"Then wasting time speaking with me seems contra-indicated, does it not? One last thing, though, stay out of harm's way."

"Now you tell me."

"I mean it. If I have to attend your funeral, I'll be very displeased."

A new nurse walked into his room in a strange mood. Some might say she was downright chipper.

"Now who's ready for their first round of physical therapy?" She was singing it. She walked over to the bedside and unclipped the lines to his heart monitor.

"What are you doing?"

"You can't do therapy all hooked up." She didn't even look up from her work.

"I got shot," Sweetwater said. "I was in a coma. I don't need therapy."

"Stop being a baby, Luther," Warden said. "And stop fighting the nice lady."

He extended his fist, then slowly turned it palm up and raised his middle finger.

"That's not very nice," Warden said.

The nurse kept right on humming, ignoring him.

Sweetwater spotted a well-built man standing in the doorway. He was at least six feet tall and looked like he might have been a strong safety in high school. His body was just starting to turn from hard muscle into hard muscle wrapped in a burrito.

"This is Scott, Mr. Sweetwater. He also works in the physical therapy department."

Scott nodded and pushed an empty wheelchair to the bedside. Without any effort he lifted Sweetwater and gently set him into the seat. "I didn't hurt you, did I?"

"I don't trust this guy," whispered Cooper's voice in his ear. Sweetwater jerked his head to the sides, but he couldn't see the ghost/delusion.

"Me either," he said.

"You either what, dear?" asked the nurse.

"Uh…I either ride or walk, and I'd rather ride."

She smiled.

Scott smiled.

Sweetwater frowned.

A short elevator ride took them into the physical therapy room. It had all the regular implements of torture that you'd find in a five-star gym, including the infamous wall of mirrors. Scott wheeled him past all of them. They stopped in the corner of the room where there were a couple of folding chairs and a card table.

"Are we going to play some poker?" Sweetwater asked.

Scott smiled again, which only added to Sweetwater's suspicions; anybody who smiled as much as those two couldn't be trusted.

"Not yet," Scott said, "but we *are* going to have a bit of fun." Then he removed the armrests from the wheelchair and tucked Sweetwater's wheelchair under the table. "First things first. I need to see where you are at the moment." He plopped down a bowl of runny oatmeal, followed by a soup spoon. "Please eat some."

"Why would I do that?"

Scott grinned like they were old friends.

"To keep me from holding your nose and force feeding you."

Sweetwater doubted he would actually do that but didn't want to find out. He grabbed the spoon until electric agony shot through his ribs as if he'd been stabbed by a cattle prod turned up to max. The spoon fell to the table as he snatched his arm back and hugged his wounded side. He was left sucking air through clenched teeth. When he was able to breathe normally again, Sweetwater looked up at Scott. "Fuck you."

Scott smiled yet again. "Just go slow, we have to gauge what level of mobility you've got." He tipped his head towards the oatmeal. "Left hand this time."

Although it pissed him off to admit it, Sweetwater grudgingly conceded that Scott had a point, so he held his breath and reached out. Tremors shook his hand and sweat trickled into the corners of his eyes. He lifted the spoon, gently, like a baby bird fallen from its nest. He felt pressure across his side but not the stabbing pain of the first attempt.

He pushed the spoon around in the grayish sludge, which felt more like stirring the runny mess with a sledgehammer than an eating utensil. He scooped up half a spoonful, he held his breath and focused on forcing it closer to his lips through sheer will. It stopped just a couple inches short of his mouth. The sweat running down his face increased as he strained to push it the last two inches. Then, desperate, he lunged forward and caught the spoon between his teeth.

His arm dropped to the table, spent. He tossed back the oatmeal and spat the spoon onto the tabletop. "That was disgusting," he said, exhausted but satisfied. "If I'm gonna have to work that hard for it, next time bring me a steak."

"So, you could choke?" the nurse said, still wearing a smile that Sweetwater increasingly felt was more sadistic than sympathetic.

"At least the juice would be worth the squeeze," Sweetwater said. "Do you have a name? Most hospital personnel have name tags, but you don't. How come?"

That erased her smile. He got the impression she didn't like patients knowing her name. "Of course, I have a name. You may call me Millie."

Cooper spoke again, and while Sweetwater couldn't see him, he smelled cigarette smoke and something nasty, like spoiled meat.

"There's more to it than that."

"Millie what?" Sweetwater said, doing his best to focus on one conversation at a time.

"Just Millie."

"Oh, just one name. I get it, like Cher. But you know, even she has a last name. And as a patient, I'm pretty sure I'm entitled to know it."

The nurse's smile had been replaced by a set jaw and stony scowl. "Ratched," she said.

Sweetwater's eyebrows lifted, and he couldn't suppress one quick laugh. "You mean like the movie?"

"Yes."

She said it in a way that reminded Sweetwater of when he'd been chewed out in basic training for somebody else's screwup. You couldn't rat out your platoonmate, but that didn't mean you had to *like* eating shit that rightfully belonged to somebody else.

"Nurse Ratched," he said, shaking his head while trying to suppress a grin. "If that's not the story of my life—"

"Should I point out," she said, "that you're making jokes about the person who brings you food and determines when, or if, to change your bedpan?"

That cut through his amusement. "It's probably a bad idea."

She nodded. "Yes, it probably is."

"Can we get on with it, please?" Scott said. "That was very good, Mr. Sweetwater. Let's see how you do with liquids. Here's something to wash it down." Scott dropped a straw in a bottle of protein mix. Sweetwater took a pull and swallowed, then turned away like he'd sucked up battery acid.

"Does this hospital intentionally serve the most disgusting food available? As bad as this shit tastes, it better be good for me."

Ratched left for other duties, but the torture continued until Sweetwater had finished the oatmeal and half the protein drink.

"Add some rat poison next time, it couldn't make it taste any worse."

After which they started some light physical therapy. First, he moved his arms in little circles to loosen the muscles. His right arm, he could bend fine at the elbow, but when he used his shoulder, the ribs screamed like his Scout Sniper School instructor had done the time he'd sneezed in a hide. The left arm, though weak, moved more easily.

Scott guided him through a series of stretching and strength exercises. Each successful repetition was toasted with a sip of the protein fuel. When they finished the session, Scott gave him a tennis ball. "Use this to work on your grip strength and you'll be back in the game before you know it."

"What am I missing?" Sweetwater said, more to himself than for Scott to overhear, but the therapist did anyway.

Scott patted him on the shoulder. "You're not missing anything. You did good."

"I don't know why," Cooper said, from wherever Cooper was, "but there's something else going on here. I've got a bad feeling."

Chapter Twenty-Six

The Elvis Presley Trauma Center, Memphis, TN

Sweetwater's shirt was sweat stained from the workout. Nurse Ratched rejoined them as Scott wheeled him back to his room, patting his back and then looking at the wetness on her palm.

"Did he cry?" she said, obviously still remembering Sweetwater's earlier comments about her name. Then she used baby-talk. "I hope our big boy didn't cry."

"Not this time," Scott said, as he pushed the chair down the corridor. Sweetwater could tell from his tone that Scott didn't approve of the nurse's barely repressed hostility. "Lay off, Millie, he fought through every exercise and kept asking for more. By next week, I think we'll be on the bench press."

Sweetwater knew it was bullshit, but the kid had that unique ability that the best physical trainers possessed, a gift for pushing you past your limits to achieve more than you thought possible. And here he was defending his patient as he should have done.

"Isn't that wonderful? Keep working your magic, and we'll have him out killing people again in no time."

"What's that?" Scott asked.

"You didn't know? He's one of those LifeEnders people." She picked up a folder from the desk. "I have to make my rounds. Scott, would you take him back to his bed?" She turned and walked off without waiting for an answer.

"You kill people?"

"Yeah, you know how it is. Kill people, get paid. A guy's gotta eat."

"That explains it then. Millie lost two brothers to hitmen. She tried to have them prosecuted, but…"

"But it's legal."

"Yeah."

They were outside of Sweetwater's room, where Scott had just propped the door open, when Dottie LaForce called out from down the hallway and hurried over to them.

"You're late," she said with a mock scowl at Scott. "I need to take Mister Sweetwater's vitals before my shift ends."

"Sorry, Dottie, he was doing so well I wanted to push him."

"It's all right. Oh, that delivery man came again with more flowers, Mister Sweetwater, somebody really likes you."

"Flowers?" Sweetwater blinked, then panic flooded his brain. "Where's Teri?"

Scott nodded toward the room.

"She's asleep in the chair."

Cooper materialized and screamed in Sweetwater's ear, "Run!"

"Get her out!" Sweetwater cried.

Then the bomb went off.

Since he was standing in the doorway, Scott absorbed most of the blast's energy. It blew Scott into Dottie LaForce like a speeding bulldozer, and they both hit the opposite wall and collapsed. Sweetwater was bodily lifted from his wheelchair and slammed into the linoleum floor, where he rolled over several times before coming to a stop, face down. Dust boiled down the corridor in both directions, making it nearly impossible to breathe. The overhead lights went out and battery-powered emergency lights came alive. Sirens wailed.

Sweetwater rolled onto his back. His chest felt as if it were being crushed by an elephant. Someone grabbed him by the arm. Scott. Somehow, the physical therapist could still move. Scott's face swam in his vision as he dragged Sweetwater down the hallway. Through a semi-conscious squint, he saw smoke billowing from his room. A part of his brain recognized that it was only the bed and curtains and was no real danger. Hospital rooms didn't have much to burn.

He blacked out for a few seconds and woke to see Scott staggering out of Sweetwater's room, his shirt pulled up over his nose and sagging under the weight of a limp Teri Warden. He laid her beside Sweetwater and then slid to the floor himself, his back braced against the wall and blood oozing from dozens of cuts to his face, neck, arms, nose, and mouth. The Marine first aid course had emphasized that concussion wounds, like from IEDs, often resulted in internal wounds you couldn't see. Scott had every sign.

So did Warden, who also had lines of blood running from multiple cuts on her face. There were matching blood trails running from her ears. Her eyes wide with panic, she gasped for air. Sweetwater reached out and squeezed her arm. She looked at his hand on her forearm, and when she met his eyes there was recognition. Against the odds, they were both alive.

People in green, blue, and pink scrubs ran to and fro, some with white labs coats flapping. Not all ran toward the burning room or injured people, either. Nurses and other staff ducked into nearby rooms and pushed, pulled, carried, or threw an arm around other patients to help them into the elevators or down the emergency exit.

Pain overwhelmed him, and he whimpered, then lost consciousness again. When he woke up next somebody had placed a few of Sweetwater's personal things, plus Warden's computer and phone, near them. The laptop was closed, and cracks lined the phone screen like a spider's web. Staring at them with a vacant look, Scott held up Sweetwater's credentials in their distinctive leather case. The badge was covered in dust, but other than that it looked untouched.

Medical personnel swarmed over them, as if suddenly figuring out that somebody had been injured in the explosion. Even as they worked on him, though, Scott gasped out a question.

"Your badge number is triple seven?"

Sweetwater nodded.

"You might be the luckiest man I know."

"I don't feel very lucky," he said, as a doctor examined his eyes with a pen light. The words came out as a croak.

Hovering over him, the doctor answered instead of Scott. It was Tamika Wilson. "You got shot point-blank and survived, Mister Sweetwater. Now a bomb explodes in your room and you're still breathing. He's right," she said, nodding at Scott, "if you're not the luckiest man, you're sure as hell the luckiest one I've ever met." Then she looked directly into Sweetwater's eyes. "Why do you want to kill people for money?"

"How do you know it was a bomb?" he asked, ignoring the question because he didn't know the answer.

"This hospital is ground zero for the gang wars. It's not the first time we've been bombed."

"How is my friend?" he asked, not giving her a chance to ask the embarrassing question a second time.

"We need to get you both downstairs to the ER where we can check you out."

"Scott?" Nurse Ratched called as she rushed toward them. The young physical therapist got to his feet, using the wall as a brace. Dr. Wilson gave him a brief look over.

"Damn, Scott. Millie, help him take Mister Sweetwater and his girlfriend downstairs, then get Scott checked out, stat."

Scott nodded to Millie, still stunned and in obvious pain. Since he had been standing sideways in the doorway, his left side had absorbed the force of the blast. Blood had soaked into the fabric around holes sliced in his scrubs by flying debris.

"Let's find a gurney or wheelchair," he said. "And hurry, I'm not feeling too good."

A page for Dr. Wilson over the intercom sent her scurrying up to the next floor, where there were more casualties. The detonation had done more damage than originally thought. Alone now, Warden grabbed Sweetwater by the arm and handed over her phone. She had typed a text message which, despite the shattered face, was still readable.

bomb was for you

Sweetwater looked at her and nodded. It felt like he had a cinder block duct taped to the top of his head. She typed another message and showed him.

he knows ur here he mite b watching we need 2 run

Their eyes met. Sweetwater licked his lips and nodded. Warden was right; they had to find a way to get out of there. Holding his ribs with his right arm, Sweetwater turned and planted his left hand on the ground, grinding his teeth to keep from screaming. Then he pulled in one knee, followed by the second. With a short prayer he rose to his knees, swayed, and blinked at the red stars in his vision. There was a bumper that ran the length of the hospital corridors, probably put up to keep gurneys from tearing up the walls. Sweetwater grabbed it and pulled.

Intense pain shot through the top of his head like an ice pick, but he kept rising. Once he was on his feet, he took a tentative step, gasped, felt his legs tremble, and thought he might fall. For what couldn't have been more than a second everything went black. A craving to sleep overwhelmed all other thoughts...until a familiar and feared voice cut through his stupor.

"Is something wrong with you, Private Sweet Meat?" It was his drill instructor, Gunnery Sergeant Addison, his face apoplectic as he shrieked into Sweetwater's ear at Parris Island. *"Don't you like your fellow privates?"*

"No, sir!"

"You don't like them?"

"Aye, sir!

"Well, which is it, you do like them, or you don't like them?"

"I do like them, sir!"

"Then why did you answer 'no' before you answered 'yes'?"

"I was answering the first question, sir!"

"Am I confusing you, Private Sweet Meat?"

"No, sir!"

"Then why are you lagging behind the rest of your platoon, Private? Do you want them to get killed?"

"No, sir!"

"Don't you love the Marine Corps, Private Sweet Meat?"

"Aye, sir!"

"Good, that makes me happy. And since I'm a Marine, does that mean you love me, too?"

"Aye, sir!"

"Do you want to take me to dinner, Private Sweet Meat, buy me roses, and maybe pick me up in a limousine?"

"No, sir!"

"Now I'm confused, Private Sweet Meat, I thought you said you loved me! If you love me, don't you want to wine and dine me?"

"No, sir!"

"So, you don't love me then?"

"I—"

"You what, Private? Do you want to stand there holding your pecker, is that it? Or maybe you want to stand there holding my pecker. Do you want to hold my pecker, Private Sweet Meat?"

"No, sir!"

"Don't you like my pecker?"

"I wouldn't know, sir!"

"Do you need to see it to know if you like it? Would you like me to whip it out right here, Private Sweet Meat?"

"No, sir!"

"Then what do you want, Private Sweet Meat?"

"I want to perform my duties to the best of my abilities, sir!"

"You do?"

"Aye, sir!"

"Then why aren't you helping your friends to safety, Marine?"

"Sir, I don't deserve to be a Marine, sir!"

"You deserve to be a Marine if and when I say you do, Sweet Meat. Do you understand me? And since when does the Marine Corps send people who don't

deserve to be Marines to Scout Sniper School? Did you lie to the Marine Corps, or are you saying that my beloved Marine Corps made a mistake?"

"N-neither...sir!"

"Didn't you learn anything from me, Sweet Meat? Marines do not call Gunnery Sergeants, sir, you will address me as Gunnery Sergeant Addison. Is that clear?"

"Aye, sir—Gunny!"

"Now what is your problem? I know you have a scratch, so I assume you don't want you to strain yourself helping your friends survive. Is that it, Marine? Does your own comfort matter more than Suzie's life?"

"Her name is Teri, and she's not a Suzie, Gunny."

"I know her name, dumbass, but if you're too stupid to know she's a Suzie then maybe you are too stupid to be a Marine."

"Like hell I am!"

"Well, well, what have we here? Do I see Corporal Sweetwater finally making an appearance?"

"Fuckin' A, Gunny."

"Well, it's about fucking time. Now why are you talking to me instead of saving Suzie? Why are you sitting on your ass when you should be acting like a fucking Marine?"

Sweetwater was slipping down the wall when he came back to full consciousness. It hurt to breathe, stand, or even hold his head up, but now all that seemed trivial. He was a Marine goddamn it! He'd forgotten it until that moment. Now, finishing the mission was all that mattered; it's what Marines did.

A strong hand grabbed his arm and helped him stand straight again.

"What are you doing?" Scott asked, yelling to be heard over the fire alarms. Millie wasn't with him. With his free hand he reached down and placed the wheelchair behind Sweetwater. "That was impressive, but you're not ready. You can barely hold a spoon."

"Give her the chair," Sweetwater said. "I don't need it; I'm a Marine."

"You're going to be a dead Marine if you try to walk too much. Please, sit." He looked at Warden. "Can you stand?" She nodded and got up, slowly, the laptop tucked under her arm. Scott looped her free arm over his shoulder.

"Can you hang on, but try not to pull down too much?"

She nodded.

Smoke was still pouring from Sweetwater's room. The elevator alarm jangled from the doors being locked open, and bits of carbonized plastic tubing floated on the air currents as they moved toward it and got on. Scott released the Lock button which stopped the alarm, and once the door closed, it muffled the fire alarms.

"Y'all all right?" Scott asked, his own face drawn and pale.

They both nodded, although Sweetwater had to fight down vomit from a convulsing stomach, while Warden hugged her laptop in both arms. The doors opened to reveal blue lights flashing outside the glass emergency room doors, but no sirens. Or if there were sirens, they couldn't hear them over the continuing fire alarm horn.

People were running everywhere. The trio moved to the waiting area on the other side of the hall, where Scott found an empty chair.

He eased Warden into the seat and wheeled Sweetwater next to her. Finally, he reached down to lock the wheels without looking down.

"Stay here, okay? I'm going to find a doctor."

"Find one for you, too," Warden said.

Scott nodded and disappeared back into the elevator.

Tears made track marks in the chalk-like dust caked on Warden's cheeks. Oddly enough, it also acted as a coagulant and stopped the lacerations on her face from bleeding. Thin runners of blood still flowed from her nose and ears.

Sweetwater tried to tough it out as if Gunny Addison was standing nearby judging him, but it hurt even to take shallow breaths. When he spoke, he had to gasp out the words in bunches. "How we gonna run? Where to?" Head on his chest, he waited what seemed like an hour for her to answer.

"We steal an ambulance," she said.

"Only works in the movies. They all have GPS trackers now…and we still have the problem of nowhere to go. Erebus found me here, so we sure as hell can't go back to my trailer."

"I knew it. You really do live in a trailer." Now her face lit up with a weak smile, which he returned.

"I already told you I live in a trailer."

"I figured you were just bragging or something."

"Right, 'cause everybody brags about living in a single-wide." The bravado felt good. His smile grew until he let slip a single laugh, which made him grit his teeth and squeeze his eyes shut from a stab of agony that felt like when a goat had gored him in the side when he was 11. "Do you still have that hotel room?"

Warden shook her head. "I didn't see the point since I've been living here for the past week. My roommate was quiet and slept a lot. It was a pretty good crash pad."

Sweetwater's eyes went wide. "That's the ticket."

"I knew it would be. What are you talking about?"

Neither had bothered keeping their voices down, since the continuing fire alarm made it hard even to hear each other, but now he leaned in close.

"We're going to need Scott, or maybe Nurse Dottie. We have to keep out of sight. In the meantime, get with LifeEnders and tell them I died."

"What's the plan?"

"I haven't thought it through yet, but if somebody at LEI *is* feeding Erebus information, maybe we can use that against him. If it works, who knows, we just might live through this."

"By being dead?"

"No reason to kill somebody twice, so if I'm dead, then I'm out of the crosshairs. We get time to heal."

"He might come after me."

"I don't think so; I think you're collateral damage."

"So where are we going?"

"Right here. We have Scott or Nurse Dottie find us a room with a comatose patient and hide there. The important thing is we have to keep this a secret from the hospital. The more people who know we're here, the more danger we're in."

"That's crazy! Why would they do that?"

"Why does anybody do anything?"

"I don't have any money; not enough to bribe somebody. Besides, how do you know one of the staff didn't tip him off?"

"Yeah, okay, good point. But we've got to trust somebody."

"Skip that part, I've got an idea. What then? What's the next step?"

"You have to track down Erebus. If we keep playing defense, sooner or later we're going to lose. We need to go on the offensive."

Chapter Twenty-Seven

Adrian Erebus leaned back on a pile of pillows and stretched out on one of the motel room's twin beds while Herbert lay belly down on the other. A freshly opened can of Busch foamed in Adrian's hand, while a can of Coke sat on the floor beside Herbert, the pop-top still sealed. Together they watched the nightly news, which for Herbert was unusual; he rarely paid attention to the world at large.

"This is Diana Carlson," the late-night news anchor said. The shine from her smile was like a fluorescent flashlight in the darkness of the room. "We are back now with continuing coverage of the explosion at the Med, where an FBI spokesman has just confirmed that the explosion was intentional, although no cause has yet been given. Early reports claimed it was a bomb, but that has not been confirmed. However, the FBI and Memphis Police are no longer calling it a terrorist act. And while it is believed this was another attack connected to LifeEnders, that has not been verified either. Collateral injuries from the incident were substantial, but while resulting in no additional fatalities beyond the presumed target of the attack, three people are listed in critical condition. Initial damage estimates are nearing 30 million dollars."

Her co-anchor, grinning through enough pancake makeup for a chorus line, waggled his finger at the camera. "Another LifeEnders related attack? How many does that make?" He brushed at the silver

264 | HOY & WEBB

hair on his temple, despite it shining with enough hairspray to keep a strand from falling out of place in a hurricane.

"That's right, Jerry, another one. This makes the third fatality in the past month. We are calling the killer the LifeEnders Ender."

"Do we know the Ender's game?" Jerry asked in an obviously rehearsed ad-lib.

"Ha-ha! As you know, the actual purpose and extent of the organization has always been hotly debated, Jerry, and this killer seems to have landed right in the middle of that disagreement. They liken it to the ongoing debate over such things as UFOs, aliens, or Bigfoot. Many people who disbelieve the official government story are calling for the killer to be allowed to continue his streak."

Jerry's malleable face suddenly shifted from friendly clown to stern lecturer.

"And that is where I have to step in, Diane, and remind our viewers that this news organization is taking no sides in this debate, we will just be keeping the score. And that score is currently, LifeEnders Ender three, LEI zero. Now let me speak directly to this vigilante, if he or she is listening, there has to be a reason for your actions, and I want to hear your story. I promise you total anonymity, as guaranteed under our constitution. Call me anytime, day or night, here at the station, and I promise that I will take your call. You obviously have something important to say, and I want to help you say it."

The camera lingered on Jerry's grave face a moment and went back to Diane.

"In other news, White House spokeswoman Natalie Washwhite laughed off an alligator hunter's drone video footage that went viral last month, which purported to show a rhinoceros herd stampeding through the Louisiana bayou country. 'The CGI in that video is laughably bad,' Washshite claimed, going on to say, 'The scale was off by a factor of four, and the rhinos were orange, not gray or black. Some people will do anything to get attention.' In an email to media outlets, the Associated Center for Understanding Phenomena said, 'This is just another government cover-up, like Roswell and the Chupacabra.' This station has been unable to—"

Adrian sat forward on the bed, slopping beer, and hit the mute button.

"LifeEnders Ender," he said, "what do you think of that son?"

Herbert held up a thumb.

"Me too, me too. Think we should make T-shirts?"

His son pulled a pillow over his head.

Erebus got up and rummaged through the leftover bomb-making materials inside his duffle bag until he found a wrinkled 5x7 picture of LEI Asset Luther Sweetwater. "I'll be right back." He went to the bathroom and set it aflame, like he'd done with Shields' photo. When it had burned to mostly ashes, he dropped the remnant into the toilet and pissed on it. The streaming urine broke it apart and the ashes of Luther Sweetwater swirled away into the sewer, where he belonged.

Erebus came out of the bathroom and flopped onto his bed, knocking over his little hill of pillows. "We did it, Herbert. We finally killed the bastard that killed your mom, and it was all your idea. You're such a smart boy." He put his hands behind his head and lay back, staring up at the ceiling. "What should we do next? I've got enough savings to last another six months or so, if we're careful."

Herbert took the pillow off his head, sat up, and faced his father. He held up four fingers.

"Oh, I like how you think, son. You are such an amazing boy."

He fished his wallet out of his back pocket. There wasn't much inside, his credit cards had expired years ago, but behind one of the plastic windows was an old photo of his family outside an amusement park. He pulled it out and held it under the lamp next to the bed.

Herbert had been six at the time? No, five. It had been the summer right before Herbert started first grade, and his birthday was in late September. Tracing his finger along the edge of the picture, he couldn't stop staring at Grace Allen holding an ice cream cone between her husband and son. She wasn't smiling, but Erebus knew how tired she'd been when the kind stranger took the photo for them. It wasn't like she was unhappy or anything.

"I did it, honey. I swore that I would, and I did. I killed them."

Then a sharp, familiar pain in his head forced his eyes shut to block out the glare from the TV. The migraine felt as if someone had shoved a knife right behind his left ear. He pulled four pills from the bottle of pain relievers he always kept on the nightstand and chased them down with a swig of beer. The migraine was already starting to relax before he even had a chance to set the empty beer can down.

From the secret pocket in his wallet, where other men might hide a twenty, Erebus had stuck a note with a phone number written in pencil. He used the motel phone to make a call.

After three rings, a voice answered. "Yeah?"

"Mickey, it's Adrian."

"Oh, hey," Mickey said in a friendly voice. There was some rustling, and after a few seconds he spoke again, this time in a panicked whisper. "What the fuck, man? You can't call me here."

"You still at work? It's kinda late."

"You think? They've got us working around the clock trying to find your ass. Get the hell out of Memphis before you burn us both."

"So, they know about me."

"No, what makes you think that? You kill two Shooters and a third shows up at your house, what did you think he was there for, to sell you some cookies?"

"Good," Erebus said.

"No, you moron, *not* good. For all I know they're backtracking my cell phone signal in real time."

"Can they do that?" Erebus said, his tone reflecting panic of his own.

"Fuck if I know…no, I don't *think* they can do that."

"I'm ready for another name."

"I knew you were gonna say that. I got it. But before I give it to you, I have some other news."

"So, tell me."

"This is going to cost you. Let's say double?"

"Why? I thought we were friends."

"What the hell made you think that? This is strictly business between us."

Erebus' face went slack, showing no emotion. Once again, he'd been fooled by someone pretending to be his friend. Yet there was also something empowering about Mickey's statement, something he couldn't put his finger on. But Adrian Erebus was no longer a man to be pushed around. Now, he was a man who pushed back. The extra expense would hurt, so he'd just have to figure out how to get more money.

"I'll pay if it's worth it."

"You'll pay anyway."

"They haven't caught me yet, Mickey, and they won't. But one phone call from me and you're at their mercy."

"You wouldn't do that!"

"Not to a friend, no, but to a business associate? Maybe I would."

"I'm planning my exit, Adrian. Soon. And when I bug out of here, I'll need more cash."

"No, give me the name, and you're safe. Don't do it, or lie to me, and I make the call."

"Yeah, fine, the regular fee then. I always figured you for an honest man, Adrian."

"Did you? A friend would have known better."

"The guy in the hospital?"

"Sweetwater, yes, what about him?"

"He ain't dead."

Erebus didn't speak for more than ten seconds.

"Adrian, you still there?"

"We saw it on the news," Erebus said, his voice matched the whispered tone on the other end of the line.

"It was all shit. He's alive."

Erebus hit himself in the head with the phone receiver and then squeezed it with both hands. He pulled in a shaky breath and put it back up to his ear. "So, where is he?"

"I don't know. No one over here knows. He's gone dark."

"Gone dark?" Erebus repeated.

"He's off the grid. He's hiding."

"I thought you could track him?"

"Normally, but we lost his signal when you bombed the place. It must have destroyed his phone. If it comes back on, I'll get you his location."

"Thank you, Mickey. I'm sorry I spoke harshly to you before."

The change in Erebus' tone was too abrupt for Mickey not to notice.

"Yeah, okay, sure, Adrian. We're copacetic. Don't sweat it."

"I'm being tested by this guy, Mickey. I don't why, but I'm being tested." After a short pause, he continued, "I'll take care of him, don't worry about it. Now send me more names, as many as you can before you leave. Just pull the money from my account."

"Your account is getting low."

Erebus didn't hide the warning tone in his voice. "You told me you were getting ready to leave."

"You're right, Adrian, never mind. We're cool. I'll send it out in tomorrow's mail. If you were to set up an email, I could send it to you tonight."

"The mail is fine. Computers are how people get caught. I'm not gonna get killed over some stupid computer."

"As long as you can keep paying, I'll send it by carrier pigeon."

"Not leaving anymore?"

"Plans change…"

The happy mood of earlier faded into the rage Erebus knew so well. For his entire life he'd tried to control it, to keep the explosive anger that led to blackouts filled with violence from ruling his life. Now, it no longer seemed worth the effort. After returning the phone to the cradle, he took the last two beers out of the mini fridge, put a fresh Coke beside the two untouched ones near Herbert, and sat in the chair by the window. His son was still watching the news, enraptured by a story about a gang shootout that left a young girl dead. But as much as such stories usually cheered him, now Erebus let the darkness settle into his brain.

Staring unblinking at a fly on the far wall, he made plans.

Chapter Twenty-Eight

Southwest Memphis, TN

The fly hadn't moved for hours because it wasn't a fly; it was an old nail in the wall. That didn't stop Erebus from leaning forward on his forearms, focused on the nail's flat head like it was the face of God. Only when his peripheral vision caught movement coming from the bed did he blink, which snapped him out of his trance.

He didn't notice his urine-soaked pants, or the puddle he now sat in. The TV channel had one of the local news broadcasts on a 30-minute loop, and when the image of the sheet-covered girl lying in the street came on again—the one killed by gang members—the camera shifted to a line of residents in the background who jeered and threw things at the police. Herbert pumped his fist in the air, which Erebus had never seen him do before. It took him a few seconds to understand that Herbert was cheering the protestors on, and that washed away his gloom. His son was so much better than he deserved.

Erebus muted the sound when that story gave way to coverage of the hospital bombing. He'd seen the story three or four times now, yet every time he spotted some new detail that jumped up his heart rate. The FBI bomb and crime scene teams were crawling through the wreckage searching for clues to the bombing.

Good luck, he thought.

The internet was a wonderful thing, a resource for showing people how to build everything from bird houses to bombs, and the dark web let you buy anything you might need. His smile returned and he glanced at the wires, wire cutters, and other leftover paraphernalia on the table near the window; there was plenty for more bombs. Maybe next time he'd strap four together instead of only two.

"He's still in there, Herbert," Erebus said, pointing at the TV. "Somehow, the murderer Sweetwater survived, and is still in there. I'll bet he's got a dozen nurses waiting on him hand and foot. It wouldn't surprise me if he's planning to kill the ones who have kids." He punched the pillow on the bed beside him. "He's gotta be stopped."

When a new scene showed MPD officers searching packages coming into the building, Erebus realized the looped news had given way to a live feed. The screen changed to show a policeman standing with a dog.

"Now they've got bomb dogs? Fuck. How do I get in there now?"

Herbert sprang up to his knees, climbed off the bed, and walked to the TV. He pointed to the edge of the screen where an ambulance had pulled up and backed up to the doors of the hospital.

"An ambulance," Adrian whispered. "You're right, son; that might do it."

Pieces of PVC pipe lay scattered in the corner. Beside them was a bag of black powder and a small pile of electronics that weren't needed for the last two bombs. The last bombs hadn't been big enough; that had to be why they failed to kill Sweetwater. He wouldn't make the same mistake twice.

"We can't do it here. One look at this place, and we'll get locked up." He walked to the window and peeked through the curtain. Across the road was a liquor store. As he watched, six cars pulled in and out in the space of a few minutes. "Perfect."

He pulled the Sig Sauer from his suitcase. It felt heavy and bulky in his hands, but twice now he'd managed to face down a killer with the gun. Herbert said something that made him look up. The boy rarely spoke, so when he did it got his father's attention.

"Oh yeah, good point son," Erebus said, and put the gun back in the suitcase. Herbert was right, even if he smuggled the gun inside, how was he going to find Sweetwater? With all the cops and federal agents prowling the halls, he couldn't exactly do a room-to-room search. "So, what do I do?" Herbert answered, and Erebus cocked his head. "Really? They have those?" He didn't question how his son knew such things.

Wet stains reached to the knees of his pants as Erebus walked to the door. Cut short, spikes of oily hair stood out like an overgrown Mohawk. Beard stubble itched on his face, but anger drove him to ignore it. When Herbert spoke again, he turned in the doorway. "Yeah, I guess you're right. You're smarter than your old man, just like I was smarter than my father." He pulled out his wallet, withdrew a twenty, then tossed the wallet to his bed. "Wish me luck." Twisting the knob, he went out into the night.

Following Herbert's suggestion, he started toward the corner gas station. The night was colder than he expected, but he didn't want to waste time going back for his jacket. He stuffed his fists into his pockets and kept walking. The gas station was on the corner, not too far from the motel. He pulled the door open and stepped inside. Hot air hit him in the face.

Erebus shook his arms, as if to get the blood moving. He smiled at the man behind the counter and realized his teeth were chattering.

"Sure is cold out there."

The clerk nodded and went back to work opening cartons of cigarettes and slipping them into a display behind the counter. Erebus went to the coffee station and pulled a small cup out of the metal sleeve recessed into the table. He put in four French vanilla creamers and three packets of sugar, topped it off with coffee, fitted a lid, and walked back to the counter. That's when he spotted what he needed. Herbert had been right.

The clerk pushed the cigarette cartons to the side, out of Adrian's reach.

"That be all?" he said.

"Actually, I was wondering how much those pocketknives are?"

The clerk turned to look at the display on the back wall.

"Which one?"

"The big black one, right next to the red…upper left."

It was a folding knife, half-opened for the display. The blade was six inches long, and made it resemble more of a medieval dagger than a modern weapon.

"That one's fifteen. Want it?"

Erebus nodded. The clerk pulled a box from under the display case and scanned it with a bar code reader.

"With the coffee, it's $19.79."

Pulling out the twenty, he smoothed it on the counter and slipped it to the clerk. "Thanks."

The clerk slipped him the thin cardboard box with the knife inside. Twenty-two cents rolled down a thin steel slot and spun in the bowl at the bottom.

After scooping up the change, he stood by the entrance, took a deep breath of the warm air, and then bumped the door open with his butt. The door swung out just long enough for him to slip outside. He sipped the coffee as he walked to the trashcan.

The coffee was still too hot to drink and burned his lip. He set it down and slipped the knife from its packaging. He pressed the nub on the back of the handle and the blade popped out. He looked the knife over, peeling away the manufacturer stickers stuck to the edge. Then he folded it and put it in his pocket.

Leaving his coffee on top of the garbage can outside the store, he walked to the liquor store and back. By then, the coffee had cooled enough to drink. Arms huddled against his body in defense against the breeze, he stood outside the door and slurped the coffee. It had a faint burnt flavor. He was still standing there when Herbert walked toward him out of the shadows.

"What are you doing out here, son? You should be up in the room. You're not even wearing your coat."

Herbert just stared at his father, not speaking.

"I'm going to do it, just give me a minute to finish this." He took another sip of his coffee, but the boy kept staring at him. "It's cold out here."

Herbert's eyes never left his face, never blinked; it was the same pleading gaze Grace Allen had always given him when they had to separate for any reason. His family couldn't live without him and in return he indulged their every whim.

"Fine, fine, it's not going to get any warmer. Let's do this." He slipped around the corner of the liquor store. This was something best done out of the streetlights. Erebus emptied the cup and placed it against the wall. He pulled out the knife, clicked it open, and brushed the edge of the blade with his thumb. He felt a sting and pulled his thumb away; a thin red line formed from where he touched the blade. "Perfect, nice and sharp."

Dim illumination reached the side of the liquor store from a streetlight across the parking lot next to the gas station. Herbert kneeled, facing his father with the light behind him, so he was only a black shape…except for the faint red glow from his eyes. Erebus hadn't seen him do that for a while. It was a sign of approval.

Now came the hard part. In preparation, Erebus thought back on all the movie scenes where Japanese soldiers committed suicide. Pulling up his shirt, he put the knife tip against his belly, took a deep breath and held it. He pushed against the point until a line of blood dribbled down his stomach. A quickly growing ball of icy doubt churned in his stomach.

If the Japanese could do it, why couldn't he? He wasn't even going to kill himself. Faint reflections from the knife blade included a smear of red, which meant Herbert was still right there watching, and Erebus felt shame under the gaze of his son.

"One…Two…Three."

He placed the blade back against his belly, but couldn't push it in.

His strength left him, and he leaned against the building's cold brick wall. Summoning his courage, he looked up at his son. Herbert's eyes had shrunk to pinpoints of red, which burned like lasers into Erebus' soul. Tears leaked from the corners of his eyes; he'd let Herbert down.

"I can't do it," he said, voice cracking. "I'm so sorry, son, I can't do it." He was crying now, his chest heaving as he struggled to control himself. The knife slipped from his fingers. There was no other way to get into the hospital, and if he tried to wait until Sweetwater finally left, they'd track him down. One mistake Erebus would not make was to underestimate law enforcement, especially the FBI. They'd find him, all right. If he stuck around Memphis that much was certain. Even if he ran, they might find him anyway, but *not* running wasn't an option. If he was going to kill Sweetwater, it had to be now, and since he couldn't kill him now, then the assassin had won. There would never be vengeance for his wife.

Erebus watched through tears as Herbert bent down and picked up the knife. Herbert wiped the blade against the leg of his jeans, brushing it free of dirt and gravel. The boy pointed the tip at his father.

"Herbert? Be careful, buddy. That's sharp."

Herbert met his father's eyes, two glowing coals that reminded Erebus of the glaucoma test that used to be part of his yearly eye exams. Entranced, he leaned back, as if commanded to do so by some unseen power. Something flickered in the corners of Herbert's eyes, flames, tiny flames. Erebus felt like he was floating, watching the scene unfold in the darkness below. It was all so strange…

The spell snapped, and he understood.

"Herbert, no!"

The boy put one hand on his father's shoulder for leverage and plunged the knife deep into his gut. As the steel slipped through his flesh, Erebus heard a meaty *thunk*.

He gasped at the sudden pain, exhaling until his lungs emptied. With no air, he couldn't scream and breathing hurt too much to take a deep breath. His eyes grew wide as Herbert pulled out the blade, drops of his blood falling from the point, and slammed it into his chest. Erebus fell forward, extending his left hand to keep from hitting the pavement while clutching his ruptured stomach with his right. Blood poured in a stream from the wounds and spread across his shirt.

He felt Herbert's hand on his shoulder, followed by a shove. Erebus fell over and groaned. He closed his eyes as spasms of agony wracked his body. A red light shone through his eyelids and he looked up at his son. Herbert shook his head, the gesture of an adult, not a child, one that did nothing to hide the boy's contempt. He stabbed his father again, and yet again.

Erebus' jaw fell, hanging loose.

Herbert raised the knife high above his head, and slammed it all the way to the handle into the right side of his fathers' chest. Finally, he let go of the knife, leaving it sticking out of his father's chest, where it rose and fell as Erebus gulped shallow breaths.

Time passed. Seconds or hours, he couldn't know. The world turned dark.

Someone pulled on his arm, and some part of his brain recognized that he was being supported by another person. Disjointed images came to him like photos shown out of order. The neck of a broken rum bottle on the concrete sidewalk, the gray door handle, the features of a dark-skinned man running toward him, fluorescent bulbs shining overhead, and then...blackness, relieved at some point by the wail of a siren.

E rebus heard the ambulance driver lean on the horn when an off-duty nurse crossed the driveway that led to the Med's Emergency Room. The driver's door slammed shut as he burst from the cab, and footsteps marked him running to the back of the truck. Voices beyond the closed doors were too muffled to understand. The doors flew open and he saw blurry figures outlined against the darker background of the ER entrance.

He focused on a heavy-set female paramedic crouching next to him. Erebus wondered why she was shaking her head. He saw and heard everything like he'd fallen deep in a well.

Where *was* he? He tried to ask but no words came out.

"BP is 76 over 48 and thready," she said, calling out the rest of his vitals. Erebus didn't hear most of it as the world swam from glaring lights to utter darkness. Metallic sounds registered as dull noises. He felt a sensation of motion, of sliding, as people grabbed the gurney he was strapped to and pulled it from the truck.

There was an oxygen mask over his nose and mouth. His neck was in a collar that prevented him from seeing the knife sticking out of his chest, but the jostling from being moved caused the blade to throb in time with his pulse. His body was sticky from blood.

A small bump caused Erebus to cry out when the gurney's legs came down. The bounce made the knife move inside the wound, even though the pressure bandages were supposed to hold it in place.

"Hold on, sir," the female paramedic said as she ran trotted alongside the gurney. "You're at the Med now. They're going to take very good care of you."

There was too much going on for Erebus to keep up with, so he closed his eyes. He was so tired. Someone pinched him on the arm. He wanted to tell them to stop pinching him, but the mask and neck collar prevented him. People kept talking around him but opening his eyelids felt like too much effort.

"Do you have an ID?"

"No, he's a John Doe. We think he was a mugging victim. He was unresponsive when we picked him up. He just woke up, but his vitals are in the toilet."

A young, black female face opened an eye and shined a bright light into it. "Sir, do you know where you are?"

Erebus tried to nod his head, but all he could manage was to blink his eyes.

"What is your name, sir?"

His lips moved. Nothing came out.

"That's all right, sir, we'll find out later. You've been stabbed and we need to operate. I'm going to take off your mask, please answer if you can hear me. Are you allergic to any medications?"

He saw ceiling tiles passing overhead, so he knew they were still moving, but the room was getting dark. Distantly, he felt someone pull his mask away. Erebus tried to say no to the allergies question, but all that came out was a mumbled "nrr." The world went dark again.

He woke in a panic. Glaring lights blinded him. There was mask was on his face, and he didn't remember it being there. Someone had stuck a needle in his arm. Squirming, he tried to pull it out, but a black woman with pretty eyes held his arm down. She wore a blue mask, so he wasn't sure if he knew her or not. He tried to smile at her and blinked.

His eyes drooped; he was so tired.

Erebus awoke in a hospital room. Cords and tubes connected him to various machines arranged around the head of his bed. A line of windows, high on the wall, showed it was nighttime outside. Where was he? And why did his torso hurt so badly?

Using his left hand, which was free of tubes and lines, he pulled down the top of his hospital gown. On the right side of his chest was a thick bandage, held in place with gauze wrapped around his body. It was white with only a small spot of red in the middle. He thought about pulling the gown off so he could see his stomach, but he could feel a large bandage that was taped to his stomach.

His memory came back in fragments, fully aware that he should be dead. Maybe he was? Thinking hardly seemed worth the effort, so he decided that he was still alive and had been stabbed.

He drifted back to asleep.

The next morning, he was awakened by a nurse leaning over him, and beyond her stood a middle-aged woman in a simple brown business suit.

"Good morning, sir. My name is Dottie LaForce. How are you feeling today?" the nurse asked.

"What happened?" His mouth felt dry. A moment of double vision left him blinking. "My stomach hurts."

LaForce pulled a pen light from her pocket and flashed it in his eyes, first one then the other. He tried to turn his head.

"I'm sorry for that, sir. Can you tell me your name?"

Lifting his left forefinger, he tried to point at the bandage on her cheek, squinting to focus.

"What happened?"

"Wrong place, wrong time," she said with a friendly smile. "Can you tell me your name?"

He hesitated, thinking. Some instinct told him to lie.

"George Jones," Erebus said. The woman in the corner raised a notepad and started writing.

"Thank you, George. Do you have a middle name?"

"George," he said. It was the first thing that popped into his head.

"George George Jones?"

Unable to think clearly, he nodded.

"All right then, George George Jones it is." Even in his debilitated state, Erebus heard the doubt in her tone and cursed himself. "Do you know where you are, George?"

"Hospital." *Stick to short answers,* he told himself.

"Yes, that's right, you are at the Elvis Presley Trauma Center, the Med. Do you know why you here?"

"Stabbed."

"Yes, again! You were stabbed five times in the stomach and chest and underwent emergency surgery. Doctor Gupta will be in to see you shortly to discuss your injuries and recovery plan, but in the meantime, this is Mrs. Thomas." LaForce stood and motioned to the other woman. "If you feel up to it, she has some questions for you."

The woman in the business suit pulled over a rolling office chair and sat down at his bedside.

"If you need anything, Mister Jones, just push this button, and I'll be with you in a moment."

"Thank…you," he said as she left the room.

"Mr. Jones," Mrs. Thomas said. "You came here in such a hurry we were unable to get you into our system. Before we start, is there someone you'd like to call?"

"My wife." He said it without thinking.

"Do you know her number? I can bring you a phone."

He paused, remembering his error. His face grew pale as he stalled, trying to think of an answer.

"Don't worry, I'm sure it will come to you. If you think of the number, just let me know." She picked up her note pad. "Can you tell me your address?"

Erebus froze. He should have thought of all this before…before what? He remembered holding the knife and kneeling on rough ground…a dark parking lot somewhere, and his plan to…to…*Luther Sweetwater!* Like turning on a faucet, the memories flooded back of his plan to stab himself to get inside the hospital so he could kill Sweetwater, but had he actually done it?

"My address…" He paused and eventually remembered a house number of a neighbor from years before. "…1879 Willington St."

"Is that in Memphis?"

"East of Memphis."

"Really? The ambulance driver said they picked you up here in the city. Do you remember what you were doing?"

His mouth went dry. "I can't remember."

"That's fine." She was writing in her notebook again. Then she asked, "Do you know your social security number?"

"I can't remember." He looked away from the woman and saw his fist was curled in the blankets. He forced it flat and smoothed the sheets.

"Any chance you remembered your wife's number?"

Erebus shook his head, afraid that if he kept talking, he'd give everything away.

"That's all right, I'll go look up your address. Soon as I confirm your address, we'll get the ball rolling."

"Right." He wiped his sweaty palms on the blankets, wondering what she meant by that.

"You just take your time and get better. Leave all this to me. The police will want to speak with you."

"Yes, ma'am." He managed to raise a hand in a wave as she left.

Chapter Twenty-Nine

Memphis Police Department Secured Facility below the
Elvis Presley Trauma Center, Memphis, TN

Beneath the Med was a secret section for high-security patients. The wing contained a series of cells the Memphis Police Department used for anyone in custody who might also require medical attention. A specially designed operating room allowed the surgeons to work on patients who, despite their injuries and anesthesia, might still pose a threat to their safety. Once in recovery, the police simply handcuffed people to the bed frames in open rooms, reserving the cells for the violently aggressive. Luther Sweetwater had spent the last three days hiding in one of those cells.

"It's me," Nurse LaForce called out as she entered the room.

Sweetwater sat up, watching the door. She entered alone, carrying three foam lunch containers like the ones restaurants used for take-out orders. As fewer pain drugs were needed, his mind was beginning to clear, and clarity of thought brought a renewed alertness for danger.

"Fantastic, Dottie, I'm starved. What's for lunch?"

A delicious odor of real food filled the room, overpowering the antiseptic smells. She pulled the wheeled table to his bedside, and pulled two bottles of protein drink from her lab coat pocket. She set them on the table with a smile.

"Liquid chalk? Again? I dearly hope you're kidding," Sweetwater said, his face falling. Then his stomach rumbled loud enough to hear.

"Calm down, Luther, I brought food, too. It's what my daddy used to call…well, I won't use that language, but the Army had some unsuitable names for common foods."

She opened one of the foam containers on the table. Sweetwater could project a chagrined, boyish smile when he wanted to, and in that moment he wanted to.

"Shit on a shingle. Why do you hate me, Dottie? What did I do to you?"

"It's better than you deserve," said the moldering corpse of William Bonney, who materialized next to the bed without warning. The dead Shooter glared at him with his arms crossed and long splits in his dry skin, and Sweetwater barely gave him a glance. He was getting used to dealing with the living while ignoring the dead. Sweetwater pressed on his stomach to calm the spasms. The sight of two thin slices of white bread covered in congealed brown gravy crushed his dreams of bacon and eggs.

"Hate you, dear?" she said, not trying to hide her sarcasm. Sweetwater hadn't thought her capable of it, but clearly had misjudged her. "I have no reason to hate you. Just because you're a paid killer and I've dedicated my life to saving the lives of others, or that you got one of our rooms blown up, or the fact that poor Scott faces six weeks of physical therapy and probably PTSD, why would any of that matter to me?" She moved around the room, checking the machines and generally acting fussy. "Besides, I thought you were a military man. You're supposed to like eating that kind of stuff."

"We were served it; I'm not too sure how many of us liked it. But isn't my diet controlled by a nutritionist? White bread and watery gravy doesn't seem particularly geared to a man who recently had surgery."

"Enjoy it while you can, butt-breath," Bonney said. "When you're dead, you can't taste anything anymore."

"I didn't kill you, asshole," Sweetwater said, turning to face Bonney. "And I'm not responsible, either. Go jack off before your dick shrivels. And if you see Shields, tell him to fuck off, too."

Laforce paused from re-tucking the corners of his bedsheets, eyebrows raised.

"I beg your pardon," she said.

"Sorry for my language," he said, "flashback to boot camp."

That brought a hint of sympathy to LaForce's face, and no sarcasm tinted her answer. "Most of our patients are gang-bangers, dear. I doubt there's anything I haven't heard."

She came around the bed and removed the first foam container and flipped open the lid of the second one. She added a plastic spork and napkin to his table and pushed it back into place. There was a slice of buttery Texas toast covered in thick ground beef gravy flanked by green beans and mashed potatoes.

"*That* looks fantastic, Dottie."

Sweetwater pushed himself a little higher up on his bed, dug the spork into the potatoes, lifted it halfway to his mouth, and stopped. "Thank you, Dottie." Then he popped the food into his mouth. His eyes went wide as he finally tasted flavor for the first time in almost a week and a half. He finished chewing and swallowed. He cut a piece of the toast and rolled it in the gravy. "How come?" he said between bites.

She didn't need clarification. "I'm a religious woman, Luther. I believe everything happens for a reason, whether I understand that reason or not. That means God has a part for you to play, and if Jesus was here, he would love you despite your sins." Then she shrugged, as if she'd said everything she had to say. Luther stopped chewing and nodded. "For my sake, just stay hidden so I don't have to dodge any more explosions. You do that, and I'll call it even." She gently inspected his bandages, probing the worst of the wounds. "Now, how are you feeling?"

"Better. Relinda—I think that's her name, Scott's replacement— had me walking earlier today. I figure next weekend I'm going fishing. I need some time on the water."

"Don't we all? How is the pain?"

Sweetwater talked around another bite of his breakfast. "It aches but nothing to worry about. I'm fine."

"They monitor the narcotics, but I might be able to find you something."

He took another bite and waved the spork. "Really, I'm good. This food is what I needed. I'm not afraid of a little pain." He shoveled in another bite. "The biggest thing is just to thank you for keeping my secret."

She nodded and sat a bottle of protein mix beside his meal. "I know you don't like it, but it's good for you, dear. The protein will help you heal faster."

"Yes, ma'am, anything for Nurse LaForce." He saluted her with his fork.

She turned to go, but stopped in the doorway and, without turning around, said, "I'm glad you didn't die." She disappeared around the corner, and, less than five seconds later, Teri Warden entered.

"I'm glad we didn't die either," she said.

He took a swig of the protein shake. "She meant that for me because I'm so cute. Nobody cares about you."

"Nobody?" One corner of Warden's mouth curled upward, along with her eyebrows.

"So maybe somebody does."

"I wonder who that could be." She continued without giving him a chance to respond, "Something smells good."

"Dottie brought food."

"I saw her in the hallway. She was smiling so I figured you died or something." She grabbed the remaining container and popped it open. "Well now, I hope it tastes better than it looks." She showed it to Sweetwater.

"Hey, no fair, you got meat loaf."

"I wasn't shot." She poked at it with her spork, tore off a small bite of meat and bread, and popped it into her mouth. "Nope, can't do it. It's terrible." She closed the lid and put it on the window ledge.

"I'll take it if you don't want it."

"You Memphis people like some weird stuff."

She retrieved her breakfast and slid it onto Sweetwater's tray.

"I'm not from Memphis, I'm from Semple."

"Same thing."

"Don't say that in Semple. What did you learn?" he asked while chewing.

"Nobody would tell me anything until I called Witherbot, then they couldn't shut up. They were righteously pissed, but they gave it up. They said the bomb could have been a lot worse, but the pot they used for the flowers was some metal alloy. It focused the explosion up, which is why it blasted into the room above more than yours. Also, your door being opened probably saved my life because it channeled most of the blast force away from me. It was a cheap pipe bomb, just like the one that took out Mark last week."

"Who's Mark?"

"Mark Shields. Don't you remember you met him?"

"Was he the Crispy Critter?"

"I think you called him Barbeque Boy."

"Oh yeah, him. He wasn't very happy about being dead."

"I doubt many people are. Anyway, you had a talk with him. I could only hear your part, which didn't tell me much, but there were long gaps so I think he did most of the talking. Anyway, his code name was Mad Mok; he was another Shooter here in Memphis. It looks like Erebus stuck a pipe bomb under his car, which means he's not just looking for you anymore. We think he's declared war on LEI itself. That puts all assets in danger."

"Good God, have you notified HQ?"

"Of course, this is currently the top priority across all of LEI North America."

"Do they know how this guy got his info?" Sweetwater asked.

"That is job number two on the list."

"Any guesses?"

"That's confidential, but I don't think I'm leaking anything to say it has to be a mole, and finding a mole takes time."

"Y'know, if I was gonna sell confidential company data, I don't think I'd do it to a corporation that kills people as its business model."

"People are whack, dude," she said. It was a hard point to argue.

Sweetwater picked up Warden's breakfast and held it over his own empty container. "You sure?"

She waved her hand.

"Knock yourself out."

Sweetwater dropped her container into his open box. "Were you able to get anything off your computer?"

"Yeah, the screen shattered but the hard drive was good. So, I slaved it to a new machine the company overnighted, and I'm back in action. Hey, are you getting tired? Suddenly you don't look so good."

He pushed the container away. "I think I ate too fast, but I'm all right. So, let's pretend I understood what you just said; what's next? Who does LEI have running things?" he asked.

"That's complicated. BB assigned you the contract."

"What?" Sweetwater grimaced as he washed down the last food particles with a gulp of the protein drink. "I'm strapped to a hospital bed. What are they thinking?"

"You're not actually strapped in anymore."

"There's gotta be more to this."

"I told them you were ready to get out of here and get back to work."

"I think you're the one that's whack."

"So just how long are you planning to stay locked up in this little hidey-hole? I thought you were an ex-Marine."

"You're *always* a Marine."

She held out her hands. "Okay, listen up. I figured you were smarter than this, but you're still on meds so I'll give you the benefit of the doubt. We've got a mole, right? In here, you're a stationary target—"

"In a secure facility!"

"That's the point. Witherbot has people stationed all over the hospital from LEI, FBI, MPD, and every other alphabet agency you can think of. There is no way Erebus gets to you down here."

"I like the sound of that!"

"No, you don't. Think about it, Luther, while you're in here he's not coming after you, so he's free to hunt anywhere without us having a track on him. Or go to ground and wait for you to finally come out. LEI and the LEOs can't keep assets committed to this case forever, and if you go that route, you're at his mercy. But if he thinks you're back out there now…"

"He might come out looking for me."

"There's no 'might' in there. The dude is cocoa bananas."

Sweetwater's jaw closed with a snap. The steady *beep-beep-beep* of the heart monitor increased its pace.

"You wanna turn your back?"

"Fuck no."

"Fine, get my pants." He lowered the side rail of the bed and slipped his legs over.

Warden just sat in her chair and tried to hide her smile by covering her mouth, which Sweetwater took as a sign of approval for his actions. His gown opened in the back and he didn't try to tie it closed. If she wanted to stare at his butt, that was fine by him.

"So, I'll get 'em myself," he said. Sweetwater eased one leg down until it touched the floor. He grabbed onto the side of the bed with a death grip and gingerly slipped off the bed until he was standing. The room spun twice and then stopped. He was still on his feet.

He took a deep breath, pausing when he felt the stabbing pain in his ribs, held his breath for a slow ten count, and exhaled. He caught Warden's eye. Her expression showed surprise.

"Yeah, so you can stand, big deal. Can you get your pants off the chair or walk to the doorway?"

He glanced at the chair and the door. The door was closer, about four yards. Ten baby steps, maybe twelve. Gripping the pole connected to all his tubes and lines, Sweetwater took a tentative step. His legs trembled as he shifted his weight from one foot to the other. He locked his focus on the doorknob and took another step. His jaw was clenched as he focused on the handle. Step, take a breath, next step, exhale, repeat. Inhale on the right step, exhale on the left. The doorknob grew closer.

Finally, he reached out, grabbed the handle, and pulled the door open.

"What the hell?" said a startled young black woman who had been about to enter. Sweetwater regretted what had happened to Scott, but not that Relinda was now his therapist. Involuntarily, he gave her a bright smile, although pain made him grind his teeth and blink. Sweat ran from his temples as exhaustion dragged at his body, but he wasn't about to show Warden how tired he was, much less his pretty physical therapist. That's not what Marines did.

"I think maybe it's time I get out of here."

"Well, you can just rethink that, can't you? Does your nurse know you're out of bed without hospital staff present?"

"I don't need permission."

"Oh, you're one of *those*. Fine, hotshot, you want out? Go ahead, I won't stop you."

"Uhh…"

"Yeah, I thought so." She grabbed Sweetwater under the armpit. "I think you've done enough for today. Back to the bed." The back of Sweetwater's hospital gown stuck to his skin from sweat.

"Men, huh? Or was this your idea?" Relinda asked Warden.

"He's gullible."

"So, it *was* your idea."

"Wait, what do you mean I'm gullible?" Sweetwater said. Warden ignored him.

"I baited him," Warden said, "but did you see how far he got? I think you're being too easy on him."

Sweetwater straightened his legs in the bed and Relinda pulled the blankets up to his waist. As she bent over his bed, the top of her scrubs hung low for a split instant and he had to curl his knees slightly to avoid embarrassment. He made as if to brush his hair back, but he was really just hiding his face.

"I am not gullible!"

"Good job," Relinda said to Warden. "Sometimes, getting them to take the first step can be the hardest."

"He's a Marine."

"Oh," Relinda said. "No wonder you're with him."

"It's not like that," Sweetwater said in protest.

This time Relinda *did* respond to him. "If it's not like that, then you aren't just gullible, you're not very smart. She's a catch." Relinda grabbed his wrist, fingering it until she found his pulse. "How far did he get?"

"From the bed to where you caught him," Warden said.

"I'm sitting right here, y'know," Sweetwater said. "You could just ask me your questions."

"As you know, I have been instructed to act as if you're dead—"

"I thought—" he said, cutting her off.

"Luther!" said Warden, cutting him off in turn. She gave a short shake of her head. That was an LEI matter, not to be shared. As far as the hospital records and staff were concerned, he *was* dead.

Relinda looked from one to another before continuing. "We're going to do your physical therapy down here. We have a room with a treadmill and cross-trainer down the hall, and enough space to stretch and do simple exercises."

"I feel like a rat in a cage." Sweetwater grabbed the safety bar on the side of the bed and pulled it back up, locking it in place. "I need to get out of here."

"Less than two weeks ago you were in a coma. It wasn't a week ago that you were in a bombing. Give your body time to heal."

"How much more time?"

"I'm just your physical therapist, those are questions for your doctor."

"I've yet to meet a doctor that gives a straight answer to anything. But that's not your fault, so fine, let's do the work down here. I'm going to get better and get out of here."

"And probably break all the speed records doing it." Relinda smiled and left.

"I think she likes you."

"Yeah?"

Warden's grin faded some. "Why, do you like her?"

"Shouldn't I? She's pretty hot."

"Oh, she is, huh?"

"Why do you care?"

"I don't care."

"Then why are you asking me?"

"Just asking, that's all. Making conversation."

Now it was Sweetwater's turn to smile. "That's all?"

"What else could it be?"

"I don't know, but Relinda's smokin'."

"I'm glad you think so."

"What did I do?"

"God, you're stupid."

Warden rose and stalked to the door, stopping only when he blurted out, "Your butt wiggles funny."

"What? Do you know how wrong it is to say that?"

"No, I didn't mean any sexual, it's just that one side—never mind, sorry."

"My right hip is a half inch higher than the other. Are you happy now?" Halfway out the door she turned back. "It doesn't affect my walk but yeah, it makes my cheek jiggle. Some guys like it, I'm sorry it bothers you."

"I didn't say—"

"The British Bitch is coming to check on you in person."

The door slammed behind her.

"What did I do?" he called after her.

Chapter Thirty

Intensive Care Unit, Elvis Presley Trauma Center, Memphis, TN

Adrian Erebus remembered little after squatting in the dark alongside the liquor store, only fragments of memories of lights and people talking. The surgeon making his rounds two days later expressed amazement at how lucky he was, since the stab wounds all managed to miss vital organs. The worst injury was a punctured lung, but even that one only nicked it. It missed all the major blood vessels.

It was, the doctor said, like the assailant knew precisely where and how deep to make each wound. He'd never seen such a thing and would be talking about it for years. Erebus still had close to a hundred stitches in him, but overall, the prognosis couldn't be better.

The problem was Mrs. Thomas. She kept running his information and coming back with holes in his story. The address he gave didn't exist, which he explained away by claiming to have transposed two numbers. Then, of course, was the fact she looked up the phone number that was registered to the house. The people that answered the phone confirmed the address and told her they had never heard of a George Jones. Erebus knew the time had come to act.

The doctor wanted him to sit in a chair for short periods, three times a day. He asked for some clothes to replace those cut away during surgery or taken by the police for evidence by pleading he had no one to retrieve any for him. They brought him some gray sweat pants and an old green Sansui T-shirt with holes under the armpits from the lost and found. Once he was alone, Erebus pulled off the wires and removed the IV. He hissed at the sudden pain and held his arm for a minute until the sting subsided.

Peeking out of his room, he spotted an arrow pointing right that said "Elevators." There wouldn't be a second chance for him to find and kill Sweetwater. He timed the move for shift change, when fewer employees would be in the halls, but he still needed to hurry before somebody discovered he was gone. Within five steps, the pain nearly bent him double. The blade might have miraculously missed killing him, but it hadn't missed the large abdominal muscles. They spasmed as he trudged toward the double doors down the hallway. The doors required pushing a button for admittance, which no doubt led to someone at a nurse's station.

Should he push the button? Did they have a camera monitoring the hallway? He didn't see one, but you could never tell. He couldn't just keep standing there, though.

The problem solved itself and left Erebus thinking that God was on his side. An orderly pushed a withered black woman from a nearby room through the door. He sped up to pass through in the wake of the wheelchair, even though it hurt so badly he wanted to cry.

The hall stretched on, but the woman pushing the wheelchair turned into a room. Erebus lowered his eyes and kept walking, following another arrow. The hallway ended with another pair of doors, and luckily these had a push-bar handle. He slipped through before anyone spotted him.

The corridor opened onto another long hallway that split in a T. He turned right and finally came to the elevators. He took them up a level and retraced his steps on that floor, above the recovery ward.

Except two handlebar doors wouldn't open. He took a step back and saw a badge reader on one side.

Damn it!

Short of stealing a badge, his plan of searching the hospital for Sweetwater was over. He took the elevator back to the first floor and headed back to the emergency ward with less urgency. Now, if they found him wandering the halls, he could plead a temporary blackout or something. That might give him time to think of another way to track down Sweetwater. Soon enough he found himself outside the emergency ward, which had a badge reader on the door.

"Shit," he said, loud enough to startle himself. He turned his head, looking around for someone with a badge.

Behind him, he heard the sound of a door closing. He looked up and caught a reflection in the curved mirror overhead. Somebody in civilian clothes was heading for the nurse's station at his back.

Was that the woman who broke into his house? He reached up and rubbed the side of his head, using his arm to block his face. It was her, he felt sure of it!

He turned to see where she'd come from and saw a short hallway behind a column, partially hidden to the left of the main hall. Beyond that were double doors, and he couldn't see any badge readers. He carefully angled himself to get a better look. Beside the door was a sign that read "Memphis Police Department."

Action followed observation and he crossed the hallway diagonally, well within sight of the nurse's station. Nobody noticed. The green Sansui shirt looked a lot like the hospital scrubs, at least from a distance. Without hesitating, he pushed on the door, and the latch clicked. He opened the door an inch; there was no one in sight. Erebus slipped inside.

Behind the door was a service elevator to one side and a fire exit stairway leading down to a small landing, and another stairwell that ended in a steel door. Taking the elevator seemed only marginally less attention grabbing than blowing an air horn, so Erebus took the stairs, leaning heavily on the steel handrail. He opened the door without hesitation. Either there were cops on the other side or there weren't.

There weren't.

The halls of the hospital were now dingy reminders of once soothing pastels, faded now into a grimy industrial palette so typical of public facilities. When first built, the waiting areas would have had soft, comfortable chairs with televisions mounted in the corners. They were all still there, but the chair seats only hinted at the color of the original fabric, and most of the TVs didn't work.

Once he passed into the police section all that changed. The walls were a dull but clean gray, only half a shade darker than the linoleum floor. There were no soft stuffed chairs, only metal folding ones beside a wall of lockers colored the same gray as everything else. The area was empty.

There was a wall of lockers at his back and the hallway stretched out before him. There were only five other doors, and four of them were already open. Being barefoot, he walked silently to the first open door and peeked around the corner.

There was an empty bed in the room and nothing else, so he crept on to the second room. Like the first, it was empty except for the simple hospital bed. Erebus then moved to the third door. It was closed, and inside he could hear the regular beeping of a heart monitor.

A wire-reinforced glass window mounted in the door let him edge along until he could see someone occupied the bed. He had to bend his knees to avoid being seen, which strained his ruptured stomach and chest muscles. He felt the agony, but when the sleeping man in the bed rolled over and Erebus saw his face, euphoria washed through his mind and overpowered the pain.

It was Sweetwater.

"There you are," Erebus whispered, his dirty teeth revealed by a snarl. "Third time's the charm."

In place of a doorknob there was a push-down lever. Gently as possible, he applied pressure, but it refused to move. Heat reddened the tips of his ears. A locked door was not going to prevent his righteous revenge from sending Sweetwater straight to hell. He eased away, careful not to wake the man in the room.

Even in his enraged and partly drugged state, Erebus realized that he couldn't break through the door without rousing Sweetwater and probably triggering an alert. Nurse Dottie had filled him in about the comings and goings of the security people from multiple agencies and how they were concentrating on screening everyone who came into the hospital. That explained why he hadn't seen anybody yet, and why the ceiling mounted cameras hadn't given him away; nobody was paying attention to the *inside* of the hospital or the video monitors. They were all securing the perimeter. They would have him on recordings, but then it would be too late. But if he wasn't careful, a dozen security agents would be on him fast, and Sweetwater would get away again.

He moved back to the lockers, none of which had locks. Moving slowly, afraid of a squeak from a rusty hinge, he opened every locker. They were all empty except one, which was filled with cleaning supplies. Bottles of disinfectant and a scrub brush stood inside a metal pail, with rubber gloves hanging over the edge. Nothing that could be used as a weapon. He briefly considered what he could do with the plunger at the back but rejected that when he saw the broom with replaceable head. Perfect! By unscrewing the wooden handle, he essentially had a spear. The Shooter deserved another bullet.

With his improvised weapon, he climbed into an empty locker to wait. It was a hospital after all, and someone was bound to check on Sweetwater before too long.

Squeezed into the locker, Erebus jumped when he felt a tug on his pants leg. Barely able to turn his head enough to look down, he saw two glowing red dots at his left elbow.

"Herbert," he said, in a low whisper. "Oh God, son, I'm so sorry, I got stabbed and forgot all about you. How could I do that? I don't know, it must be the drugs. Forgive me."

"Kill him this time," Herbert said.

Erebus nodded. "I won't let you down again."

Now that Herbert was with him, Erebus was resolved to finish the job. He stood in the dark for what seemed like hours, holding the door closed without letting it latch. Downward sloping vents allowed him to see a portion of the floor. He was careful not to make any noise, but he was growing antsy.

Eventually, he heard the loud *ding* of the elevator, and he tensed. He dared to crack the locker door half an inch and he saw a well-muscled woman in scrubs pulling a treadmill out of the elevator. It appeared to be stuck. Grunting and cursing, she didn't hear Erebus step out of the locker and come up behind her.

Erebus raised the broomstick over one shoulder. She must have heard something, or maybe she sensed something was wrong, because she half turned from struggling with the treadmill, eyes wide at the wild-eyed man in the bloody T-shirt hefting the broomstick like a baseball bat. Erebus didn't realize his wounds had opened, leaving streaks of dark red across his torso, but he was so pumped full of adrenaline he didn't feel any pain. That allowed him to put all his strength behind the swing. The woman reflexively brought up her arm to catch the blow. The broom handle shattered.

She bent over, gasping out a low wail and cradling her injured arm. Holding the splintered wooden shaft, Erebus realized it now had a sharp, vicious point. Although less than half its original length, it was a true weapon.

He raised it overhead like Van Helsing preparing to stab Dracula with a stake and jammed the broken shaft deep into the side of her neck. The lithe woman tried to dodge to one side, but Erebus was faster. The jagged end penetrated four inches into her neck, just below the left ear. When Erebus pulled it back out, blood spurted from the hole and streaked his face and shirt.

She fell to her knees, her face registering shock, and Erebus saw how pretty she was. Her lips moved as she tried to speak, and he had the funny thought that his grandmother used to do something like that. "Chewing her cud," his mother called it, though he didn't know what that meant. Now the young black lady was doing the same thing, and he couldn't help giggling. Finally, she fell forward, the blood making a juicy, splattering sound when she hit the floor.

Erebus stepped back from the corpse. Blood covered the elevator floor, and both the treadmill and the woman's body were blocking the doors. Would anybody get suspicious that the elevator was stuck down there? He couldn't send it up like it was, and there likely wasn't time to clean it before somebody either saw him on the cameras or came down the stairs. Maybe the woman who'd broken into his house would come back, or a doctor, or a nurse.

Looking at the body, he spotted a ring of keys on a retractable cord attached to the lady's waist. He unbuckled it and advanced on the locked door, the blood-covered stick in his left hand. His best chance now was speed.

He pushed three keys into the lock before the fourth one slipped cleanly inside. Erebus pushed the door open and charged inside, ready to strike, but two steps inside he stopped. The bed was empty.

Something smashed into the back of his head.

Sweetwater woke to the click of the door handle and a soft rattle from the door as somebody pushed against it. It didn't open but, after a few seconds, the same thing happened again. He was about to drift off to sleep again, when through the fog of narcotics his brain flashed a warning; staff would have a key to unlock the door. Whoever was outside the door obviously didn't.

He scanned the room, confirming that Warden hadn't returned after storming out. The only sound was the heart monitor's continual beeping. Listening, muffled noises came from the hall outside. The sense of danger grew.

Apart from the furniture, he didn't see anything useful as a weapon. Taking a deep breath, he swung his legs off the bed, grabbed his IV pole, and stood. Using it for support, he shuffled to the door. Tubes and lines hung from it in case he needed intravenous drugs again.

The distinct and unmistakable *crack* of breaking wood drew his gaze to the door's window. There, crouching in the open doors of the elevator, beside the bleeding figure of Relinda, was Adrian Erebus, the man who'd shot him. Sweetwater watched Erebus paw at Relinda's body. After a few seconds Erebus stood, holding a ring of keys.

The deranged man was coming to kill him. Most people would have panicked, but while the idea of killing innocent people nauseated him, killing murderers and madmen was a different story. He'd been trained to do that, and to do it well.

Leaning against the wall behind the door, he again scanned for a weapon. The sound of keys digging into the lock echoed through the room. He needed something to defend himself. Then there was a click followed by the sound of a key being driven home.

The door opened with a violent shove and hit Sweetwater's big toe. Erebus ran inside, brandishing a bloody rod. He stopped when he saw the empty bed and looked around for his victim. Out of time and by sheer, unthinking reflex, Sweetwater grabbed his IV pole in both hands and smashed it against Erebus' head.

The man fell to his hands and knees, and Sweetwater landed on his back. With a scream, he brought his fist down on the back of Erebus' neck, driving the would-be assassin onto his stomach. Under normal circumstances that would have put Erebus down, maybe killed him, but Sweetwater's blow lacked the power to do more than stun his smaller, older opponent.

The two men scrambled for control.

Erebus reached back and grabbed Sweetwater's arm. Blood soaked his green shirt but apparently he was too far gone to feel any pain. Or maybe he was drugged. Either way, Sweetwater felt himself being pushed off the man's back. He just hadn't recovered the strength for a fight. With a jerk, Erebus threw him aside, and he landed on his shoulder. Stars shot through his vision.

"You're not getting away…this time…you fucking murderer," Erebus said. Whether from pain, blood loss, or rage, he was panting between words. Even so, Sweetwater watched as Erebus tried to climb to his feet, except he was tangled amid the unused cords and lines hanging from the IV pole.

The improvised weapons training course he'd taken in Scout Sniper School told Sweetwater's brain what to do next. Survival depended on speed, so he ignored the twisting pain associated with his movements and lurched at Erebus, grabbing a handful of cords and looping them around his assailant's neck. Using them as a garrote, he pulled back and up, then crossed his hands and leaned back, relying more on his weight than muscles to cut off Erebus' oxygen.

It worked. Erebus clawed at the cord digging into his flesh. For a few seconds, it became fading strength against fading strength, the blood of the two men mixing as it puddled beneath them, but even fueled by extreme hatred, Erebus couldn't win in hand-to-hand combat against a bigger, younger Marine.

His face purpled, and his struggles weakened like a mouse in the final stages of being constricted by a python. As the rodent died, its brain lost control of its body. In its last seconds of life, a mouse's back legs ran like a cartoon animal as the flight neurons, no longer held in check by the brain, poured energy into its nervous system. Thrashing in desperation, one of Erebus' arms was caught in the tangle of cords, and the other left gouges in his own neck as he tried to clear his throat.

Sweetwater twisted harder. Erebus half turned his head, and their eyes locked. Sweetwater saw nothing in them except the cold eyes of a killer, pitiless and filled with hate. Erebus' lips turned blue, and his eyes filled with red as capillaries burst from the strain. His struggles grew feeble.

Sweetwater kept up the pressure long after his brain told him that Erebus was dead. For the first time in his life, he had actually killed someone, and he felt no remorse in doing so.

But the blood leaking from his own wounds clouded his vision. He might have slain Erebus, but Erebus might have managed to return the favor. It was like he was driving through a tunnel, but no matter how fast he drove the end grew more and more distant, until everything faded.

Warden shook Sweetwater awake. He was still gripping the cord looped around Erebus' neck.

"Is he dead?" Sweetwater asked in a less than a

whisper.

"Yes, Luther, he's dead. You killed him. Now lie still; I've called for help."

But Sweetwater couldn't lie still. Beyond Warden hunched a figure out of nightmare, like a Minotaur with human hands and glowing red eyes, and horns curving forward along a long face.

"Watch it!" he cried. He tried to roll away but was held in place by Warden.

"Luther, what is it? What's wrong?"

"Behind you! Can't you see it? Let me up!" Sweetwater's chest burned from the exertion of yelling.

Warden paused, craned her neck, and looked back at him with wide eyes.

"I feel something there, something horrible. You can see it, can't you?"

"Help me up."

The beast moved first. It bent over the dead Adrian Erebus, opened his mouth, and breathed fire down his throat.

Erebus coughed and sat up, pulling the lines loose from around his neck.

"Herbert," he said. "I knew you'd help me. You are such a good son."

Chapter Thirty-One

Memphis Police Department Secure Facility below the
Elvis Presley Trauma Center, Memphis, TN

"What the hell?" Warden backed up against the wall, her gaze fixed on the reanimated corpse.

"I thought you said he was dead," said Sweetwater.

"He was."

Unlike her, Luther could see the...*thing* standing over Erebus. Whatever it was, and whatever it had done a moment ago, had brought life back to a dead man. But now the creature was diminished by at least a third. Its head had brushed the ceiling, but now it stood no taller than he did, and the radiance from its eyes was dimmer. Then it disappeared.

Sweetwater rolled onto his side, breathing heavily, and pointed at Erebus.

"I get it. I know what thing that is."

Erebus lay flat on his back and was glaring at Sweetwater. Sticky blood covered his face.

"You don't know shit. I killed you twice, fuckhead. Now you know how it feels."

Sweetwater spotted Warden's purse still hanging off her shoulder. He'd already ripped out a lot of stitches, which hurt like hell and had started bleeding again, but it gave more freedom of movement. He got to his knees, reached into the purse, and pulled out her pistol. It felt heavier than before, but using both hands, he aimed it at Erebus' temple.

"No, don't shoot him, Luther! We need him."

"Like hell."

He moved his finger to the trigger.

"No!" Warden said, pushing his hands to the side as his finger squeezed the trigger. The gunshot echoed in the small room and it was like having his head inside a metal bucket while somebody smacked it with an aluminum bat. A light in the ceiling started flashing red and sirens blared in the hallway.

Erebus lay stiff and unmoving, his eyes dilated from the shock of the gunshot. The bullet buried itself in the cinder block wall after ricocheting off his skull. A streak gouged his skin along the top of his forehead where the bullet had ripped it open. Fresh blood oozed out, a brighter red than the partly dried mask covering his face.

Sweetwater brought the pistol back up to the other man's temple. This time he didn't have his finger on the trigger, but along the underside of the gun barrel.

"Talk to me! What the fuck was that?" Sweetwater said, yelling to be heard over the alarms.

He never unlocked eyes with Erebus. The effort of remaining upright was starting to take its toll and his vision blurred, though he tried not to let Erebus know.

"We need him," she said.

"Repeating yourself doesn't help, so maybe throw in some facts?"

"LEI has a mole, Luther. That's probably how this POS found out you weren't dead. We need him to ID the leak, or a lot more people could be at risk."

Sweetwater pushed the barrel hard against Erebus' temple. The alarms stopped ringing.

"Or I could put a bullet through his skull."

"No! Orders are to keep him alive." She reached out to grab his arm again, but he glanced over with an expression of warning. She drew back her hand. "Don't you see? This guy isn't shit; he's a worm, and the world's full of other worms like him. There will always be someone else. Being a Shooter is dangerous enough without some inside anaconda selling us out."

"Us?"

"All my personal data is in there with yours. And LEI doesn't only do private contract work. It's still on the front lines working to identify terrorists and put them down before they can do anything. Now, somebody with access to LEI databases is out there selling that info to the highest bidder. He's already gotten Bonney and Shields killed, and damned near you and me, too. We have to put him down."

"We?"

"Yeah, *we*. Because I'll do it if nobody else will."

"You'll have to get in line. So, what about you, Turdzilla?" he said to Erebus, his voice losing power. "Who do you want to kill you, me or her?"

Nobody moved as Sweetwater's stare burned into the other man. In response, Erebus closed his eyes, took a deep breath, and exhaled through pursed lips.

"I have students like you, dumb as a fucking rock. No matter how much you try to teach them, they stay stupid. If no one's going to die today, I could sleep."

"That thing…it's you, isn't it?"

312 | HOY & WEBB

"See? Stupid, like I said."

Sweetwater lowered the gun. The effort of keeping it aimed exhausted him.

"Here," he said, handing it to Warden. "Keep it aimed at his head."

She took it and, despite her tough exterior, the weapon trembled in her hands. Erebus opened one eye, then closed it again.

"Somebody should be here soon," she said, "I wonder what's taking so long. You don't look so good."

"That fits; I feel like shit. Is the elevator still blocked?"

"Oh yeah, I forgot. There's the stairs."

Sweetwater put his head down. "I don't know."

"I need to go get you help, Luther. You're bleeding pretty bad again."

"No, keep an eye on them."

"Them? Luther, talk to me, are you all right?"

Sweetwater rolled his head, seemingly half asleep.

"He's not alone. That thing is with him."

"What thing is that, Luther? I can't see it."

"It's like...like a demon."

Erebus opened his eyes, face twisted in rage.

"That's my boy, you ignorant shit. His name is Herbert!"

Banging was coming from the door that connected the police annex to the rest of the hospital. Warden looked from one man to the other. They were both lying on the floor, glaring at each other, and neither was acknowledging her.

"I have no idea what's going on, but I can't leave you two like this." Using her foot, she rolled Erebus onto his belly. He slid sideways on the bloody floor but didn't resist. "Hand's behind your back." He complied, turning his head to continue baring his teeth at Sweetwater.

"A boy needs his mother," he said. "You took that away."

"A mother needs her boy, too, and *you* took *that* away."

Warden knelt and put her knee at the base of Erebus' spine. She grabbed a cord off the floor and jerked it free of its connection to a monitoring computer. She fumbled with the cord, but eventually secured the man's wrists.

"Luther, can you hear me? I'm going to get help."

"Don't leave me alone…with that thing."

"I told you that's Herbert!" Erebus said. He tried to yell, but it came out hoarse. A long sigh followed as the last breath left his lungs.

"Damn," she said, hurrying out.

Stepping into the hall, Warden's brain suddenly felt immediately overwhelmed. Bells were ringing down the elevator shaft as the doors tried to close, were blocked by Relinda's body and the treadmill, fully opened again, and then repeated the process. Warden briefly considered trying to clear them, but the treadmill was too big. It was also a crime scene. The assault on her ears wasn't the only disorienting part of it, though. Blue lights flashed along the top of the corridor, like a slow strobe light.

She tracked bloody footprints down the hallway toward the emergency exit. Relieved, she pushed on the bar to open the door, but nothing happened. The door stayed locked. Shoving it again with both hands did no good. Then she rammed it with her shoulder, kicked the door, and finally pounded on it with both fists. Only then did she spot a small sign below the Exit sign.

A blue light indicates lockdown until opened by the Memphis Police Department.

"Damn it," she yelled, pounding on the door. "Who locks the fire exit?"

She heard pounding from the other side, a hollow *thud thud* on the heavy door. The echo of the elevator bell drowned out a voice. She put her ear against the steel and was able to make out the muffled words.

"How many?"

Warden made a fist and hit the door three times.

She yelled to whoever was on the other side, "Go get help."

Two knocks followed.

Having done all she could, Warden ran back to Sweetwater's room. For a moment she paused outside, watching the elevator doors bump Relinda's body. The physical therapist stared at her with wide, dead eyes, until Warden got the eerie feeling that told her somebody dead was standing beside her. Trembling, she stepped into the room…and found the figure of a young boy sitting on Erebus' back holding a black-bladed knife. He was using it to saw through the cord binding Erebus' hands.

"Who are you?" she said, her voice betraying terror. In her heart, Warden knew the answer. "How did you get in here?"

From the side he appeared normal, except as if viewed through a black haze. The boy's head turned and Warden backed up a step, nearly tripping over Sweetwater. Stabs of ice froze her spine. Empty black eye sockets fixed her in place like a mounted insect and sucked her deep into a well of darkness. Tongues of flame licked at his eyelids and provided the only light. He grinned, his mouth a slash that stretched nearly to his ears, filled with serrated, triangular teeth like a shark.

Warden backed to the wall, stepping over Sweetwater without looking down. Her shoes stuck in the tacky blood, lifting up strings of the semi-solid liquid like cheese from a hot pizza. As she stared at the apparition, it laughed at her, but instead of a "ha-ha-ha" sound, it was a hiss, *Sss-Sss-Sss.*

Semi-conscious, Sweetwater saw the black misshapen figure sit astride Erebus without at first recognizing the figure for what it was. Blinking, he heard a hissing sound escape through dagger fangs. The synapses in his brain lagged behind their sensory input due to the blood loss, and its corresponding drop in blood pressure, so it took a full second to realize what he was seeing. Once that happened, adrenaline shot through his body and he pushed himself away. Shaped now like a child and not the half-human half-bull minotaur, it had once again shrunk, confirming Sweetwater's theory; the *thing* revived Erebus with its own energy.

Its hissing dropped to a growl as it jerked the blade up, cutting the cord around Erebus' wrists. Wisps of smoke rose from the cord's blackened ends. The twice-dead serial killer took only seconds to free his wrists.

"Shoot it," Sweetwater called out, weakly. "Hurry, kill it."

"No!" Covered in blood and looking more dead than alive, Erebus scrambled to his knees with a quickness that belied his gory appearance. No sanity remained in his eyes. He threw his arms wide to shield Herbert.

"You will *not* shoot my boy."

No taller now than waist high, Herbert placed the knife in Erebus' hand, and he gripped the handle in a tight fist. The man's flesh sizzled, and the reek of seared flesh caused Sweetwater to flashback to the post 9/11 days of digging out bodies from the Capitol.

"Yes," Erebus said. He hefted the knife and thrust the point upward through his tongue, splitting it like a reptile's. Blood filled his mouth and ran out the corners. He smacked his lips like it was chocolate syrup.

"Thank you, my boy."

Warden already had her back against the wall but was trying to back up anyway and slipped on the bloody floor. Falling, she squeezed off a shot that missed Erebus and shattered the heart monitor screen. Her head bounced off the wall, and she landed in a heap.

Erebus swiped at her hand with the knife, cutting her thumb and knocking the pistol free. He knelt, pulled her leg taut, and stabbed the fleshy part of her calf below the knee. The blade ripped through her leg and out the other side. She screamed and kicked when he grabbed both her legs and dragged her off of Sweetwater, where he could reach her head and chest.

She kicked him in the jaw using her other leg. A loud *crack* indicated she'd broken his jaw, but Erebus plunged the blade deep into the thigh of her injured leg.

Warden's screams echoed in the room as her body trembled from the sudden, overwhelming pain. Beyond Erebus was the dark figure of Herbert, laughing as his father raised the knife for another stab. She kicked again, and this time, fueled by desperation, met the plunging knife with the sole of her shoe. The tip penetrated through the tough leather and nicked the skin below, which made him laugh.

Erebus yanked it out, held her leg, and even as she jerked and struggled, struck again, twisting the blade as blood poured onto his fist. He slid the blade free and drove the knife into her abdomen, pushing hard to drive the blade in all the way to the guard. Then he ripped it free again in a spray of droplets.

Warden's screams hadn't roused the catatonic Sweetwater, but her low moan did. Only half-conscious, he spotted the pistol lying beside his right knee in the puddle of his own blood. When he tried to pick it up, the gory handle and weight made it slip twice before he got a firm grip. Raising it was like hefting a brick. The ammo might or might not be wet.

Laughing as Warden sagged after the stab wound to her stomach, Erebus noticed Sweetwater's movement and glanced down at the half-dead hitman. The knife dripped at his side.

"I'm glad you're still alive, Two-Bit," he said. "Now I can watch you die."

Fresh hammering came from the hallway, diverting Erebus' gaze. When he looked back, the pistol was pointed at his chest.

"I hate that fucking name," Sweetwater said. He fired, unable to control the recoil, which sent the gun up and to the right. It didn't matter. The bullet hit Erebus under his sternum, passed through his body, and out the back, where it mashed flat against the cinder block wall.

The knife dropped from Erebus' fingers, and he collapsed to his knee before falling face-first into the blood puddle. The elevator bell stopped ringing, and seconds later a squealing noise came from the hallway.

Warden and Sweetwater's eyes met. She had a hand on her belly wound.

"I'm not ready to die," she said, tears forming in her eyes. "I don't wanna die, Luther. God help me, I don't wanna die."

Voices came from the hall. Sweetwater tried to raise the gun. Erebus' chest still rose and fell, although he was coughing blood, and Sweetwater only had seconds to finish him off. Warden noticed and shook her head.

"Don't do it," she said.

"Some fuckers just need to die."

The world was going gray again.

"Where is the kid?" she said.

"Gone…disappeared."

Erebus coughed a spray of blood into the pool he coughed up the last time he died.

"Is he gonna live?"

"I hope not. I've already killed him twice…so who the fuck knows?"

Sweetwater dipped in and out of consciousness. He woke under a bright surgical light for a few seconds. Next, he woke in a room, which resembled the one in the recovery ward. His stitches and bandages were back in place, as were the usual machines, hanging bags, and associated wiring and tubes. There was a second bed on his right occupied by Teri Warden. Sleeping, she looked pale, but a nurse fussing with something didn't appear panicked. *Why* he'd needed further surgery wasn't as clear but sleep beckoned, and he began drifting away.

"Mister Sweetwater?" said a deep, raspy voice that whistled when the speaker inhaled. He wore a well-tailored gray suit with black pin-stripes, a blue shirt, and red power tie. "I'm Police Director Hayes, how are you feeling?"

"Better than dead, I guess. I'd shake your hand director, but you should know I charge for autographs."

Hayes' face showed no response beyond a twitch to the left corner of his mouth.

"In the past two weeks my department has investigated four homicides and one bombing that all have one thing in common, you, Mister Sweetwater. Moreover, the only trauma center for two hundred miles has been effectively shut down to all but the worst emergencies because of that bombing, which I am given to understand was designed to kill *you*. Multiple hospital personnel have been killed or wounded. Innocent people going about living their daily lives, who came to work to help save the lives of those in critical danger of death. Memphis has its share of crime, Mister Sweetwater, and I understand that innocent victims are part of that—"

"Hey, I'm a victim here, too."

When Hayes turned to make sure neither of the two cops posted at the door were watching, even in his tired state Sweetwater didn't need instinctive warnings to know something unpleasant was coming. He didn't expect what happened, though.

Satisfied none of his people were stupid enough to spy on the boss, and that Warden was still unconscious, Hayes gripped Sweetwater's forearm and squeezed, hard. Refusing to show how much it hurt, Sweetwater grinned, biting the inside of his lower lip instead of crying out at the pain.

"I understand you were not the cause of most of these issues, Mister Sweetwater, and while I find you and your fellow—what is it you call yourselves, Shooters?—while I find you viler than a depraved pedophile, your profession is, nevertheless, legal. But you, Mister Sweetwater, are a magnet for trouble. The physical therapist who died downstairs was a single mother of three. She earned her degree at night while cleaning houses during the day, all to build a better life for her children. Had you been the manager of a drive-through fried chicken restaurant, she would have tucked those children in that night. Instead, her mother, their grandmother, had to explain why they would never see their mother again.

"I have reached out to your supervisors and requested you be removed from my city just as soon as possible. And lest there be any confusion about what I mean, let me spell this out as clearly as I can: Leave my city, Mister Sweetwater. Get out. Do not pass go, do not collect two hundred dollars. *Leave.*"

Hayes withdrew a pair of handcuffs from his jacket pocket, snapped one end on Sweetwater's wrist and the other around the bed railing.

"That's gonna be hard to do if I'm handcuffed to this bed," Sweetwater said, knowing it wouldn't help, but not caring. Hayes wasn't there for a reasonable discussion.

"This is just a safety precaution while we wait for your transfer to come through. It's for your own good. There will be no further attempts on your life. However, I'm going to unlock the door when I leave, and I'm also going to disable the automatic lock down. The next time someone comes in here to kill you, I'm going to make damn sure there is no collateral damage. That is the correct term, isn't it? If one of your assassins hits a non-involved person, that is the term for them, correct? Collateral damage?"

"Among others."

"I appreciate your cooperation, Mister Sweetwater. Now get the fuck out of town."

Hayes turned on one foot with a military flourish and strode to the door.

"Let's not do this again anytime soon," Sweetwater said.

Hayes stopped, back erect, and executed a full turn.

"Perhaps I was not clear enough. If you return to Memphis, Mister Sweetwater, then it may have dire consequences. For you."

Chapter Thirty-Two

Memphis Police Department Secure Facility below the
Elvis Presley Trauma Center, Memphis, TN

"Father?" A familiar voice cut through the black haze in Adrian Erebus' unconscious mind. "It's time we talked."

A single light source, like a high-intensity spotlight, came from above, making a wide illuminated circle on the floor. Erebus sat up and saw he was wearing his favorite old teaching suit with all of the little nicks and tears mended and the elastic in the suspenders not overstretched. He felt comfortable in the suit, which allowed him to revel in doing what he most enjoyed: teaching.

"Herbert, is that you, my boy? What a pleasant surprise."

The boy walked along the edge of the shadows, half in, half out of the light. He wore jeans and a T-shirt with a butterfly on the back. Erebus smiled a father's warm smile at Herbert, trying to see the reciprocal love in the boy's eyes, but something was wrong. It hurt to look at his son's eyes, so he turned away. He looked at the T-shirt instead.

Erebus didn't remember getting up, but he found himself standing on a hard surface.

"Hey, buddy, I missed you." He dropped to one knee and held his arms. "Give your dad a hug?"

"Of course."

The boy stepped closer and embraced his father.

"Ow." Erebus felt a sting on his neck. It hurt, but only for a moment. "Did you bite me, son? Why did you do that?" He pushed the boy away and held him at arm's length. Something on Herbert's shirt caught his eye, a single drop of red spreading into the surrounding fabric. It could have been spaghetti sauce.

"I'm sorry, father. I'm just so hungry."

"We talked about not biting people a long time ago."

"Yes, Father. I'm sorry. I won't bite you again."

"That's all right, buddy. These last few days have been hard."

"Are you all right, Father?"

"I feel a headache coming on."

"Oh."

Erebus felt something in the air change. The room, or wherever they were, grew a bit colder. Then two boy-sized hands lifted his face so he could stare into the vacant nothingness of his son's eyes. The sight made tears well in the corners of his eyes.

"I'm so sorry, son."

"Why, Father? Without you I wouldn't exist. I am you."

"You're dead because of me."

"No, you're wrong, I *live* because of you. Come, Father, I have something to show you. Let's go for a walk."

Erebus took his son's proffered hand. As they walked, the bare ground turned into a cobblestone path. Tufts of grass sprung up here and there, growing denser until both sides of the trail was a green field. Erebus realized the darkness was slowly growing lighter, as if dawn was breaking.

Together they strolled through the countryside. Off to the left, he spotted a brook winding its way through the green field. Everything was so tranquil, so idyllic. It was the type of place Adrian Erebus, dedicated schoolteacher, had dreamed of living.

"You picked a winner of a spot, buddy. Where are we going?"

"We're almost there, Father." Herbert pointed with his free hand. "Just over that hill. Do you see?"

Erebus squinted and could just make out a thin ribbon of smoke rising from behind the hill. The path wove back and forth and turned to follow along the little ridge. As they rounded the hill, the path fell away and snow covered the ground, bright and shining in the morning sun. The trees along the route were evergreens, their branches dusted in snow.

"Look, Father, one for you and one for me." Herbert picked up two woolly coats hanging from a tree branch.

"Well, that's just perfect," Erebus said, smiling and patting the back of Herbert's neck. They each put on a coat and resumed walking. Around another bend in the path, Erebus spotted a cottage. It had yellow walls and a blue roof. The smoke was coming from a stone chimney, merrily puffing little black clouds like from an old man's pipe. The house was ringed by a picket fence. Erebus had never seen this house before, but he recognized it immediately; it was the sanctuary he'd retreated to all those nights when his drunken mother went on a rampage.

He bent down and lifted his son in his arms.

"Are we home?"

"Yes, Father. It's just like you told me."

Erebus lifted his son and trotted toward the log and stone house. As they came closer, they could see a Christmas tree in the picture window. Holding Herbert in one hand—the boy weighed less than he remembered—he pulled open the gate and followed the path to the front door. He sat Herbert by the door and turned the knob.

The warm smell of gingerbread enveloped him. "Adrian, is that you?" It was the musical voice of Grace Allen, his wife. "Don't forget to wipe your boots off."

He looked down and saw he was wearing snow boots. He stomped them on the welcome mat and stepped inside. Grace Allen stepped out of the kitchen with a warm gingerbread cookie in each hand.

She was just as Adrian remembered her. Her gorgeous red hair was bundled on top of her head and she was wearing a plaid dress and a spotless white apron. Her adoring smile always made his heart race. Leaning out to kiss her cheek, she stopped him.

"Boots first, kiss second." She pointed to a wooden bench beside the door. "I will not have you tracking snow through this house."

Erebus sat and pulled his boots off, then he picked up Herbert, plopped him on the bench, and unlaced his boots. He remembered Herbert being older, somehow, eight or ten instead of sixish, but no matter. He pulled the boy's boots off and placed them beside his own just to the right of the door. Grace Allen put a cookie in Herbert's eager hand, wrapped her arms around Erebus' neck, and kissed him more deeply than she had ever done before. When she finally released him, he could still taste her lips on his own. She popped her second gingerbread cookie into his mouth.

"Only one cookie each. Dinner is in thirty minutes. We're having Christmas lasagna; my father's recipe."

He watched her backside as she walked back to the kitchen. They were the perfect couple.

He felt his son tug on his shirt sleeve. He knelt on one knee and brought his head down to his son's height.

"What's up, buddy?"

"Father, I found Mommy," Herbert said. "You can stay here with us if you want."

Erebus crushed his son in a bear hug. "I never want to leave."

Sweetwater jerked in his sleep. He needed pain meds, but that was a no-go; the doctors wouldn't prescribe any more. Apparently, the whole "do no harm" thing only went so far. So, when Grace Allen Tarbeau appeared next to his bed, Sweetwater had no idea if it was a dream or not.

"Be careful, that's not my son," she said.

Sweetwater knew she meant the horned thing.

"Then who is it?"

"It's Adrian."

A slight noise roused Sweetwater enough to crack open one eye. Seeing who it was sitting in the chair near his bed, he closed it again and lay still.

"Will you be pretending to sleep for much longer, Mister Sweetwater?"

Damn!

328 | HOY & WEBB

Sweetwater took five seconds to run through an old meditation trick he learned in sniper school.

"Hmmm…oh, Ms. Witherbot, what are you doing here?"

"Keep your voice down, your roommate really is sleeping. I have left my comfortable office in Dallas because the Memphis Police Department informs me that you do not play well with others." She crossed her legs and placed her hands on her knee.

"They said that?"

"More or less. Do not think me unaware of the strained relationships between LEI and some law enforcement agencies across the nation. Our company tries to maintain a working relationship with the local police departments, but sometimes it does not work out, through no fault of ours. In this case, however, the fault *is* ours, or more specifically, yours and Miss Warden's, so now I'm here to clean things up."

"Meaning?"

"I do not like repeating myself, and as this concerns you both, I will wake Miss Warden first."

"Which of us will be getting waterboarded?"

"Are you volunteering? Because that did cross my mind."

"On second thought, no. What's the point of this little talk?"

"You have a lot of maturing to do, Luther."

"It's Luther now?"

"Only because we are alone at this moment. As I said, you have a lot of maturing to do, but as you are doing the growing up you should already have done, there is one thing I will *not* abide. Under no circumstances are you to hurt Miss Warden. Do we understand each other?

"I would never hurt her."

"That is not an answer."

"Yes, I understand. But what's this about?"

"If you do," she said, side-stepping his question. "I will take whatever action I deem appropriate."

Teri Warden groaned and tried to roll over onto her side but couldn't. Pulling in a deep breath sent spasms of pain from her stomach into her chest. Slowly, with several false starts, she opened her eyes in the dimly lit hospital room.

She wasn't alone. It wasn't what she thought of as her "psychic powers" that alerted her to another presence, rather it was that feeling all humans get when they're being watched. Squinting, the single floor lamp drew her eye to a slim, forty-something woman in a black pants suit, her hair drawn back so tightly into a bun she would never need a facelift, her face frozen in the familiar disapproving scowl. It was Cynthia Witherbot, the British Bitch herself.

"Mom?" Warden tried adjusting the bed up to see her more easily, but it hurt. "What are you doing here?"

"Mom?" Sweetwater asked from across the room.

Witherbot lifted an eyebrow.

Uh-oh, Warden thought. She knew what that meant.

"Do you wish for me to focus my attention on *you,* Mister Sweetwater?"

"No, I'm good."

Witherbot turned back to her daughter.

"We have two Shooters gone forever, a third lies on death's door, and my only child is sliced up like a mackerel ready for grilling. Pray tell, where else should I be?"

"Uh, thank you?"

"You falsified your report."

"What? I did no such thing."

"You reported that you and Sweetwater were heading the investigation to catch Mr. Erebus. In reality, Mister Sweetwater was incapacitated."

"Not completely. Plus, we caught him."

"Semantics, Teresa?"

"Teresa?" Sweetwater asked. This time Witherbot ignored him.

Warden scowled and let out a huff, even though it hurt.

"Please don't call me that, Mother. You know I hate that name."

Sweetwater couldn't help calling out. "How does it feel?"

This time Witherbot turned fully in her chair, which Warden knew to be a very bad sign.

"I have convinced the staff to reintroduce medications to control your pain, and also to feed you something other than yesterday's leftovers. They will do this provided we move you soon, and I have agreed. Would you like me to nullify that agreement? Do you enjoy pain that much?"

"Not really."

"Then don't say another word, Mister Sweetwater. Now, Miss Warden, your catching Adrian Erebus was a fluke."

"No, it wasn't. Luther laid a trap, and I went along."

"This was *his* idea?"

Warden nodded. "And it worked."

"After the target murdered a hospital employee and a patient in the room above Mister Sweetwater's when that bomb detonated."

Warden looked away and said nothing.

"But the killer fell into your trap, right?"

Again, Warden said nothing.

Witherbot rose and paced the room. Warden knew *that* was a good sign; it meant she was deep in thought.

"If Erebus thought Mister Sweetwater was deceased, then how did he discover otherwise?" Stopping, she turned to Warden. "This is our other problem, isn't it?"

Warden nodded, pulled the blankets up to her waist, and smoothed them flat. Her mom could make her feel like a naughty five-year-old, even when she didn't mean to.

"Damn. Very well then, I'm here to take you both back to Dallas."

"Why are we going to Texas?"

"Moving forward, we need the cooperation of the Memphis Police Department. They have formally requested that we remove the two of you from their area of responsibility, and given the havoc of late, that seems like a reasonable request. I'm also here to claim Mr. Erebus, who will be undergoing some rather nasty debriefing. I believe he has some information about possible holes within our security. Technically, Miss Warden, you are not under my direct authority, so I'm extending to you an invitation to join us for the trip. Some of the LEI management feel that you might have acquired some first-hand information that may aid us in the future."

Witherbot leaned on the railing at the foot of Warden's bed.

"Are you waiting for my answer?"

"Please allow me to clarify your options. You may join us as we travel to Dallas, you may return to your home in Atlanta, or you may remain here in Memphis. The latter two seem fraught with danger, given your current physical state, but the choice remains yours."

"What do *you* want me to do?"

That stopped Witherbot, and for the briefest instant her scowled dropped into something much less severe.

"Why would I care?"

"I'm not asking the British Bitch, the assistant director, I'm asking my mom."

Witherbot didn't answer right away. Then she approached Warden's right side, bent down, and brushed a stray lock from her daughter's forehead.

"Given the choice, her mother would prefer to nurse her back to health in Dallas."

"Her daughter would like that, too."

Straightening, Witherbot now pointed at Sweetwater.

"Consider this a confidential briefing, Mister Sweetwater. Revealing what occurred here could have deleterious consequences for you.'

"I don't know what that means, but I won't do it."

"Smart. Now, before I leave, there is someone you need to meet. He is one of our top assets, and I have asked him, as a favor, to oversee your safety during this move." She waved her hand as a tall, well-knit man wearing a beautifully tailored suit but no tie, attempted to come through the doorway...until a uniformed policeman blocked his way.

"You should move," the newcomer said.

The cop stood two inches taller and was much broader across the chest, but the newcomer dominated the moment. Warden sensed something in him, something extremely powerful and...familiar?

"It's all right, officer," Witherbot called to him. "He is here at my request."

"I don't answer to you, ma'am," the cop said, albeit in a shaky tone.

"And you'd best be glad you don't!" she replied. The man stepped back like she'd raked talons across his chest.

The man in the suit nodded once.

"Thank you," he said and entered.

"Luther Sweetwater, Teri Warden, this is Steed."

Chapter Thirty-Three

23,000 Feet Altitude, Somewhere Over Texas

Cynthia Witherbot never walked anywhere, not even down the center aisle of the LEI Learjet 75 in rough air. Rather, she stalked in a way that drew all eyes toward her. So, when she passed Steed, and his head turned to watch her backside, with the same peculiar swing as her daughter, it didn't surprise her at all. She also didn't mind.

"Are you sure he's out?" she asked the large male nurse sitting beside Erebus two rows behind Steed. She wasn't willing to take chances with such a dangerous prisoner, despite his grievous wounds. The nurse was in his first week of Shooter training. That allowed him wide latitude in dealing with Erebus.

"Yes, ma'am. He's been unresponsive for the past twenty-four hours, and he was just administered an additional sedative. If he's not in a coma, he'll be asleep for the next twelve hours."

"Thank you, Robert," she said. "Please slip on your headphones; we need to discuss something. You too, Steed."

"What about Two-Bit up there?" Steed said.

Witherbot sighed loud enough to hear, meaning it was for effect.

"I suppose that cannot be helped."

She pointed toward Warden, lying on a specially installed folding bed two rows back, and tapped her own ears. Once all of them had donned microphone-equipped headphones, she began.

"Needless to say, this conversation is strictly confidential. Robert, what that means is that if you breathe a word of what is said here, even if by accident, then you are in, shall we say—"

"Deep shit," said Steed.

Although visibly annoyed at the interruption, Witherbot let it pass.

"Just so. It is never wise to break the rules of an organization whose chief source of revenue is killing people. Now, to put it simply, we have a mole inside LEI. How to find him or her is the point of this meeting. I want to hear your ideas."

She sat back in her chair and crossed her hands.

"Did you verify this is an internal attack?" Warden asked.

"On that count, you were right. Our database can only be accessed behind our firewall, and we track all IPs that touch it. I am reliably informed that no hacker on Earth could enter our system without our knowing it, although I understand that our technicians would likely say that regardless of its truth. They are the ones who set up the system, after all, and the ones responsible if it is hacked. Still, I'm fairly certain this is an internal breach, but if so, whoever is doing it knows how to cover their tracks."

"I'm not a computer guy, but I'm a fan of keeping things simple," Sweetwater said. "Follow the money and that will lead back to our man."

"After checking the logs, that was the second thing we tried. Unfortunately, there have been no anomalous changes in our employees' accounts, not that we can find."

"What about the ones you can't find?" Steed said.

"Meaning what?"

"Cash, jewels, gold, dummy corps, crypto-currency…"

"None of which can be easily investigated."

Steed used his chin to point at Sweetwater. "Boy Wonder over there still nailed it; tracking the money is the best way to find him."

"Or her."

"Or her," he said. "I don't know how else you'd do it, not at this point."

Sweetwater and Warden turned to look at each other. They shook their heads, until Sweetwater held up his finger.

"What about my death?" he said.

Steed answered before Witherbot could.

"I wouldn't volunteer if I was you, she might take you up on it."

"This is serious shit, Mister Steed," Warden said, with far more fervor than seemed necessary. Injured or not, her words had power behind them. "You should give the assistant director the respect she's due."

For the first time, Steed looked closely at the girl. Witherbot saw it, and knew she needed to change the subject, fast. Given time, Steed *would* figure it out.

"Thank you, Miss Warden, but Mister Steed is not singling me out for disrespect, he treats everyone that way. He thinks it's cute, no matter how many times he's told that it's not. Now, Mister Sweetwater, you were saying?"

"I don't really understand how all this works. Does everyone at LEI have access to the contracts?"

"No, only those whose duties require them to have such information."

"Okay, but when LEI announced that I died from the bomb, what was put in the database? Was my file marked dead?"

338 | HOY & WEBB

"If you are asking who could access the logs containing your true status, then, as I said earlier, that avenue has been thoroughly checked. The number is small, and every person has been checked out. They are all clean."

"And yet Erebus knew."

"This is not new information, Mister Sweetwater."

Sweetwater unclipped his seat belt and slid to the edge of his seat. "But somehow Erebus found out I was still alive, even though LEI had me on record as dead."

"Now you're repeating yourself."

"Then you explain it," he said.

Witherbot's face turned stony. Steed grinned.

"Yeah, boss, you explain it."

"Dial down the testosterone everybody," Warden said. "You, too, M—" Steed leaned forward. "Ma'am. Sweetwater might be onto something. I called you directly, so who might have heard that call?"

"Hold it." Steed put out his hands to stop the conversation. He examined the girl until she squirmed. "What did you almost call her?"

"Steed—" Witherbot started, but he held out a palm to stop her.

"I don't have to answer your questions," Warden said.

"Walk down the aisle," Steed said.

"Fuck off! What kind of perv are you?"

"One with a haunting suspicion that I've been lied to for the past twenty years," Steed said, speaking through clenched teeth.

"Look, buddy," Sweetwater said, "I don't know what your deal is—"

Witherbot cut him off before things got out of hand. "He's not a pervert, Teresa." Witherbot raised her chin. Her square face could not have been stonier if it were chiseled beside Teddy Roosevelt on Mount Rushmore. "He's your father."

Warden and Steed gaped and blinked for ten seconds, until Steed rose and walked the length of the plane without looking back. Sweetwater knew enough to shut up. He considered trying to comfort Warden, but realized that was a bad idea, too.

"Certainly, you must have many questions," Witherbot said, "but now is not the time. We have a mole to catch."

"Not the time? *Not the time*, Mother? For twenty years you've told me that my father was dead! Twenty years! Why? Why is my last name Warden instead of, instead of whatever my real last name should be?"

"Steed is your father's last name. It's his preferred name."

"You really *are* the British Bitch, aren't you?" Warden asked, turning to look out the window.

"Perhaps so, but as I am also the assistant director of LEI and, at the moment, I have field operatives who are dead because someone in my organization values money more than life. Finding that person is my current priority. Once that is done, you may castigate me in whatever way you choose, and for as long as you wish."

"Does that go for me, too?" Steed asked, walking back with a glare.

"You're my father?" Warden said, with an expression like she was trying to process it.

He sat and ran hands through his hair.

340 | HOY & WEBB

"The instant I saw you I knew something was different. I—I can't explain how I knew that, but I did. Now it makes sense."

"How long were you together?"

"Teri!" Witherbot said.

"Together? We were married."

"You—what?"

Witherbot stood. "Enough! We land in twenty minutes, and we still have no plan for catching our mole. Lives are at stake, and regardless how angry you both are with me, that is our only concern at the moment. May we, therefore, move on to the issue at hand? I believe we were just starting to make progress."

"Fine, Mother, but this is far from over."

"I have no doubt of that."

The anger had not drained from Warden's tone, but she pressed on. Every few seconds she glanced up at Steed.

"I think we have something with the time we reported Luther as being killed by the bomb. If you're positive those with access to the database didn't do it, then that only leaves our phone call."

Her mother reclined her chair a few inches. "Go on."

"How many people know you came to Memphis?"

"I am the assistant director; everyone knows when I am gone from my desk."

"But how many know who you're bringing back with you?"

"Other than me, they are expecting only you and Mr. Erebus. And Robert, of course."

"Not Luther?"

"No. As I said before, only a small circle knows that he still lives, and the few who do believe he was too badly wounded to move for many weeks. Even I am astounded at his recovery. Although I have seen this sort of thing before."

"So, most people think he's dead, and the rest don't know he's coming?"

"Correct."

"Has anyone updated the passenger list since then?"

"I don't know."

"Then maybe you'd better find out," Warden said.

Nobody at LEI had ever spoken to her that way, nobody. Yet Witherbot said nothing, merely rose and walked toward the cockpit, steadying herself as the plane began its descent into Dallas-Fort Worth. There she pulled a white phone from the wall.

"Adam, have you been in contact with Dallas?" She paused while the other person answered. "Have you submitted a passenger list?" Another pause. "No, I don't want that information shared at the moment. Please continue regular communication about the flight, but nothing about any of the passengers. That will be all. Thank you, Adam." She hung up the phone and returned to her seat.

"All right, Mister Sweetwater's presence on board remains unknown. What are you thinking?"

"What if you spread the word that the Memphis Police have him in custody for all the murders, which technically is their legal right? That he was being questioned when you left and wanted to make a deal?"

"That could work," Steed said, not bothering to hide his anger, though for the moment focusing on the task at hand. "Whoever this person is, they know that Luther here isn't dead, so use that. Tell everybody the Memphis cops want him to help get Erebus to confess, in return for a deal."

Grateful to have buried the subject of her daughter's paternity, even if only for a little while, she added her own thoughts to the plan. "And what if the Memphis Police want whoever sold Erebus the information as an accessory to murder and are willing to make a deal to get the name?"

Aside from the whine of the jets, the cabin fell silent.

"It seems we have a plan," Witherbot finally said.

"Father."

Adrian Erebus blinked sleep from his eyes and focused on Herbert, who was tugging at his arm like a lab puppy wrestling with a shoe. Snug and warm under the covers in the bedroom of their cottage, he rolled his head to one side and smiled, as he saw curly red hair covered the pillow beside him. A naked shoulder disappeared as Grace Allen groaned and pulled the quilt over her head.

"Mom's asleep," he whispered, raising a finger to his lips.

"Father, I think someone is going to try and hurt us."

Wrinkles crossed the child's forehead. From the intensity of his expression, Erebus knew Herbert meant what he said.

He slipped out from under the quilt and pulled on a T-shirt that was sitting on top of the dresser. The shirt read, *Dad—The Man, the Myth, the Legend.* Grace Allen had the shirt printed for him one Christmas after seeing a picture of some biker guy who described himself that way.

"All right, buddy, let's go downstairs so you can tell me about it."

The boy led his father down the steps. The stairs ended in the sitting room, where the Christmas tree stood next to the picture window with presents piled up to the lower branches. Snow glistened outside. Erebus eased into his recliner. Herbert sat on the couch. It was the perfect Christmas morning, just like it had been yesterday, and the day before, and the day before that.

"So, what's wrong, bud? Did you have a nightmare?"

The boy shook his head. "I saw it in the other place, Father. Someone wants to hurt us."

Erebus leaned closer and sipped from a mug of hot chocolate that appeared on the table beside his chair.

"I'm not sure what you mean. What other place?"

Herbert picked up a pair of bright orange plastic binoculars. He held them tightly in his hand as he talked to his father. "Before we came here, you were somewhere else. It was a place where bad people hurt you, but you couldn't always hear me when I talked to you."

Erebus reached up and massaged a temple with one hand; a headache was starting to press from right behind his eyeball. He could tell the headache would grow into a full migraine. "Hold on, buddy," he hissed as his temples started throbbing. "I can't think about that right now. It hurts." The last few words were said in a near-whisper. The headache kept growing. Erebus leaned back in his recliner, his hands pressed hard against his temples, like a vice. He groaned. "My head."

Herbert reached out and touched the side of his father's head. The pain disappeared instantly.

"What?" Erebus asked, looking up to his son's eyes. Flames flickered where his eyes should have been. It only seemed that way for three seconds, and then Herbert blinked. The eyes returned, looking like they always did.

"Did you do something?" he asked.

"I took the pain away." Herbert kept his hand on his father's temple as he spoke. "There are some bad people who want to hurt you. They want you to tell them something about your friend, and that will break up our family. They are going to take you from Mommy and me."

Erebus took a deep breath and put his hand on his son's knee. Had his son shrunk?

"If you can help me find 'em, I'll tell them to leave us alone."

Herbert's head fell. Erebus saw his shoulders shaking, and his voice quavered. "It won't work." Herbert sobbed. "They are going to try to hurt you. They might even kill you. Father...they want to kill *me*!"

"Buddy, oh buddy, I won't let that happen. I'm not going to let anyone hurt you or break up our family."

"They are going to kill us," Herbert insisted. "I heard them talking."

"I'm not going to let 'em. I'll do whatever I have to do." He nodded to the orange binoculars. "Is that how you saw them?"

Herbert's eyes widened, larger than Erebus ever remembered them and hot tears ran down his face. A trickle of snot covered his upper lip. "They are going to kill you, Father. I know it. And they will kill me, too." He hugged the toy binoculars close to his chest.

"Hand me the binoculars, son."

Herbert laid the plastic toy in his father's palm. It had the slick, oily feel that cheap plastic toys have. He turned them over but didn't see anything special about them. Herbert's tears told him there had to be more to it, so he started to raise them to his eyes. His son reached out and stopped his hand.

"Father, you're going to need this." Herbert reached into a crease of the couch and pulled out the long, black pocketknife they'd bought at the convenience store, the one that had cut him up so badly. With a sudden thought he peered at his stomach, expecting cuts or scars, not the smooth skin he saw. A sense of unease seeped from the blade. He didn't want to touch it, but...

"Take it, Father."

"All right, buddy." He took the knife. Where the binoculars were light plastic, the knife was heavy steel. Something terrible was about to happen—he could feel it—and he knew he couldn't stop it.

"Don't let them take you away from us," Herbert sniffled through the tears. "Don't let them hurt you. Kill them fast."

"Who are you?" Erebus said with a sudden clarity of mind.

"I'm you, Father. You've always known that."

Erebus nodded as a new comprehension filled him with resolve. Herbert was right. Herbert was right, he *had* known it. They were one.

Raising the binoculars to his eyes, what he saw didn't make any sense. There was some sort of tunnel-like room, filled with sunlight, dark swivel chairs, and a blue carpet. He heard people talking, adults, and some of them were familiar. Still holding the binoculars to his eyes, something pushed in the small of his back, something powerful.

After a momentary sensation of falling, Erebus blinked and found himself strapped to a stiff, uncomfortable platform. He recognized the interior of an airplane even if he didn't know how he got there. In the seat beside him sat a large man in scrubs. He wore noise cancelling headphones with a fold-down microphone, and his attention was on the people in the seats in front, not on Erebus.

Along with his sudden shift from the cottage to the airplane, he recognized his clothes had changed. He was dressed in a full set of blue pajamas, but not the comfortable ones he had at home. These were stiff, as if they had never been worn before. He also felt his feet were enclosed in a thin pair of slippers. He still held the binoculars and the knife.

Over the insistent whine of the jets, he heard snippets of the others talking. It was Sweetwater again; that bastard was still alive! Rage stabbed his brain like a surge of electricity, but instead of driving him to desperation, it had the opposite effect. Instinct told him this was the last chance he'd have to avenge Grace Allen. Outnumbered and with only a small knife for a weapon, he had to be smart.

First, he worked slowly against the limited freedom afforded by the straps. Eventually he was able to slip the plastic binoculars into a pouch on the bulkhead to his left. Conveniently, the knife was already open, and he began sawing through the heavy, threaded cloth. Someone shifted in their seat to check on him, and Erebus quickly tucked the knife under his leg and closed his eyes, mimicking a comatose state and trying hard to slow his breathing.

Chapter Thirty-Four

20,000 Feet Altitude, Somewhere Over Texas

Steed sat up, alert, like a birddog flushing a covey of quail.

"What?" Witherbot said.

"There's an immediate threat," he said.

"How do you know that?" Warden said.

Witherbot waved at her. "Ssshh. Where, Steed?"

"It's—I can't pin it down. Something's interfering."

"How is that possible?"

"I don't know..."

Sweetwater decided it was time to speak up.

"Do any of you folks believe in ghosts?"

Through slitted eyes, Erebus saw the agitation of the people in the seats. The man beside him, however, hadn't yet noticed. Awake now, he focused on the approaching ground out the window. If Erebus was going to strike, it had to be now. He chanced sawing the straps faster until the first one parted, giving him leverage to cut the other one more easily.

"Hey!" cried a strange man, half standing from a seat in front.

The man beside him grabbed his wrist. A hard thrust of the blade ripped open his neck from bottom of the chin to Adam's apple, and

347

he fell back, blood gurgling through his fingers as he tried to seal the fatal wound. Erebus' wounds hurt as he stood up from the gurney. The muscles were tight from new scar tissue, but he couldn't let it slow him down. Protecting his family mattered more than a little pain.

Sweetwater was already on his feet, blocking the aisle as the older man tried to push past, brandishing a pistol. Without thinking, he held the knife outstretched in both hands, and charged toward them.

Witherbot and Warden had craned their necks around the seats when Robert cried out and watched in horror as the formerly comatose Erebus cut Robert's throat. Erebus' face was twisted into a visage of demonic fury as he attacked Sweetwater. Both women had to throw themselves backward to avoid the black knife.

The downward angle of the plane's descent added momentum to Erebus' attack. Sweetwater had regained some of his strength, but he was really just starting to get his feet under him. Walking was still an effort, and the last time he'd fought this man, he had barely avoided dying. But in the seconds as the raging Adrian Erebus ran downhill toward him, Sweetwater's brain registered tiny flames in the man's eyes.

A fist holding a pistol braced on his shoulder and two shots rang out, both hitting Erebus high in the chest. The impact stopped him cold, like he'd been slapped. Then, with a roar, he came again. Sweetwater felt the hand tense as Steed squeezed the trigger…and the plane banked forty degrees to the left.

Steed didn't fire. He and Sweetwater both lost their footing and slammed into the port bulkhead, falling in a heap. Steed cushioned Sweetwater's fall and absorbed the punishment. He appeared stunned, with a long contusion on his right cheek. The pistol was nowhere in sight.

Lacking his former core body strength, Sweetwater gripped the seat back to try and pull himself away from the unconscious Steed. Muscles quivered as his arms strained, and he was half standing when Erebus appeared in the aisle. Blood was spraying his face and torso, just like the last time. He held a black knife aloft, just like the last time. It was the same knife as at the hospital, the one the boy had given him, the boy with the flaming red eyes, the boy that disappeared. The boy that Sweetwater knew wasn't a boy at all and never had been.

Knees bent, with Steed underneath him, he planted his feet. One way or another, Erebus was going to die. Sweetwater wasn't going to let him carve up the women, even if it cost him his own life. *That* was why he'd joined the Marines, to protect others, and by God he was going to do just that.

Like brains tend to do in combat, his slipped into hyper-mode. Forget the dodge, he told himself. If he accepted the blade, he would have the opportunity for a counterblow. A Marine goes down fighting, so he balled up his fist and aimed for Erebus' throat.

"Sweetwater, down!" Witherbot yelled as the engines throttled-up to a deafening whine.

There was no time, as once again the floor tilted sharply to the left, throwing Sweetwater off his feet. Only this time Erebus fell on him.

Even with blood pouring from the new bullet wounds, Erebus drove the knife downward with great strength. Sweetwater grabbed the killer's wrist and stopped it, but Erebus was too strong, and the point inevitably reached for his face. Using his right fist, he pummeled his attacker. Although his core strength remained weak, his arms were as strong as ever. His right hand flew into the broad nose, smashing cartilage over and over again with sprays of blood. But he was stopped by the floor, unable to draw his arm back. None of them had enough power to disable Erebus.

The knife point pricked his left cheek, where his jaw met his ear. Three more inches would be fatal.

The barrel of Steed's Sig Sauer P320 touched Erebus on the right side of his head. The gun was being held by Cynthia Witherbot.

"Not even you can survive without a brain, Mister Erebus," she said in her cold British Bitch voice. "Put the knife down or die right here, right now."

"No," he said, somewhere halfway between a hiss and a growl. "I have to save my family."

"Your family is dead, and it's your fault."

Erebus lost focus and turned. His hate twisted his face and gave Sweetwater a clear shot at his throat. Bloody knuckles drove Erebus' Adam's apple backward, and he rolled off Sweetwater, gagging. The knife flew out of his hand.

"Even maniacs gotta breathe," Sweetwater said through gulps of air. "Who's got handcuffs?"

"We're not cops. Let me see what we have in the back," Witherbot said, handing him the Sig. "Don't kill him, Luther. You hear me? We need him."

"No promises."

"He won't," Warden said, coming into the aisle now that it was safe. "Luther's not like that, but if we don't get him medical treatment ASAP, he's gonna die anyway."

"I wouldn't be too sure," Sweetwater said. "Those two bullets are both potentially fatal hits, but you saw what just happened. And I learned that punch in the Marines, it's meant to be lethal."

"What are saying?" Witherbot said.

"Nothing yet."

Raising an eyebrow, the assistant director of LEI went to look for something to restrain Erebus.

Sweetwater pushed to his feet as Erebus started to recover, pushing himself up from the floor. Pistol whipping somebody wasn't like they showed in the movies, it usually resulted in damage to the gun and/or the hand holding it, so instead Sweetwater maneuvered for kicking room. Warden beat him to it with a heel to the forehead.

While Erebus moaned on the floor, she reached into the overhead storage to rummage through her backpack, checking each pocket until she pulled out two pairs of cuffs.

"Tell Mom they fell out of the overhead."

"Only if you tell me later why you had handcuffs in your bag. Or better yet, show me."

"Jeez, Luther, don't be disgusting," she said, wrinkling her nose while also smiling.

What the hell does that mean? he wondered.

After handcuffing the semi-conscious Erebus to a seat support, Sweetwater roused Steed and helped him into a seat. The knot on his head darkened to a reddish purple. Then Sweetwater collapsed into his own chair.

Witherbot knelt beside Robert, stood, and shook her head.

"Fuck," Sweetwater said. He was breathing hard, but his ribs didn't hurt as much this time. "Maybe you could change the policy about bringing demonic madmen on the plane?"

"That rules out all her exes…except me, of course," Steed said as Warden touched the knot on his face.

"This needs ice," she said.

"We'll be on the ground in a few minutes. As to your suggestion, Mister Sweetwater, I'll take it under advisement."

"You called me 'Luther' a minute ago."

"Yes, and now I'm calling you Mister Sweetwater. Do you have any idea where he got a weapon?" Since she was the only one still on her feet, she searched for the knife. "Found it." She pinched the black blade between her gloved finger and thumb and held it up.

"Son of a bitch," Sweetwater said. "Yeah, I know where he got a weapon. You're just not gonna believe me."

"You'd be surprised what I would believe, Mister Sweetwater."

Steed laughed with his eyes closed. "She's been around, Two-Bit, more than you think."

"I hate that name," Sweetwater said.

"And the more you say how much you hate it, the more your fellow Shooters will use it." He paused and then added, "If nobody objects, I'd like to decapitate that bastard now."

"I'm still waiting for Mister Sweetwater to tell me how Mister Erebus smuggled this knife aboard?"

"He had help," Sweetwater said.

"Obviously. But the only suspect is Robert, and I'll be shocked if he was able to manage that. It makes no sense."

"Because that's not how he did it—it was the boy, or whatever he is."

"Oh my God, Luther," Warden said, covering her mouth.

He only nodded.

"Would someone fill me in?" Witherbot asked.

"I think it was a ghost," Sweetwater said, "or something like a ghost."

Witherbot held his gaze. At one point he'd fantasized about having an affair with her, but now, as she bored into his eyes, he squirmed the way he'd done when he tried to lie to his grandmother. Except he hadn't lied.

"Be certain of your answer, Mister Sweetwater. This may affect your future involvement with LEI."

"He's not lying, Mother," Warden said.

"Quiet. I was not speaking to you. I want to hear *his* answer."

"When we were in the secured area of the hospital, Erebus came to kill me, and I fought him to the ground—"

"You have already told me this more than once."

"But not this part; I left it out. I was afraid you'd think I was mentally unstable. Teri came in and tied his hands behind his back, and then went to get help. While she was gone, an—I guess you'd call it an apparition—showed up. I'd seen it twice before that."

Steed interrupted him next, and Witherbot said nothing. To Sweetwater, that showed the power Steed commanded within the company. "What does that mean, you'd *seen* him? Like a shadow figure?"

Damn! He'd been afraid this would happen, and now there was no hiding it.

"No, I see dead people. Not all the time, and not everybody, it just happens sometimes. But there's nothing blurry about them. I wish there was."

Witherbot met Steed's glance, and something went unsaid between them. Sweetwater noticed.

"What?" he said. "I'm not lying."

"I do not think you are lying, Mister Sweetwater," said Witherbot. "We will talk about this more in the future, but in five minutes we'll be on the ground, so please finish your story, and do so quickly."

"The first time I saw him, he wasn't a boy, he was like a man-bull, with horns and stuff—"

"Like a minotaur?" Steed said.

"I don't know what that is."

"Never mind," Witherbot said. "Get on with it."

"Okay…Erebus was dying, or maybe dead. The bull breathed fire into his mouth, and he came back to life. The next time, the min-now-whatever was smaller. The third time is when he looked like a little boy, except he was all black, had this giant mouth full of sharp teeth, and no eyes. There might have been fire in them, too, but by that point I was pretty far gone."

"Then how can you be certain all of this is real?"

"I saw the boy, too," Warden said quietly, as if remembering something terrible. "He was just like Luther says."

"Erebus kept calling it 'my son' and 'my boy.' Teri had hogtied his hands and the…ghost, or whatever, cut Erebus free using *that* knife you're holding. Then he disappeared. One second he was there, the next he wasn't."

"He's telling the truth, Mom. Like I said, I saw the kid, too. Right before that psycho stabbed me in the leg."

"Is that the only ghost you've ever seen, Mister Sweetwater?"

Reluctant to say more, Sweetwater shrugged. "No, I've seen them off and on my whole life, but the others kept coming around after they'd been dead a while, and...I don't know how else to put this, but they looked as rotted as their bodies must have been."

"I see," Witherbot said. "Thank you for telling us that, it changes things a bit. Can you summon these ghosts at will?"

"I don't know, I never tried."

"I think it's time we find out."

Chapter Thirty-Five

On Final Approach to a Private Airfield near Downtown Dallas, TX

Steed laid a blanket over Robert's corpse. Technically, his death wasn't a police matter because he'd been killed by the target of a legal contract, which made him both collateral damage and an LEI licensed operative in pursuit of executing said contract. Therefore, preserving evidence wasn't necessary.

Once finished, Steed stood and gave him the Gunner's final salute. Making a pistol with his fingers, forefinger extended straight with the other three tucked, and thumbed cocked, he held it in front of his face, pointed it out at a 45-degree angle, and pretended.

"Well done, Shooter. Be seein' ya."

He turned to see Sweetwater watching.

"Remember that," Steed said.

"Please, take your seats," the captain said over the intercom. As Steed turned to walk away, Sweetwater saw him reach back and take something out of the pouch affixed to the bulkhead, over the bench where they'd strapped Erebus.

Once seated, Sweetwater looked at the window as the ground rose to meet them. Aside from an adjacent runway, he only saw a distant chain-link fence.

"This isn't DFW," he said.

"No, it is not," Witherbot answered. "This field belongs to LEI. We are its owner and sole user."

"But we've been flying over the city for a while now."

"We have indeed. Before other matters distract me Luther, I want to thank you for standing against Adrian Erebus. You gave me the time I needed to call the pilot. I had to use my satellite phone, and that takes longer to connect. I realize you are still weak from your previous encounters, so again, thank you."

"Wow," Sweetwater said, "I don't know what to say."

"Don't spoil the moment, please, Mother," Warden said.

Witherbot lifted an eyebrow, then spoiled the moment. "But we still must discuss your previous actions."

The aircraft skipped twice off the runway, then settled and taxied toward a small glass building with several vehicles parked in front of it, among them two ambulances.

"As should be obvious by now," Witherbot said, "our plans are no longer relevant, and we have no concrete ideas on how to find our information salesman, unless one of you have had a sudden epiphany? Mister Sweetwater—Luther, you seemed to have had an idea earlier."

"I don't know, ma'am, it's pretty out there."

"Your ghosts?"

"You're not as surprised as I expected."

"The world is far stranger than you imagine, but the paranormal is outside my realm of experience. That vile man on the floor, you two, Mister Steed, our mole, budgets, stockholders, all of those types of problems, I can deal with. But the spirit world, if such a thing exists, is beyond my scope of knowledge. So, please forgive me for repeating myself, but do you have any idea how we can find the mole?"

"Maybe," Sweetwater said.

"I do," Warden said at the same instant.

Witherbot pointed for her daughter to go first. The plane turned off the runway and slowed.

"Instead of hiding what happened in Memphis and on the plane, what if we go the other way? Blast the news through LEI, hold a press conference, tell everybody that Erebus came to Dallas to cut a deal, and that he's here to finger the mole. Watch to see who bolts."

"Part of that is good, but he wouldn't need to come to come to Dallas to give us the name. We also can't announce company-wide that we have a mole. That information can never get out. If it did, our customers would lose faith in us. Our confidentiality is the real service we offer. If we couldn't secure the secrecy of our contracts, LEI would be out of business."

"You're all overthinking it," Steed said. "You don't announce anything and there's no deal involved. We drag Erebus into the Kremlin and show people who they've been tracking as a way of including them in his capture. Then we announce we're about to interrogate him the LEI way. If the traitor is in that control room—and he's either there or in Mexico—he'll know what that means. Have security seal the building."

"And if he's in Mexico? Or Cuba, or someplace else with no agreement of cooperation?"

"Then we cross-check border crossing and airline records against the company's absentee list. There can't be that many people who know how to intercept phone signals."

Witherbot snapped her fingers. "No, there cannot. That's how he did it then. All right, that's plan A then. Luther, stand by; you're plan B."

The moment the jet's staircase touched the ground, EMTs swarmed the aircraft and loaded Warden and Sweetwater into one ambulance and Erebus into another for the trip to LEI Corporate Headquarters. The convoy took only 15 minutes to reach the down-sloping entrance to the building's secure underground parking garage. Guards armed with shotguns stood on both sides of heavy iron gates, the approach to which had to be navigated through a series of concrete pylons. Beyond the gates, a GAU-8 Avenger 30mm, seven-barrel Gatling-style gun covered the entire driveway from a steel-reinforced concrete bunker. A humorous sign low on the bunker wall read "No Truck Bombs Allowed," with a diagonal line through the words.

"I'm still surprised you allowed that," Steed said, when the armored Mercedes sedan he was sharing with Witherbot passed the bunker.

"I didn't," she said. "I had it painted over."

Steed raised his eyebrows. "He overruled you on *that*? It seems too trivial to attract his attention."

"He does that sometimes, to remind me that I'm only the assistant director."

"Huh. Well, he's a hard man to read. He's got the perfect poker face."

"Being dead has that effect."

"Is he? Dead?"

"I don't know."

"You don't know? *You* don't know?"

"That's right, I don't know."

"You know who might find out, don't you?"

"I thought of that the moment he mentioned speaking with the dead. Luther Sweetwater may turn out to be more useful than he appears at first glance."

Beyond the entrance defenses, stood two large doors marked "Authorized Personnel Only. All others will be shot." Iron-faced guards fingering automatic weapons ensured there would be no mistaking it for another humorous message. The ambulances pulled up in front of the doors and the EMTs took their passengers into a small but lavishly equipped trauma center. Several of Witherbot's assistants met her and Steed outside the doors and led her off to a private office. Left alone, Steed found a waiting room with four chairs and checked his messages.

A few minutes short of an hour later, Teri Warden found him and sat down.

"You look exactly like her," he said.

"I've got your chin."

Steed cocked his head to both sides and studied her face. "You do, don't you? I—I'm not even sure what to say, what to call you."

"Anything but Teresa."

He laughed. "Fair enough."

"I'm gonna call you 'Dad.'"

"Don't be insulted if it takes me a while to answer. That'll take some getting used to. My last girlfriend was your age, maybe a little younger."

"We're swerving into creepy-perv-dad territory here."

"Why don't we save this discussion for when this is over?"

"I think that's a good idea."

"You and Luther, are you two a thing?"

"A *thing*? Seriously? You already sound like a dad. Not that it's any of your business, but no, we're not hooking up."

She smiled and smacked his arm and Steed flashed back 20 years, to a time when Cynthia Witherbot had the world's sexiest British accent and her sense of humor hadn't yet been hammered into a perpetual scowl. He started to say that when Witherbot's administrative assistant found them.

"The assistant director would like you to join her and Mister Sweetwater."

Once inside an examination room, Steed saw Sweetwater being attended by a frumpy nurse whose application of fresh dressings to his wounds was closer to an art form than medicine, and a youngish doctor whose erect bearing and manner of speech indicated a military background.

"I have just finished reviewing the data supplied by the trauma center in Memphis, and it appears Mister Sweetwater exacerbated his injuries during today's HTHC—"

Sweetwater saw Witherbot raise an eyebrow, and interrupted at the exact instant Steed did the same thing.

"Hand-to-hand-combat."

"Yes, correct," the doctor said, allowing his tone to vent displeasure at being interrupted.

Must've been an officer, Steed thought.

"As I was saying, Mister Sweetwater's wounds partially reopened during the altercation, as did Miss Warden's. Both will need light duty, or no duty, for four to six weeks, with continued physical therapy. I am putting both on oral antibiotics as a precaution."

"What about Mister Erebus?" Witherbot asked.

The doctor crossed his arms and leaned against the sink.

"According to what I've been told, Erebus has sustained multiple mortal wounds both today and in the recent past, yet he is still alive. I have not studied the previous wounds in much detail, but either one of the two fresh gunshot wounds or the acute laryngeal trauma should have been fatal. I cannot tell you how he is still alive, Madam Assistant Director. If medical science has an answer, it is beyond me to understand."

"*Could* medical science have an answer?"

"I reached out to a colleague at the Wake Forest School of Medicine who is a researcher for the CDC and other organizations. She has no explanation either."

"So, it's a miracle?"

He shrugged. "If you believe in such things."

"Is he awake?"

"Against all odds, yes."

"Thank you. I'll send for him when ready. And doctor? Take no chances. Adrian Erebus is a very dangerous man."

"With all due respect, he is at death's door, Madam Assistant Director."

"Yeah, well," Sweetwater said, "he's been there before."

Chapter Thirty-Six

LifeEnders Inc. Worldwide Corporate Headquarters, Dallas, TX

Once the nurse finished rewrapping Sweetwater, Witherbot led them through a series of locked doors and elevators. Finally, they came to a steel elevator door. There was no elevator call button, but there was a keyhole to the left of the door. Witherbot pulled a thin billfold with the LEI logo, exactly like a Shooter's credentials' wallet except in black leather not red. Inside, along with her LifeEnders badge and license, was a laminated ID card which she pressed against the wall over the keyhole. A sliding door six inches wide and eight high opened, behind which were located additional sensors. After she pressed her fingerprint on one sensor, let a retina scan read her eye, and used a proffered swab to get DNA from the inside of her cheek, which she inserted into a slot, a blue light flashed four times and turned green. The doors of the elevator opened.

"I've seen witch doctors with simpler rituals," Steed said.

"If that's how you open the door, what's the lock for?" Warden asked.

"That's how we turn the lights on." Witherbot held out her hand, inviting the others to board. Three seconds after they boarded, the doors closed.

Sweetwater instinctively looked for a row of buttons. All the walls were made from sheets of diamond plate steel. There was recessed lighting along the elevator's ceiling, but there were no other markings or controls. He could feel the elevator moving in his stomach, but he couldn't tell what direction they were moving. "So, are we allowed to talk yet?"

"Yes. From here on you will be in one of the most secure facilities in the United States. I might say the world, but that is a hard thing to judge. No one really wants to share information on their secure facilities."

"When I was upstairs, I had no idea any of this was here," Sweetwater said.

"What you have seen so far is nothing, Luther. Just a secure garage, doctor's office, and elevator. What you are *going* to see is an altogether different matter."

Sweetwater nodded and started counting the trip, a habit from his childhood. Times had sometimes been tough, and it was a way of distracting his mind from pangs of hunger. When he reached 47 the doors opened. The first thing he noticed was that the walls were lined with copper mesh. Steed noticed his wrinkled eyebrows.

"It's called a Faraday Cage," he said. "The mesh is designed to block any electromagnetic fields. There's no way, outside of an access port, to reach the rest of the world."

"What about the SAT phone?"

"An external antenna, Luther," Witherbot said, having overhead them. "Welcome to the Kremlin."

Four guards awaited them when the elevator stopped. Two stayed behind, the other two led the quartet down a short copper-clad hallway that ended in double blast doors. Ten feet before reaching them, Witherbot went through the same procedure along a section of blank wall as at the elevator. Once finished, a hidden side door of six-inch-thick steel opened, and she stepped through. More guards were waiting inside.

"What's in there?" Sweetwater said.

"Everything," Witherbot replied, a tinge of pride to her usual laconic tone. "That is the Kremlin, the administrative heart of LifeEnders, Incorporated. This is the War Room."

The room was a techie's dream. Workstations were grouped in rows facing a wall of enormous monitors, with a long table in front of them that held a giant mixing board. The opposite wall was floor-to-ceiling glass, separating it from a stadium-shaped area beyond. Recessed spotlights shone down on rows of desks that faced a speaker's podium and a giant monitor.

Sweetwater stopped in the doorway, stunned at such a display of advanced technology. Steed nudged him ahead, so he joined the others at the mixing board, where a pale man in his early thirties awaited them. Fluffy black muttonchops covered his cheeks.

"This is Jason," Witherbot announced. "Jason is our communications supervisor."

Her eyes went to Steed, who gave a curt shake of his head.

Jason started pressing a row of buttons, which brought the wall of monitors to life. Their glow illuminated that side of the room.

"I have asked Jason to channel all the security camera feeds down here," said Witherbot. Each monitor displayed an entrance to the building or a group of workers.

"Where's Denton Poole?" Steed said, cutting his eyes to Warden and Sweetwater. "Denton's the head of security; shouldn't he be here?"

"He is coordinating our response from the field," Witherbot said.

Warden pointed at the video feeds. "What's our time frame here?"

"We are about thirty minutes before the announcement of your touchdown at the airfield," Jason said without looking up from the screens. "I wanted to get a visual baseline. The displays are running three times live. The announcement reached us at approximately sixteen hundred hours, roughly the middle of the second shift, so there shouldn't be much activity at the exits."

Sweetwater located the monitor showing the front door to the building. Where he had stood less than a year ago, working up the courage to come inside. On the screen, Sweetwater saw Jason enter the building. "That's you?"

"Yes, I work first shift, which is 0400 to 1200 hours, but I couldn't stay away."

On the screen, others started entering the building, from the front door and through the basement parking area. Other cameras focused on the secure entrances that fewer employees had permission to use.

"I'm guessing this was when the news went out?" Witherbot said.

"Yes, ma'am, about ten minutes before. Most are the extra security you requested."

"And you are certain that everyone heard that Mister Erebus was cooperating?"

"Yes, ma'am, absolutely."

They each scanned the monitors, looking for anyone leaving the building. There was activity in all the rooms, and there were people at the entrances, but they were all entering the facility.

They kept watching. Soon enough they saw their own convoy navigate the basement security maze.

"C'mon, c'mon," Sweetwater said, "he's gotta be there."

"Don't assume it's a man," Steed said, pacing back and forth, his arms folded.

"This was our chance!"

"How unfortunate," Witherbot said. She thought for a few seconds and motioned Steed over for a brief whispered conference. Steed's face betrayed nothing. He nodded when she finished, headed for the door, and motioned for Sweetwater to follow. Surprised, the younger man fell in step. On his way into the hall, he heard Witherbot speaking to Jason.

"I'm sorry, Jason, but I must ask you to stay."

S teed took a left, said something to one of the guards, and followed them from the War Room.

"What's going on?" Sweetwater said.

"We're running a con."

"On who?"

"Fuck if I know."

"So where are we headed?"

"To the break room. It's been a long day and I could use some coffee."

"They have soda? Maybe some chips?"

That made Steed smile. "I'd be surprised if they don't."

The guards turned left, stopped, and pointed to an open door. The break room was lavishly stocked with free drinks and food, including more substantial fare such as salads and soups, along with shuffleboard, pool, foosball, and other game tables. Aside from them it was empty.

"How ya feelin'?" Steed asked once they were seated.

"I wouldn't mind a beach and a few months to sleep. Man, I hurt, Steed. Down deep, y'know? I just wanna crawl into bed. So, what are we really doing here?"

"We're trying to flush the mole. Cynthia—the assistant director—thought it might be Jason, but it's not. So now we're trying to panic whoever's guilty into making a mistake."

"How can you be sure it's not Jason?"

Steed sipped his coffee, which Sweetwater knew was a stall to give him time to think of an answer. People always thought he was naïve because of his age, accent, and background, and he was getting damned tired of it.

"And don't lie, like you're fixin' to."

Steed lowered the cup, slowly, his eyes never leaving Sweetwater.

"That's a dangerous thing to say to anybody, Luther, but say it to the wrong Shooter and you'll be dead. Don't do it again. There's more to this world than you can possibly imagine, and the hard truth is you're low man. You don't have the clearance to know more than you already know."

"I just hate being talked down to."

"Grow a pair, Marine. If you can't tell the difference between friends and enemies, you're in the wrong business."

"Yeah? What do you know about service?"

Steed's cheeks flushed, and his nostrils flared. "I was in the room."

Sweetwater began to speak, stopped. His expression changed from angry to awestruck.

"With bin Laden?"

"That's right."

"Oh."

"Can we move on to current business now?"

"Yeah."

"Never mind how I know it's not Jason; I know and that's all that matters. You and I are supposedly interrogating Erebus using whatever methods necessary to make him squawk. Then we go back in there and see who runs."

"What if nobody does?"

"I have a way of reading people, so I'll try that."

"I thought I was Plan B? Since we've gotta burn time anyway, let's go see Adrian. The mole might have accomplices who can tell him if we don't."

"That's a good point, Two-Bit. Sure, what the hell? Let's go see the sonofabitch."

"I might have to lie about some things."

"We're all sinners."

Chains tied Adrian Erebus to the hospital bed. Multiple PICC lines hung from his arms, and electrodes, a feeding tube, and oxygen mask obscured most of his face. But he was not unconscious, and his eyes followed Sweetwater and Steed when they entered with the doctor and nurse.

372 | HOY & WEBB

"He should be dead and buried," the doctor commented while checking the monitors. "Instead, he's healing faster than any patient I've ever treated. Heart rate, blood pressure, oxygen saturation levels are all back to normal. Considering the volume of reported blood loss, that should be impossible."

"Are the bullets still in there?" Steed asked.

"No, the assistant director said to keep him alive, so I performed emergency surgery, but scar tissue formation was well advanced in his chest. His larynx was entirely whole; other than some bruising, there were no signs of trauma. And then there are the bullets." Reaching into his lab coat pocket, he placed them in Steed's palm. "I can't explain any of this."

If he hadn't known their origin, Steed wouldn't have recognized the lumps of pitted gray metal as bullets. He showed them to Sweetwater.

"Looks like they were dipped in acid."

"Doctor, could you and the nurse give us the room? We need to speak with this waste of resources privately."

"Sure thing."

"And please, could you take out the feeding tube? I really don't care if he starves."

The nurse moved to comply and wasn't gentle.

"I can't guarantee his oxygen levels if you take the mask off."

"I'll risk it."

"Before you go," Sweetwater said, "I need something sharp, like a scalpel or scissors, and a bone saw."

"A bone saw?"

"You've got one, right?"

"I've got a hacksaw in my trunk if you'd rather have that."

"Sure, that'll work."

Erebus laughed in a soft, raspy voice.

"You're not scaring me, asshole."

Steed made to reply, but Sweetwater held up a finger and Steed let him take over.

"It's not you I'm trying to scare."

"Goddamn if you aren't the stupidest fool I've ever met."

"You might want to leave God out of this, since you're probably gonna be having a conversation with him soon."

"Stupid, like I said. You killed the love of my life, now you wanna kill my boy. I don't care what it costs so long as you die."

Sweetwater laughed and shook his head. "If only you were half as smart as you think you are, Adrian. You must've been the teacher everybody made fun of."

Erebus strained against his restraints the same moment the doctor returned carrying several scalpels and a hacksaw with rust in the teeth. Teeth champing, he snarled and growled and mumbled curses against Sweetwater.

"Did I walk into *The Exorcist?* Do you want guards in here?"

"No," Sweetwater said. "I've killed him three times, and he won't stay dead, but he will the next time."

That made Erebus throw back his head and cackle. "You *can't* kill me!"

"I'm not going to."

The doctor looked from Sweetwater to Steed and back again. "Be careful with the hacksaw, the rust might cause infection."

"I'm not worried about him getting an infection."

"Me either," the doctor said. "I meant for you."

"Thanks. If you hear screams, just ignore 'em. Oh, and I want to apologize in advance; I'm afraid it's likely to get messy in here."

Once they were alone again, Sweetwater laid out the instruments on the ubiquitous hospital-style rolling steel table. Everything in his body above the waist felt like he'd gone fifteen rounds with the world MMA heavyweight champ and lost. Fatigue weighted his limbs, but even after all he'd been through, he realized that moment was the first time he *wanted* to kill somebody. Up to that point it had all been defensive. Now his fingers itched to slice Erebus into slabs...and circumstances wouldn't let him do it.

Erebus said something. Sweetwater gripped the largest scalpel like a knife, whirled, and jammed it through the sheet into his right leg above the ankle. Screams echoed in the room and a spreading circle of red stained the sheet. Steed settled against the HVAC system to watch.

"See, Adrian, I didn't kill Grace Allen. Neither did Bonney. You've been going after the wrong target this whole time."

"Bullshit," Erebus said, "you're just saying that so I don't kill you."

Sweetwater glanced at the sheet. The bloody circle seemed to have stopped growing, exactly as he'd thought it would.

"I went there to kill her, but I couldn't go through with it, so her husband pushed her over the side."

"You're lying! I'll bite your eyes out!"

"Nope, not lying, so let's stop with the threats, both ways, okay? You're not gonna kill me, and I'm not gonna kill you. I *can't* kill you. I know that now...at least, not until I kill Herbert."

"My boy! Keep your fucking hands off my boy, Sweetwater, do you hear me? Leave my boy alone!"

"Your boy is dead, Erebus, and he's *been* dead for years."

Erebus went into spasms of rage so violent they moved the bed. PICC lines popped out, and he bit at the chains.

"That thing isn't your boy; that thing is *you*. It's feeding you energy to keep you alive, but every time it does, it shrinks a little. So, all I've gotta do to kill it is to keep torturing you."

"It is Herbert, you lying sack of shit! It is, it is, it is! My boy isn't dead!"

"You want me to leave him alone, Adrian? Do you want me to leave Herbert alone?"

The madman calmed immediately, wary but listening.

"Yes."

"Give me the name of the mole."

"And you'll leave Herbert alone?"

Sweetwater nodded.

"You swear?"

"I swear by all that's holy."

"I didn't like him anyway," Erebus said.

Chapter Thirty-Seven

They reassembled in the War Room. Steed whispered something to Jason, listened to the answer, and went back into the hallway with Warden in tow. All of the War Room technicians kept their heads down, pretending to work, but human nature caused them to look up when they thought it safe. Guards entered and headed for the glass wall overlooking the much larger Kremlin. Steed positioned himself near the door.

"Fuck!" cursed a stocky man in the last row, pressing a jury-rigged lever on his desk. Alarms rang throughout the building. The guards drew their weapons. "Fine, I'm your guy, but if you shoot me you're all fucked. I've got a tank of sarin wired into the HVAC system."

"Mickey!" Jason said, aghast. "Why?"

"It's the usual pathetic story," Witherbot said. "Drugs, women, gambling. Mister Erebus told us everything, even the message board on the dark web where they met. There is no way out of this, Mickey."

"Then we'll all die together, won't we? How did you know?"

"Adrian Erebus gave you up, of course. Now put the gun down and let's forget this lockdown nonsense. You know what happens if you shoot one of us."

"Did you miss the part about the sarin?"

"I did *not* miss it, I heard you. I simply do not believe it."

"If he shows himself, I can take him. No problem," Steed said in a loud voice. "You know my talent."

"No, Steed, Mickey can buy back his life by coming clean," Witherbot said. "We just need to determine the extent of the damage."

Mickey had crawled under his desk, was out of sight for a few seconds, then reached up one hand where they could see it. His thumb was on a red button.

"I'm standing up now."

The round head of Mickey Riggle appeared over the top of his personal monitor. A bad combover did nothing to hide his thinning hair or distract from the odd pistol in his left hand and the detonator in his right.

"Looks like a toy," Sweetwater said.

"It's real enough! Stop talking or I'll blow us all to hell and back!"

"Steed?"

"Could be a homemade pistol. If that's a ceramic barrel it won't be very accurate."

"That would explain getting it past the metal detectors," Witherbot added.

"For a smart guy, you're really stupid Mickey," Jason said.

Witherbot's scowl could have withered a bouquet of roses.

"Quiet."

"All of you shut up!" Mickey said and waited for silence before going on. "This is what we're going to do. The assistant director and I are going up the elevator together, up to the roof. One of you is going to call for a chopper to take me wherever I want. Once I'm gone, I'll let her go."

"Why should we believe you?" Sweetwater asked.

"If I kill her, the government will pressure whatever country I land in to either extradite me or let a Shooter take me out. I'm not suicidal unless you don't give me a choice."

"What about the sarin?"

"You'll figure that out. Let's move. Anybody shoots me, this bomb goes off, and they'll be scraping us all off the walls. Now get over here, ma'am. I don't wanna die, and you don't either."

"Steed?"

"He's capable of doing it."

"Very well then, Mickey, I'll go with you. On condition that you first let all of your fellow employees walk out of here."

"No!"

"Yes," she said, making clear it was not negotiable. "You're also going to have to lift the lockdown. With the elevators down, how do we reach the helipad?"

"Let me take him, boss," Steed said.

"No, it's too risky. And his logic is correct, if he kills me, he might as well put the next bullet in his own mouth. Mickey, let these people move into the Kremlin. They've been your friends and colleagues for years; do you really want to hurt them?"

Mickey licked his lips. "They'll be safe once we're out in the hall."

"Very well," she said.

"Hey, Ace," Sweetwater said, "if you hurt her, she's right, you'd best eat the gun before I catch up to you."

"We," Steed said, "before *we* catch up to him."

Witherbot joined Mickey at the end of the row of workstations. Every gun in the room tracked him, but the tableau held, and nobody fired. Sweetwater glared at the man as they walked across the room.

"I'll see you soon."

M ickey didn't reply.

Witherbot walked through the doorway first. The guards had backed away, guns at the ready, except for one to the right of the door. She was focused on him, so she only saw in her peripheral vision her daughter's arm and a hand wielding a shoe, swinging at Mickey's face as he exited the War Room. The shoe missed Mickey's nose and smacked his chin, spinning him sideways.

Reflexively, he pulled the trigger. The gun exploded in his hand as the homemade barrel couldn't contain the blast of the gunpowder. Fired from a distance of only three feet, the bullet hit Warden in the right flank, and she went down. Jagged shards sprayed Mickey's hand, arm, and left cheek, but hit the guard in the eyes. He staggered backward, hands to his face, and dropped his pistol.

Witherbot had her head turned so she missed being wounded, but her position blocked the other guards from shooting. She saw her daughter sink to her knees, which drove all thoughts out of her brain except killing Mickey. She balled her right fist and pivoted without looking, aiming for Mickey's face…and missed. He'd gone to one knee to retrieve the guard's weapon. She kept rotating her body in a continuing motion, and her left fist struck his forehead. Mickey rose fast and used the pistol barrel to hit her with an uppercut to the chin. Without hesitating he shot her in the stomach.

"Anybody moves, and I shoot her again," he cried, his voice trembling as he realized what he'd done.

The sound was unlike any gunshot Sweetwater had heard before, and it took milliseconds to recognize it as an explosion. It wasn't the suicide vest, something smaller; the homemade gun. Then a second shot echoed from outside the War Room, this one the telltale report of a Sig Sauer P320, the standard handgun used by LEI at all levels.

Slowed by his injuries, Steed beat him to the door but stopped. Although unarmed, Sweetwater joined Steed and saw Mickey supporting a bleeding Witherbot as they walked backward toward her private elevator. The bank of employee elevators was down a branch hall, behind a guard station. Then Sweetwater spotted Warden on her knees and holding her stomach, blood spilling onto the floor. He raised his fist and stepped toward Mickey.

Mickey was using one hand to help Witherbot walk, which left him to choose between fingering the suicide belt detonator and holding the Sig to Witherbot's head. He chose the latter.

"Hold up, kid," Steed said. "You'll just get her killed. Help my daughter instead."

"Wait," Mickey yelled. "Stop!" He took a shaky breath. "Everyone, just wait a second." Panicked, he looked around, but kept the gun pressed against Witherbot's head, above her right ear. A hole in the side of her suit jacket hid the extent of her wound. A grimace of pain barely registered on her stony countenance, but Sweetwater knew her well enough to see it.

Warden was on her knees, hugging her abdomen as blood flowed between her fingers. Sweetwater knelt beside her. At the sight of her wound, his lips pulled back, showing all his teeth, like a dog about to attack. Ripping off a piece of her shirt, he applied pressure to the wound.

"You're a dead man," he said, jabbing a finger at Mickey.

"Shut up," Steed said in a stage whisper. "That's not helping. Consider this advance Shooter training." Raising his voice, he spoke so everyone could hear. "Don't listen to him, Mickey. He doesn't know how these things work."

Jittery shakes and flitting eyes showed Mickey was on the verge of doing something crazy.

"And you do?"

"Yeah, I do. Cynthia, how bad is it?"

Mickey blinked rapidly as control of the situation slipped away.

"Don't talk to her, talk to me!"

"Listen to me, Mickey. Listen to me," Steed said. "You're only alive as long as she is, do you understand me? She lives, you live; she dies…"

"I'll blow us all up!"

"No, you won't. Everybody else lower your weapons."

The guards glanced at each other. They'd never seen Steed before and didn't take orders from strangers.

"Do as he says," Witherbot said.

Reluctantly they all lowered their pistols.

"One of you slide your weapon to my fellow Shooter, here."

"No!" Mickey yelled, "I'll kill her, I swear."

"Here's the deal, Mickey, when I shoot, I never miss—never. If you let go of the assistant director to reach for that detonator then

I'll have no choice but to put a bullet in your head. If you shoot her, you'll be dead before she is. And if she bleeds out standing there…well, you get the idea. The only way you leave this hallway breathing is by surrendering before any of that happens. Now slide that weapon over."

One of them did as Steed asked. Sweetwater didn't release pressure on Warden's wound to pick it up, but eyed it like a gambling addict eyed a stack of chips traded for their paycheck.

"Now there's a wild card, Mickey. Mister Sweetwater here is a lot younger than you or me. He's impetuous and does things without thinking. He's also a Marine and graduated from Scout Sniper School. That means he doesn't miss either. I've told him not to shoot you, but he has a crush on my daughter, and you shot her, too."

Sweetwater heard the words even over the powerful underground blowers, but he didn't react. Warden heard them too, and squinted despite her pain.

"She's losing a lot of blood," he finally said. "We've gotta get her to the OR, fast."

"Hear that, Mickey? Time's running out for both of them. So what's it gonna be?" Steed said.

"Stop rushing me! Lemme think!"

"Hey, Luther," Warden whispered with a tiny smile, "please tell me I can still wear a bikini."

Blood covered his hands, but the words drove into Sweetwater's brain like hot nails. Mickey was standing directly to Sweetwater's right, with his and Witherbot's body' turned at a right angle, putting him at the extreme edge of Mickey's peripheral vision. Dangerous or not, Sweetwater forgot everything else, snatched up the pistol, steadied it with both hands and fired.

Sensing movement, Mickey started to turn when the bullet struck. Sweetwater had aimed for his ear canal, but the slight twist brought Mickey's Sig into the line of fire. The round vaporized most of his trigger finger and hit the trigger, driving it forward with such force that it jammed. Half a second behind Sweetwater, Steed fired twice. Both shots hit the Sig, and it flew out of Mickey's hand.

Screaming, Mickey released Witherbot and reached for the detonator, but Sweetwater got there too quickly. Tackling the computer tech, he was able to drive four punches into the man's nose before Steed and some of the guards dragged him away.

Gurneys and medical personnel swarmed the two injured women. LEI's bomb squad rushed in to disarm the suicide vest. Once it was off, one of them held it up so Steed and Sweetwater could see it.

"Fake," he said.

In the corner of the ICU room, Sweetwater lay in a wheeled recliner, snoring. Teri Warden blinked awake and focused on the room's second bed, where her mother was focused on a tablet computer.

"How are you feeling?" she asked in a low voice without looking up.

"Terrible, you?"

"Irritated."

"Mmmm…" Sweetwater said, rousing. "Hey, look who's back. Are you all right? Did it hurt?"

Witherbot closed her eyes and shook her head but said nothing.

"Of course, it hurts, dumbass. I was gut shot." In contrast to her words, Warden gave him a weak smile. "Plus, you ripped my shirt up to get a look at my bra."

"What?" he asked, sitting up. "That had nothing to do with it."

"Do you have a preferred method of dying, Mister Sweetwater?" Witherbot said. "I can write that into the contract."

"Hey—what? What did I do?"

"Aside from sleeping with my daughter, you developed a romantic relationship with a fellow employee, which is strictly against company policy."

"I did not! Tell her, Teri! Tell her we never did anything. I never even kissed her."

"Mister Sweetwater, I am not deaf. On the plane, I heard what I heard. It gives me no pleasure, but rules are rules. And her father insisted."

Leaning on the door jamb, Steed joined in. "That's true, kid, sorry. Diddle my daughter, you gotta die."

That's when Sweetwater's brain finally woke up enough to notice Steed and Warden were suppressing laughs.

"Yeah, yeah, okay, make fun of the new guy. Now I get it."

"I hope the doctors did a better job on me than what they did on you," Warden said. "You look like a chopping block."

"I was shot in the chest, there's important stuff in there. You were shot in the belly. It hurts, sure, but everything there is squishy." He paused. "Wait, how do you know what my chest looks like?"

Witherbot looked up from the computer and did something she rarely did; she smiled.

"Busted."

"What about you, ma'am?" Sweetwater said. "He shot you, too."

386 | HOY & WEBB

"Mine was a through and through. They said the bullet went through my intestines. There was a bit of surgery, but I'm fine."

"And Mickey?"

"Mickey has agreed to fully cooperate, so he will be fine...until he isn't."

Chapter Thirty-Eight

Five Weeks Later

Somewhere in the West Texas Desert

After a five-hour drive, the stifling heat made Adrian Erebus gasp shallow breaths of the hot air. He reached to wipe the sweat from his forehead. For the fifth time, his hands were stopped by the chains. He was secured in handcuffs and leg cuffs, joined by a length of chain.

"It's hot in here!" he yelled and kept yelling.

There was no response.

The trucked rocked a bit as if they had turned off the road and eventually came to a stop.

Erebus looked up at the sound of a key turning in the door lock. Multiple shotguns were pointed at him, but an explosion of sunlight blinded him. Unable to shield his eyes, he could only close them and turn away. Hands grabbed him and dragged him outside, where he fell to the dirt.

"I can't see," he whined. "Take these fuckin' chains off. I can't see!"

The guard holding Adrian by the armpit gave him a sharp hook punch to the gut. He tried to curl up, but a second guard grabbed him and hauled him up straight.

"Boo-fucking-who," said a familiar voice. It took a minute to place it—the man who killed Grace Allen. Now it all came back.

Erebus tried to say something, but the dust hung in air so hot that it hurt to breathe, so he only wheezed. It felt like the moisture was being leached from his eyes, and his lungs were blistering. He stopped resisting and went limp, and the two men dragged him into the desert.

Four guards surrounded him in addition to the two holding his arms. Alongside Sweetwater walked a man in his late 30s or early 40s…Steed—that was his name—with a younger female holding a scoped rifle on the other side. He knew her, too. Teri Warden.

The dryness of his mouth made it hard to form words. Staring at Sweetwater, all he could eke out was, "You…Grace…not right."

Sweetwater ignored him. He accepted a bottle of water so cold that condensation dripped like a melting icicle. Erebus' hated enemy drank deeply, smacked his lips, and cupped hands his around his mouth.

"I'm calling for the entity known as Herbert," he said, the words swept up by winds and thrown over the desert. High overhead, a prairie falcon circled on the thermals. "We intend to kill this man as many times as it takes for him to stay dead. I know that reviving him reduces you, but our fight is only with him, so it's up to you whether to keep existing or not."

"My boy…won't abandon me," Erebus managed to say.

Someone set a bench in the dirt and a guard pushed him down until he lay flat on the wood. Rough hands pinned him while someone else used thick straps to secure him tightly to the boards. Last, they wedged a hard plastic bookend on either side of his head. All he could do was stare straight up as the sun burned through his eyelids.

The entire bench was lifted upright, bringing him back to his feet. Now that the sun wasn't right in his face, he could see vague images.

Fifty yards away, a distant umbrella had seats arrayed as if folks were tailgating at a football game. Erebus watched one of the men put a long stick with a "Y" at the top into the ground. The Warden woman lifted her rifle into the notch and pointed it at him.

"Hello, Father," said a voice from below.

Sweetwater stood, holding binoculars up to his sunglasses. "He's here."

Erebus could only move his eyes to look down, but it was enough. Playing in the dirt at his feet was Herbert.

"Son, what are you doing here?" He tried to twist his body, but the straps held him tight. "We've got to get you out of here; it's dangerous."

Herbert stood up. "Yeah, about that." He brushed dust from his knees. "I think it's time I went my own way, Dad."

"What do you mean?"

"See, it's like this. When Mom died…well, not *my* mom, my mom is your mom. But when your wife died, you created me from this reservoir of your—language doesn't really do this justice—this reservoir of your all-consuming hatred. You summoned me from hell to become part of you, to get revenge on those you believed harmed you. I helped. When I stabbed you, I knew it was the only way to get you close enough to your enemy to kill him. You opened this world to me, and I was grateful. It was our…let us call it our *bargain*."

A green laser dot appeared on Erebus, right over his heart. Slowly the dot climbed up his body to stop between his eyes.

"But now you're a liability. As long as you're alive, I'm bound to restore you, to heal you using the energy that makes *my* existence possible. And things aren't looking too good right now, you know? You're tied to a bench in the middle of the desert, and even I can't keep reviving you forever. But this isn't goodbye, Father. Rather, it's more like a welcome, because, now, instead of me being part of you, *you* will be part of *me*."

Then his face began to change. Herbert's pale blue eyes turned into flames. His face lengthened and widened into something resembling a bull, with a mouth stretched into a wide slash filled with sharks' teeth. Standing on his toes, he reached up and touched the green dot.

"Aaaaiiiiieeee!" Erebus screamed. As if an embalmer was sucking out his bodily fluids, he could feel his life force flowing into the thing called Herbert.

"You're cleared to shoot," Sweetwater said, watching in horror as the black thing doubled in size.

Warden couldn't see the entity, only the green dot, and squeezed off a single round. The 50mm bullet passed through Herbert and struck dead center in the laser mark. Blood, bone, and brain matter splattered against the bench, which toppled over with a softball-sized hole blown through the wood.

Herbert nudged the partially decapitated body of Adrian Erebus, turned to lock stares with Sweetwater, snorted fire, and vanished.

Epilogue

Four Months Later

Luther Sweetwater's Trailer, Southeast Fayette County, TN

The Wolf River, as it passed south of La Grange, TN, expanded into something less like a river and more like a shallow lake, then narrowed again and flowed west-northwest to bisect Memphis before its eventual confluence with the Mississippi River. Pre-dawn light allowed Luther Sweetwater to load his new Toyota pickup with everything he'd need for a half day of fishing. He'd missed the spawning season, but catching fish was beside the point; it was the first day he'd been cleared for a return to normal activities, and just the act of going fishing signaled life getting back to normal.

Whatever that meant.

Two texts already received from LEI had gone unanswered. A mysterious death in Dallas coincided with Sweetwater's release from the hospital, and Witherbot wanted to know if he knew anything about it. She also warned him that with Shields and Bonney gone, that left a shortage of Shooters in the region, and he'd get all the work he wanted. Sweetwater almost, but not quite, told her that he didn't want *any* work. His boss lifted an eyebrow at his stammered "great" but let it drop.

Returning to the trailer for a cooler of water and sodas, the last thing to load, he'd lifted it and turned back to the front door when a figure standing there startled him so much that he dropped the cooler. Ice, soda cans, and bottles slid across the linoleum floor. One soda burst open and spewed sugary brown liquid all over his furniture.

"Goddamn it!" he said, pissed that his warning sense hadn't alerted him. "Grace Allen?"

Outlined against the pale dawn and having already turned out the interior lights, Sweetwater couldn't see many details of the ghastly spectre in the tattered dress and was glad he couldn't. It took a moment for him to realize that the flashes of white were bone. Few strips of flesh still clung to her skull.

"Who else would it be?" she said, the jaws clacking when she spoke. Any traces of a human voice were gone, her vocal cords and larynx having rotted away, leaving her with only a hissing growl.

"Sorry."

"Are you?"

"Well…yeah."

"What are you sorry for?"

"A lot of things, Grace Allen, starting with causing your death."

He tried to keep his face neutral and not show revulsion at her appearance, but failed.

"You *did* do that, Luther, you know that don't you? I'm a moldy corpse because of you. Maybe if you'd turned down the job, somebody else would have killed me, or maybe Dennis Roy would have done it himself…or maybe I might still be alive. We'll never know."

"No, we won't."

Sweetwater sat on the red naugahyde couch opposite the flat screen TV and stared at the big rip in the floor. For all he'd done to try and move past his guilt, there was the rotting manifestation of it standing in the doorway.

"I'd make it up to you, if I could," he said.

"You mean that?"

"I do."

"You sure? My whole life, men told me anything I'd wanna hear 'til they got what they wanted, then I never saw 'em again."

"That's not me."

"Not now it ain't. But you saw what I looked like...before."

"You were gorgeous."

"But not smart. I believed in men of poor character."

"Like me."

"I don't know about that...I think you are genuinely sorry for the part you played in my death, and one day you're gonna have to explain it, but not to me." The apparition of Grace Allen Tarbeau paused until he glanced up to see if she was still there. "What would you do for redemption, Luther, for me to forgive you?"

"Anything in my power, except kill another innocent person."

"Is it within you to kill?"

It was the question he feared more than any other, the one he'd been thinking about for months. To his surprise, Sweetwater found that he had an answer.

"Yeah, it's within me. If they deserve it."

"Who decides if it's worth it?"

"Me. I'm the one who's gotta answer for it."

"Then get revenge for me," she said. "Adrian is in hell now, where he belongs. And you may not know it, but my second husband Dennis Roy Tarbeau, the man who *did* kill me, well he's dead now too. They found him on the sidewalk outside the Renaissance Building not a week ago now and ruled it a suicide. The detectives figured he just couldn't live without his wife."

"Do tell," Sweetwater said.

"He tells a different story."

It took Sweetwater a few seconds to understand what she meant by that.

"He's with you?"

"Let's just say he can't ever get away from me again. But there's still one man left who needs killing, the man who raped me the night my Herbert died. You do that for me, and I'll put in a good word for you when the time comes."

"You're a fine woman, Grace Allen. I wished I'd known you in life."

"I was a little old for you, Luther."

"Not that much older."

Maybe it was his imagination, but Sweetwater thought he saw a softening in the empty eye sockets. The jaws parted in what might once have been a smile. Grace Allen Tarbeau then dissipated like smoke in a breeze, never to reappear, but her final words echoed through his trailer.

"Thank you for Dennis Roy."

The three-hundred pound bulk of John Cleve Stuart huddled over the emaciated deer, dressing the animal even as it bleated in agony. He'd come across it on the long dirt trail that acted as a driveway into the deep woods, where his makeshift dog-fighting arena sprawled on the private property of an absentee owner. A whole carload of fresh bait dogs guaranteed a big crowd that night, with lots of cash, and he'd have Marcus grind the deer meat into burgers and sell them for ten bucks apiece. Even as his knife cut through the tendons of the animal's left hind leg, it craned its neck to scream for mercy. A slit carotid artery would bring death in seconds, but the truth was that John Cleve Stuart liked seeing things suffer.

A single gunshot from close behind his left shoulder made him jump to one side. The bullet struck the suffering deer between the eyes and ended its misery. Stuart struggled to his feet holding the dressing knife in his right fist, but squinted at the two men standing ten feet away, one with folded arms and the other holding a smoking pistol. The taller of the two was both lean and heavily muscled, but short; Stuart knew him from around Semple but couldn't remember his name. He wore the usual camo and held the pistol with wisps of smoke leaking from the downward pointing barrel. The other man was the Sheriff of Fayette County.

"Sheriff Knickermeyer," he said, using the sheriff's proper name instead of substituting the highly offensive n-word in place of 'Knicker,' as he did among his friends. The black man's grim expression didn't change, nor did he unfold his arms. He and Stuart had a long, long history together. "What's the problem, there's no hunting season on deer in this county."

"Nope," the sheriff said, "and that one clearly had wasting disease, and I wouldn't care if you ate infected meat for the rest of your life. But not to kill it first…that's low, even for you, John C."

"It ain't against the law."

"I could probably take you in for animal cruelty, maybe even make it a felony, or for trespassing on private lands again, but I'm not gonna do any of that."

Stuart cocked his head and squinted. He wasn't a smart man, but he was clever in the way that most criminals were.

"What's the catch?"

Knickermeyer nodded with his head. "This here is Luther Sweetwater; you might have seen him around town some. He grew up around here, not too far from your momma."

"Whoopee shit, so what?"

Sweetwater smiled. "So the sheriff is my client and led me here so I could do the job he hired me for."

"What does that mean? You pickin' up trash outa the ditch?"

Using his left hand, Sweetwater pulled a sheet of paper out of his top shirt pocket along with a single one dollar bill. As he did so, his focus never left Stuart, and his right hand never let the pistol drop.

"This is a binding contract offered to me through LifeEnders, Incorporated, who employ me as a licensed Shooter. As you can see, it's been duly signed and notarized. That means I'm legally obligated to kill the person named on the line where it reads 'target.' Can you see what's printed there? That's your name, Mister Stuart."

"But…huh? Wait a minute, you can't do that! Tell him, Sheriff! Take me in, I'll confess to whatever you want."

"Sorry, John C., that's not on the table now," Knickermeyer said.

Stuart started forward, but didn't get a step before Sweetwater lifted the battered Sig Sauer P320 in his right fist a scant three inches, his finger on the trigger and the barrel now aimed at Stuart's forehead.

"Remember Grace Allen Erebus, Mister Stuart?"

"She was my old lady's daughter," he answered, wariness in his whispered tone.

"Correct. She was also the young lady you raped the night her son was murdered and she fled to her mother for help and comfort."

"I don't—"

"Shut up you piece of shit, or I'll use every bullet in this magazine to make you suffer the way you did that deer, the way the sheriff tells me you've been doing with dogs for the last 30 years. If I could prolong your suffering I would, but something tells me you're gonna spend all of eternity begging for mercy. If we lived in Shelby County, or Hardeman, or McNairy, I would have done this pro bono for Grace Allen. That's what I came here for. But you see, this is *my* home too, and it sickens me that assholes like you hide behind the courts and the law, when what you really need is a bullet. When the sheriff told me about you, what you've done all these years, then it became personal."

"Grace Allen, yeah, I get it now. You must have fucked her like everybody else in the county," Stuart said, managing to sneer despite the situation. Maybe he thought it would help. Instead, Sweetwater lowered the gun, fired, and blew out Stuart's right knee.

The huge man collapsed into the dried leaves and sticks covering the shoulder of the dirt road, howling like one of the bait dogs he sent to its death in the ring. Rolling in the dirt, a jagged branch cut a long slice in his cheek, but the pain of his destroyed knee overrode the minor wound. Sweetwater knelt near the man, the Sig less than two feet from Stuart's right jaw.

"Like I was saying, I would have done it for free after hearing Grace Allen's story, but when I let the sheriff know you'd be turning up dead, he insisted on paying me. After I heard your story, I downright refused to take his money, and he downright refused not to pay me. We were at an impasse. Since I didn't want to be paid to kill you, and the sheriff wouldn't hear of not paying me, well, we compromised. Your life is worth precisely one dollar, Mister Stuart. A single fucking dollar."

In between sobs, Stuart mouthed pleas for mercy, even appealing to the sheriff's well-known religious beliefs.

"Vengeance is mine sayeth the Lord," Stuart said. Dirt stuck to his wet face, making his bloodshot eyes appear whiter than they actually were. "That's what the bible says, Sheriff; that's what it says! Reverend Milthouse said so hisself!"

"Romans 12:19, John C.; you're right. I've heard him give that sermon three or four times, an' it does my heart good to know that you love the Lord. It kinda makes this easier. But you see, what the Lord doesn't say is what tool He will use to exact His vengeance. In this case, I believe He is using Mister Sweetwater here, much as he did Samson, except instead of the jawbone of an ass, Mr. Sweetwater uses a Sig Sauer chambered for 9mm rounds. You see the similarity, don't you, John C.?"

"That's not what God meant!" Desperation gave volume to Stuart's words.

Knickermeyer shrugged. "Much as I'd enjoy debating theology with you, the day's getting on. Oh, last thing, John C., I promise. Don't count on a proper Christian burial. I talked to Sam Hart before coming out here—this is all his land, as I'm sure you know— and he gave me permission to leave your body right here. You remember what Clint Eastwood said about vultures having to eat, the same as worms, don't you, John C.?"

"I—"

The second gunshot sent a flock of grackles flapping skyward in a nearby field, which the two men could see through a thinner stand of trees. The bullet struck Stuart about four inches short of the chin and blew off most of his lower jaw, leaving a flap of skin and splintered bone flopping as he tried to speak. But it didn't kill him. The horror on Stuart's face was a grotesque sight which finally sated Sweetwater's desire to avenge poor Grace Allen. In his mind, it didn't square things between them—nothing could—but maybe it would give rest to her soul. A third bullet shattered Stuart's skull like a pumpkin.

Sweetwater policed his brass while the sheriff strolled back toward the cruiser.

"You killed me," a voice said from the ditch behind Sweetwater. "You really did it."

The translucent figure of John C. Stuart stood with hands outstretched in disbelief.

"Yeah, John C., I killed you. I wish I could do it again."

"You know I'm gonna get you for this," Stuart said, as if Sweetwater was too stupid to understand the consequences of his actions. "You *know* what's coming at you."

For the first time in a long time, Sweetwater chuckled.

"*You're* not gonna do anything, John C., except learn how to live with being dead. And if you're thinking that any of your scumbag buddies will try to kill me, I hope like fuck they do. But I'd think you have more to worry about than me."

"If I'm dead, what do I have to worry about now? Except maybe hell."

"Maybe the spirits of all those dogs you tortured."

"Dogs don't have spirits!"

"No? I heard they did, and that they like to bite people who treated them bad. I guess you'll find out which of us is right, but that sounds a lot like hell to me."

He turned to join the sheriff. Sweetwater knew that Knickermeyer couldn't see the dead man. He wasn't sure how he could communicate with the dead, but he knew that others couldn't see or hear them.

"I didn't say you could go," Stuart yelled out. "Please don't go, man; I'm scared."

"So were all those dogs you killed."

"They were just fucking *dogs!* You killed me, asshole; now stay here. You owe me that much!"

"Go to hell," Sweetwater said, smiling at the pun.

Stuart dissipated like mist, but where he'd been standing stood three other figures, all of which were little more than skeletons. Two raised bony middle fingers and, by their builds, he recognized Bonney and Shields. The other saluted...Cooper. Then they followed Stuart into the netherworld.

Knickermeyer returned with a sign made from black paint on an old piece of wood nailed to a long, sharpened board. He jammed that into the ground beside Stuart's body.

"Did I hear you sayin' somethin'?" the sheriff asked.

"Just a prayer."

"Yeah? I didn't figure you for a prayin' man. For John C's sake, I hope God's got more forgivin' in His heart than I would."

"I wasn't prayin' for John C. He can burn for all eternity as far as it concerns me."

"Who then? Can't be all them dogs, no way a dog goes to hell."

"Me," Sweetwater said. "I was praying for me."

"Oh…yeah. Son, I sure as hell ain't the man to speak for God, so I can't say whether in His eyes you're a good man or an evil one. But I meant what I said to John C. He gives us tasks to accomplish according to our talents and uses us to bring about His grand plan."

"And you believe that?"

"I surely do, Luther."

"You know, Sheriff, cops don't generally like Shooters very much, and the other way around, but you and I just might get along."

"Before this, I hated you people," Knickermeyer said. "I shouldn't have—the Lord says not to hate anybody—still, I'm paid to keep folks alive, not help 'em die. But you know, this is the law of the land now, and in certain cases like this one, it might just work out better."

The sheriff sucked on his cheek and scratched his neck then, and Sweetwater knew the man wanted to ask him a question, probably the same question *everybody* wanted to ask a Shooter. He decided just to get it over with and not wait for Knickermeyer to ask it.

"The idea of killing somebody who hasn't done anything wrong bothers me a lot, Sheriff."

"Oh," Knickermeyer said, taken aback.

"Can I tell you a secret, Sheriff? Something nobody else in the world knows?"

"You sure that's a good idea?"

"I think so, yeah. Leastwise, if you swear not to tell, I'll believe you."

"Long as you're not confessing to a crime committed in Fayette County, or anywhere else, I guess, then I swear to keep your secret."

"Not a crime, no, it's kind of the opposite. I've killed people, Sheriff, two so far, and both had it coming, but I've never killed anybody for a contract. I was supposed to, and I took credit for it, but I didn't do it."

Knickermeyer picked an acorn out of a crease in his sleeve, tossed it into the ditch and then let his eyes roam over the field beyond.

"So you're confessing to *not* killing somebody?"

"Pretty much, yeah. I can't give you details about it, without maybe opening you up to a lawsuit, but I checked and what I did, it's not a crime. LEI tells you it is, but it's not, it's a breach of contract, a civil matter."

"So they won't kill you for doing it?"

"They'd kill me in a heartbeat. That's like Rule Number One of things for a Shooter not to do."

"Why are you telling *me*, Luther?"

"I don't know, exactly; I just felt like I needed to tell somebody."

Knickermeyer smiled like Sweetwater always wished his dad would have smiled at him.

"You have a conscience, and I think you're gonna find that a moral compass ain't such a good thing in your business. I wouldn't go 'fessin up to just anybody, either. Trust ain't so common as you might think. Now, how 'bout I buy you dinner at the Donutman?"

"Donutman sounds good, but I'm payin'. I can afford it now."

LEI allowed Shooters to do pro-bono work for a good cause, and Sweetwater had found his. Whether he could ever kill anybody to fulfill a contract or not remained to be seen, but Fayette was his home county; he knew the people because they were *his* people. The sign alone wouldn't stop the John Cleve Stuart's of the world from making money off the suffering of animals that scumbags would pay to see tortured, and that's where he came in. Grace Allen hadn't died for nothing after all, her death led him to find John C., and that had given him a purpose. Riding in the front passenger seat of the Sheriff's Department cruiser, Sweetwater saw the sign in the side mirror and read it again.

This is what happens to rapists and dog fighters in Fayette County.

Cast of Characters

Luther Sweetwater – Ex-Marine sniper and Probational Shooter for LifeEnders, Inc.

Teri Warden – Contract consultant for LEI.

Cynthia Witherbot – Assistant Director for LEI.

William 'Billy the Kid' Bonney – Shooter for LEI based in Memphis.

Adrian Erebus – Former high school math teacher.

Grace Allen Tarbeau – Adrian Erebus' ex-wife.

Herbert Erebus – Grace Allen and Adrian's son.

John C. Stuart – Grace Allen's mother's former boyfriend.

Eamon Cooper – LEI contract target.

Mark Shields – Shooter for LEI based in Memphis.

Steed – LEI Shooter.

About Larry Hoy

Larry is a contributing author for a collection of anthologies, most of them dipping into the horror, supernatural, and mystery worlds. He is also a contributing member of the Malice in Memphis & Memphis Writers clubs.

When not writing, Larry can be found on the back of his motorcycle. Trips have taken him through a healthy bit of America and some of Europe. Over those years, he has collected an endless supply of stories. Now, on days when he isn't thundering down backroads, he has been spotted putting some of his stories down on paper. This is one of those stories.

Other high water marks in his life include his wife and daughters. Together they have shared many adventures and somehow come out safe on the other side. The family also trains in Kempo-Karate, where they earned enough belts they can all hold up their pants.

If you are fortunate enough to see him out and about, please wave him down and tell him how much you loved the story.

To find out more, you can contact him at https://larryhoyjr.wordpress.com/

* * *

About William Alan Webb

Despite persistent rumors, Bill does not have Besquith ancestors, and he is not the result of a failed genetic experiment; he just looks that way. Born in the badlands of West Tennessee, he foraged for food and shelter in the perilous world of his parents' home until age 21. They used the term 'mooching;' he saw it as wilderness survival.

Regardless of semantics, a lifetime of sloth and hedonism convinced his wife Kathy that he was a great catch, and by the time she realized her mistake, it was too late. There were kids and dogs and bills and a mortgage, and he had correctly calculated that she would decide that kicking him to the curb was too much trouble.

Having more time than brains, he attended the University of Memphis while majoring (more or less) in Creative Writing. (The university's English Department would say 'less.') Ignoring the standard four-year schedule, he instead chose the more leisurely 38-year plan. This allowed him to be heavily involved in his children's lives, which repeatedly embarrassed them in their teenage years. That, of course, was the point.

Then, in one fevered year, 2014-2015, he wrote the two books that launched the writing career the world had successfully avoided until that moment. The rest, of course, is infamy.

Bill now lives in [REDACTED] with [REDACTED].

Follow Bill on social media:
Twitter: @jointhebrigade1
Facebook: https://www.facebook.com/TheLastBrigade/
Facebook: https://www.facebook.com/keepyouupallnightbooks/

The following is an
Excerpt from Book One of The Devil's Gunman:

The Devil's Gunman

Philip Bolger

Available Now from Blood Moon Press

eBook, Audio, and Paperback

Excerpt from "The Devil's Gunman:"

I eased the door open and braced for gunfire or a fireball.

I got neither. I swept the entryway with my rifle's sights. Nothing more offensive than some high school photos glared back at me, and I didn't hear anything running down the hallway or readying a weapon. There were no shouts from police or federal agents, either.

What I did hear, from the living room, was incessant chatter underscored by the occasional interjection of a laugh track. The chatter was accompanied by the soft peripheral glow of my television. Whoever had broken into my house was watching a sitcom.

"I'm unarmed," a man's voice rang out. "So put down the rifle, and let's have a talk."

"The fuck we will," I shouted back. "You broke into my home!"

I moved down the hallway, keeping my rifle on the opening to the living room.

"That's part of what we have to talk about," the voice said. I peered around the corner and saw a young Caucasian man. His pale features and dyed blue hair did little to mask the malicious smirk on his face. He was dressed in an oxford shirt and slacks with a skinny tie, as though he couldn't figure out if he wanted to look like he'd just joined a band or an investment firm. He wore a silver tie clip with a red blood drop on it.

I stood there with my rifle sights on his head.

"I'm here as a messenger," he said and flashed his teeth. I saw pointed incisors. That was enough for me. "This is peaceful, Nicholas. No need to be violent."

I lowered the rifle. I didn't like the prick's condescending tone; he sounded like he enjoyed the sound of his own voice. Those types were always eager to give up information.

413

"Okay, let's talk. Who's the message from?" I asked.

"I hold the honored post of Emissary of the Lyndale Coven," he said politely, examining his nails. "We've taken a professional interest in you, and Coven leadership sent me." "Oh yeah?" I asked. "What for?"

"To dictate the terms of your surrender," he said, locking eyes with me. His hands twitched, then curled slightly. I imagined him leaping off the couch and knocking me down. I fought the urge to bring the rifle to bear, keeping it at the low ready.

"Thought your kind needed an invite," I said.

The man snarled.

"We both know who built this house. I have a standing invite. The coven master says that the Duke no longer wants you, so you're fair game. Our agreement, which I have right here, has the details."

He pulled a no-shit scroll out of his suit jacket and put it down on my coffee table. I glanced at it. The Lyndale Coven seemed to be under the impression that I belonged to them. I read the word "slave" once, and that was enough for me to decide I wasn't interested.

"No dice," I said.

"These terms are much more charitable than those the Coven Master wanted," he said, warning in his voice. "Oath breakers aren't normally given this kind of clemency."

I didn't have much idea what he meant about oath breakers, but I wasn't going to play ball with this pompous fuck.

"Not charitable enough," I said. "Why do you guys want me? Running out of blood from young clubgoers and runaways?"

The young vampire smiled again, flashing his teeth with what I'm sure he thought was menace.

"It'll certainly improve our coven's standings with the Duke if we prove we can clean up his loose ends. I'm sure you'll make an excellent blood thrall. We'll be taking a pint of blood every month, as—"

I raised the rifle and sighted in on his head. He sighed, and rolled his eyes.

"Look, you primitive ape, guns won't—"

I fired three times, the rounds earth-shatteringly loud in such a tight place. He screamed in pain and terror as the holy rifle's bullets tore through him, the wounds leaving bright blue caverns of light.

His screaming echoed in my head, so I kept shooting. I fired the rest of the magazine until there was nothing left but a corpse, riddled with holes and glowing softly, and me, standing there in my gunpowder-fueled catharsis.

I dropped the mag and slapped in a fresh one, savoring the sound of the bolt sliding forward and knowing that if the emissary had any friends, they too, would be introduced to the kinetic light of St. Joseph.

"Anyone else here? I got more."

* * * * *

Get "The Devil's Gunman" now at: https://www.amazon.com/dp/B07N1QF4MD.

Find out more about Philip S. Bolger and "The Devil's Gunman" at: https://chriskennedypublishing.com/philip-s-bolger/.

* * * * *

The following is an

Excerpt from Book One of The Shadow Lands:

Shadow Lands

Lloyd Behm, II

Available Now from Blood Moon Press

eBook and Paperback

Excerpt from "Shadow Lands:"

The combatants, for lack of a better term, were both resting at the edges of the dance floor. To the left was a very butch-looking blonde in what looked to be purple leather, along with her entourage, while to the right, a petite, dark-skinned Hispanic in a princess outfit stood, surrounded by meat popsicles wrapped in leather. Vampire fashions make no damn sense to me, for what it's worth. There were a few 'normals' huddled against the far wall, which showed signs of someone's face being run along it, repeatedly. Sure enough, the London 'Special' was in the DJ booth. He killed the sound as soon as he realized we were standing there.

"Ladies and gentlemen, may I introduce the final players in our little drama, the Reinhumation Specialists of the Quinton Morris Group!" the Special said into the mike.

"Fuck me running," I said.

"With a rusty chainsaw," Jed finished.

The two groups of vampires turned to face us.

"Remind me to kick Michael in his balls when we get back to the office," I said.

"You're going to have to get in line behind me to do it," Jed replied.

"You can leave now, mortals," the blonde said with a slight German accent. She had occult patterns tattooed around her eyes, which had to be a bitch, because she would have had to have them redone every six months or so. Vampires heal.

"Like, fershure, this totally doesn't involve you," the Hispanic said, her accent pure San Fernando Valley.

"Jed, did I ever tell you how I feel about Valley Girls?" I asked, raising my voice.

"No…"

419

"Can't live with 'em, can't kill 'em," I replied, swinging my UMP up and cratering the Valley vampire's chest with three rounds into the fragile set of blood vessels above the heart. Sure, the pump still works, but there's nothing connected to it for what passes as blood in a vampire to spread. On top of that, company-issue bullets are frangible silver, to which vampires have an adverse reaction.

With that, the dance was on. The damn Special in the DJ booth at least had the good sense to put on Rammstein. *Mien Teil* came thundering out of the speakers as we started killing vampires. Gunny ran his M1897 Trench Gun dry in five shots, dropped it to hang by a patrol sling, and switched to his ancient, family 1911. I ran my UMP dry on Valley Vamp's minions, then dropped the magazine and reloaded in time to dump the second full magazine into the Butch Vampire as she leaped toward the ceiling to clear the tables between us and the dance floor. As soon as Butch Vamp went down, the remaining vampires froze.

"Glamour," the Special called, stepping out of the booth. "I can control a lot of lesser vampires, but not until you got those two randy cunts thinking about how much they hurt."

"You. Fucking. Asshole," I panted.

Combat is cardio, I don't care what anyone else says.

"Yes?" he replied.

I looked him over. He was wearing a red zoot suit—red-pegged trousers and a long red jacket with wide shoulders over the ubiquitous white peasant shirt, topped with a red, wide-brimmed hat. He even had on red-tinted glacier glasses.

I felt his mind try to probe mine, then beamed as he bounced off.

"My that hurt," he replied.

"You know, we don't work with Michelangelo for nothing," Jed replied. Apparently the mind probe had been general, not specific.

I went through the messy side of the business—staking and be-heading—assisted by Capdepon. Crash helped Jed sort out the normal survivors, followed by prepping the live lesser vampires for transport. The Special leaned against a wall, maintaining control of the lesser vampires until we could move them out. Once all the work was done so the cleaners could move in, and the lesser vampires were moved out of Eyelash, I stepped wearily to the Special.

"What's your name?" I asked.

"You can call me," he paused dramatically, "Tim."

I kicked him in the nuts with a steel-toed boot. Even in the undead, it's a sensitive spot.

* * * * *

Get "Shadow Lands" now at:
https://www.amazon.com/dp/B07KX8GHYX/.

Find out more about Lloyd Behm, II and "Shadow Lands" at:
https://chriskennedypublishing.com/imprints-authors/lloyd-behm-ii/.

* * * *

The following is an

Excerpt from Book One of The Darkness War:

Psi-Mechs, Inc.

Eric S. Brown

Available Now from Blood Moon Press

eBook and Paperback

Excerpt from "Psi-Mechs, Inc.:"

Ringer reached the bottom of the stairs and came straight at him. "Mr. Dubin?" Ringer asked.

Frank rose to his feet, offering his hand. "Ah, Detective Ringer, I must say it's a pleasure to finally meet you."

Ringer didn't accept his proffered hand. Instead, he stared at Frank with appraising eyes.

"I'm told you're with the Feds. If this is about the Hangman killer case…" Ringer said.

Frank quickly shook his head. "No, nothing like that, Detective. I merely need a few moments of your time."

"You picked a bad night for it, Mr. Dubin," Ringer told him. "It's a full moon out there this evening, and the crazies are coming out of the woodwork."

"Crazies?" Frank asked.

"I just locked up a guy who thinks he's a werewolf." Ringer sighed. "We get a couple of them every year."

"And is he?" Frank asked with a grin.

Ringer gave Frank a careful look as he said, "What do you mean is he? Of course not. There's no such thing as werewolves, Mr. Dubin."

"Anything's possible, Detective Ringer." Frank smirked.

"Look, I really don't have time for this." Ringer shook his head. "Either get on with what you've come to see me about, or go back to wherever you came from. I've got enough on my hands tonight without you."

"Is there somewhere a touch more private we could talk?" Frank asked.

"Yeah, sure," Ringer answered reluctantly. "This way."

Ringer led Frank into a nearby office and shut the door behind them. He walked around the room's desk and plopped into the chair there.

"Have a seat," Ringer instructed him, gesturing at the chair in front of the desk.

Frank took it. He stared across the desk at Ringer.

"Well?" Ringer urged.

"Detective Ringer, I work for an organization that has reason to believe you have the capacity to be much more than the mere street detective you are now," Frank started.

"Hold on a sec." Ringer leaned forward where he sat. "You're here to offer me a job?"

"Something like that." Frank grinned.

"I'm not interested," Ringer said gruffly and started to get up. Frank's next words knocked him off his feet, causing him to collapse back into his chair as if he'd been gut-punched.

"We know about your power, Detective Ringer."

"I have no idea what you're talking about," Ringer said, though it was clear he was lying.

"There's no reason to be ashamed of your abilities, Detective," Frank assured him, "and what the two of us are about to discuss will never leave this room."

"I think it's time you left now, Mr. Dubin," Ringer growled.

"Far from it," Frank said. "We're just getting started, Detective Ringer."

Ringer sprung from his seat and started for the office's door. "You can either show yourself out, or I can have one of the officers out there help you back to the street."

Frank left his own seat and moved to block Ringer's path. "I have a gift myself, Detective Ringer."

Shaking his head, Ringer started to shove Frank aside. Frank took him by the arm.

"My gift is that I can sense the powers of people like yourself, Detective," Frank told him. "You can't deny your power to me. I can see it in my mind, glowing like a bright, shining star in an otherwise dark void."

"You're crazy," Ringer snapped, shaking free of Frank's hold.

"You need to listen to me," Frank warned. "I know about what happened to your parents. I mean what really happened, and how you survived."

Frank's declaration stopped Ringer in his tracks.

"You don't know crap!" Ringer shouted as Frank continued to stare at him.

"Vampires are very real, Detective Ringer." Frank cocked his head to look up at Ringer as he spoke. "The organization I work for…We deal with them, and other monsters, every day."

Ringer stabbed a finger into Frank's chest. It hurt, as Ringer thumped it repeatedly against him. "I don't know who you are, Mr. Dubin, but I've had enough of your crap. Now take your crazy and get the hell out of my life. Do I make myself clear?"

The pictures on the wall of the office vibrated as Ringer raged at Frank. Frank's smile grew wider.

"You're a TK, aren't you?" Frank asked.

"I don't even know what that is!" Ringer bellowed at him.

"You can move objects with your mind, Detective Ringer. We call that TK. It's a term that denotes you have telekinetic abilities. They're how you saved yourself from the vampire who murdered your family when you were thirteen."

Ringer said nothing. He stood, shaking with fear and rage.

"You're not alone, Detective Ringer," Frank told him. "There are many others in this world with powers like your own. As I've said, I have one myself, though it's not as powerful or as physical in nature, as your own. I urge you to have a seat, so we can talk about this a little more. I highly doubt your captain would be as understanding of your gift as I and my employer are if it should, say, become public knowledge."

"Is that a threat?" Ringer snarled.

Frank shook his head. "Certainly not. Now if you would…?" Frank gestured for Ringer to return to the chair behind the desk.

Ringer did so, though he clearly wasn't happy about it.

"There's so much to tell you, Detective Ringer; I'm afraid I don't even know where to begin," Frank said.

"Then why don't you start at the beginning, and let's get this over with," Ringer said with a frown.

"Right then." Frank chuckled. "Let's do just that."

* * * * *

Get "Psi-Mechs, Inc." now at:
https://www.amazon.com/dp/B07DKCCQJZ.

Find out more about Eric S. Brown and "The Darkness War" at:
https://chriskennedypublishing.com/imprints-authors/eric-s-brown/.

* * * * *